OPERATION DOCKSUNK

Operation Docksunk

Ted Bass

SERENDIPITY

Copyright © Ted Bass 2005

First published in 2005 by
Serendipity
Suite 530
37 Store Street
Bloomsbury
London

All rights reserved
Unauthorised duplication
contravenes existing laws
British Library Cataloguing-in-Publication data
A catalogue record for this book is available from the British Library
ISBN 1-84394-135-X

Printed and bound by Antony Rowe Ltd, Eastbourne

Dedicated to the Artificer Branch of the R.N. especially the Submariners and in particular the class of September '53 with whom I recently attended a 50 year reunion. Also to the finest Officer I have ever served under who was at the time Commander Fieldhouse Skipper of H.M.S./M Dreadnought.

Many people, too numerous to mention individually, have helped me and reminded me of events and times and have had a good laugh at both triumphs and failures. Nigel Davies who has both helped me with detail and constructive criticism. Also to my good friends at W.I.L.L.O.W. who helped me with mysteries of computers. Finally to my two daughters who have given me loads of encouragement to produce this book with lots of false starts over more years than I care to remember.

List of Illustrations

'V' Type Hunter Killer	8
'Mother'	19
HMS Adamant	20
O & P Class Type Boats	26
Baggy	53
Baggy's Modifications	56
Area of Operation	65
Baggy's Approach Track	70
The Target	81
Securing Freeflood Grill	86
The Ungodly	94
Assistance	97
Map According to Click	120
Guess Who?	163
Roughers on the Pond	175
Fred	180
Let's Twist Again	182
'Q' Ship - The Conversion	200
Re-visit Routes	214

Contents

	PREFACE	
CHAPTER 1	Finale	1
CHAPTER 2	Problem	4
CHAPTER 3	Plan	7
CHAPTER 4	Players 1	12
CHAPTER 5	Players 2	35
CHAPTER 6	Training	51
CHAPTER 7	Passage 1	60
CHAPTER 8	Briefing	69
CHAPTER 9	Preparatory 1	77
CHAPTER 10	In	88
CHAPTER 11	Ungodly	92
CHAPTER 12	Docked	99
CHAPTER 13	Fix	106
CHAPTER 14	Out	109
CHAPTER 15	Cavalry 1	112
CHAPTER 16	R&R	123
CHAPTER 17	Cavalry 2	131
CHAPTER 18	Rendezvous	136
CHAPTER 19	Evacuate	140
CHAPTER 20	Meanwhile	146
CHAPTER 21	Kidnapped	152
CHAPTER 22	Evacuate 2	156
CHAPTER 23	Exit	160

CHAPTER 24	Lift	169
CHAPTER 25	Shufti	177
CHAPTER 26	Boom	184
CHAPTER 27	Washup 1	188
CHAPTER 28	Preparatory 2	197
CHAPTER 29	Passage 2	204
CHAPTER 30	Revisit	213
CHAPTER 31	Attack	222
CHAPTER 32	Search	228
CHAPTER 33	Takeover	237
CHAPTER 34	Exodus	250
CHAPTER 35	Trip 1	256
CHAPTER 36	Trip 2	259
CHAPTER 37	Washup 2	264
CHAPTER 38	Epilogue	267

Glossary

AA	Aircraft Artificer
AFD	Admiralty Floating Dock
AMS	Auxiliary Machinery Space
AWOL	Absent Without Leave
AWACS	Airborne Warning and Control System
Asdic	Underwater detection equipment
Ballast Pump	Boat's Most Important Trim Pump
Below	Warning Cry when Lowering – Throwing Item
Bent	No not that! Tied as in String or Rope
Big Spit	Vomiting – Calling Bill and Hughy
Black Lighting	Very Low Level Lighting – Usually Red
Blood Wagon	Ambulance
Boats	Submarines
Bootneck	Royal – Royal Marine
Brick	A Naval Shell
Brow	Gangway to Link Ship to Ship or Shore
BMH	Base Medical Hospital
Buffer	Chief Boatswain's Mate, Jimmy's RH man
Bunting Tosser	Communications branch rating (flag wagger)
COQC	Commanding Officers Qualifying Course
Casing	Free Flood upper deck, bit seen when surfaced
Celanese	Natives of Ceylon – now Sri Lanka
Chippy	Shipwright Artificer
Chit/Chitty	Piece of paper for permission or instruction
Coxswain	Boat senior Chief Policeman, Doctor, Caterer
Clacker	Pastry
Comforts	Special Issue Food for Boats
CPO	Chief Petty Officer
Crabfats	Members of the RAF (Colour of Uniform)
Crushers	Leading Patrol Men – RN Police Constables
Dabtoe	Denigratory term for Seaman
Deck Ape	Denigratory term for Seaman
Deckhead	Ceiling
Deep Six	Oggin* Deeper than Old Heaving Line Length
DF	Duty Free
Dhoby Dust	Wash Powder (Daz-Tide-Surf etc)
DQs	Detention Quarters (Naval Jail)
Desiccate	Dry Out using Compressed Air

DO	Divisional Officer – Head of Branch
Donk Shop Horse	ERA* in charge of Boat's Engine Room
Ditch	Throw Something Over the Side (e.g. Gash*)
Divisions	Formal Parade for Special Occasions
Dyso	Malta's Waterborne Hand Driven Taxies
EO	Engineer Officer
ERA	Engine Room Artificer
ECM	Electronic Countermeasure Mast
Fanny	Cylindrical Mess Trap
Fast Black	Official (Black) Saloon Car/Any Taxi for Jack
Ferchrisake Wire	Arrester Cable Nearest Carrier's Sharp End*
Fifth Five	To sign on for 5 more years after doing 22
Fish	Tin Fish* – Torpedo
Flags	An Admiral's Flag Lieutenant
Float Test	Ditch* Something Overboard
Fore-Ends	Forward Torpedo Compartment
Fruit Salad	Medal Ribbons
Fizzer	On Report – In Trouble
Furious Palmtree	Jack's name for Helicopter
Gash	Rubbish, Surplus to Requirements
GPS	Global positioning by satellite
Greenies	Any member of the electrical branch
Guvvy	Government (Private) Work
Guz	Plymouth
HP	High Pressure
Homers	Hospitality for Jack when away from home
Heads	A Vessel's Latrines
IC	In Charge
IG	Imperial Gallons
In	In Tomato Sauce e.g. Herrings in/Sardines in
Jaunty	Master at Arms – Joss Man*
Jimmy	Jimmy the One, Warship's First Lieutenant
Jolly	Trip for Pleasure with no Useful Purpose
Joss man	Master at Arms*
Jury Rig	Temporary and Emergency Arrangement
Jews March Past	Examining Wallet/Pocket Contents for Funds
Killick	Leading Hand: Name of Badge, Killick Anchor
LCT	Landing Craft Tank
Lagging	Kit, Clothing
Lashed Up	Provided Generous Hospitality
Liberty Boat	Small Vessel to Transport Libertymen
Malta Dog	Sickness and Diarrhoea (Malta's bad water)

Mag Amps	Magnetic Amplifier Switching Devices
MFV	Motor Fishing Vessel
Metal Moths	Rust
MI	Military Intelligence
MO	Medical Officer
MOD	Ministry of Defence
MV	Motor Vessel (Compression Ignition Engined)
NM	Nautical Miles
Nautical Mile	Two Thousand Yards (not 1,760)
Neaters	Undiluted Rum – Grog
NAAFI	Navy Army and Airforce Institute
OD	Ordinary Seamen (below able rate – AB)
Oggin	The Sea
OIC	Officer in Charge
On	Favours Owed for Services Rendered
OOW	Officer of the Watch
Oppo	Opposite Number Watchkeeping (friend, pal)
Panel	Boats Diving Surfacing and Mast Control
Paraffin Budgie	Jack's Nickname for Helicopter
Ping Bosun	Asdic* Operator
Pipe	Whistle Call Informing Crew of Daily Events
Pompey	Portsmouth
Pond	Atlantic Ocean
Pongos	Army (where the Army goes the Pong goes)
Pot	Diving Compression Chamber
Pussers	Royal Naval
Queen Mary	Large Articulated Lorry and Trailer
Ratted	Well Drunk
Rattle	On Report (In Trouble)
RA	Rationed Ashore (Living at Home)
RBG	Rich Brown Gravy
REA	Radio Electrical Artificer
REM	Radio Electrical Mechanician
Retirement Age	After 22 years Compulsory Unless FF*
RFA	Royal Fleet Auxiliary (RN Supply Fleet)
RIB	Rigid Inflatable Boat
RM	Royal Marines
Roughers	Rough Seas
RPO	Regulating Petty Officer (RN Police)
Runner	Senior Officer's Assistant (Messenger)
RV Point	Rendezvous Point
Scran	Food

Scran bag	Sculling* Gear Collected
Sculling	Lying or Rolling About on the Deck
Scratcher	Bosun's Mate – Second Coxswain*
Sea Spew	Sea Sick
Set	Full set of facial hair
Sharp End	Warship's Bow, as opposed to Blunt End
Shitehawkes	All Classes of Seagull
Show the Flag	Diplomatic visits to Foreign Ports
Shuddering Shithouse	Bootnecks* nickname for a Chinook
Shufti	Arab Word – to take a look
Slop	Liquid Waste (slopping out water)
Slops	Cash Clothing Store
Snort	Run main engines at periscope depth
Somali	Native of Somalia
Steam Catapult	Aircraft Launch Mechanism, British
Subby	Sub-Lieutenant RN
TG	Turbo Generator
TGM	Torpedo Gunner's Mate
Three Badge	Chevrons – One/Four Years Undetected Crime
Tiffs	Artificers – Tradesmen
Tin Fish	Torpedo
Tot Time	Rum issue time approx. 11.30–12.00
Trim	Submarine's State of Neutral Buoyancy
Townie	Oppo* coming from same area
Troop	To be put in the Rattle*
Troops	Collective term for Jack
Tunnel	Shielded Passage to Aft over Reactor
2IC	Second in Command
Two and One	Diluted Rum – 2 water, 1 rum – Stop Hoarding
Up Homers	Family Hospitality when away from home
US	Unserviceable
UWT	Under Water Telephone
Up Spirits	Pipe* to initiate rum issue
Van	Vanguard – Advanced Guard – Forefront
Wardroom	Officers/Officers Mess
Washup	Post Exercise Analysis and Discussion
Wiggely Amps	AC (Alternating Current)
Wrecker	Outside Tiff* Sees to All but Propulsion
Yarpy	White Native of South Africa
Zeds	Sleep, as in Zizz-Zonk (Knock out a few)

Chapter 1

Finale

I make no apologies for what I've done! As far as I'm concerned I've done my duty, and I've done what I had to do, and my conscience is clear. Not only that, I'd do it again if I had to, given similar circumstances. Anyway I'm knackered and I could do with the rest, and it's nice to be on my own for a bit of peace and quiet.

I'm up in front of the Beak tomorrow and no doubt with a bit of luck he'll send me down for an extended rest. It'll give me a chance to put pen to paper, and try to put the record straight, and sod Their Lordships and the Authorities.

The charge, Manslaughter! I'd topped my best mate of 45ish years, the rub being that he was still my best mate when I snuffed him, and I was still his best mate to the very end. It wasn't hard, he'd been in and out of hospital for over ten months or more with the stints in dock getting longer and more frequent as time went on, getting weaker by the minute, (sometimes it felt like ten years). He'd been ill at home for some time, but had deteriorated to such an extent that his wife couldn't cope full time any longer. She did her very best, no one could have done more. The awful thing is she hates me, she's hated me for years, ever since he started to be ill, and her hatred of me has increased over the years as her husband's health has deteriorated, because she blames me for his illness, which, in the final analysis is true. The really bizarre bit about the whole thing is that I was the best man at their wedding, and at the time, according to her, was the finest thing since sliced bread.

For some considerable time he'd been asking, then pleading for the last three months to do something for him, because his medication was becoming less and less effective. We were both convinced it had been the 'operation' which had started his problem, bowel and bone cancer! Over the years he'd had bits and pieces removed, bits added, transplanted, and resectioned, you name it he'd had it, but the big 'C' kept up its relentless advance.

What to do? We discussed it at some length and in great detail, every time I visited him in that bloody awful hospital. They'd put him through every possible indignity, just to postpone the inevitable. The awful thing was that it was never his style. If you had ever suggested to him that something like that would happen to him he'd have laughed at you and said, 'I'll top myself first', but by that stage he just wasn't physically capable. Every time I saw him in that state I used to think of my old man, who lived on his own, and always said that when he couldn't cope he would put himself in a home. But it never came to that because on a trip to the local shops he fell down stone dead. It wasn't very good for us relatives, but at least he didn't suffer, and that's the way I want to go. Anyway I knew that my mate had a fully paid up pension, so what I had to do was make it look like natural causes, or manslaughter by person or persons 'unknown' if his missus was to benefit.

I'd conned the hospital staff into believing that I worked permanent nights, and was allowed special dispensation to visit after normal hours. This ensured that I didn't clash with his Trouble and Strife. So the plan of action we decided on was to wait until he'd had his night time medication, which was towards the end of my visiting time, although in the case of terminally ill patients it was flexible to say the least, but equally, so were my visiting hours. For this reason we had to be very careful, because timing was crucial to the plan. After taking his medication he always dozed off for minutes at a time, which was a critical element in the plan, another was the fact that this hospital's pillows had a plastic inner case, so it was going to be a piece of cake!

Medication, doze off, pillow over face, hold it down tightly, make it look as if we were talking intently, so that nosy parkers walking past wouldn't twig, check lack of pulse with free hand, return pillow and plump up, say 'tara' as usual, walk away smiling sweetly, job done. So much for good plans!

What we had both failed to notice were the internal security cameras, hidden discreetly either end of the ward. Next thing I know plod calls and starts asking daft questions and then suggests that I should accompany him – – – – – !

After a short while, it was time to meet the Beak. To keep the story live (no pun intended) I pleaded not guilty, and although my brief did his best, worked hard and sounded very plausible, it didn't do me a bit of good, but at least I've got my wish for a rest and peace and quiet that I'd promised myself. The only good thing to come out of this whole mess, is that his missus will be financially secure.

As I've promised myself before, I will now have the opportunity to get down on paper the whole truth and sod the lot of them, the Authorities, the Official Secrets Act and their Lordships of the Admiralty. This isn't a book as such, more a record of what really went on to keep this country of ours safe, and the sacrifice that a few good and true men and women made to make sure it happened, as has happened before, and I'm sure will happen again in the future. I hope it will also show that there are still the Saddams, Stalins, Hitlers and Amins out there ready to sacrifice many lives and World Peace for personal glory and gain. A great bonus for me though, is that I don't have to worry any more about food or accommodation for a while.

I'm not much good with words, and make no apology for it, as I'm an Engineer not a writer, but I have to set the record straight, so instead of getting all tied up with descriptions and explanations, I've used drawings and sketches so that detailed blurb is unnecessary.

Chapter 2

Problem

It's on record that a certain East African dictator had delusions of grandeur and had friends in high places in the southern area of Africa. It's also a known fact that this same despot had strong connections with a certain Cuban 'Dignitary', who in turn had the ear of the Kremlin.

Historically the MOD* had supplied (obsolete) military equipment to the Southern African States. It is also on record that in the mid seventies the nuclear powered Hunter Killer class submarines of the 'Valour' class were near the end of their useful life with the advent of the new Polaris fleet. Most of them were laid up as Greenpeace was at odds with Their Lordships regarding method of disposal, but one was sold at a knockdown price to South Africa on the understanding that it would be used for training purposes only! Some months later it was reported to have mysteriously sunk at its moorings, 'fortunately' with no loss of life, and was a total write-off, and so had been raised, towed out to deep water and scuttled, much to the chagrin and exasperation and protest of Greenpeace.

Also historically 'boats'* based away from HM Dockyards with minor defects requiring dry docking, such as a damaged propeller to be replaced, would use the locally moored AFD (Admiralty Floating Dock). In Nore Command, on the west coast, with the advent of Polaris boats no expense was spared and the base was expanded massively which included a shore-based state of the art docking facility. This of course made the local old AFD* redundant and, as it was too small for Polaris anyway, it was sold for scrap and eventually uprooted (it had been moored in one place for a long time) and towed to a destination down south.

Subsequent reports revealed that the poor old AFD, while under tow heading south in the Irish Sea, had floundered when a sudden squall had blown up, which is not unusual in that area, but fortunately with no loss of life. It is a know fact that AFDs tow like waterlogged bricks at the best of times, and therefore did not surprise anyone in official circles.

A shrewd and imaginative, but very bored, member of Military Intelligence seconded from the RN sifting through various random reports from diverse sources including the Merchant Fleet, Warships, Coastguards, and civilian sea goers of all shapes and sizes, started to come across all sorts of strange, and what can only be described as bizarre, and in isolation, extraordinary accounts. A few examples follow:

Mr and Mrs J. Mellor, transiting from Inverkip Marina to Londonderry in their Motor Sailer *Capricorn*, reported to the coastguard that whilst passing between Arran and Ailsa Craig in heavy seas and poor visibility they both sighted what they described as 'two tall rusting grey structures with lattice tops not moving in the swell'.

Captain A Stavros, the Master of MV* *Spero* carrying general cargo bound for Belfast noted in his log and sent a signal to the MOD that a sighting had been made of what appeared to be a strange looking oil rig type structure adrift off the east coast of Ireland. Coastal Command Prestwick scrambled a Sea King, which conducted an extensive box search of the reported area, which tended to reinforce the report of the sinking.

Round the world, Yachtsman Stuart Knott reported back to his home base that, about to attempt to round the Cape of Good Hope in heavy seas, he sighted in the heavy hazy distance what appeared to be a very large orca (killer whale) with a large distorted dorsal fin.

Report in the local *Bostuta Evening Standard* (Lower East Africa).

> Local fishermen came ashore today having abandoned their traditional fishing grounds because they said it had been taken over by a 'Big Black Devil' that churned the water around them and scared them off. Our intrepid reporter went hot foot to the area but found nothing to indicate anything untoward, apart from a crowd of hysterical natives whose individual stories did not correlate, and so dismissed it as local superstition.

Geologist Dr Justin Knowles conducting a seismic survey for Mostin Chemicals off the east coast of Africa included in his report that he had come across unusually high levels of radiation in the area of the Aldabra Islands, which lay to the south of the Kananga River. He also reported that on subsequent visits to the area it still showed high radiation readings, but reducing exponentially in magnitude. This information was forwarded to Mostin and also to the *National Geographic* and onward to the MOD.

Portuguese fishermen operating in the Bay of Biscay reported to the Portuguese Navy that they had sighted what appeared to be, they all claimed, what could only be described as a block of flats under construction. When questioned they admitted that there was a long high swell running with intermittent dense fog banks. A Portuguese Navy Frigate was dispatched to the reported area but found nothing, mainly due to increasing fog density, which is not unusual for the area, although a strange radar contact was noted fleetingly. The radar operator also commented that the echo appeared as a double blip.

Unconfirmed reports have filtered through to the National Press of some sort of natural disaster occurring on the banks of the River Kananga in east Africa. Natives of a large area around the tragedy site have fled and appear to be badly traumatized, but none of them are either able or willing to offer an explanation for their actions. Further investigation by the United Nations is being discussed at a high level; a decision is expected soon.

A small article in *Pravda* states that a small nuclear device had been successfully tested! Watchers and listeners in the west detected a nuclear explosion in the area of the Russian Stepps, its intensity in the order of XX megatons.

Intelligence sources, through 'diplomatic' means, suggested that the device was in fact a nuclear warhead fitted to a conventional sized torpedo, therefore able to be launched from a standard 21' torpedo tube in a conventional boat or a Nuclear Powered Hunter Killer boat. The article in *Pravda* continued in the vein that the government was looking for financial assistance because of their ailing economy.

Captain Reg Vardy, Pilot of DC3 *Spirit of the Sky,* part of the fleet of 'Vardy Transport S. A', (the other part of the fleet was another aging DC3) reported to Air Traffic Control that he had sighted what looked like a large barge-like object making very heavy weather of being towed eastwards. Position was sighted, 20 miles southeast of Robben Island, South Africa.

Our intrepid MI* Officer, realizing that there may be some connection, collected all these snippets of information and a few more together and passed the file in to his superiors who, having sucked their teeth and picked their noses, decide to make further investigations and enquiries.

Agents were sent out to survey the area but came back empty handed. They couldn't get anywhere near the area because of very many large native gentlemen with very real AK Automatic rifles.

The 'Management' therefore decided that further investigation was justified and a series of high level photographic reconnaissance flights were organized, which proved relatively inconclusive. Plan 'B' sent in a combined operation ground and sea-borne force, which was energetically repelled, but not before it was discovered that the whole area was comprehensively covered by very sophisticated surveillance equipment, including radar and an underwater sonar array. This force was very lucky in extricating itself with only minor injuries and no fatalities. That's when the shit hit the fan!!

Chapter 3

Plan

The meeting was called to order by Nore Command Admiral Sir Arthur Hopgood, a rather brusque florid man of ample proportions, who explained the gravity of a developing situation without being specific, as if he hadn't a clue what was going on.

He then introduced Commander S. Westerman, a very different kettle of fish. He was a tall slim and fit looking man with a Boats Dolphin badge above a couple of ribbons, he also sported Wings and a Divers Badge on his sleeves, (a bit of an all rounder). He stood stock still in front of the mass of service high ups and boffins and waited till the general hubbub slowly died away to an expectant hush. He then strolled around stage left, and made a signal and the lights dimmed, and a large screen illuminated so intensely it hurt. A quick click and up popped a picture of a 'Mushroom'. His voice came over slow, steady and firm with very little emotion.

'Gentlemen, this picture is of a nuclear device detonation. This will happen in the near future unless we can prevent certain events taking place. We don't even know what the target will be, but we know it will not be the only one.

'And now gentlemen to specifics, (another click and up came an aerial photograph). This is the River Kananga on the east coast of Africa, and the little black oblong thing there is a floating dock! To be accurate, Ex RN AFD 69, last reported sunk in the Irish Sea in a freak squall!' another click.

'This gentlemen is an aerial photograph of the approaches to the same River Kananga. The little black thing bottom left is (another click) now blown up to reveal a submarine! To be accurate this is in fact Ex HM Sm. *Victor*, sold to a South African state on the understanding that it would be used for training purposes only. This vessel was last reported to have sunk at her moorings and been written off and subsequently disposed of by scuttling in deep water.

'Our sources tell us that the Soviets are attempting to raise funds by selling nuclear armed torpedoes to an unspecified African state.

'So putting two and two together, whatever your answer, we have to come up with a plan quickly. You have to go away from here and come up with a solution. We must not, I repeat, not cause an international inci-

'V' Type Hunter Killer

dent or be identified, and we must have absolutely minimum fatalities, but we must completely destroy this facility. We reconvene at 0800 tomorrow with solutions or else!'

Sir Arthur closed the meeting with a warning about secrecy, and the need for strict security.

Came the dawn and all the Brass trooped back into the lecture room looking rather glum. Westerman strode to the front, mounted the rostrum and spun round to face the gathering.

'Well gentlemen?'

Complete and utter silence. Admiral Hopgood took to his hind legs and pleaded with the assembly to no avail. His face started to change in colour until it increased to a dark shade of purple and then he exploded.

'If you, as professionals cannot give me solutions, you will make yourselves available for answers to specific requests for material and equipment. You are all Heads of Departments or Supply Units, and you will furnish whatever is requested immediately, as it is demanded if not sooner. You are dismissed' He fumed.

'You' Pointing an accusing finger at Westerman. 'Commander, my office now' he barked.

He shoved Westerman through the door and slammed it behind him, went behind his desk and slumped in his chair.

'What the hell's wrong Stan?' They were old shipmates having served as Skipper and Jimmy in both conventional and nuclear driven boat.

'I dunno Sir but it's a bit of a bugger expecting immediate answers with all the restrictions we're imposing.'

'Well, because of just that I'm going to lumber you with the whole damned problem.' The Admiral said with an accusing look. 'You will go away from here, surround yourself with whoever you consider can help you, and all that mob of no hopers are at your beck and call for whatever you want. Come back tomorrow with a solution. DISMISSED.' He barked, swivelled his chair around 180º and slumped even deeper into it.

A bemused Stanley wandered down the base main drag ignoring all the passing salutes that were thrown at him.

As I passed him and he didn't respond to my salute I made my first big mistake. I said,

'You OK Sir?' Nothing. 'SIR' – at which he swung round and stared hard at me. Then his eyes seemed to unglaze and he eventually recognized me.

'Hello Chief, sorry, miles away, how's things?'

'I feel better than you look Sir, what's up?' I could talk to him like that 'cos we'd served together. I'd been his Wrecker* and later Donk Shop Horse* and when he was Jimmy* on the first of the conventional 'O' boats, and then Wrecker first and eventually Chief Tiff on *Vectra* when he was Jimmy. He suddenly seemed to come alive, looked a bit happier, turned, stared at me for a bit and said, 'You may be able to help me Chief, d'ya fancy a run ashore, a couple of bevies and a natter?'

'Yes Sir, OK, I'll throw on some civvy lagging*, and meet you at the main gate in half an hour.'

Thirty minutes later we were bombing down the road to the city lights. He pulled up outside the boozer I'd never been in before; it was out of the way and very quiet. He got the beers in and we sat down in a darkish corner, and then he shut down again.

'What's up Stan?' he was miles away again, but suddenly he came to life again and said, 'Between you and me, how would you disable an AFD?'

'You're winding me up,' I said, laughing.

'No, I'm deadly serious.'

'Well in that case it's easy, all you do is lay a line of plastic (explosive) along the line of keel blocks, on detonation the ballast tanks rupture, it loses buoyancy, its back breaks from fo'rard to aft, the sides collapse in and it sinks!'

'How would you get the explosives there?'

'What're you on about? You just stick it down and put detonators in it.'

'No, it has to be done in secret.'

'Now you ARE pulling my plonker, why would anyone want to blow up an AFD in secret?'

'Trust me and just answer the question, how?'

'I dunno,' I said, 'I suppose I'd wait for a vessel to be docked down and do it under cover of darkness using the vessel as a cover.'

'What if the vessel was a submarine, what then?'

'That's easy, you hide in the ballast tanks!'

'Now it's you pulling mine.'

'No I'm not, you can hold a dance inside a boat's ballast tank, well, almost. Don't forget I've wrecked for you on two boats and we've docked them both down, and one of the final jobs of the outside gang is to check ballast securing straps, wedges and keeps and fastenings of the actuating mechanisms of main vents within the tanks (boats have pig iron ballast in the bottom of the tanks and main vent operating linkages run through the ballast tank tops).'

'Could the explosives be placed anywhere other than by the keel blocks, where they might be spotted?'

'Yeah, string a necklace of plastic under the damned thing on the centre line the effect would be the same, if not better due to water pressure, but it'd be a bit more difficult to rig.'

His eyes went to tilt again for a while then suddenly he leapt to his hind legs, shot out the door, jumped in his car and roared off leaving me stranded, so I stayed and got smashed, thumbed a lift back to base very late, very pissed, and died.

It felt like we'd hit some harry roughers 'cos I was rolling around badly, but a voice was droning on in the background.

'Chief, wake up Chief, Chief, Commander Westerman wants you in the Main Conference Room one one two.'

Bloody 'ell, I couldn't even find a clean shirt. Eventually I managed to get my act together, just, and dashed to the conference room, barged in and stopped dead in my tracks. I'd never seen so much gold braid and scrambled egg since the Coronation. All heads turned, all eyes glared at me 'till Commander Westerman rescued me by ordering me to take a seat at the back.

He carried on spouting something or other about logistics, then a Boffin stood up with his hand raised. Stan Westerman looked up, saw him and said huffily 'Yes?'

'This is all very well. But how do you propose to get there?' in a very supercilious manner.

'Initially, to get near, the team will sail to the outer dock area in a locally familiar type of vessel on the pretext of being broken down, because of heavy surveillance. Then the attack team will transfer to hitch a ride on a submarine that is about to go upstream to dock down for maintenance.

'Don't be ridiculous!' was the rejoinder that really angered Stan.

'Chief, CHIEF!' I was miles away, 'Up here please.' By now he was looking very agitated.

'Tell this –ah- this gentleman how you can hide in a submarine.'

'Yes Sir, you hide in the ballast tanks!'

There was a general ripple of incredulity and the same Boffin snorted and said 'Absolutely ridiculous!'

'No Sir, ballast tanks are evacuated initially using high pressure compressed air in a short blast to give slight positive buoyancy and then when surfaced and the conning tower hatch is opened the low pressure blower is started and fully evacuates the ballast tanks of water through stonking great holes in the tank bottoms with perfectly good fresh air drawn in through the conning tower hatch, even if it is a bit oil misted and stale smelling, and when you open the main vents to let the air out and the water back in the boat sinks, easy!' With a confused look, and snort, the boffin sank back into his chair. Westerman continued addressing his audience.

'Thank you Chief, as per Admiral Hopgood's instructions you will supply me and my team with all, I repeat all, our needs. That's all for now, I will be in touch, thank you gentlemen! Come on Chief, we have a job to plan.'

As he hurried down the main road with me dragging up the rear I shouted at him.

'But Sir I already have a job!'

'You have a new job now, you heard what the Admiral said, you're now part of the team.'

Chapter 4

Players 1

For me it all started with an advertisement at the back of the *Radio Times* calling for apprentices in the Royal Navy, so I wrote off for details. What came back was great, but an exam had to be sat. I also had to have parental permission and Headmaster's OK to sit it. My mother gave her permission and signed the consent form. My Headmaster was another kettle of fish, he positively sneered at me and as much as said I had no chance, which made me all the more determined. To be quite honest I think his negative attitude was my inspiration, to prove him wrong, but to this day I don't know if he took this course of action on purpose.

To cut a long story short I passed the exam, don't ask me how, we went down to Pompey* for the interview, practical exam and medical, passed them all and was in, and went home to await instructions. Mum was pleased for me, and when I finally got my orders she gave me a fag case and lighter because she knew I smoked, and off I went at 15 years old to sign on for 12 years from the age of 18, fifteen whole years, a lifetime when you're that age.

What a different world it was, a load of 15 year olds thrown together from all walks of life to do an apprenticeship in the Royal Navy. The good thing about an RN apprenticeship is that they try you out at every skill they require, and when you enjoy a particular skill you do it well. That's how you choose your trade; it works well. That's the way it was done in our day anyway.

Thrown together you soon make friends, not close friends because the RN keeps you on the move, but now and again it's different. That's how it was with Smith and me; we seemed to hit it off from the start.

John Henry Smith, Smith for short or H to his friends, was the thinking one; I was the practical one, that's why we made such a good team. Most of us managed to weather the rigours of apprenticeship, and came out the other end as good tradesmen. I still believe that the RN apprenticeship is the best you can get. The snag is they don't train you to cope with the numerous pitfalls of civvy street after they chuck you out!

Anyway, we ended up in the fleet, I got lumbered with an old up and downer (reciprocating engines) Loch Class Frigate, out the Persian Gulf for 18 months, H got lumbered with a similar Bay Class Frigate doing South Africa, which for both of us was leaking steam and slinging hammocks.

After sweating cobs out in the Gulf, Karachi, Crater City, Djibouti and the Suez Canal I was drafted to HMS. *Lochinvar*, South Queensferry, and guess who turned up, Smith! We eventually got fed up of commuting to Rosyth Dockyard most days and decided to volunteer for submarines. In the meantime we both got drafted to the Gareloch and HMS *Adamant*, Submarine Depot Ship. Soon after we joined, it was off on a DF* run to Portugal, a superb run ashore. We were both laid on the beach at Estoril watching a couple of our sailors who were Shallow Water Divers who, having smuggled fins out of the diving store, were showing off in front of the local talent, and very nice they were too. There and then we decided to slap in for a Shallow Water Diving course. That was a mistake!

When we arrived back in UK our Draft Chits to the Diving School at Rosyth Dockyard had arrived, in a very cold, very snowy February. By now we were Third Class Tiffs entitled to wear three gold buttons on the sleeve cuffs and be addressed as Chief, all the rest of the course members were mainly OD's*, and Killicks* so we thought that we would be treated well. Not a bit of it. It was every man for himself, we did our dips off the deck of an MFV* in the tug basin of Rosyth Dockyard, having to sweep the snow off the deck beforehand. Then it was a mad scramble to get a decent suit. They (the suits) were all hung up on coat hangers in the hold, and the only way to get a good one was to be first down the ladder. Once down you had to look for chalk, because chalk was used on the rubber dry suits as a dressing for new units to stop them sticking when first manufactured.

Some of the suits were a disgrace, patched up with bike puncture repair patches. The next problem you had was to get into the damned thing. You first put on thermal underwear, which in those days was abwool, which was very itchy and also very absorbent. Once you had the jersey, socks and long johns on you climbed into the dry suit through the neck hole, which is all very well until you're in it up to your waist, then you need help. Someone has to grab a sleeve and the neck hole on the same side and in a co-ordinated lunge, the prospective wearer has to plunge his arm into the gaping neck hole and hit the sleeve hole or else. Then you have to perform the same manoeuvre for the other arm, then it's the dreaded neck band, an oval steel band that's fitted inside the suit neck hole, then the hood is pulled over the head, and the skirt is then arranged over the now expanded neck hole.

A large jubilee type clip is then slotted over the head and tightened over the sandwich of neckband, suit neck and hood skirt. If you think that's complicated, you ain't seen nuthin yit. It's the breathing set next, an oxygen rebreathing set with high pressure oxygen storage cylinders on the back with an envelope arrangement underneath which contains a quantity of 4 oz lead balls to assist you in sinking and a quick release pin on the envelope to jettison the contents to assist in surfacing in an emergency (more about 4 oz lead balls later). Strapped to your front is a breathing bag with a large canister connected to it, which contains soda lime. Now this granular chemical has a very useful property in that it absorbs carbon dioxide (CO_2) the poisonous gas that we exhale. That is why it's called a re-breathing set, because you breathe in the oxygen from the cylinders on your back via a reducing or demand valve breathing bag and the soda lime canister. Exhaled unused oxygen is stored back in the breathing bag and the generated CO_2 is absorbed by the soda lime. The reason for this seemingly complex system is to prevent discharging any give away bubbles when you're on covert operations, so when you watch a film with Frog Men in it inspecting enemy beaches or shipping, and streams of bubbles keep appearing, you know they are breathing air and the film's rubbish!

The diving course itself was truly terrible, but it did have its lighter moments. The accommodation was disgraceful, it was an unlined wartime Nissen hut, the only heating being an old cast iron pot bellied stove, the fuel, coke. Have you ever tried lighting that sort of gadget in the freezing cold with wet coke?

It's easy, you nick a full breathing set cylinder, a bit of newspaper on the grate, a few sticks on top, then fill the whole thing up with soggy coke, light the paper and give the whole thing a blast of the old O_2. It burns like rocket fuel!

But I digress, to recap; we have the suit and the breathing set on, next come the dreaded wrist bands which are just very wide lazzy bands, the idea being to prevent ingress of oggin* up the cuff of the suit. In actual fact all they do is cut off all circulation to the hands, which in extreme cold ensures that all feeling to the digits is completely lost. Next comes the even greater dreaded nose clip, which is constructed of two half-inch diameter rubber pads connected together by a looped coil spring. The two pads are prised apart and placed over the flare of the nostrils and released, thus closing the nostrils rather firmly so preventing water ingress to the nasal passages but which, after a time, tends to bring tears to the eyes. The snag with me is that I'm rather well endowed in the bugle department and due to that, had to have two springs, which after a while felt like I had a G clamp attached to my face. Now the mask, you have to gob on it (on the inside) and rub it in, it was supposed to stop it steaming up, not that it made any difference in the tug basin, you couldn't see your hand in front of your face.

And now the mouthpiece – you open the bottles, check the demand valve is working, and the tricky bit, you stick the mouthpiece in your mouth and operate the way cock, which is positioned in front of the mouthpiece. This cock is in fact a two-position valve, either open to the atmosphere or to the oxygen system. The object of this gadget is to evacuate the lungs of air so that the soda lime is not contaminated, and unwanted nitrogen is eliminated. The method is – way cock to atmosphere – exhale – way cock to oxygen system – inhale deeply – repeat at least three times. I forgot to mention that you are now wearing either fins for swim work or heavy boots and lead loaded belt for bottom work. A lifeline is attached to your harness, the quick release buckle on your harness is checked and with a tap on your head you put your hand over your mask and jump, that's all there is to it! Your next problem is sinking, you're floating like a beached whale, but all is not lost, on the back of your hood is a bit sticking out that looks like the inflation nozzle of a balloon. It is in fact a non-return valve, and the reason you're floating is that all that abwool has air trapped in it, so now you have to tip your head forward and the hood valve allows the trapped air to escape, and then you sink. That's the theory, but it doesn't always work out that way – have you got enough weight, or too much? Either way you're in trouble! Anyway, just suppose you've got it right, you're now in another, alien world of no light and very little sound, apart from the thrashing of the tug propellers, which totally ignore the 'Diver in the water' signal flag.

The bloke in charge of the whole training programme was Chief Diver Sidney 'Pancho' Powers. Pancho was a great bloke, but a stickler for accuracy and detail. His instructions to you on the start of a dip might be to head out to a floating fag packet and retrieve it without being seen. It sounds easy, but in reality, with no point of reference, you lose all sense of direction and eventually you have to come up for a shufty* to get your bearings. Beware showing too much above the surface, 'cos the next thing you know is Pancho pelting you with 4 oz lead balls very accurately, and they don't half hurt.

Working on the bottom in lead boots and belt is an entirely different kettle of fish. A 'Shot' line, consisting usually of a concrete block weighing a stone or so with a metal ring cast into it with a two inch or so rope attached to it is dropped over the side and secured to a bollard on the deck of the MFV. You are then dropped over after it equipped with a light half-inch lead line. The idea is that when you reach the bottom, you attach your lead line to the shot line and walk away from it whilst paying out the lead line (so that you can find your way back). That's the theory – in reality, once you hit the bottom you are thigh deep in thick glutinous mud. Having attached your lead line, to try to move you have to lean forward almost horizontally and start paddling in the mud, paying out the lead line as you go. You can't guess your actual progress, but you feel you're doing real well and when all your lead line is paid out you're pretty exhausted. You stand up and turn around to go back and hit the shot line with your lead line coiled at your feet.

To add to your misery, whether swimming, or on the bottom, the cold and the leaks get to you. The cold takes its toll particularly on your hands as they are totally exposed and as previously explained, the pressure of the suit cuffs and wristbands reduces circulation badly. But by far the worst were the leaky suits. You start the dip and slowly this damp feeling starts and gets slowly worse and colder. But by far the worst snag with leaks though are that they make you get heavier and heavier and you have to keep opening the regulator bypass to allow a bit more buoyancy into the breathing set, but there are limits. The heavier you get, the harder it is to work with progressively increased exhaustion.

The other thing you have to be careful of is a 'cocktail', which is caused by salt water leaking into the soda lime canister, as this causes a violent chemical reaction. This nasty mixture then erupts through the mouthpiece with no warning with extremely horrible results.

Regarding leaks, one amusing incident involved H. As usual we were waiting for the signal to go below and get suited up. H had pulled a flanker and manoeuvred his way to be nearest the companionway. The order was eventually given and H was down below like a rabbit down its burrow, and lo and behold he had chosen a beautifully chalky white suit, it must have been brand spanking new. We all got suited up and rigged in our sets etcetera. H went in first in his brand new suit, sank like a stone and immediately shot back up to the access ladder protesting violently with gestures. But Pancho would have none of it and kicked him back down and told him to get on with it. By the end of the dip, a very sad and very sorry and very very cold H emerged. It transpired that the suit he had chosen was a very old but unused type, which was rigged with a pee hole and a blanking plug on a short lanyard. Unfortunately, on this unit the lanyard had broken and the plug was lost and H hadn't noticed. As he entered the water an awful lot of very very cold oggin hit his nether regions, which is why he tried to exit like a rocket. So at the end of his dip, poor old H's legs were full to the brim and the water had capillaried up to his armpits as abwool acts as a very good wick. He just about managed to drag himself out weighing a ton, convinced that his sex life was ruined. After that he never failed to check any suit he chose thoroughly before getting dressed.

With visibility in the Tug Basin being zero, to check our technique we did dips in the Olympic swimming pool at HMS *Caledonia*, the Shore

Establishment H and I had completed our apprenticeship in. The good thing about this was that you didn't have to prat about with a suit, the only snag was the pool itself, being of Olympic standard it had the normal shallow end and a very deep deep end. The problem was that Pancho insisted that in swimming lengths of the bath you hugged the bottom with the inevitable change in buoyancy. When going from shallow to deep you lose buoyancy because of the compression of oxygen in the breathing bag of the set. This compression can compensate for cracking the bypass valve of the regulator for just a little burst to increase buoyancy, but beware the return trip because if you've overdone it, when you come back up the slope towards the shallow end, oxygen starts to leak out of the sides of the mask, or even worse, you end up surfaced. The next thing you know, Pancho is either heaving 4 oz lead balls at you, or jabbing you in the ribs with a very long bamboo pole whilst shouting at the top of his voice 'OXYGEN WASTER'.

Another amusing incident involving H was one of these training sessions. To amuse ourselves, and with Pancho's blessing, we used to hold races to see who could get into the water first. Our sets were lined up along the deep end wall. We would line up along the water's edge facing our own sets. On the command you dashed to get your set on, clear the air from the set with three out and in cycles. On this occasion H was first in, but shot straight out again coughing and spluttering because, in his rush to win, he had miscounted and left the waycock in the atmosphere position and guffed up half the pool.

Other techniques practised were changing sets under water and rescuing somebody from the bottom by sharing one set, with the ever vigilant Pancho at the ready with the bamboo pole and lead balls.

Throughout the course classroom work was very important, as was the workshop practice where we serviced our sets and pumped up our set cylinders from larger storage cylinders. H and I had no real trouble with either element, but some of the lads struggled and even with our help eventually dropped out. We also kept losing men through illness, mainly heavy colds, until eventually we were the only two left. He wouldn't give in 'cos I wouldn't and vice versa, the main reason being that we were nearing the end of the course. The final irony was that one of the last elements of the course was the decompression chamber dip on the next Monday.

On the Friday before our scheduled dip, Pancho took us into a deserted area of the dockyard and there in all its glory, on a shingle covered, weed infested patch was a dirty, rusty, skid mounted cylinder called a decompression chamber connected to an engine driven compressor. Pancho suggested that, as we were Tiffs, we should check things over. On inspection we discovered that it was a bit unusual in that it was dual fuel, starting on petrol and changing over to diesel when warmed up. The starter battery was flat as a fart, so we drew a fully charged unit out of the Dockyard Stores on Pancho's slop chit and tried again with no joy. By this time we were getting very suspicious of Pancho's motives! Doing a compression check (to check piston and valve condition) we found that three of the four cylinders were well below acceptable values, and no wonder, H had found traces of charred rag in the air intake. Some silly sod had obviously tried starting the thing on diesel using an old and very frowned on trick of removing the air intake filter and holding a burning oil-soaked rag near the air intake whilst turning the engine over and so preheating the combustion air. Unfortunately whoever did it got the whole burning rag too close and got it sucked in. We buttonholed Pancho but he denied any prior knowledge but we didn't believe him, but when we explained our fears that it might have bent valves, his uncompromising answer was that if it couldn't be fixed the course couldn't be completed. H and I went into a huddle and decided that as we'd come this far it would be daft to give in at the stage we were at so we decided to give up our weekend to see if we could fix it. By the time we'd made this decision it was getting dark, but there was no lighting around, no power points and we tried but failed to borrow a generator, so it was going to have to be daylight.

So, early on Saturday morning we bummed some tools and started to do an engine top overhaul. On removing the cylinder head we found charred rag under three inlet valves, and out of four, you don't stand any chance of running it up. On stripping the head down we found no bent inlet valves but two burnt exhaust valves that were nothing to do with the rag job but still needed attending to if we were to stand a chance of success. These valves needed precision grinding, so we decided to bum off 'Cally' (HMS *Caledonia*) our old stomping ground. We found the workshop Regulating Chief Stoker, and H sweet–talked him into opening up the tool room for us and gave us permission to use the valve grinder, but it was designed to grind larger valves, so I turned to and made a centring sleeve. Eventually we had everything ready to reassemble before we lost the light. Sunday morning dawned bright and cold, and we got down to it. We begged, borrowed, and stole grinding paste for lapping valves in, jointing compound for the rocker cover etc., packing for the cylinder head joint and feeler gauges for setting tappets. Having finally got it all reassembled, we checked petrol, diesel fuel, (having first drained off nearly half a pint of water from the tank), cooling water and oil for the engine and oil for the compressor, and both air intake filters. Came the moment of truth just before dusk, we tossed for it and I won so H pressed the tit which caused just a whirring noise and nothing else. He tried again with the battery slowly giving out when suddenly a couple of smoke rings puffed skywards, and then 'Verroom' and it was away. The governor took over and it warmed up nicely and then was switched over to diesel. It gave a couple of coughs and then came back onto the governor. The compressor clutch was engaged and a satisfying hiss emanated from the open hatch of the pot. We shut it down and shook hands, all we needed then was for the cylinder head joint to last out till the next day's pot dip. We cleared away the debris, got a quick wash and brush up and thumbed a lift into 'Dumps' (Dunfermline) our old apprentice days stomping ground, and got pissed.

Came the dawn, a bit worse for wear, Pancho came into the classroom looking quite glum and asked how we'd got on and was gobsmacked when we told him it was fixed.

We did the classroom bit about procedure and safety and then went to the tank to do the 'Dip'. We started the engine with no trouble, then climbed into the pot, Pancho shut the hatch and engaged the compressor clutch and slowly raised the pressure to represent the equivalent of 100ft depth, equivalent to three atmospheres, stayed there for the regulation 10 minutes and then slowly decompressed. Due to the previous night's run ashore we were not in very good condition, but survived and

'Mother'

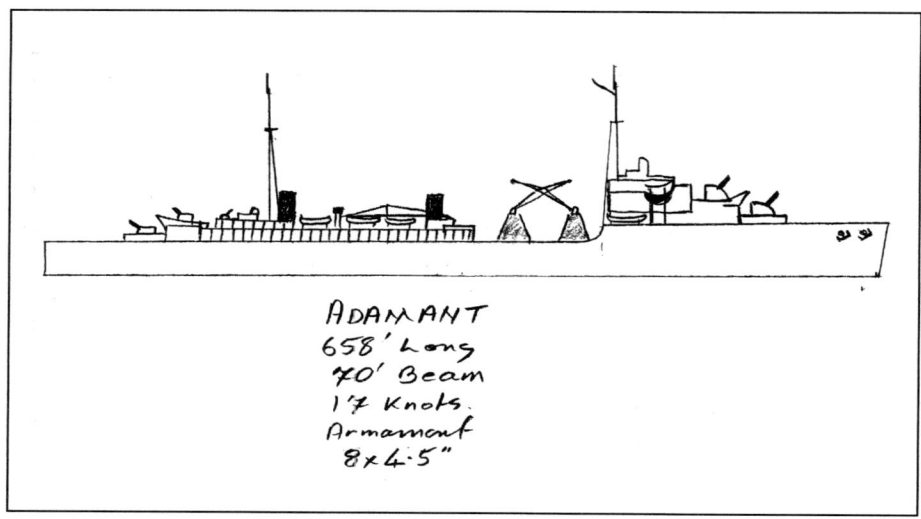

ADAMANT
658' Long
70' Beam
17 Knots.
Armament
8 x 4·5"

on return to the diving school had a couple or so guffs of oxygen and felt a lot better, and we eventually finished the course. We were awarded our shallow water diving badges of a gold divers' Hard Hat and divers' log book, sewed the badge on the right sleeve above the three buttons and felt very pleased with ourselves.

We were both then drafted back to *Adamant* to work in the workshops, I in the light machine shop, H in the heavy machine shop. Depot ships are amazing vessels, fully equipped to cope with any job and any emergency. The snag with all this expertise and up to the minute equipment when things were slack, which was often 'Guvvy'* reigned supreme. You could get anything (for a price) cars being one of the best money or tot spinners. New exhaust systems, accident repairs, chassis welding, you name it – it could be done. Most branches deep down hate 'Tiffs'* because of their rapid advancement, but they knew where to go for help when they were in the shit!

Even the Master at Arms or Jaunty (The Senior Regulating CPO*) God to most, asked me if I would have a look at his car. It was an old sit up and beg Rover 90. Just the tappets and a bit of an exhaust blow, he said! It turned out that H and I spent all weekend again. The tappets were overhead inlet and side exhaust valves, a bugger of a job with no room to work. The exhaust was even worse, a complete new system was required which passed through the chassis members and used triangular connecting flanges, a right sod of a job. We had to use a lot of 'on'* to get it ready to fit.

But in the long run these sorts of jobs pay dividends as in this case. One of our number in the Tiffy's mess had transgressed and was in the rattle. Some time earlier he had done a guvvy for the Admiral's Chief Steward. Unfortunately he was busy when the Tiff went to collect his dues but rather than turn the poor lad away he sat him down in the steward's pantry, plonked a large bottle of gin and a bottle of orange cordial and a glass in front of him and left him to it. David 'Tugg' Wilson (all Wilsons are Tugg in the mob) didn't have the heart to tell him that he didn't like gin. Still, he thought, I'll have one to show there's no hard feeling. Unfortunately he began to quite like it, eventually, when the bottles were empty he decided to sod off and was last seen by a particularly snide junior member of the regulating branch staggering into the heads* wherefrom disgusting noises emanated. Fortunately one of our mess stewards saw said RPO* legging it to the Jaunty's office, and told us what he'd seen. H decided to see if having a word with the Jaunty himself would help, as being drunk onboard was a serious offence. We didn't know what H had said, and he wouldn't tell us, but whatever he said, it worked. Tugg got a right bollocking but nothing more. The snag was that if he'd been trooped the steward would have been implicated and also trooped, so H got a good result.

We, that is H and I, eventually got very bored with the general day routine and both volunteered for submarines! It seemed to be a good idea at the time. So we both slapped in (requested in writing) to join the Boats*. To my dismay, H's request was granted and he was told he would be drafted in time for the next submarine course, whilst my request was refused! I was gobsmacked, and slapped in through my Divisional Officer to question why I had been turned down. My DO came back to me, and in an embarrassed manner, told me he had made me an appointment with the base MO*. He would not be drawn on the reason, so I had no option but to wait until my appointment came up. The consultation was short and sweet, the MO*, a Surgeon Commander came straight to the point and told me that I had been refused my request on the ground of my habitually contracting sexually transmitted diseases. I was absolutely floored, as although I'd had my moments, nothing like that had befallen me. I protested and asked to see the file that he had been consulting. He was good enough, as he was not obliged to show it to me. Waves of relief passed over me as the file was not mine, but someone of a similar name. To cut a long story short, the correct file was found, my request was granted and we both went down to HMS *Dolphin* together. The Sick Bay Tiff (Sick Berth Attendant) was given a mild bollocking for getting the wrong file, so no real harm was done, and honour restored!

The boats course was great, the technicalities were no problem for either of us. We had a great set of course mates who all helped each other, and of course H and I also combined our efforts, which made things even better, and a lot easier.

Three things of this period stick out in my memory, the Canadians who trained with us, the first sea trip in the boat, and the tank.

The Canadians were great blokes who integrated so well but couldn't get their heads round the English weather! Jim Matiatchuk from Saskatoon Saskatchewan was heard to utter in a loud despairing voice, having experienced, in a corrugated iron roofed building, spring sunshine, heavy rain, and snow,

'God damn it, all we need now is hailstones and we've had the whole damned lot.' And the heavens obliged with deafening results.

The sea trip! To me it was everything I'd volunteered for. We were split into small groups and at various times, joined a boat and went on a day trip. Our ride was an old, weary, but very happy HMSm *Trite*, an old wartime 'T' boat with a good record in the Mediterranean theatre. She had a riveted hull as opposed to modern welding, and was still fitted with four inch gun sited forward of the conning tower.

Visitors to boats for sea trips are limited in number because of both the amount of room available, but mainly the number of escape equipment sets that are carried. We guests huddled in the control room, could hear all the orders coming from the Bridge and also the responses. I was amazed at how calm the crew were at going about their business. A message came over the tannoy to 'open up for diving' and the crew still went calmly on. Eventually the klaxon sounded, down came the bridge crew, the conning tower lid was shut and then what appeared to be nothing else, no dramatics, nothing. The officer of the Watch ordered open Main Vents, the Tiffy on the panel operated some levers, and that seemed to be it. The Officer of the Watch seemed preoccupied with the panel between the planesmen, then I looked at the depth gauge and realized it was moving. We were moving but there was no sensation of it. The Captain had the rear periscope raised and swung round once, then invited us visitors to have a look. To my amazement and delight the view was incredible, and so clear, being able to use the high power effect was better than high magnification binoculars, also to elevate and depress and, being binocular, object ranges could be measured. We then were given a Cook's tour from stem (torpedo room and fore ends) to stern (motor rooms and after ends), the complexity of which overwhelmed us all. After the official tour we were given leave to do our own thing for half an hour. A few of us ended up talking to the Chef, a rather laconic Glaswegian whose work place (Galley) was an alcove off the main passageway. How he managed to cater for the whole crew in such a confined space was a matter of wonder, which led one of us to ask him if he had had any hairy moments? He started chuckling, and explained in a broad Glaswegian accent,

'Ah rrmemba uonce ah was dooin dinnah fer the wardroom an some verra verra important visitors. It was rroast poork an aall the trimmins, and A wer just aboot to dish up an a'd forgot the green beenz, so ah grabbed a tin o em an banged em int oven, one thing a forgot was t peirs the tin an carrid on dishin up. Shuddenly there was such a bang, ah ended up wearin the oven dooor an there wer green beenz evera were, what a bloody mess. Evera thing wer covered in f – -in green beenz, and ah wer charged wi abuse o government property, but the Skipper saw the funny side o it and let me off wi a bollokin.'

The tannoy called us visitors back to the control room, and the Skipper told us that his crew, for our benefit, was going to demonstrate a 'gun action' exercise, and warned us not to get in the way.

Action stations were called, and a few personnel changed places. The Skipper called for periscope depth and did a quick all round sweep, and ordered 'Stand by for Gun Action' and suddenly the control room is full of very stern looking guns crew, all in wet weather gear? (The weather up top was perfect!). The gun layer, Breech Block slung on a lanyard round his neck, stationed directly under the gun hatch. The next order gave serious concern to us uninitiated.

'Pressurize the boat', and the panel operator, who was now the outside ERA* (Wrecker*) opened a compressed air valve to the atmosphere and our ears started to feel the effect like going downhill very fast. The Wrecker was checking the atmospheric pressure gauge, zero being normal, and either side being plus for pressure and minus being vacuum. When the pressure reached the gauge maximum the Wrecker stopped blowing and reported the boat pressurized. The next set of orders came thick and fast, 'down periscope, increase to 140 revolutions, blow main ballast, planes to dive!' I found out later that the idea was to surface as quickly as possible and get off the first round as soon as possible. So blowing main ballast to give positive buoyancy, planes to dive counteracts the first action and increased speed helps. The next thing to look for is a tendency for the depth gauge to reduce, at which time there is another rush of orders. 'Stand by Guns Crew, reverse the planes, open the Gun Hatch.' With that your lungs feel as if they're bursting, there's a roaring as the built up pressure releases through the Gun Hatch, and also blowing the Gun Layer with it onto the casing with a column of water pouring back into the boat, the rest of the guns crew follow and quicker than it takes to tell there's a sharp crack of the first round away. To the uninformed this evolution is both confusing and frightening but to the trained eye it is an extremely precise exercise, which was extremely effective during the last world war.

The tank was something else, the object of the course being to train the boat's crew to escape from sunken vessels, in this case from 100 feet depth. The first thing that has to be done is to check your buoyancy! Most people are naturally positively buoyant; a very small minority are big boned and just plain sink. Guess who sank, you've got it, H, so for the rest of the practical part of the course he had to wear a red hat. The course was good and the training was excellent, and in those days the escape method was free ascent, which means you use your natural buoyancy to rise 100 feet. When you are at a depth of 33 feet one extra atmosphere is pressing on you but you don't notice because your lungs are at the same pressure. At 99 feet you are at 3 atmospheres but again it is equalized internally. The snag comes when you depressurize when ascending because the air in your lungs expands and the body's natural reaction when underwater is to hold on to it, which will over pressure and burst the lungs. So one of the first things you are taught is that you must force yourself to breath out for the whole of the 100-foot ascent. It takes on average 22 seconds to rise 100 feet; you try blowing out hard for that length of time!

It's all quite clever really, the Tank is about 20 feet in diameter and 115 feet tall, the extra 15 feet being a mock-up of the interior of a typical boat with a hatch in the middle. A small group at a time are herded into the mock-up dressed in cozzies, and, in H's case, a daft hat, carrying a demand valve on a short length of hose with a male instantaneous coupling (known as a PCL). The entrance watertight door is shut and sealed behind you and then the fun starts. A twill trunk is rigged by removing closure boards from round the escape hatch and the canvas tube is pulled down and held in shape at the bottom by a steel ring sewn into the skirt. The top end of the tube is secured round the hatch with a watertight joint. The lower ring of the twill trunk ends up about 30 inches above deck level and secured rigidly by four light lines to ring bolts set into the deck. Now comes the tricky bit, the compartment is flooded, which is when we plugged our demand valves into the PCL sockets, which ran in rows in the deckhead of the mock-up compartment. As the compartment flooded and the water rose so did the pressure, and with the dull emergency lighting, a heavy mist formed to give a very eerie atmospheric feeling. With the water up to our chests the pressure equalized and our instructor, who had an extra long air hose, ducked under the rim of the twill trunk, climbed into the trapped air pocket and released the clips of the hatch which flew open to release the trapped air. The instructor then returned back to the compartment to supervise our exit. It sounds easy but it isn't that simple, first you have to shuffle along changing PCL sockets as you go, then it's your turn and you take a last breath, discard your demand valve, duck under the trunk rim and up you go forgetting all your training about breathing out, but suddenly you are grabbed and thumped in the gut, which makes you breath out rather explosively. What happens is that a Swim Boy has spotted your omission and has swum out from his alcove, in which he has a refreshable air supply, and given you a sharp reminder, and then popped back to his billet to peer out of his sight glass looking for his next victim. You're still not out of the woods though because the human body is less than aerodynamic and tends to shoot off at angles rather than straight up so the Swim Boys pop out, spin you round and send you on your zigzag way. You eventually end up bobbing about on the surface very disorientated and very relieved, but also quite elated at having done The Tank.

The rest of the course went ahead apace, eventually passing out as makee submariners, and after a good party in the mess H and I found we had draft chits back to Gareloch and *Adamant* as spare crew, kicking our heels again, which was not our style, so we started making a nuisance of ourselves in the draft office. Eventually we got lucky, H went to a new 'P' boat, and I eventually got the first of the brand new 'O' class, and joined our respective vessels within days of each other as part threes.

A part three is the lowest of the low, he knows nothing and has to start from scratch learning all the systems, both mechanical and electrical, and also all the various fixtures and fittings. You can always tell a part three as he is always very grubby with a note pad and pencil appearing from the bowels. Every one has to do it when they join a new boat, even Officers, including a new Skipper. When you think you are ready an oral examination is conducted to find out how little you know. Eventually you are allowed to keep an accompanied watch, for us Tiffs it was in the engine room, but it was a bit boring as this type of boat was diesel electric where all the manoeuvring was done by the Greenies (electrical department). The only taxing bits being crash dive practice and starting and stopping snorting, so I made a few noises and got myself the second job as dickey outside ERA commonly known as the Wrecker, as the incumbent, Wally Hart was shortly leaving the service. It suited me down to the ground being varied with unusual tasks and challenges, and I sure got to know the boat very well indeed. A couple of instances, I was sat off watch in the mess when Scratch (the 2nd Coxwain) came in asking if anybody had seen the sewing machine. Someone said he'd seen it in the spare stowage locker in the fore ends but he understood that it was bust. I decided to go with Scratch to see what was what. Sure enough we found it where we were told it was and sure enough it did-

O and P Class

n't work, but to cut a long story short, I found that someone had tried to use an oversize shuttle which was jammed. I managed to prise it out with no damage, and loaded and threaded the right size one and tried it out successfully on Scratch's bit of sewing, after which I got to do most of the machine sewing (which to be honest I didn't mind as it kept me busy). Another little challenge was the film projector. When a boat went on an extended trip Their Lordships in their infinite wisdom considered that up to date entertainment would keep Jack happy and so supplied vessels with up to the minute film releases and of course a projector and screen. Unfortunately just after we left for an extended exercise the incumbent projectionist, a killick* greeny, discovered that the projector was defective and I was invited to try and fix it. I found that the take up spool drive pulley bearing bush had collapsed and its securing screw was missing. So I went back aft and down to the shaft space where a little 4 inch lathe was installed and got to work. The measure of the importance of film shows can be judged by the fact that I was excused watch keeping to complete the repair. The next evening came the big trial with me doing the projecting. It went down a bomb; half a dozen laced together Tom and Jerrys, 'Good old Fred'. I was, as a result, voted senior projectionist and projector maintenance engineer, well whoopee F-in do! After a while I was talked into going back into the Engine Room and eventually was made Donk Shop Horse (Tiffy in charge of the Engine Room).

Suddenly everything changed for me because of the advent of Nuclear Powered Propulsion and the building of the RN's first nuclear powered boat. I waited impatiently for H to come in from patrol and took him on a run ashore, poked a couple of pints down his throat, not that he needed any persuading, and broached the subject of us volunteering to do the nuclear course. I thought he was going to choke, because he went a funny shade of purple, and refused point blank to even consider it and no amount of cajoling would change his mind. It was upsetting for me, and I respected his decision, but I was determined to be in with the new technology and slapped in next day to attend the next nuclear course. My request was eventually granted and at the appropriate time my draft chit came through and I was off down south to join HMS *Sultan* the RN Engineering School.

A dozen of us started the course, all of us technicians of one sort or another, ERA's EA's Mechanicians and Electrical Mechanicians. It was all very different to what we'd been used to and it was all classroom work, and very hard too. It was long before calculators were available and we had to be taught to use slide rules before we could start on any other subjects. Subjects like higher maths, calculus, water chemistry, reactor physics and PWR design (Pressurized Water Reactor), to name but a few. We even got homework to do, and many an unhappy hour was spent in the recreation room wrestling with a formula as long as your arm to solve a reactor design problem. It was very hard work with no let up apart from one amusing incident that involved me.

I was one of the few on the nuclear course who lived aboard *Sultan* so was subject to weekend duties, a pain in the bum but unavoidable. Having three buttons meant that one of my duties was witnessing the Troops* rum issue. This particular Saturday the rum ration came up spot on time at twelve noon, with all the troops left aboard queuing up with their tongues hanging out. It was my duty to witness the consumption of their tot on production of their Station Card. The tot was an eighth of a pint of 100 proof dark Demerara Rum and a quarter of a pint of water, known as two and one, that had to be consumed on the spot, which was the reason for me being there. All went well for a while, but after a short time I thought I recognized one of the sailors in the queue. He showed a station card, got his tot, turned away from me and downed it in one and sort of slid off. It got me thinking how many more were at it, and damn me if meladdo wasn't back again ten minutes later for yet another tot, which was taking the urine. I let him get near the issuing table and then called him to one side and told him, in a very quiet voice that could not be overheard, that two tots was one too many and if he didn't piss off and take his cheating mates with him I'd troop the lot of them. The result was dramatic, as he walked slowly down the queue almost half of them peeled off and disappeared.

The course continued at breakneck speed and we were all hard pushed to keep up, but one advantage for us not RA* was that an instructor who had been in the States to do the nuclear course but who had not been able to join the first nuclear boat due to ill health. John Redwood was an outstanding instructor and also a Chief Tiffy, who lived aboard like us. Being Tiffs we shared the same mess and John was always on hand to give us help, but he had an awful problem, or should I say we had a problem with him. He looked a lot younger than his years, in fact he was near retirement age*, and had served in the Second World War, but not in the mob, in the RAF and he had medals to prove it. For this reason nobody wanted to know him when we were on Divisions* because if you were to stand anywhere near him, the Inspecting Officer would stop at John and suggest that he had the wrong medals up, so John had to explain that he had been a rear gunner in Lancaster Bombers in the last war, which was all very well for him as he was congratulated, the snag was that the Inspecting Officers entourage ranging down the line were staring at you trying very hard to pick holes in your turn out. At the order to fall in, blokes would pull all sorts of strokes to be as far from John as possible.

We on our course all passed eventually and went our separate ways, and guess where I ended up? You've got it, back at Gareloch spare crew waiting for *Vectra* to come in from patrol as I was drafted part three to her. Whilst waiting, H's boat came in and we had a good run ashore, swapping notes and getting arseoled. He told me he was thinking of volunteering for Periscopes, which was a very sought after billet, but it didn't sound right coming from him. I took him on another run ashore a couple of days later, and after a few wets I broached the subject of Periscopes, to which he ummed and aad a bit, then he admitted he'd met this bird and reckoned that it was the real thing. Now H had been around a bit and had known plenty of girls, you could almost say he was a bit of a lad, but I'd never known him act like this, this was serious stuff.

Shortly after this revelation, *Vectra* came in, did a quick turn round and I was away, part three again. It felt good to be off again with a new challenge, and guess who was Jimmy, Lieutenant Westerman who had been the Sublieutenant spare hand on my last 'O' boat. Having got successfully through my part three I was appointed second dickey Outside Wrecker with all the same challenges as before and some new ones like electronic rather than manual controls, transistors, magamps* and lots and lots of room in this revolutionary vessel, or so it seemed. Anyway, my idea was to get aft and get involved in the nuclear propulsion side of things. I eventually got the wrecker's job and got a second dickey to train up. 'Chippy' Carpenter was good, with a mind like a computer and a photographic memory, the one failing he had was that whatever job we did together, I ended up with shit up to the eyeballs and he came out clean as a whistle. All very infuriating, but he was good and I increasingly left him on his own while I did my own thing. I was particularly interested in the sonar set we had fitted. It was state of the art at the time, using transistors, (it was before microchips were invented) and needed heat sinks and a cooling water system, which is why I was able to get in on the act and befriend the Tiffy in charge of the electronics and general maintenance of the set. 'Bunny' Warren, an REA (radar Electrical Artificer) who joined boats to specialize in sonar, and looked more like a prop forward than an electronic whiz kid. The set he looked after was, at the time, so good and so secret that the Yanks would have given their eyeteeth for it. It would do a series of pings, process the return echo, photograph the results and back project them onto a one metre square screen every 45 seconds where a couple of Sailors would mark in chinograph pencil possible contacts and erase them if they did not develop. Their Lordships also required a 35-millimetre record of the same screen, so I was given the task of mounting a camera in a suitable position, which I did between two watch keepers, and rigged it with a remote shutter release, so that all one of the operators had to do was his normal job and then check the camera view was clear and press the release as it had automatic wind on. Unfortunately a newly qualified Sublieutenant had joined us as a spare hand and took a particular interest in the sonar compartment and would spend all his spare time peering at the screen. One particular operator, a laconic TGM* from the Outer Hebrides, always seemed to be on the watch when the nosy Subby was in attendance and he was always in the way when the photo had to be taken. Eventually he got so fed up of asking the Subby to please excuse him and have him apologize that eventually as he turned, with the Subby in the way yet again, he held up his hand and said in a loud voice:

'Don't bother moving Sir, just turn sideways and I'll take it through your F - -ing ears'. Exit very red faced Subby never to be seen in the sonar shack again.

Being a new and proper submarine rather than a submersible we were in great demand for exercise purposes with all the NATO fleets, especially with our sonar set to help us. An incident I was involved in which gave me great satisfaction was when, just after one such exercise had started, our super-duper sonar set packed up. I went to see Bunny who told me that the micro switch-sequencing shaft was inoperable so the Skipper was going to have to call the whole exercise off, so I talked

Bunny into letting me have a look. Having seen the damage I reckoned I could have a fair chance of effecting a repair, so we had a word with the EO* who in turn spoke to the Skipper who reckoned that we had nothing to lose and to go ahead. So it was back aft to the up market Lathe where I turned up a gear blank the same size as the existing damaged one in brass and cut out the damaged section of teeth, then cut a section out of the blank and epoxy resin glued it in. Then came the tricky bit, re-cutting the teeth as it was a helical gear, but careful use of needle files saw the job done. Bunny and I refitted it and gave it a quick whirl and lo and behold it worked and the exercise went ahead after a short delay. The sequel to the story is that my recommendation that future units be fitted with gearwheels manufactured in yellow metal instead of aluminium was adopted, and I won an award of a glass bottomed pewter tankard from the Herbert Lott Trust Fund (or as we called it, the Herbert Trott Lust Fund). When it finally turned up along with a few other blokes' awards and promotions we were all called into the wardroom where the Skipper did the presentations. When it came to my turn he opened a can of beer and said he wanted to christen it and poured it into my new tankard and straight onto my boots and the Wardroom carpet so I had to go away and mend the damned thing, the story of my life!

One amusing incident occurred just before I left the Wreckers job to go back aft. We had been having trouble with the fresh water plumbing in that the automatic change over system was not working correctly because a sensor had malfunctioned and we had no spare so we would have to wait till we returned to base. The one good thing about a nuclear boat was that fresh water was really quite plentiful and was stored in two relatively large tanks, one being in service whilst the other was being filled by the back aft distillation unit. With the automatic change over system out of action it was PO Stoker Steve Cutts' job to do it manually. All tank-operating movements are performed using compressed air so that when Steve changed over fresh water tanks his routine was to depressurize the on line tank, divert the distiller output to the now depressurized tank and isolate it from the supply system. The other tank has now to be isolated from the distillation line, opened up to the service line and then pressurized to give adequate supply pressure at the taps. It sounds complicated but in fact it takes no longer than it takes to read this explanation. Our Skipper at this time was one of the best Gaffers I've ever served under and shall remain nameless as he now holds a very senior position indeed. At the time of the incident he was a very senior three ringer, not too tall and rather portly to say the least. I was on watch at the panel on a deep dived transit, so everything was quiet and everyone was alert but relaxed, when the fresh water low alarm went off, so I called Steve up on the intercom to have him change over the tanks. Steve, who was also not very tall, and also portly, came up into the control room to do the biz on the air tank system. He had just depressurized the nearly empty tank when this apparition appeared at the entrance of the passage leading to the wardroom and Officers bathroom. All eyes in the control room focused on the figure of the Skipper with a flowery bath hat on, a skimpy towel round his ample waist, covered from head to foot in very heavy soap lather. Poor old Steve couldn't contain himself and burst in a very loud uncontrollable laugh. Our beloved Captain stood in all his glory, now with a bright red, almost purple face and exploded with the words,

'Shut up Fat Bastard!!'

And the whole of the control room collapsed in a big heap of hilarity, whereupon the Skipper spun on his heels and as dignified as possible marched off back to the bathroom with the noise of very loud laughter ringing in his ears.

Shortly after this very amusing little incident my request to go back aft was granted and there was I, part three again, but I had a bit of a head start, as I knew all the auxiliary systems having been Wrecker. My first watch-keeping billet was the fresh water distillation unit, which converted seawater into pure drinking and steam generator feed water. Then onto the steam generator level control panel and its associated testing and chemical treatment of feed water. Then onto the engine room proper looking after Main Engine Turbines and the Turbogenerators and the associated closed feed system.

Eventually I made it to my ultimate goal, the manoeuvring room, starting off with the main engine control panel, which was a doddle as the only time anything really happened was entering and leaving harbour apart from the odd rev change.

The next stage was the electrical distribution panel, which was a lot more of a challenge. One of the tricky operations being paralleling up the TGs*. It goes this way, the Engine Room Tiffs run up the off the line TG and when happy with it, hand its control over to the gaffer (OOW*) of the manoeuvring room who then tells the panel operator to do the biz. Then comes the tricky bit, getting the incoming genny to run at the correct speed. It's called the synchronous speed, which means that both gennys are running at exactly the same speed, which is achieved by the operator using a speeder switch, which remotely adjusts the gennys' governor and so the rotor speed. The next tricky bit involves the synchronization gauge, which is like a clock face but with only one hand, which is adjusted by careful use of the speeder switch to rotate it slowly clockwise approximately once every 5 seconds. This means that the incoming unit is running minutely faster than the loaded unit, the breaker (big switch) used to bring this off line unit in, in parallel is prepared by priming the breaker operating switch when the synchronizer hand is at 5 minutes to twelve and rotating at the right speed. Now comes the *really* tricky bit 'cos you have to do it all again, the problem is that the minute speed difference is controlled electro-magnetically and is not always steady and the rotating hand can become somewhat erratic. The snag is that this time the switch is operated; the main breaker slams in and connects both TG's together, locking them electrically. If you get it wrong the best that can happen is there is a slight thud and the lights dip momentarily and a cheer goes up throughout the boat, causing you some embarrassment. But if you get it badly wrong there is an almighty bang as two great lumps of machinery try to stop to phase lock together. It has been known for this type of incident to cause severe reduction gear box damage entailing extensive downtime and expensive repairs, and of course a very rough ride for the unfortunate panel operator. I've seen trainees reduced to quivering wrecks trying to make the final switch, even having to be relieved by an experienced operator to show them that the trick was to take your time and not to worry if the delay was prolonged, as it was his responsibility not to be rushed.

The final qualifying hurdle was the reactor control panel, which to the newcomer was awesome, the reason being its massive power potential, or to put it another way, destructive force if something was to go wrong. For this the safety systems were extremely complex such that all control parameters were in triplicate and an automatic two out of three logics was operated by bank upon bank of electronics racks containing row upon row of magnetic amplifiers, as this was still the days before microchips. One of the snags with mag-amps was their susceptibility to temperature fluctuation, the solution being to install huge air conditioning units, which was, as a spin off, also good for the crew.

Basically the system was that very pure water at very high pressure was pumped round the reactor core picking up a high temperature without generating steam, because of the high pressure, and passing it through the steam generator, which was just a big heat exchanger on the secondary side of which was water which generated steam because it ran at a lower pressure, and there you have it in a nutshell.

I did all the qualifying and eventually made Chief of the watch, and then also Chief Tiff of the boat, which gave me great satisfaction. Shortly after this last event we took the boat round to Rosyth for an intermediate dry docking in company with old faithful *Adamant*, and guess who was in the spare crew mess, yes H. After a bit of backslapping he told me he'd volunteered for periscopes and it had been granted. I was real pleased for him, as it was a very complex job, which included all types of masts, not just periscopes. We went ashore to Dumps and our old haunts, chewed the fat and got pleasantly pissed. Dockyard routine was very boring and nine to five, so H and I decided to re-qualify as Shallow Water Divers, but found that the Rosyth School had shut down. But we were told that across the river Forth in HMS *Lochinvar*, our old haunt, was a Clearance Divers depot and School so we got in touch with them and were invited to join them anytime. This was where we met Andy Bromfield, one of the instructors, a nutter. All Clearance Divers are nutters, but Andy was tops, complete and utter, well who in his right mind would want to grovel about in all sorts of murky water digging up live explosives and defusing them? He made us do all sorts of daft things, one of the daftest being to go round the jetty when the tide was out, no problem you may say, but you'd be wrong. Anyone who knows *Lochinvar*, which is now a public Marina, will know that the jetty is extremely long and will also know that when the tide's out, half the length of the jetty is soft oozing mud. That pillock Andy made us all wear full rebreathing gear and fins, you want to try running in mud wearing fins, the only way it can be done is to run backwards! It was exhausting, but the penalty for coming last was to have to do it again, the sadistic sod, because it was always me or H who lost. We had some good runs ashore afterwards though and got to know Andy and Edinburgh a lot better, and got our diving qualifying dips in.

Eventually the refit ended and we went our separate ways again. I had some bad news that a more senior Chief Tiff was appointed over me which pissed me off more than a lot, even more so because on enquiring of the Chief Engineer why, he couldn't give me a satisfactory explanation, but insisted it was nothing to do with my performance. So I immediately slapped in for a Draft because I didn't get on with the new bloke, but I was told I would have to give him a good hand-over period, which pissed me off even more. I stuck it out and eventually got my draft to Gareloch base, where I met up again with H, who was still in periscopes and still enjoying it.

The periscope shop had been transferred from the Depot Ship to a brand new shop in the base so he and I had a few runs ashore. Then he told me that the girl he'd met earlier was the same one he'd mentioned a while ago, and it was obvious that it was serious stuff, to cut a long story short they got engaged and eventually got married and as I said I supported them and like to think that I helped. I was their Best Man and pleased to do it and so life went on with H living happily ashore in Helensburgh.

At the base I was made IC workshops, but not all personnel were submariners as, with the advent of the larger boats and double crewing, volunteers to the service were becoming scarcer than rocking horse dung, so general service bods were employed on the base and I had some G. S. Tiffs in the workshops. One such Tiff was a third class rate by the name of Norman Kaye, Danny to his friends (all Kayes are Danny in the Mob). He intrigued me in that he was a real good grafter and built like a brick shithouse, who was 3 or 4 classes ahead of us in apprentice training but still only a third class rate. He was a good all rounder, was a fitter and turner by trade but taught himself to weld, I don't mean tacking like most of us could do but coded good quality stuff. One of his hobbies was cars and motor bikes, the same as me, and we ended up collaborating on a few guvvy jobs, and also going to a few road race meetings on an old spring hub Triumph Thunderbird with his Manx Norton strapped to an RSC which was secured to the chassis in place of the side car, we went all over to race meetings, he never did much good because he was far too heavy, and the Manx too old, but we enjoyed ourselves, he as the racer and me as his pit manager. I also introduced him to H and we all ended up having a few good runs ashore when we were able to spring H, but Danny was a bit of a lunatic when he'd had a few too many, but more of that and him later! Things were going along nice and smoothly until Stan Westerman caught up with me.

Chapter 5

Players 2

I was called into the Base Engineer's Office and was abruptly told by him that he didn't know what was going on and didn't want to know, but it was very inconsiderate and inconvenient of me to want to be reassigned. My protests of innocence went unheeded and I was told I had to report to some 'special operations department' office somewhere in a remote area of the base.

Reporting as ordered, a rather tasty Wren ushered me into a poky little office to be confronted by none other than Commander Stan Westerman.

'Ah, come in, I'll be with you in a jiffy,' and promptly shot out before you could say kiss my arse. He came back in a few moments later with a bundle of papers under his arm.

'Excuse me Sir but what the Hell's going on? I was quite happy where I was.' To which he just waved his arm at the paperwork he had brought in.

'Just have a skeg at that lot before you get carried away and say something you'll regret.'

I started reading and it slowly dawned on me that the gist of the file was to do with what Stan had discussed with me earlier, which I had forgotten all about. But this report went much deeper with lots of detailed planning. The more I read, the gloomier the scenario got, concluding with the prediction of an 85 percent chance of a nuclear holocaust.

'But what's this got to do with me?'

Stan stood up, started pacing for a while deep in thought, then taking a deep breath,

'I know it's presumptuous of me, but after we had our chat and the subsequent meetings I've been working flat out trying to come up with a plan that would be approved by the powers that be. I now have that approval and all I need now is the wherewithal to carry out the plan, part of which is a reliable team.' I tried to interrupt but he held up a restraining hand and bashed on.

'I'd like you to help me choose the team and also help lead it because you know boats, you know diving, you know and can lead personnel, and I need someone I can trust!' He then slumped in his chair and stared at me with piercing eyes.

I really didn't know what to say but I did wonder how the details of the plan were going to be worked out. Eventually I voiced these thoughts and was assured that all would be sorted out or revealed once we had a team we could work with. So after a little time to chew it over in my mind I decided to run with it and told him I was in.

A huge grin split his face; he leant over his desk and shook my hand furiously, pushed a button on the desk and told me to come back at turn to in the morning. A discreet knock on the door and in swept the dishy Wren.

'Take the Chief out, show him round our little empire, feed him coffee then kick him out. Till tomorrow then Chief, and see if you can come up with any names, time is of the essence.'

Wandering back to the mess in a bit of a daze, I wondered what I'd dropped myself in for, but the die was cast so I resolved to make the most of it. So I went back to the Mess, got changed, and wandered over to the Chief and PO's canteen and had a few wets while I chewed over in my mind the latest developments.

I was rudely interrupted by the Base Engineer's runner*, a right snide, who had come over especially to tell me that his boss was not best pleased with me and that my future in the mob looked decidedly bleak. To which I suggested that he urinate away, or words to that effect, but he insisted on staying and giving me earache. I even suggested that he go forth and multiply which still had no effect, by which time I started to lose my temper, so I put one on the end of his nose. The next thing I remember through a curtain of red rage mist was Danny lifting me off him, and I mean lift. He grabbed me by the waist and lifted me over his shoulder and carried me away. The lads ganged upon our local unfriendly, bleeding, snide, with threats of further 'unpleasantness' should he feel inclined to troop* me. But all to no avail, the canteen Manageress who answered to the name of Miss Ruby, a right old battle-axe and a stickler for order and discipline, reported the incident to the regulating office, and I was duly ordered to attend Commander's defaulters at 0800 the following morning.

Standing in line like a common criminal the next morning feeling very hung over, as I had decided to drown my sorrows after the incident. The Joss Man came out with his regulation clipboard and was about to do his thing when he spotted me, crooked his finger, and motioned me over to him, and told me I wasn't on his list and to get lost before he put me on it for wasting his time, with a slight grin. It took me no second bidding and I was off like a rat down a sewer pipe.

Reporting to my new place of graft, I was greeted by the dishy Wren, who curtly told me I was late, and to go into Commander Westerman's office immediately. Feeling more than a little miffed by her attitude, I knocked on his door, which produced a loud 'enter' to which I obliged, to find Commander Stan looking less than happy.

'You're late.'

'Yes I know Sir but ...'

'No excuses, we have urgent work to attend to.'

'Yes I know Sir but ...'

'No buts ...'

'SIR, now just a bloody minute, I was quite happy where I was, then suddenly you appear, I have a criminal record, I'm up to my eyeballs in skulduggery, and can look forward to a very uncertain future, and you have the bare faced effrontery to tell me I'm late and you don't want excuses! Well you can stuff your job up your arse, you and your snotty Wren can go and get knotted and I don't give a toss if you put me in the rattle, at least I'll be away from this crazy set up.' At which point, while I paused for breath, the bastard burst into uncontrollable laughter, which really pissed me off. Eventually I saw the funny side of it and Stan called the 'snotty' Wren in, who was giggling, and he introduced her to me formally as his wife, who apologized for giggling, but had heard our little conversation over the intercom, and had found it quite amusing, much to my embarrassment.

After this little incident things settled down and we got down to the serious business, getting on like a house on fire. Stan explained that we would have two distinct groups, the assault team and the support party. The first group had to be divers and preferably submariners, but it wasn't essential. The second gang had to be good all-rounders, with at least one who was a diver or knew diving techniques and equipment, and at least one who could deal with mechanical breakdowns, the rest to be sailors, as in yachts and canvas.

I had a couple of suggestions in the back of my mind but decided to bide my time until I'd been given a better idea of the plan of action. Stan proceeded to give me an outline of the suggested operation, with a promise of strict confidentiality, which involved transporting the whole kit and caboodle down the Indian Ocean complete with its local type waterborne transport by legitimate Merchant Navy Freighters or similar. At an appropriate position, under cover of darkness the whole shooting match is unloaded, the deed done and the teams reassemble and go home, easy peasy!

Now that I knew a few more details of the operation I decided to open the batting with the suggestion that my mate H join us because, as I explained to Stan, he had as much if not more experience than I and was also a qualified Shallow Water Diver the same as me. H's name was duly noted and an interview appointment set up. Stan then proposed that he himself would be part of the assault team, which brought anguished protests from his wife Penny, (the dishy Wren) all to no avail. For my part I was quite happy, as I knew that he would be a first class leader. Stan then pointed out that the active team should be limited to a minimum and suggested that four should be ample, so I quickly pointed out that we had to have an explosives expert with us, then suddenly the thought struck me, Andy Bromfield, the crazy clearance driver from Port Edgar. The question was, had he left the mob and would he fancy the job? Penny took details of his last know whereabouts and initiated a search through her Wrennery connections in the Personnel Records Office.

Next came the problem of the backup team, the first being, we both agreed, a diving expert, then both together we said in unison Pancho Powers, we knew he had done a Fifth Five* but didn't know more than that, so wheels where put into motion to track him down. The next priority we both agreed was a good all round mechanic, so I suggested Danny Kaye and again an appointment was set up for an interview with him the following day. I pointed out at this stage that we needed a team leader for the backup party, at which point Stan leapt to his feet declaring that he'd been thinking the same thing and had just come up with the ideal solution, Captain RM* 'Dusty' Miller, who he explained he had met out in Aden during all the troubles there. It appears that Dusty was involved in the who-ha in Yemen but nothing much was said about it, but it transpired that he had successfully gone native for a while and spoke fluent Arabic, a meeting with him was duly arranged.

That being all that could be achieved for the day the meeting was adjourned and reconvened in Helensburgh in one of our favourite bars where we discussed some of the lighter moments of our respective careers. We had Penny in stitches with the one about Pancho when he was instructing H and I on our diving course, when one of the lads asked him why we weren't issued with divers' knives (very large, very sharp, double edged, non magnetic instruments). The surprising reply being that one of his early students had been attacked by a particularly vicious Man Eating Pudding Fender and had almost cut himself out of his suit and had also received some rather nasty self inflicted wounds. Penny was laughing but looked a bit quizzical, so Stan explained to her that Pudding Fenders are made of what looks like knitted rope in the shape of a sphere, hence the name Pudding, the filling used being grass (a type of rope that floats). It has a securing rope attached to it which sinks, when one has become damaged it is usually just dumped over the side, becomes waterlogged and sinks because the securing rope drags it down, but only till enough of the said rope is on the bottom when the buoyancy of the Fender takes over and it ends up lurking in suspension. The poor unfortunate diver, in zero visibility, bumped into it, which unnerved him, what he didn't realize was that it was on its way back to him, but with a bit of velocity. When it hit him back it was out with the knife and slash and stab with disastrous results.

Stan came up with the story of a colleague he had served with (I also served with him at a later date). This chap had recently qualified, and at the time of the incident was OOW in the control room on a routine dived listening transit, which is very boring. To liven up the proceedings the rest of the wardroom (negative skipper) decided to wind him up. They knew that he was fluent in Russian and Morse Code, so one of the perpetrators who also had Russian wrote out a bogus message listing soviet naval manoeuvres and passed it to the Communications Officer. They then went back aft to the shaft space, which is where the main propeller shaft disappears into the stern gland. Also down there is a main bearing called a Plumber Block, which is fitted with a 'wrong direction transmitter'. As the name implies, if the man on the manoeuvring panel answers to the telegraph in the wrong direction a big red light comes up on the steering and diving panel. The swines down the shaft space started sending their pre-prepared message on the wrong direction transmitter. Said unfortunate took it in hook line and sinker, started reading the flashing red light, grabbed a pencil and pad and started scribbling, on completion he grabbed the intercom mike and in an urgent voice called 'Captain to the Control Room'. Out came Mon Captain looking a bit peeved at having been disturbed, and went into conference with the victim, his face started to distort and change colour, suddenly he grabbed the intercom mike and yelled into it for an immediate relief for the OOW. Stan shot out of the wardroom, thinking it was an emergency and took over the watch, but much to his dismay and amazement the Skipper dragged our poor unfortunate mug into his cabin, whence the verbal volume was horrendous.

Penny by this time was almost hysterical, so I told her another story about the same chap. The poor sod got a draft chit shortly after this incident which is where I came across him on *Vectra* where I was wrecking. As I went back aft to start qualifying, he had just qualified as OOW in the manoeuvring room, and the engine room watch keepers were awful to him as Jack* was always keen to exploit any weakness. He was a nervous character at the best of times, and the rotten sods made his life a misery, much of it self-inflicted. For instance, on start up when steam is first exported back aft, all the steam lines become waterlogged (full of water) and the automatic steam traps couldn't cope with the sheer volume, so trap bypass valves were fitted which were operated with great care, apart from the one in the far corner just outside the front of the manoeuvring room, which the bloke operating it wanged wide open after giving the appropriate warning signal to the rest of the manoeuvring room gang. The result was an horrendous roaring of escaping steam, with spectacular effect on the said OOW, who would leap about a foot in the air trying not to panic.

Another rotten trick that was pulled off was the Kensitas scam. Kensitas cigarettes used a bright red paper strip to pull out the first fag from the flip top packet. It's not surprising how boredom can bring out the worst in Jack. The idea was to remove the red strip, lick it, stick it at an angle on the cheek, stick the fingers, well splayed so that the red showed through well, then with an ear splitting scream stagger past the manoeuvring room door groaning loudly. This brought me-lad-oh almost diving out of the room in sheer panic to comfort a junior stoker grinning like a Cheshire cat.

By this time the object of all this effort had developed a rather nasty nervous twitch, and an even nastier looking skin complaint, which required medical treatment to his hands and plastic gloves to protect them. The last straw was another cruel trick the engine room watch keepers pulled off on him which involved the emergency manoeuvring position. On Captain's rounds he always praised the engine room for its cleanliness, apart from the state of an area behind this position which was inaccessible due to big red hand wheels which were meant to be used in the event of the manoeuvring room throttle control position being disabled. They were situated tightly up between the main engine casings, so the stoker, whose part of the ship it was, asked the tiff on his watch to undo the nuts securing the hand wheels to their respective spindles, highly irregular but needs must. The tiff duly obliged, and the stoker was able to remove both hand wheels and squeeze down the resultant gap to clean the offending area. This routine was passed onto the stokers of the other watches and the said area was kept pristine, much to the Skipper's and Chief Engineer's delight. The only problem was that the securing nuts were left hand tight, which was not really good practice. Nevertheless, some bright spark thought up another spiffing wheeze to terrorize the said nervous wreck. Again it was in the silent hours, dived in transit, all very steady and boring. He unshackled the hand wheels, and took the ahead one (the biggest) and, on command the whole engine room watch started a hell of a racket by banging hammers and wheel keys, then the perpetrator bowled the hand wheel past the manoeuvring room doorway. The target literally fell out into the passage in sheer panic to view the grins of the whole of the engine room watch. He left shortly afterwards, back to General Service (nearly a basket case). Penny, although laughing, looked a little pensive and both Stan and I realized she was sympathizing with the poor unfortunate. Stan therefore explained that the man was not boats material, and the kindest way career wise was to remove him medically, rather than label him generally unsuitable, which would have ruined his career in the Navy completely. In actual fact he went on in General Service to do rather well. On that note, well oiled, we retired to start afresh the morrow's urgent selections for the coming operation.

Came the dawn, Stan and I met in his office as was arranged to put together a team. Stan had jumped the gun a bit and told me he had invited Captain RM Collin 'Dusty' Miller to meet us because, as he explained, Dusty as an Officer was, we both agreed, allowed to know some of the details so that he could be in on the interviews of other to give an impartial opinion. I suggested that I be excused on the grounds that I was lower deck, but Stan would have none of it, explaining that it was teamwork that mattered regardless of rank. With that he called through to ask Penny to show Captain Miller in. The door opened and a rather stocky dark skinned man marched in, snapped to attention, chopped off a salute, broke into a broad grin, took his hat off and gave Stan a very vigorous handshake. I was introduced and he was invited to take a seat. What followed was an edited explanation of the operation with Dusty's eyes getting wider and wider, and his excitement increasing by the minute. Stan concluded by explaining that we needed a back up team leader, and would he be interested in the job, at which point Dusty almost leapt over the desk at Stan, thanking him profusely. It appears that after his efforts in Aden and the Yemen, his superiors decided that he needed a rest, and had given him a desk job, which was driving him barmy. He confided in us later that he had been contemplating resigning his commission.

The next thing Stan suggested was that we each take on a prospective team member to do an initial assessment into suitability of volunteering for the operation. Stan said he'd look up Pancho Powers, he asked Dusty to see if he could chase up Andy Bromfield the Clearance Diver, and asked me to look up H and Danny Kaye. I made a suggestion that an official chit from Admiral Hopgood giving us authority to dig around a bit might help us oil the wheels. Stan agreed and had the said chits within the hour, it read:

> *To whom it may concern,*
>
> *The bearer is authorized by the undersigned to pursue his investigations and enquiries in any way he sees fit. Any enquiries regarding the holder or his actions or purpose should be addressed to this office.*

Then a horrible scribble, but followed by his official stamp, which worked wonders.

My ploy with Danny and H was to organize a run ashore so that I could do a little groundwork on them. It was my birthday on the Saturday, which gave me the perfect excuse, and they both accepted my invitation. I lashed them up to a few bevies and manoeuvred the conversation round to how my new job was going and how was theirs? Danny admitted that he was a bit pissed off, and was bored to tears with the sheer repetition of the job. I hinted that I might be able to relieve his boredom if he was interested in a bit of excitement, to which H jumped in and asked what I was on about, so I implied that it wouldn't interest him as he was happily married. H admitted that things weren't too brilliant at home and he could do to get away for a bit, and that he could also do with a bit of excitement. We had another couple of wets, by which time I really had them dangling, and left them after promising to get back to them the very next day. I then jacked it up with Stan to interview them in the afternoon and then dashed around the base to get them both relieved from duty. It gave me particular satisfaction to flash my authorization chit at the Base Engineer, who asked what it was all about, and I took great delight in telling him that it was strictly confidential and that I was not at liberty to say and left him fuming, with a copy of Hoppy's chit in his sticky little fist.

It appeared that the interview went well with Stan and Dusty in the chair as I excused myself on the ground that I had a vested interest and would be biased in their favour. After the initial interview it was explained to them that they were recruiting for a special operation that may contain some degree of danger and how did they feel about it? Danny said straight away that he was up for it, H said yes with the proviso that he cleared it with the 'trouble and strife'. On the strength of this we had another run ashore and had a good natter about the coming job, without me giving too much away, which only added to their frustration.

Stan eventually tracked Pancho down on HMS *Reclaim*, the old diving vessel. He was serving as Chief Diver, but *Reclaim* was about to be scrapped and Pancho was reluctantly contemplating leaving the service at the end of his Twenty Two. When Stan suggested a special job for him and his skills if he was interested, it appears that Pancho said yes right away and was nearly in tears with gratitude. Dusty had a bit more trouble tracking Andy down. He found out that Andy had left the service as he had signed on for 'seven and five', which meant that he'd do seven years of active service and five years in reserve, and was at this time on reserve. He had also found out that his home address was in Hull so he asked me to accompany him to look for Andy as he knew that Hull was also my home town, and also that I knew him. We went down south in civvies and stayed in Paragon Station's Royal Station Hotel, and as soon as possible got out the telephone directory and looked up the Bromfields. So as early as was decent the next morning we started the ball rolling. There were only three listed and, sod's law being what it was we struck lucky on the third one. A lady answered and I asked if I could speak to Mr Bromsfield. She replied that he was at work and asked who was calling, so I explained that I knew him from the Navy and just happened to be in the area and would have liked to renew our friendship if it was possible. She explained that he worked for a local builder, which I knew of, so I thanked her and said that if she didn't mind I would be in touch later, to which she said she would look forward to it. Dusty and I discussed the situation and decided to go down to the builder's office to see if we could find out where he was working, so we took a cab to the firm's offices. Dusty stayed in the cab and I went into the office, gave the receptionist my name and asked if she could put me in touch with Mister Andy Bromfield. She asked me for the reason, and when I explained that I was an old friend from his Navy days she picked up the phone, spoke a few words and the next thing I know Andy's coming through the rear office door.

'Stone me, what are you doing here?' as we shook hands, with a big grin on his face.

'Can you get time off to come out and have a natter for a few moments?'

He spoke to the receptionist and explained with a wink that he was going to visit a site, disappeared for a minute and reappeared with his jacket and coat.

'Come on then, where do you want to go?'

I pointed to the cab and introduced him to Dusty,

'Which is your favourite boozer then Andy? We'll go there and have a heart to heart, cos' we've got a proposition for you.'

Andy gave the driver directions and we ended up at The Lambwath on Sutton Road, went into the restaurant with beautifully carved panels, and ordered lunch.

'Come on then, what's it all about?' So Dusty started.

'I'm a Captain RM and he and I are part of a team who are about to embark on a special operation, and we're short of specialist team members. One of those specialists we require is a diver with explosives expertise, and he (pointing to me) suggested you, and as you're still on reserve we'd like you to volunteer. What do you say?'

Andy looked hard at both me and Dusty, and then just stared into space for what seemed like an age, then a big sigh and said,

'My prayer's been answered, I've been wondering how to get out of this rat race for a long time, when will you want me?'

Dusty replied that we were both delighted that he had accepted the job and would be sending a letter of recall and draft instructions immediately as time was of the essence, and so he was going to ring the instructions through, and should receive his orders the next day, or at the latest the day after.

That all settled, Dusty made his phone call to Stan to organize the paperwork and Andy invited us back to his house where we met his delightful wife and two children, were lashed up to tea and pleasant conversation, omitting the pending operation. I then suggested that if a babysitter could be organized Dusty and I would be very pleased an honoured to take them both out for a meal and a drink on us, which was graciously accepted. The evening was a great success and a lot of tall stories were told and a lot of reminiscing was done, then we arranged a cab, and took the Bromfields home, carrying on back to the hotel to pack and caught the night train back up north and managed to get our heads down for a while.

Next day we had another meeting to give everybody a chance to give a progress report and any relevant comments and observations. H had swung it with his Missis, which meant that we had a full diving team of Stan, Andy, H and me. We had the backup of Pancho for the diving side and Danny for the mechanical bits, so the question was what else was required?

Then Stan sprung it on us.

'Gentlemen, I forwarded a plan for this operation some time ago now and have had official approval at the highest level. The most I can reveal at this stage is that the area of operation is the Indian Ocean, and consequently our mode of transport will be an Arab Dhow.' Which brought a loud groan from the audience. Stan held up his hands for silence.

'Not one of your scruffy Persian Gulf jobs, but a large modern seagoing job, the type the smugglers use, with up to date high powered engines and navigational aids. So what we need is a crew to sail it. Dusty will go native as he's done it before in Yemen and will be in charge of the crew. I can do the navigation but we need at least four bodies to work the sailing side. Has anybody got and ideas on recruitment?'

Danny piped up, 'You need bodies that can handle canvas and cordage and know sailing generally, so why not advertise for volunteers from the Faslane Sailing Club?'

'Good idea Danny, I didn't know that such a club existed up here, I'll make out a notice straight away and you can stick it up in an appropriate position. By the way, I've got a special job for you to do a mod on the dhow that we are about to acquire.'

It appears that Stan had negotiated the requisitioning of an impounded smuggler's dhow, the owners having been jailed, and was on its way to Faslane by kind permission of the Royal Fleet Auxiliary vessel *Hannibal* as deck cargo with its masts unstepped.

Danny's project, with the help of 'Hoppy's Chit', was to snivel round the Shipwright Department to design and build a type of cofferdam with a cover to the main saloon, the idea being for the diving team to take to the water from the interior of the vessel, but disguised to pass close inspection undetected. It wasn't too difficult for him because he knew most of the Chippies*, as they were messmates. Meanwhile Stan had put out the notice as promised:

VOLUNTEERS

Required for special operations

Must have extensive sailing experience

NAME	*RATE*	*BRANCH*	*DEPARTMENT*

About a dozen names had been added in only one day, so Stan had to start interviewing straight away.

Eventually R. F. A. * *Hannibal* arrived in Gareloch and the dhow was unloaded, so Danny and his gang of wood butchers got stuck in. Having a good look round his domain he was over the moon. It was fitted out with twin variable pitch props driven by supercharged six litre Chrysler engines so new they had only just been run in, complete with a full set of spares, tools and emergency equipment.

Now came the problems of the hull modifications, the purpose being to cut away a section of the hull planking but leaving the keel intact for rigidity purposes.

To ensure maximum rigidity was maintained, the first thing to do was to add stainless steel cheek plates to the exposed keel section, chemically treated to remove its reflective qualities, then the box section was added to the interior of the hold. Leaving the keel intact meant that the aperture either side of the keel had to be wide enough to allow the passage of a diver in full gear. Fortunately this type of vessel was shallow drafted but wide beamed, which was ideal for this type of modification. It had to be disguised and one of the Chippies came up with the idea of a luxury double bed, to which suggestion the rest of the gang fell about laughing, but I told them to hold hard, as it wasn't such a bad idea. I ran Stan to ground and explained the suggestion to him, he looked a bit sceptical but encouraged me to continue. I explained that the first commission for me was when I was out in the Persian Gulf aboard *Killisport* on the Armilla Patrol where we had to show the flag and stop and search dhows suspected of smuggling arms. If the suspect vessel, when hailed to heave to, had something to hide they dropped the lateen sail, opened the throttles on high-powered engines, arse down and away. With only one boiler flashed up and on line, and the second one taking at least fifteen minutes to bring on line, our only action was to fire star shell over them as a futile gesture. The only time any of them hove to was when they had nothing to hide so that they could take the piss. The routine was to come alongside, and the senior Somali* would use a loud hailer to order the vessel to heave to in Arabic. The boarding party was made ready, boots, webbing, belt and gaiters, and also arms, Lanchesters for the lads, side arm for the officer in charge.

I was involved in one such operation with a large, smart seagoing dhow, to everyone apart from Their Lordships, a definite non-runner as a smuggler, but it had to be done. The guy in charge of this particular fiasco was our Engineer Officer and I was his Second Dickey as a lowly Fourth Class (Petty Officer) tiffy. The slow motorboat was lowered and we went alongside and boarded, the engineer explaining to the dhow skipper, via our Somali interpreter, the purpose of our visit. The skipper didn't seem very pleased and started giving Ali, our Somali earache until another Arab appeared and calmed him down. He obviously was well to do, dressed in fine white flowing robes, who introduced himself as the owner. He spoke perfect English and invited our OIC to be his guest and to search his vessel as thoroughly as he wished and afterwards to take tea with him, which the Engineer very graciously declined. In the course of our search thousands of watches were discovered, and when queried the owner was abjectly apologetic as only an Arab can be, but explained that he had to make a measly living, and India and Pakistan were lucrative markets for his cargo. He offered all our ships company a watch each to turn a blind eye, but the gaffer declined, much to everyone's dismay and disgust, explaining that we were only looking for arms. In the course of the search the Engineer and I as 2IC entered what must have been the main saloon which was out of this world. The furnishings and décor were as you would imagine the set of an Arabian Nights film, a veritable harem complete with two females who quickly adjusted their Yashmaks and disappeared into a forrard compartment. The owner, wringing his hands, was most apologetic about the disgraceful state of his humble accommodation in typical Arabian understatement.

So as I explained to Stan, furnish the main compartment as luxury living accommodation with the raised central feature of a bed, then he got the message and went on to suggest a few females to complete the illusion. We had further discussions on the subject and Penny was detailed off to recruit female volunteers, and I went back to tell the conversion gang that the double bed idea was a goer.

The next couple of days were frantic, what with Stan interviewing the volunteers for sailing crew and Penny choosing the visual diversion. It appears that Stan had a sudden inspiration, chased up Admiralty records and found that a lot of the Somalis who had been employed out the Persian Gulf by the RN had settled in Britain. By sifting through the records he came upon one Ali Hassan, whose address was in Portsmouth (where *Killisport* had decommissioned). Stan went to see him, his beautiful wife and five equally good looking daughters. When asked if he would like to join the RN again for a limited period he gave an emphatic affirmative and actually travelled back to Faslane with Stan, he was that keen. This meant that there were now two Arabic speakers in the crew and Ali could also speak a couple or so East African dialects, which could be very useful.

Meanwhile Penny had come up trumps, keeping in mind that the décor of the dhow had to be in the Eastern style, she had recruited a Wren of Asian decent. Leading Wren writer Anna Kharche of Goan origin who was also a linguist, having English, Indian (Hindu and Urdu) and Portuguese. It appears that when Penny introduced Anna to Stan he was very impressed but asked if she had any other volunteers, she said yes – she was. Stan looked a bit confused, so Penny with a twinkle in her eye explained that she wasn't prepared to let him out of her sight with Anna as an attraction, to which Stan, after a rather weak protest, had to agree.

Things were coming together fast now. The Chippies has finished the coffer dam arrangement, and had made other modifications of concealed stowages for men and equipment. The stone ballast had been changed to lead for a better volume to weight ratio, so giving even more room in the bilge to hide even more gear in case of searches. Penny and Anna now had a field day shopping for exotic silks, soft furnishings, trinkets, decorations and cushions. They got some of the gear from Glasgow, but insisted that they had to go over to Edinburgh and 'Jenners'* to get items unavailable elsewhere, but it was suspected that this was not the only motive. They turned up back at Falane loaded down with boxes and bags and parcels which incurred the wrath of the Stores Department who wished to know what on earth silk and gold woven saris and exotic assorted gold jewellery were required for, and how it could possibly be justified. A copy of Hoppy Hopgood's Chit was sent to the offended party and no more was heard of the matter.

Meanwhile Pancho and Andy had turned up, and Stan had interviewed all the applicants and had chosen three. The first was a three badge Killick Seaman, John 'Nobby' Clark, who lived for sailing and was a senior crew member of a private yacht owned by a local whisky magnate who was a personal friend of Admiral Hopgood, so Nobby was always available for sailing, he was a dab hand at splicing and the use of a Palm and Needle. Another choice was Petty Officer RO (Radio operator) David 'Curly' Hannam who whenever possible crewed for the official Faslane 'Moody 35' as Forepeak man, and so was well used to handling canvas and would also be useful as a communications expert, and was also a qualified day skipper. The third member to be chosen was REA Howard 'Sharky' Ward (Radio Electrical Artificer 3rd Class), an avid sailor who would crew for anybody wherever and whenever he could bum a berth. He would also be helpful with the maintenance of the electrical and electronic equipment, he also enjoyed and was good at navigation.

Stan decided that the time had come to call a meeting of all those personnel recruited for the operation. He also requested the attendance of Admiral Hopgood so that he could be brought up to speed and also meet the team.

All attended and Stan started off by introducing them all to Hoppy by name rank and team duty, starting with himself:-

Lt. Cdr. S. Westerman RN 'Stan'	Operation Leader and Navigator Diving Team Leader.
Captain D. Miller RM 'Dusty'	Deputy Leader and Backup Team Leader.
J. H. Smith. ERA1 'H'	Diving Team, Engine Room Watchkeeper, General Maintenance.
A. Bromfield. PO Seaman 'Andy'	Diving Team, Explosives Expert.

Me. CERA 'Ted'	Diving Team. Engine Room Watchkeeper, General Maintenance.
S. Powers. Chief Diver 'Pancho'	IC Diving Team. Diving Training.
H. Ward. REA3 'Sharky'	Dhow Skipper. Electrical Maintenance. Second Navigator.
J. Clark. Leading Seaman 'Nobby'	Dhow Crew. Rigging Maintenance.
D. Hanam. PO RO 'Curly'	Dhow Crew, Sail Master. Radio Operator.
A. Hassan. Somali PO 'Ali'	Dhow Crew. Interpreter.
N. Kaye. ERA3. 'Danny'	Dhow Crew. Engineer.
P. Westerman 1stOff. WRNS 'Penny'	Chef. Cover Story.
A. Kharche L. Writer WRNS 'Anna'	Chef. Cover Story.

Stan then went on to explain that he wanted the two groups of Diving Team and Dhow Crew to start intensive training. The Divers under the watchful eye of Pancho, the Dhow Crew driven by Sharky, with the cover story that it was part of an exhibition of sailing vessels through the ages for Navy Days down south.

'I have organized a largish pontoon to be moored in the loch for you divers to practise on, but not to destruction please.'

He then asked if the Admiral had anything to say, but Hoppy declined saying he would have a word in private after the meeting. With that Stan asked if there were any questions, and Dusty stood up and asked if he would have a word with him after the meeting, but Stan said that if it was relevant to the job he should bring it up for all to hear. So Dusty got to his hind legs and suggested that although the training of the two groups was well covered in their own areas, they would collectively be inadequate in a fire-fight. He suggested that one of his marines join the crew to teach self defence, firearms drill and techniques and general fitness. This Stan thought was an excellent idea and essential to be prepared in the event of trouble, and asked Dusty to go ahead and organize it. The meeting was adjourned after Stan had told the gang that the training schedules would be issued in the morning and warned that anything to do with the operation was strictly secret and confidential, and that their own safety was at stake. He then went off to get his ear bent by Hoppy, and Dusty went off to 'volunteer' a Bootneck. And so James 'Spike' Redwood joined the crew, it appears that he served with Dusty in the Yemen with distinction. He was a trained killer and knew all the techniques and all the modern weapons of war. Royal Marines are hard men trained to perfection but Spike had the ability to pass this ruthlessness on without appearing to do so.

Chapter 6

Training

A small accommodation block in a remote area of the base was allocated to the team, which helped maintain security, all shore leave was cancelled and training began in earnest. The Diving Attack Team was able to get to grips with a decommissioned 'V' class boat which had its reactor core removed ready for scrapping. It was ballasted to normal buoyancy and secured alongside the pontoon that was already moored in mid Loch. Pancho had us practising suiting up at speed, refreshing our memories on maintaining and servicing our breathing sets, charging oxygen bottles, and finally getting fit by distance swimming as all four of us had, to say the least, let ourselves go a bit. Then there were the attack exercises which involved suiting up in a small shed at the water's edge, entering the water, swimming to the V boat, diving and entering a ballast tank, isolating our breathing sets to conserve oxygen, as if in the real thing, and breathing ballast tank air. The air in the ballast tanks, was kept fresh by a diesel driven compressor that was parked on the pontoon.

One problem that immediately cropped up was visibility within the ballast tank once inside. We discussed it at some length to no avail, until Andy said he'd seen something on television's *Tomorrow's World* a while ago, something about a chemical light but couldn't remember any more about it. Unbeknown to the rest of the team, Stan got busy on the phone and shortly afterwards a box the size of a standard egg box was delivered. Stan assembled the diving team in his office that night, and having closed the door, gave each of us what looked like long ice sticks, the sort kids get from the corner shop. He asked Pancho to turn out the light, which left us in complete darkness, then asked us to gently break our sticks in the middle, then as if by magic, a beautiful pale green glow gently flooded the room. It was a chemical light developed from research carried out on fireflies. Stan explained that we would try them out the next exercise, but with light blinds to cover the free flood holes once we were inside to test their effectiveness.

We now went on to carry out an attack from the ballast tank to the pontoon, but this is where things went a bit pear shaped, as Andy hadn't quite worked out what type and where the explosives should be placed. He went to have a word with Stan and suggested that he went to see his old gaffer at the Clearance Diving School in South Queensferry to seek advice. Stan agreed and said he would go with him as two minds were better than one.

Meanwhile Sharky was trying to get to grips with the intricacies of sailing a dhow. It had arrived with the masts unstepped and all the cordage and standing and running rigging, but all in a big heap. To get the full picture, the name dhow is European in origin and includes many types of Arabian sailing vessels. The one our gang had acquired was a Persian Gulf 'Baghla' and so was affectionately christened 'Baggy'. Baggy's vital statistics were, Length 70 feet stem to stern, Keel length 50 feet, Depth of railing to keel 18 feet, and so was wide beamed and shallow draughted. Sharkey and Curly were still struggling with the intricacies of Baggy's sail rig and getting nowhere. The only member of the crew not totally confused was Danny who was completely at one with his engine room and its auxiliaries.

There was a very gentle tapping on Stan's office door late the next night when everybody else had left. He shouted come in, a few seconds later another gentle tapping on the door, by this time Stan was angry at being disturbed, leapt to the door, was about to explode and rove it open to reveal a very timid looking Ali.

'Come in Ali, sorry I was a bit abrupt, sit down, what can I do for you?'

'Well Sir, I don't really know how to start.'

'The best way is to start at the beginning, so just calm yourself down and let loose.' Which is what he did, and then he and Stan went into a huddle for quite a while, then the next morning Stan called a meeting of the sailing crew and enquired now the shake down was coming along, the reply being that it wasn't.

'Well gentlemen, I have some good news for you all, it appears we have an expert in sailing dhows among us, so I now appoint Ali as your new Sail Master. It appears that he has crewed on vessels similar to Baggy for quite some time and so should be able to give us all the benefit of his experience'. With that all the lads crowded round and shook his hand and slapped him on the shoulders.

With the advent of the new Sail Master things went from strength to strength. The first thing that Ali organized was the stepping of just the main mast, because as he pointed out it was best for all to learn and practise altogether on one bit at a time. Ali explained that the main mast was raked well forward because there are no forrard shrouds and no forestay because of the type of sail. The next step was to bend (tie) the mainsail to the yard (spar). The cordage (sheets and brace) were then connected to the sail, the parrel (the loop that connects the yard to the mast) is

rigged. The yard complete with sail is then hoisted up the mast with the yard head forrard. When it was vertical the decision had to be made as to which side of the mast the sail was to go, depending on the wind direction and the direction you want to go. Ali told the crew that a favourite saying of sailors of this type of vessel was 'No one but a madman or a Christian would attempt to sail to windward in a dhow.' In other words dhows do not tack very well. The decision made, the yard is manoeuvred to that side and the brace hauled in to pull the head of the yard down outside the shrouds, the main sheets passed outside the shrouds and the one opposite to the side the yard is hauled in. The shrouds on the yard side are then slacked off to allow the parrel to be shortened in to bring the yard close to the mast. The sail is then unfurled, the wind fills it and is trimmed using brace and sheet adjustments, that's the theory anyway! In practice, to start with, it was quite different. Early each morning the crew used to take Baggy out into mid stream, kind permission of Danny and his beloved engines, manoeuvred into the right position and direction and practised rigging the Mainsail as described, but used to get in all sorts of tangles and bunches of bastards, to coin a phrase. Eventually though, after great frustration and loss of temper, teamwork prevailed and a fair degree of proficiency was achieved, thanks mainly to Ali's patience and perseverance. So Ali ever the optimist decided to progress to practice tacking (changing sides with the sail) which meant that the boat had to go head to the wind, slacken the parrel to give clearance between the mast and the yard, the brace and sheet let go, then one or two of the crew members haul on the yard till it is vertical and the sail allowed to blow forrard, the now windward shrouds are tightened and the leeward ones slackened. The opposite sheet is then hauled in, the parrel re-tightened and the sail trimmed again by the use of brace and sheet. This exercise has to be performed in one smooth operation, timing it to perfection as the vessel begins to turn into the wind. This operation could be compared to dipping the gaff on a Whaler. If the operation is executed too fast the mast may be damaged due to slack shrouds, and if too slow way may be lost, with the vessel ending up in irons. Again that's the theory, in practice though it was a different kettle of fish, and again lots of practice was required to get it right. The next step was to split the crew into two teams to that one team at a time could practice getting underway and then tacking. The final stage was when both teams had managed to become reasonably proficient and to rig the Mizzen mast and have both teams performing simultaneously. To start with they got in each others' way, but quickly managed to sort themselves out and actually began to compete against each other and enjoy the competition, and as a result began to get quite proficient.

Meanwhile Stan and Andy had returned from HMS *Lochinvar* with the answer regarding the type and placement of the explosives for maximum effect. Stan therefore organized a get together of the diving party and had Andy explain in detail the operation. The explosive to be used was a new form of very high power plastic which was enclosed in a canvas tube with small but powerful ceramic magnets. Two lengths would be deployed from either end of the underside of the dock on the centreline from forrard to aft. Three reasons were given for this, firstly deployment would be twice as quick, secondly being separately fused if one unit fails to detonate the other would at least deal a very damaging blow, and finally manhandling would be easier in two lumps. The fuses would be hydrostatic being primed by increasing water pressure. Once primed a pre-set timer would take over, the setting of which to be determined at the target site, depending on the prevailing circumstances. Some dummy canvas tubes complete with magnets were manufactured and fitted with small pencil detonators which when armed gave a delay to allow the water to be vacated before activation. So the attack exercise was repeated with the dummy explosives, but two snags reared their ugly heads, firstly the explosive ribbons, when coiled were quite weighty and tended to be negatively buoyant, and also the magnets were very good on bare steel, but the pontoon was weed and barnacle encrusted and had to be scraped, very noisily, before they could be attached. Andy came up with the solution: instead of magnets, make the ribbons positively buoyant and when transporting them to the target, weight them to give neutral buoyancy, and once under the target cut away the weights and then string them out. The problem then came up how to make the damn things buoyant, and suddenly I remembered a frost damage prevention innovation which involved what looked like heavy duty bubble wrap in a strip which was inserted into the vulnerable pipe, so I suggested that this type strip replace the magnets in the explosive strings. A dummy set of explosives was again rigged up, but this time with the buoyancy aids fitted and it worked a treat, but Stan wasn't satisfied because he had doubts about the effectiveness of the explosive strings being unattached to the hull, so he went to see Hoppy to request, against his own orders, permission to do a live exercise on the pontoon, which was granted. The V class boat was relocated away from the pontoon and to add some realism the exercise was conducted at night.

The explosive strings were made up with the buoyancy aids and weighted accordingly, the fuses were the type used on the first dummy run with the detonator delay after arming set to thirty minutes to be sure the team were clear of the water. To allay any fears the Base and the local Constabulary were informed that some demolition was to be carried out and a notice to shipping was issued to that effect. Came the dusk we suited up, checked our gear and were landed on the pontoon, our two teams split up and off we went, launched our ribbons dumped the ballast and strung out the explosive, set the fuse and made our exits. As the countdown approached zero a hush descended on the crew, and then a muffled 'crump' then nothing, no great flash, no great wave or splash, so very disgruntled and disappointed it was decided to call it a day and find out what had gone wrong in daylight the next day. Came the dawn the gang assembled early and repaired to the jetty to survey the scene. Nothing. There was no sign of the pontoon, which was puzzling, so Andy who after all was the explosives expert, volunteered to take a dip to find out what had happened to the damn thing. He suited up quickly and swam out to the last known position of the pontoon, dipped under and in less than no time was surfaced, ripped his mask off and was yelling and waving his arms and then thrashed his way to us on the jetty. When we'd dragged him out and calmed him down he told us that the pontoon was folded neatly in two. On further inspection although Andy was right and the damage for the amount of noise and disturbance was

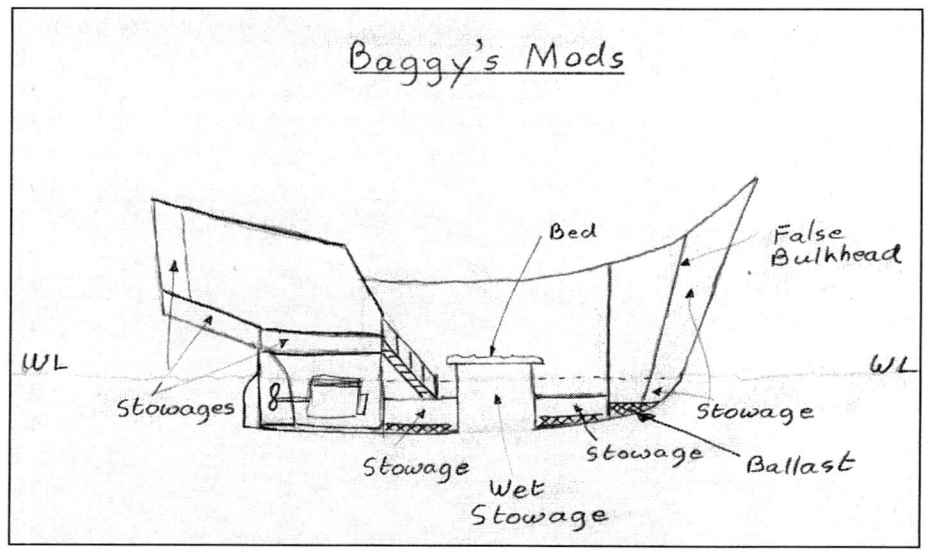

spectacular, Stan was of the opinion that the rupture line on the underside of the pontoon was not in a straight line and over a greater length as in the AFD could cause possible miss-alignment of the rupture with subsequent mission failure. Pancho came up with the solution, suggesting that a horizontal 'shot' line be rigged with a magnet at each end, which would be attached to the blunt ends of the dock just above the waterline where there would be no fouling (weed and barnacles). Stan and Pancho then went into a huddle for half a day and a method was worked out.

Two lines, each two thirds the full length of the dock, were to be rigged with a powerful ultra thin ceramic magnet at one end suitably camouflaged, and a self clenching cleat at the other, the cleats each to be fitted with half an Ingerfield clip. Two of the team would each carry a line, attach the magnetic end to the dock centreline at either end of the dock as already described, then swim towards each other, connect the two halves of the Ingerfield clip, collect the free end of the line and swim back to whence they came. The whole line was then tightened automatically in a straight line with medium tension to be used as a guide line for deploying the charges. By this time, another pontoon had been 'borrowed' under duress and the method tested with complete success.

Baggy was then turned over to the diving team so that we could practice our own evolutions. One of the main problems was how to stow all the gear, and to this end false bulkheads and extra ballast space had been built at the same time as the bed/cofferdam was being constructed, but to make sure it all fitted properly it had to be stowed in the right position and order. Being good Submariners, three of us were well versed in the art of utilizing space to the best advantage, but Andy was a mess, literally. He had no more idea than the man in the moon about tidiness, and it was a constant battle to keep him in line. One good plan evolved was to use the inside of the cofferdam to stow gear that could tolerate total immersion, such as large oxygen storage cylinders, spare breathing set cylinders, cordage, magnets and of course explosive ribbons. It was imperative to be able to retrieve or stow gear in emergency. Another procedure to perfect was to get in and out of our suits and sets in a hurry, in a confined space, all four at once. But the main evolution to practise was getting in and out of the Coffer dam, out being the most critical as a wet saloon deck could be a dead giveaway, so a routine was adopted where cleaning gear was always at hand and a deck ape was available at a moments notice to be messman and do the swabbing out.

One of the final exercises was to work Baggy under canvas in a seaway and deploy divers and recover them. So, with a safety boat in attendance, Baggy was sailed down the Gareloch through Rhu narrows and into the Clyde, out to starb'd leaving Gourock to port and then left hand down a bit where the exercise started off Inverkip Marina where a fresh breeze had stirred up a fair old lop. It very soon became obvious that the main hazard in this area was nothing to do with ourselves but the damned Caledonia McBrain Ferries which stop or divert for no one and nothing. I know the rule is power gives way to sail, but a proviso should be added, with the exception of Scottish Ferries.

Anyway the exercise went ahead with a few minor hitches, and a lot of lessons learnt, and Danny was able to gloat a little over the sailors because on diver recovery the sail arrangement did not allow for accurate positioning, so Danny was called upon to run up and manoeuvre his beloved engines. We eventually fought our way back to Faslane (with Danny's help) and at the washup we were congratulated on a reasonable outcome where valuable lessons were learnt. Then came the bombshell when Stan announced that a similar exercise was to be conducted at 'night' whereupon a big groan went up.

'Shut up and listen!' Stan roared.

'We can't guarantee weather conditions or time of day when this thing is going to come off, so get on with it and do your best. That is all,' he snapped and stalked off.

The night exercise was an unmitigated disaster from beginning to end. First off we went aground at Rhu narrows and suffered slight bow and forrard keel damage, which was minimized by Sharky's quick reflexes and Danny's equally quick response as he had his engines up to temperature and ticking over ready for just such an emergency. The next mishap was the antics of our safety boat which nearly ran us down as he had lost visual contact with us, and had started flanging around in a haphazard manner. We were running without navigation lights and we found out later that his radar was not very sensitive, and was being wood and not carrying a radar beacon, it was a real close shave.

The weather was calmer than the daylight job but there was no moon and the night was 'as black as yer 'at' as H was heard to comment. Us divers deployed with no bother, but the pick up was a complete pig's breakfast. It shouldn't have been that hard because we were all equipped with ultra violet lights and Sharky and Pancho had UV scanners, clever and simple you say? Andy and I stuck together and after a planned half an hour in the water were expecting our pick up as before. Eventually after nearly an hour when we were getting a little chilly and concerned, we heard Danny's engines burbling and Baggy's dark shape suddenly appeared out of the pitch darkness, so we dipped under and popped up inboard and splashed out into the blinding light, freezing and more than a little peeved. Looking around we both realized that things were not all 'hunky dory'.

'What's wrong?'

Penny burst into tears.

'We haven't found Stan and H, that's why we're late getting to you.'

'Well then Curly, I suggest you man the radio telephone full time because they're either going to be picked up, or get ashore and ring Faslane. Oh, and Curly call up the safety boat and tell them to do the same and also to stay abeam us 100 yards to starb'd, and ask Sharky to furl all sail and switch on all navigation lights and get Danny grouped up, and match the safety boat speed.' I blurted out.

'And Penny and you Anna, get a brew on, me an' 'im's freezin'. We'll do one more sweep and if no luck back to Faslane to stand by the phone.'

With that organized, Andy and I unrigged and went on deck with the rest, armed with binoculars, started all round sweeps. We passed Kip heading South, went a couple of miles past, came about and headed north again when, just before reaching Kip again Curly leapt out of his shack yelling that our erstwhile souls had just rung from Inverkip Marina, so I got Curly to call the marina Commodore on the radio for permission to berth in his domain to pick up our lost souls, while I went to give Penny the good news. Permission to enter the marina was granted so Baggy and the safety boat moored up, left a sentry on the mooring and went ashore to the restaurant/bar and found Stan and H half cut, surrounded by curious rubberneckers plying them drinks. Penny was over the moon and a bit tearful, but she soon regained her cool.

We all had a couple of wets to celebrate the reunion before we returned to our vessels which had gathered quite a large admiring audience, but our cover story of the Navy Days Exhibition down South held good and we slipped with no trouble and arrived back in Faslane very late but thankfully intact.

At the washup Stan admitted that his and H's UV lights had been tested and found to be defective, and that new design and more reliable units were to be supplied. The incident of the grounding was put down to poor GPS use and he and Sharky were organized to go on an intensive navigation course, and the damage caused in the grounding was relatively minor and had been effectively repaired. The incident with the safety boat was put down to an inexperienced skipper but was considered of no consequence as a safety boat would not be in on the real McCoy. One good thing that came out of the washup was a suggestion from Andy that instead of dry suits with the associated problems of getting dressed and undressed, and as the waters were temperate couldn't wet suits be used instead? So wet suits were acquired and tried out to the whole of the diving team's satisfaction and, as Andy predicted were much easier to handle in all respects. H also came up with a good idea, suggesting that a signalling system be installed between the sea side of the coffer dam and the bridge, so that if necessary divers in the water could communicate with inboard to check if the coast was clear to come inboard. So Sharky and the greenies of the base staff got their heads together and rigged up a system of lights and switches and devised a simple code, fast flash danger, slow flash help.

The final training programme was Dusty's protégé, James 'Spike' Redwood, Colour Sergeant RM who took us all including Dusty to the highlands to an old war time army training camp complete with firing range. We trained with knives, SLRs, stun grenades, and hand grenades, but the worst bit was the hand-to-hand stuff. Each day Spike paired us up with someone different and made us fight each other, and if he thought you weren't putting enough effort into it he'd show you one at a time how it ought to be done, and he was brutal, which made you a little more keen to give your opponent a good going over if possible. The snag was that I'm the original bloke that gets sand kicked in his face, and I got a right good pasting from them all.

At the end of this exhausting course the general consensus was that Spike Redwood was brutal but nice with it and he would make a better friend than an enemy, and we considered that he would be a great asset to the team, so he was asked if he would become our 'Defence Co-ordinator', to which he readily agreed. He would also make a good deck ape able to handle spars and cordage as he was built like a brick shit house.

Chapter 7

Passage 1

Stan went to see Hoppy to tell him that we were as ready as we would ever be, and was given the okay to ship out to the Indian Ocean. The timing was critical, and our intelligence bods had been working flat out to gauge the best time to execute the operation. It was decided that the Suez Canal was not a good area as there were far too many Arabs who were far too nosy for their own good. The snag was that when a vessel got to Port Said, bow and stern lights had to be fitted before going through the canal in convoy, and every Tom Dick and Harry attempts to get aboard purporting to be the official lighting party and sniff around to see if they can drum up any gossip or information useful for espionage. If not, thieve something, anything that isn't nailed down.

So the plan was to go round the Cape of Good Hope. In what, may you ask? To show how important Their Lordships rated the operation, they lashed us up to the very latest in supply vessels, none other than our old friend Royal Fleet Auxilliary *Hannibal*, the biggest, best and newest of the RFA* Fleet. She was tanker, stores ship, heavy lifter and home from home, and she arrived in Faslane unannounced to transport us and Baggy to our destination.

We all helped to unrig Baggy and make sure all the gear was stowed on board or available on *Hannibal*, then the whole kit and caboodle was lifted out of the water with *Hannibal*'s massive Sampson post crane and specially designed slings and settled on a purpose built cradle and lashed down in one of her holds. Bunks and furniture had been rigged in the hold with a separate cabin for the girls which made us a compact and secure unit away from the prying eyes and ears of the world.

Hannibal slipped at 23.59 after a couple of days and we were on our way, sliding into and down the Clyde, past the Cumbraes, Pladda to port, Ailsa Craig to starb'd and then Sanda Island to port and then across the top of Ireland as it was decided that the weather forecast for the Irish Sea was not good and that stretch of oggin can be treacherous. Out in the Atlantic there was a fair swell running but nothing too bad, and we got down to keeping fit, telling tall stories, and most importantly running through each stage of the operation trying to cater for all scenarios.

One thing bothering me was the lack of ability to keep the lads' hands in with the sailing practice so I made a few measurements and calculated that with a minor modification to a section of the hatch cover we could have Baggy fully rigged and able to keep the lads there on their toes, and the bonus would be the fact that we would be able to unload fully rigged at the other end which would save a lot of time and anxiety. I told Stan of my fears and possible solution and he was all for it, so he went to see the RFA skipper who told Stan that his orders were to co-operate in any way possible and he would get his engineering department to assist in our endeavours, so it all went ahead and our Deck Apes* were practising in no time at all. A spin off was the slight modification that we made to the lifting slings that made it easier to enable my suggestion of a fully rigged launch which only required the sails to be unfurled and hoisted.

Time passed as we steadily headed south and the Bay of Biscay was transited no problem, but as we passed Portugal it reminded H and me of the time we were laid on the beach in Estoril, and as he pointed out to me, if we hadn't been there we wouldn't be here now, sod's law eh. Time marched on as we plodded south, we had just come abreast of Madeira heading for the Canaries when the bombshell hit. The tannoy called Stan to the bridge and when he returned we could tell it was trouble 'cos his facial expression was that of a bulldog chewing a wasp. He called us all together and gave us the bad news.

'We have to turn back and go to our destination via the Med and the Suez, the one thing we didn't want. The reason is that one of our latest frigates has broken down on its way to the Persian Gulf and *Hannibal* is carrying the spares that are required and we have to deliver to Aden dockyard where the frigate is laid up'.

So we about turned and slotted through the Pillars of Hercules and into the calm blue Mediterranean, which is when the weather turned nasty. Don't let anyone kid you, the Med can be treacherous, and to prove its point, we got a right good pasting with a beam on sea. Our main concern was Baggy's securing which was taking a bit of pounding. The snag with strapping is that once it works loose it can only get progressively worse. Danny made eyebolts and welded them to the hold deck, braces were made to fit high up inside the hull, like horizontal building supports, to prevent crushing and extra straps and ratchets were rigged and tensioned up which stopped her working. The original straps were slackened off one at a time, more internal braces fitted and the straps re-tensioned, after which there was no more problem apart from mal-de-mer (sea-spew).

As we passed Malta the weather abated and we were able to get back to some form of normality and a bit of sunbathing was the order of the day, Penny and Anna caused a bit of a stir in *Hannibal*'s crew as they were both stunners and the bikinis didn't help. As we headed East leaving Crete to port the RFA skipper mustered his ship's company and us in the well deck and explained to all concerned the need for tight security at Port Said, and told us all to be extra vigilant.

'Everything has to be stowed away under lock and key, if it isn't secured or nailed down it will be thieved. The brow is to be double manned at all times, only one 'lighting team' allowed aboard at any one time. The 'team' to be escorted one on one at all times, and a constant deck patrol will be required. These measures will be required for the duration of our stay alongside in Port Said, and side arms will be worn by all those on duty. The Special Operations Team may be required to help in these duties. That is all, dismissed.'

I knew what he was on about because I had the honour to be one of the crew of Loch Class Frigate HMS *Killisport*, the first RN vessel to go north to south through the Suez Canal after the Suez crisis. We carried a detachment of Royal Marines who had been in the vanguard and served with distinction during the conflict. I remember vividly that as we came alongside in Port Said we were about to get mobbed because the quarterdeck was low and level with the jetty. Then the entire marine detachment came onto the quarterdeck in full dress uniform and you could see the whole mob recoil as if they'd hit a brick wall, because they recognized their uniforms and knew their reputation. The bootnecks wouldn't let them aboard but allowed them to put their clockwork tin toys on but not get them off, which caused a bit of consternation and a few crushed fingers from strategically placed beetle crusher boots, so I knew what to expect this time. I happened to mention this incident in the mess at dinnertime and Spike admitted that he'd been in the thick of it, and said we should have stayed and finished it once and for all instead of pussyfooting about and listening to waffling politicians. Andy piped up with vehement agreement and all of us swung round to face him in disbelief.

'Don't look at me like that' he exploded, 'I was one of the silly bastards who had to clear all the bloody mess in the canal. They put mines all over it and in it, booby trapped the vessels they sank, and generally made a right pot mess it, I hate the arseholes and Egypt in general.' Loud applause followed and Andy gave a small grin and looked embarrassed.

We found out that Andy had done this clearance work nonstop for months on end along with a lot of other nutters, and had been awarded a gong which had been richly deserved, for making the canal safe and navigable again. You can still see the raised hulks abandoned in the Bitter Lakes.

We eventually arrived at Port Said with the not unexpected shambles and organized chaos. As we came alongside they tried to mob us as expected but the skipper's plan worked, especially with the side arms combined with pukka RFA uniforms. One unplanned development was the Bum boats that came up on the outboard side of *Hannibal*, so our Baggy team dealt with them to allow the *Hannibal's* crew to concentrate on the inboard side. Our strategy was simple, fire-fighting hoses were rigged and we gave the would-be raiders an early bath, and guess who were on the business ends of the fire hoses, you've got it, Andy and Spike, who were thoroughly enjoying themselves. Eventually the official 'lighting team' was sorted out and escorted as planned and eventually when their gear was fixed up and tested they made to depart and the brow chained off but still manned by an armed guard. Came the dawn, the convoy was assembled and each vessel had to take a pilot on board, although why I'll never know 'cos apart from the Bitter Lakes you couldn't go far wrong, it was follow my leader in a straight line.

The daft thing is that every time I think of the Suez Canal it reminds me of the film *Lawrence of Arabia* when he and his companion reached the Suez, and all you saw was lots and lots of sand and flat desert and the top works and funnels of ships appearing to glide past in the sand. I remember it from when I was wrecking on *Osprey* and I'd inherited the projectionist's job, and we'd a good load of the latest films 'cos we were going on a three month fishplay exercise off the east coast of America in the Gulf Stream. Anyway, to get to the point, the first film I showed was *Lawrence of Arabia* and the beer sales trebled. But I digress, something in the back of my mind was niggling me, but it wouldn't come forward, I knew it could be important and I knew the operation might depend on it but it just wouldn't come. I was leaning on the guardrail on the starb'd bridge wing staring blankly at the vast expanse of nowt but sand. Stan came up alongside, leant on the guardrail and asked me what was wrong, so I explained that I thought we were missing something important but I couldn't put my finger on it.

'Ah, if it's that important it'll come to you, but for god's sake cheer up, you look like you've lost a bob and found a tanner.'

We got through the Bitter Lakes and then a bit more canal and then we were in the Gulf of Suez where we got rid of the 'pilot' who'd been about as useful as an ashtray on a motorbike. The convoy dispersed, with us trundling down the Red Sea, and it reminded me of the last time I was in this neck of the woods in the old Loch Class Frigate on route to the Persian Gulf. We made a courtesy call on a small island, the name of which escapes me, but I was informed that it was used as a quarantine stage for Africans on pilgrimage to Mecca. The skipper went ashore with his entourage on official business as the island was a British protectorate at the time. The weather was good, I was off watch and propping up the handrail of one of the Pom-Pom sponsons watching fascinated at an old chap on the shore fishing. It was a very clever method, he collected the net in a special way and with a sweep of his arm threw it in a very skilled fashion so that it spread out in a perfect circle before it dropped into the water. He let it sink, the edges first because they were weighted, and then he hauled it in on an attached lanyard and the net closed like a round purse and then hauled it in. Having caught nothing, a small boy who had been squatting watching and talking to the old man got up went to him, grasped his hand and led him to another spot to try again, and I then realized that the old man was blind and the boy, no older than five, was his eyes. It made me feel very humble and very thankful.

'And so we bashed on down the Red Sea towards Aden passing Djibouti to starb'd, where if you shook hands with a native, you could easily lose your watch and your paybook without even knowing it and where, if you consorted with the local talent on the way back to UK, as some had done after our Gulf stint, you could guarantee stoppage of leave when you reached Pompey because you left with more than you went with and your course of treatment was not complete. Try explaining that away to your wife or girlfriend!

Turning to port on exiting the Red Sea we headed for a pre-determined position due South of Aden. Stan managed to arrange this so that the required spares could be transferred to another vessel without arousing interest in *Hannibal*. Aden was bad, if not worse than Port Said, as it was a cosmopolitan hotbed of intrigue and skulduggery, and the less was known of our presence in the area the better. At the rendezvous point we hove to. Then an LCT (Landing Craft Tank) appeared, signals were exchanged, and she came alongside. The required spares were transferred easily because, although it was bulky, *Hannibal*'s Sampson Post Crane dropped the gear straight into the open topped cargo space of the LCT and was let go and steamed off back to Aden.

We turned south and headed in the opposite direction and settled down to a long steady transit, Anna shouted to us that she'd mashed a pot of tea so we all migrated to the mess table for a brew. She never could remember how we liked our tea so all she used to do was put the teapot in the middle of the table with a pot of milk and a bowl of sugar, half a dozen spoons and enough enamel pint pots to go round. It's funny how different people prefer a mugga! Penny was miles away as she was adding milk to her tea and stirring it noisily in the enamel mug. Sharky attempted to bring her back to reality by jokingly asking her why the ringing pitch of the spoon in the mug went down the more sugar that was added. Penny didn't hear a word he'd said, but Stan not realizing it was a wind up, explained quite seriously that the adding of the sugar changed the density of the tea and caused a change in the resonant frequency of the mug. The daft things folk talk about when they're bored, and this explanation raised a cheer and a round of applause, and then it hit me like a hammer blow.

'Stan I want a word with you in private right away, it's most important.'

'Why, what's up?'

'Just come with me, it's urgent.'

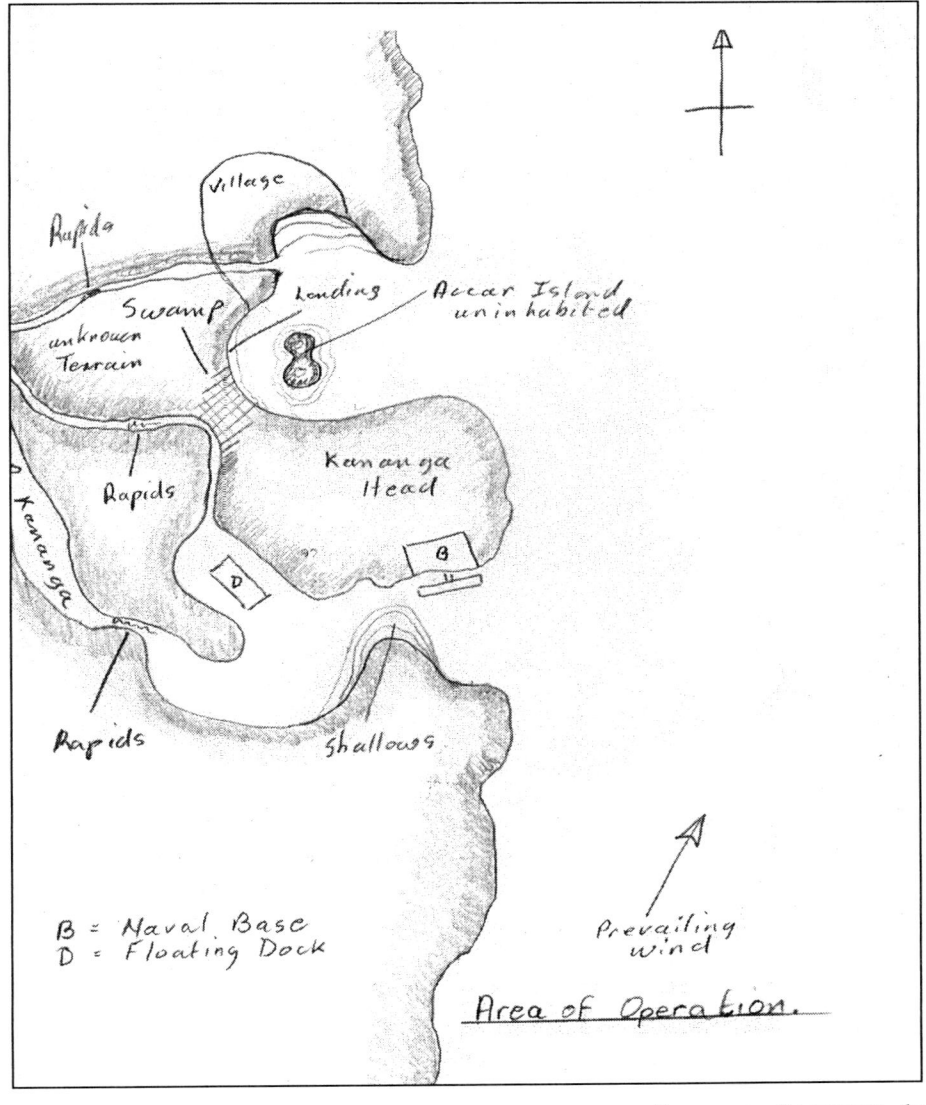

I took him on the upper deck and asked him what the Jimmy and chief stoker did before each trip in the boat?

'Work out a static trim*'

'How?'

'Oh, come on, you know better than me, you check weights, number of bodies, weight of extra stores, extra storage tank contents, fuel load, anything that changes overall weight, what are you raving about?'

'Just bear with me, now you've set a static trim, you're in a position to do a trial dive to catch a trim. What do you have to arrange to have done just before?'

'Check sea water density!'

'Yes you check DENSITY, that's what's been niggling me, you always take a sea water density check because that's what determines the final pre-dive trim adjustment, doesn't it?'

'Yes but what's that got to do with us and the operation?'

'The target is moored on the Kananga River, but is its position in the tidal section or in the fresh water flow section, because if it's in the fresh water section our explosive ribbon flotation aids will be inadequate and we're going to need more buoyancy.'

Stan turned ashen.

'Christ, it's just as well it came to you eventually, well done, but I'm trying to think what we ought to do now?'

'Well I reckon we ought to cover all possibilities but work on the assumption that sod's law reigns supreme, then the worst case scenario is it's fresh water.'

'You're right. I'll get on with the re-organization right away, come on, we'll have to send a signal off to Hoppy, and I want you to do the encoding. I've decided that we won't tell the others, it'll only unsettle them, and we don't want to do anything to upset morale.'

Stan went to see the skipper for permission to take over the radio shack, and then we got down to it, a signal to Admiral Sir Arthur Hopgood.

URGENT TOP SECRET
Ref Operation Docksunk

1. Request urgent investigation into density of water at target area.

Imperative. Operation depends on value.

2. Supply by air drop 100 yards item 18 of stores schedule, advise time of drop to project time of position, urgent reply required.

I encoded it and we got *Hannibal*'s Sparks to transmit it, and then it was up to Hoppy. So life went as boring as ever with either Stan or I hanging about the Radio Shack waiting and hoping for a reply signal. Eventually our hopes were realized and a coded signal was received which, when I had deciphered it was good and bad news, it read:

RFA Hannibal SPECIAL FORCES

Ref 1 Your signal. Agent lost on mission, cannot re-appraise in time.

Ref 2 Your signal. Item 18 available. Report your estimated position At 0900 tomorrow.

Stan shot out of the Radio Shack to have an urgent meeting with the Skipper. They pored over the relevant chart and decided on a position for that time, so Stan leapt back to the Shack for me to encode it, it was sent, and acknowledged as received. So all we could do then was to wait for the dawn, and when it broke we, that is Stan and I, enlightened the rest of the team as to what had gone on and what was to be expected.

But what really happened was most unexpected. At 0900 sharp there was the faint sound of an aircraft in the distance, which just got louder and louder until with an ear splitting scream it shot dangerously low straight over us, pulled up and waggled its wings and did a quick 180 degree turn and came back slowly, then slower and slower until it hovered over the foredeck, it was a Harrier and it was going to land. A message came over the Tannoy for all personnel to take cover and sure enough in a haze of exhaust and paint flakes the Harrier touched down and settled on its haunches and the engine was cut. We all came out from shelter as the canopy of the Harrier slid back to reveal a swarthy Flight Lieutenant with a huge grin.

'I've got a parcel for a Commander Westerman.'

Stan stepped forward and thanked him and enquired where the parcel was as it was obvious that there was not enough room in the cockpit.

'It's in the wing pod's commander', he said as he climbed down from his lofty perch. All our team was up on the foredeck by now as the pilot introduced himself to Stan as Flight Lieutenant Bob Khan, who asked if he could be given a helping hand to secure his aircraft and unload the cargo pods. So we all turned to with a will and worked to his instructions, and in no time at all we were manhandling the pods down to our hold. Bob was invited to come with us and was amazed to see Baggy and admired it immensely having been shown round the interior, but had the good sense not to ask too many questions. Stan invited him to stay for lunch but he declined, explaining that there was a Refuelling

Tanker tooling about up top waiting to give him some 'Motion Lotion' to get him home.

'Where's home Bob?' Anna enquired with a sort of dreamy look in her eyes. 'Would you like a cup of tea?'

'In that order, Crete, and yes please, two sugars.'

According to Bob, the Navy (Hoppy) had requested transports to urgently deliver vital supplies to a vessel in the Indian Ocean due south of Aden, as a critically important operation depended on it. So the RAF really pulled out all the stops, and a scheduled RAF Transport Command VC 10 to Crete was routed via Glasgow's Abbotsinch Airport to pick up the item and landed at Crete's Iraklion Airport, which is both commercial and military, where Bob was waiting with his Jumpjet. The parcel was split into two and loaded into the air pods, he was given a map reference and told to get on with it, the Refuelling Tanker also had its flight plan. Plan 'A' was to drop the pods as near to the RFA as possible as they had self deploying parachutes and were watertight and positively buoyant, but as he explained, as he flew past he saw a nice wide open expanse of deck, and thought if that guy could land a Harrier on a container vessel during the Falklands crisis so can I, which, let's face it, had guaranteed delivery without a lot of mucking about with recovery. So we toasted him with tea, he shook our hands, gave Anna a lingering kiss, then we all went up on deck and he climbed back into his giant Hover mower. We unshackled him and took cover, he lit the blue touch paper and away he went in another shower of exhaust fumes and paint chippings. He shot off forrard, did another 180 turn and came back low at full chat with a final head-shattering flypast. You didn't so much hear the noise as feel it, then on a climb he waggled his wings and was away.

This incident reminded me of a trip to Elvington Airfield while I was on leave once. The occasion was a Model Aircraft Exhibition and Display, and a friend who made and sold model aircraft kits and had a stall at the show invited me. He promised me I'd enjoy it as there were not only the models flying but also the real full sized jobs giving displays. He was right, it was all good stuff, but the best bit was, yes, a display by a Harrier. There was one snag, the Flight Line (spectator/runway distance) was a lot less for model displays, so the lovely record length runway was no good for the Harrier display as it was too close to the spectators. The display was therefore performed to the rear of the runway on the 'grass'. It was the finest display of a Hover mower ever, everybody got a bit of grass, some more than others, but it didn't distract form the wonderful display of aerobatics.

CHAPTER 8

Briefing

So we were on our way again getting steadily further South, the weather getting marginally warmer as we approached and then crossed the Equator. All the fellas had done the crossing the line routine but Penny and Anna hadn't and lived to regret it, but Stan was forgiven eventually.

After we'd crossed the line Stan decided that it was time for the final briefing, so he called us all together, unveiled the final chart pinned to a blackboard and started.

'You all know the object of the exercise is to sink an ex AFD, you also know the method, and you know we're going to get to do it, but what you don't know is the nitty gritty of the operation, so here goes. Firstly the real reason for sinking the Dock is to prevent boats of a potentially hostile nation being serviced, in particular an ex 'V' class nuclear propelled boat, which may, in the not too distant future, acquire a nuclear armament capability so we're here to prevent that possibility.'

'How are we going to be able to guarantee disabling the 'V' boat unless we know its exact itinerary?' Andy enquired.

'I'll answer that fully when I've finished the briefing Andy, along with any other questions if you could all be a little patient. The plan is to approach the Kananga Naval Base from the south, which is with the prevailing wind and clue up at the base jetty with engine trouble, OK Danny?'

'Yes boss, water in the fuel system.'

'Right, the story is that we were heading south for Dar-es-Salaam, we'd already passed the mouth of the Kananga River when engine trouble struck. The only sensible thing to do is to bend on sail and head for the nearest safe haven, which, with the prevailing wind was north to the Naval Base. We time it for when there is a boat alongside the jetty. Now then, any questions?'

'How are you going to ensure that a boat will be alongside when we arrive?' Sharky piped up.

'Ah, that's the bit I've been keeping to myself until now. We have company up top, our very own resident Nimrod spy in the sky floating about. Conventional boats (non nuclear) are regular users of the docking facility, so as soon as a boat appears to be approaching the jetty we'll be the first to know. Then we go alongside and get aggravation and

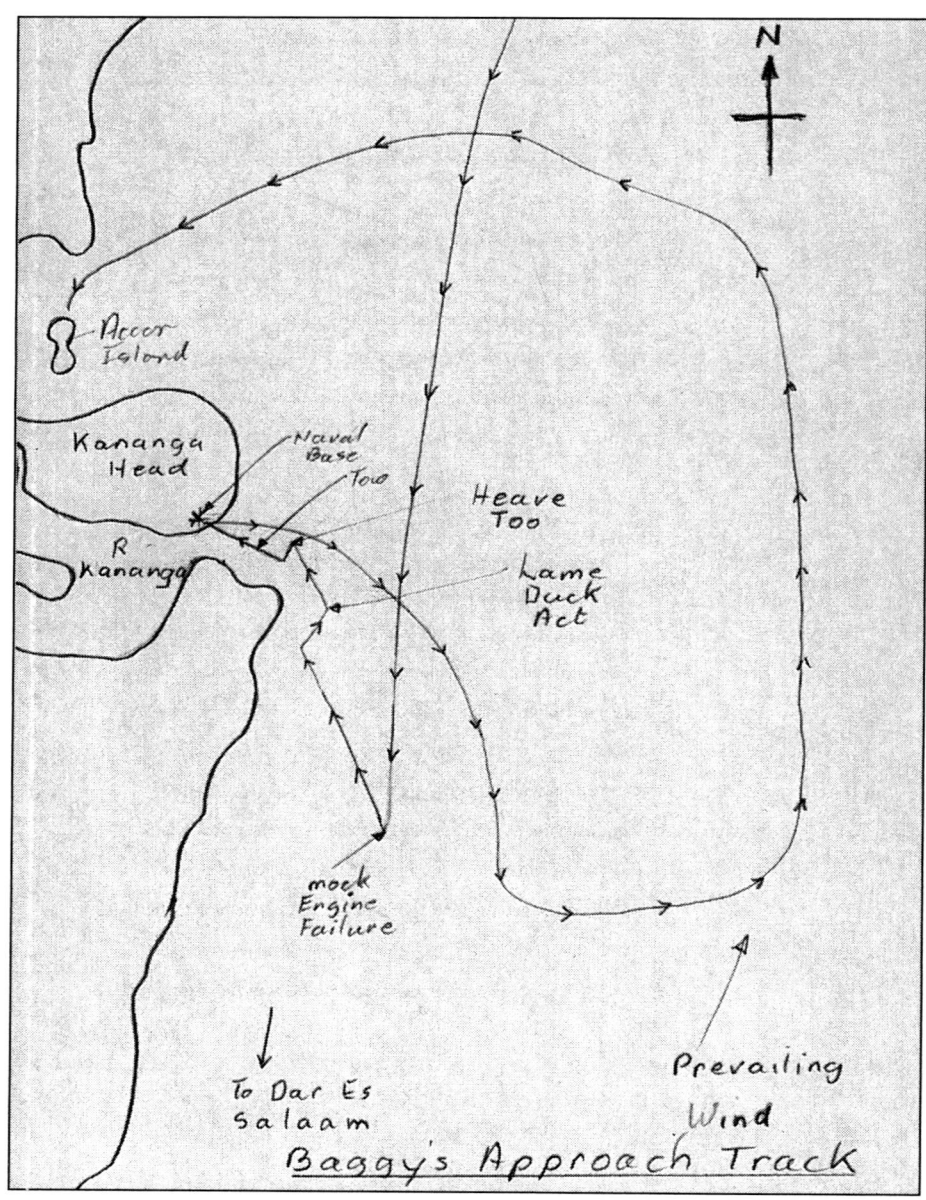

searched by which time the diving team will have transferred.'

I had trouble with this bit so I stood up and Stan asked me if I had a problem.

'Yes Stan, how can you guarantee that the boat won't go straight up river?'

'Good question Ted, boats can only get up river between half an hour before and half an hour after high tide because the narrows at any other time are too shallow, and I have the tide tables for this area, so in the unlikely event of the tide being in the opposition's favour we just wait for the next one. OK so having transferred the diving team, Danny will then have the engines clear and run up and Baggy will depart with profuse apologies and head south as the opposition would expect, then under cover of darkness double back in a wide sweep to the east, and once past the river mouth turn west to hide to the north of Accar Island. Meanwhile we of the Diving Team will be transported to the Floating Dock by kind permission of the opposition. Come the silent hours under cover of darkness, when all is quiet we will deploy the horizontal shot line and lay the charges as practised and then make our way up north across the swamp, and rendezvous with Baggy and away we go up north to be picked up.'

'How do we ensure that we disable the 'V' boat?' piped up H.

'The first time the dock is flooded it primes the detonators by hydrostatic switches, then our Eye in the Sky takes over so that we know when the 'V' boat is docked down. Fitted to the detonators are state of the art microwave radio receivers, we wait till the target has been docked down for a couple of days before detonation to hopefully have a few hull valves removed to ensure maximum damage. That's the plan, we will be in touch at all times with each other by radio, so we can all be kept up to speed. Any questions? Yes Ted?'

'What about this buoyancy problem Stan? We've got to sort it out asap. The only way I can see to do it is to attach the extra flotation aids, and add more ballast to make the strings neutrally buoyant in salt water, but make the ballast up with lots of small weights so that if we do hit fresh water we can always jettison bits at a time to compensate for possible gradual change in density.'

'Sounds good to me, see that it's organized Ted, please. Any more questions? Spike you're looking a bit pensive, what's up?'

'I was just thinking that if we end up with heavy aggravation we ought to have some sort of pre-arranged signal to go from passive to active reaction. Although I understand Arabic I'm not good enough to suss out potential conflict, so I suggest that Dusty and Ali arrange something between them to alert us all.'

'OK that's up to you lot because we'll be long gone by the time anything like that is likely to happen, but for heaven's sake act servile, snivel if you have to because the last thing you need is aggravation and conflict as you lot are our gang's ticket out! Any more questions? No, OK then let's all run through the plan and your own parts in it in your own mind and if anybody has any queries please don't hesitate to bring it up however trivial you may think it is. Now we just wait for word from up top, so everybody try and relax and enjoy the wait.'

Anna mashed yet another pot of tea and we all sat round the mess table yarning. One of the funniest stories that came out at that time was from H about when he was Wrecking on his 'P' boat. The boat was alongside *Adamant* at Faslane one evening when the shore phone rang in the Control Room. The duty Tiff 'Nobby' Clark answered it, H was investigating a suspected hydraulic leak on the panel at the time. Suddenly Nobby shouted across the control room and asked H if he would do him a sub (substitute). H, not being able to go anywhere because he had his fault to attend to, said he would, but it would cost, to which Nobby agreed, talked a bit more on the phone, and then shot off towards the mess. The next thing H remembered was Nobby in no time at all, leaping up the for'ard hatch and away ashore all dolled up and smelling gorgeous.

When a boat comes in from a long patrol or exercise there are usually a few major defects that require inboard (Depot Ship) assistance. This particular time some brazing was required and 'Jumper' Collins came aboard with his gear to do the job, he was a good hand, (for a general service rating) and one of the best coppersmiths around. The boats senior rates all knew him from previous jobs and he was always invited to the mess for a Tot and Lunch.

Nobby, his tongue loosened by his tot was telling, no, bragging about the previous evening's evolution.

'I was on duty when the shore phone rang in the control room. I answered it and a nice female voice engaged me in pleasant conversation eventually getting round to telling me how lonely she was and that I sounded nice, and if I fancied I could bring a bottle of whisky and see what developed. So H did me a sub, she gave me her address, a block of flats in Dumbarton, I got cleaned up, threw some civvy lagging on, got a bottle of Famous Grouse and went up Homers, we saw the Skey off and had one hell of a night. I've been invited back tonight.'

Lots of catcalls followed with crude and other type comments. The subject eventually changed and a few other topics were discussed, during which Jumper was heard to ask Nobby which block of flats it was in Dumbarton because he thought he knew who it was.

'It's McAllister House and there's no way you could possibly know her.'

'Don't they call her Jean Logan the girlfriend of the Scratcher of that O boat that's just left on patrol?'

'No, they call her Craig and she was unattached until last night.'

'Oh sorry, my mistake.'

And so the conversation meandered on until turn to.

That evening Nobby got tarted up again and literally floated ashore he was so hyped. Two hours later he was back aboard, fuming and threatening GBH. Eventually he'd calmed down sufficiently to tell us what was wrong.

'I got me bottle, caught the train to Dumbarton, went up to the flat, rang the bell, the door opened and there's that snide bastard Coppersmith with a half empty bottle of Whisky in his fist, and tells me to F – – off and slams the door in my face.'

With that the whole of the mess collapsed in a big heap of mirth.

'Jumper always was a quick flip to the front, how do you think he got his nickname?' someone chortled.

'That'll teach you to keep your trap shut Nobby!' another threw in.

For those who are confused, in Scotland, flats in cities are very common and have intercom systems with occupants' names against flat numbers.

This story reminded me of an incident that occurred to me, so I related the story to the gang about another Coppersmith. I was Wrecking on *Osprey* and Stan was Jimmy and I'm sure he'll remember the incident.

Ever since I'd joined *Osprey* there had been a compressed air leak behind the main panel in the control room where the planesmen were stationed. The only time it became apparent was when we were at silent routine, when carpets were laid on deck plates, fluorescent lights switched off, because of a slight frequency buzz, and all crew off watch turned in, and then you could hear this quiet whistle/hiss. It was considered not bad enough to warrant repair because it would mean a major strip down and a right bunch of buggers behind the panel until an electrical fault behind the same panel, which forced the issue. So the next time we were alongside *Adamant* the panel had to be stripped out so it was decided to repair the air leak at the same time as the Greenies did their own thing.

A coppersmith was sent down, it was the first time I'd met him, I showed him the job and he seemed quite confident and went inboard to organize his gear while I isolated the offending pipeline and drained the high pressure air from the defective section. The pipework was cupro-nickel-iron thick wall 1½in bore connected together in this case by a capillary brazed union, which is a 4in length of thick wall tube of the same material which is a good fit over the main pipe work. Recesses are turned just inside either end of the tube and filled with fluxed braze metal (a similar system to fluxed solder in Yorkshire fittings, but with a much higher melting point). The two ends to be joined are parted and the sleeve slid on one end, the two ends are then brought together and the sleeve slid back to half way so that it is centred over both ends. Heat is then applied, the braze metal melts and fuses the sleeve to the parent pipe work and the join is complete and tested when cooled. Unfortunately our leak was a flaw in the fusing of a union in one little area. The solution was to cut the existing sleeve in half, part the two ends and heat them up one at a time to melt the braze metal and slide the ends off. Then clean up each end, slot on a new capillary brazed union, realign the pipe ends and as already explained slide the sleeve half and half again, apply heat, cool down and test.

Our new coppersmith seemed to know what he was doing and had organized asbestos millboard and cloth (this was before the asbestos who-ha) to protect the surrounding area from heat. I'd cut through the old leaky union, he applied heat and slid the two halves off no problem, cleaned up the ends, slid the new sleeve on, applied heat, let it cool down and I went to test it. High Pressure Compressed Air is one of the mainstays of a boat, it is stored in external (outside the pressure hull) bottle banks and piped into the boat via HP Hull Stop Valves. Compressed air at 4,000 PSI is both powerful and dangerous if mishandled and very unforgiving.

The Hull Valve to allow air back into the repaired section was well forrard by the forends hatch. I left the coppersmith in the Control Room and went up front to open the hull valve. You have to open it slowly to allow the pressure to equalize slowly. A loud hiss tells you that you are bleeding air into the depressurized section and as it diminishes you open the valve a little more until eventually the hiss diminishes to silence, indicating that the pressure has equalized, so I opened the valve fully and then heard that all too familiar sound of an air leak but quite loud this time, so I started to shut the Hull Valve. As I just about had it shut there was such a bang and a thick cloud of asbestos dust flew up the passage enveloping everything. All the crew converged on the Control Room and as the dust settled there was no trace of asbestos left at the repair site and no sign of the coppersmith either, and we all feared the worst. Eventually he was located just coming round, but very dazed with his upper body bare and pebbledashed, laying on the wardroom door which was laying on the wardroom table, with his oxyacetylene torch still in his hand. What had happened was that as I'd opened the Hull Valve he's heard the leak and without thinking had re-applied his torch to reheat the joint as the pressure had equalized at 4,000 PSI the braze metal had melted and the built up pressure had exploded out. Inspection of the said pipework showed that the two ends had been blown a foot apart due to the reaction of the expelled air and no amount of heaving with pull lifts and chain blocks could get the two ends back together and a foot length of pipe had to be fitted with two Capillary Brazed Unions. The lesson to be learnt, don't mess with HP air, it may damage your health or in this case the coppersmith's, also your ego and your credibility.

That got Andy going about taking liberties like when he was stationed at HMS *Lochinvar*, South Queensferry. At the East end of the establishment was the Bomb and Mine disposal depot equipped with a large shed that was used for gear storage, a lecture theatre and an armaments and munitions display area. One of the exhibits was a 5,000 pound bomb that had had a lump of casing cut away to show the detonator and the filling which everyone was assured had been emptied of explosives and filled with harmless wax. This particular display unit was parked near an exit and everybody used to kick it or pick a bit of wax out of it. That is until a newly qualified Sub Lieutenant joined the Disposal Team and took a keen interest in the 5,000 Pounder, had it shipped down to the beach, rigged a hired steam generator and steamed the 'wax' out of it and set it alight. It went up like a volcano, because it was the real thing, Amatol.

Penny got on the bandwagon about taking liberties. It appears that she joined the WRNS on the lower deck, but quickly gained promotion. It was when she was promoted to PO and was drafted to HMS *Raleigh* at Torpoint in Cornwall where one of her duties was Film Projectionist. One of the films she had to show was to graphically illustrate a lecture to young new recruits on sexually transmitted diseases. To start with it was very difficult and embarrassing and she used to sneak into the projection room by the back door, but eventually she got used to it, and in fact became quite blasé about it. The audience, however was always new. They started off as Jack the lad, looking forward to a good laugh and lots of crude comments, but as the film progressed things quietened down then there were a few groans, some just looked away, others rushed outside to be physically ill. Eventually she used to make a habit of walking the full length of the lecture hall to get to the projection room when this particular subject was to be shown, to a chorus of jeers, catcalls and whistles, and at the end of the lecture and film show, getting great satisfaction in walking back down the hall with a wry smile seeing all the pale faces, and all those who had been ill looking so pathetic.

Spike showed us a battered cigarette case and told us that was caused by him taking a liberty.

'Never run in front of a window when you're house clearing.'

It appears that he was in the first wave of Bootnecks to go in at the start of the Suez Crisis. He made the mistake of running in front of a window and was shot. What saved him was his fag case, which he kept in his left breast pocket. He was in a coma for three days and it was touch and go as to whether he would make it at one time, but he never took liberties any more.

A few days later *Hannibal* was tooling about well to the southeast of the target area when a signal came through and the shit hit the fan.

Chapter 9

Preparatory

Our Eye in the Sky passed us an encrypted signal, so Stan called Curly in to decode it. It read:

URGENT IMMEDIATE

Required Item approaching relevant area.
Position @ 0100
4 deg 44 min 25 S – – 45 deg 32 min 14 E
Estimated speed 12 Knots
Course 276 deg
Acknowledge.

We sent a signal confirming receipt of the sit rep, and then got our heads down over the chart with *Hannibal's* Skipper to work out a strategy to bring us to the Naval Base Jetty to coincide with the oppositions boat being alongside and the tide being in our favour. We had to be as near as possible to the boat's position, but out of sight and radar range. The good thing was that when Baggy was launched she would easily have the legs on the boat on 12 knots, and we would be a very small radar target, so we should be able to get quite close before detection. The snag was that timing was critical and we couldn't calculate progress accurately because we had nothing to work on, so we sent a signal to the Nimrod asking them if they could give us a progress report of target regarding position, speed and course every 2 hours, and any dramatic changes in those parameters immediately.

The cryptic signal came back:

WILL DO

Stan then called the whole team together to update them on the latest situation and remind them of the importance of the operation, and then ran through the sequence of events and the salient points to remember, he then asked for any questions or comments.

Ali stepped forward and explained that he and Dusty had a possible solution to Spike's problem of how to warn the rest of the crew of imminent conflict. He explained that as he was to be the spokesman, being the most fluent in Arabic, it was up to him to judge the mood of the opposition and give the signal. He explained that it would be the adoption of a typical Arabic resting position of squatting on his haunches with his elbows resting on his knees, hands together, the execute signal was elbows still on knees but hands outstretched, palms up. As he explained, the potential aggressors attention would be focused down on him which, as he explained, would be to our advantage. He then gave a demonstration, and all the team agreed that the signal was unambiguous and was unanimously adopted.

Curly was seconded to the radio shack so that he could update the situation regarding the position, course and speed of the Subject boat. All the rest of the team busied themselves as best they could, checking and rechecking equipment, but a general air of inertia prevailed, as if they were reluctant to believe that the crunch was about to come. Then, as Curly reported the latest information it put the boat nearing the base, and everybody suddenly realized that it was the real thing and were re-motivated and got stuck in. On the lighter side, Dusty organized a fancy dress parade, where all the home team got dressed up in their Arabic rig of the day, and used plenty of liquid sunshine to darken the complexions. The sailing crew looked a right motley gang of cut-throats and very authentic in their well worn and non too clean Jibbas. Dusty was the owner, dressed in luxurious linens and silks with gold lame', 'His Girls' did nothing for the reduction of male blood pressure, they looked stunning, and Ali the Eunuch Attendant to all his masters needs, and his mouthpiece.

Dusty then did a rig (dress) inspection to check that nothing was out of place, and he reckoned that on the whole it was a good turn out apart from the odd missed bit of bottled bronzy, the only real let down was Pancho of all people who had forgotten that he was still wearing his Rolex Submariner which would have been a dead give-away as, being a hairy arsed dhow crewman he could hardly have afforded a Timex egg boiler.

Spike did his rounds of Baggy, checking locations of secreted arms and ammunition to be sure that they were well concealed but readily available should the need arise, and that those involved knew there location. He also warned everyone not to hide arms about their persons in case of body searches.

Curly had an update on the subject boat's position which was a bit confusing as its progress up to this point had been steady and consistent until this last one. The course was still the same but the position had suddenly leapt forward suggesting a speed in excess of 25 knots which was impossible for a conventional diesel driven boat, which baffled us. After discussion with Stan and Sharkey this anomaly was put down to a tracking error, but a consequence was that the time for the deployment of Baggy was brought forward.

Hannibal's Skipper, Stan and Sharkey had a meeting to discuss the timing of the parting of the ways as *Hannibal* was picking up a faint radar transmission which meant that we were nearly in range, it was therefore decided to reverse course, wait for the cover of darkness and launch Baggy that same night. So, as the sun dipped below the horizon, the hatch covers were removed, the slings shackled up, the whir of winches, and in next to no time Baggy was in the Oggin, and the gang embarked, a last good luck from the Skipper and *Hannibal* melted into the blackness to tool about out of range till we called for her, we were on our own.

Danny had the Chrysler engines flashed up, and in no time at all we were creaming our way north making a good 19 knots leaving an almost brilliant fluorescent wake.

The Nimrod was informed of our changed status and gave us an update of the subject's position which, when it was plotted, was not good news, as if its projected ETA was correct would enable it to clear the narrows before the ebb tides half hour deadline. Danny was talked into getting a bit more out of the engines, so he increased the boost pressure to near maximum and got a magnificent 22 knots out of her. The problem was: would it be enough? Sharky explained to us that we would have to keep going at full chat until the opposition's radar pinged us, but one good thing in our favour was that our ECM (electronic counter measure) sensor rigged in the main mast would give us warning of any such radar transmission and because it was passive could not be detected by the opposition. That being the case the engines could be secured in plenty of time and sail bent on to give the right approach speed consistent with the wind speed. One bit of good news was that the weather was freshening which gave us a bit of an edge in our request for a safe haven. So we ploughed on trying to win time and beat the tide, but it was going to be a close run thing, especially if we were to be stopped and searched in open water for any length of time. One thing we had to do at this stage was to prepare for possible confrontation, so all the home team got dressed in the native rig and bundled their western gear up, weighted it and gave it the float test, whilst we, the away team, donned our wet suits just in case. The following sequence of events is as told to the away team by Dusty and Sharky.

Eventually the inevitable happened when our ECM told us it was time to act the lame duck, and Danny shut down the engines and cosmetically sabotaged them, and the sailing gang got to do their own thing, and remembered to unrig the ECM sensor. We of the away team made ourselves scarce, secreting ourselves behind the forrard false bulkhead, the reason being that if the opposition did a head count it may cause confusion and possible problems in the future whilst we were doing our own thing. In no time at all, as dawn was breaking a low hulled grey Patrol boat appeared out of the morning mist, and a loud hailer blasted the ether with a demand in Arabic to heave to. Sharky put the helm to starb'd, brought Baggy head to wind and ordered the sails lowered using Ali to shout the orders in Arabic. As way was lost the Patrol boat came up alongside, and a boarding party of half a dozen black sailors armed to the teeth leapt aboard and took up very aggressive stances. Then the obvious Gaffer of the outfit stepped aboard. He was the spitting image of Idi Amin, covered in gold braid and badges, and wearing a permanent sneer. He spoke in a loud guttural unintelligible African dialect, to which Ali replied in Arabic. It appears that he demanded to see the person in charge, to which Ali had replied that his Master was in his State Room and would be honoured if his lordship would join his master to take coffee or something more substantial, and discuss his master's misfortunes that Allah had seen fit to bestow upon his humble servant. The brute was ushered below with much bowing and scraping, and his eyes widened in disbelief as he surveyed the scene.

Dusty looked the bees knees and played the part superbly, but the girls were the perfect attraction to keep the unwelcome visitor wrong footed, with Ali in attendance, doing a wonderful job of grovelling. Dusty explained in Arabic that his miserable dog of an engine minder had made the engines not work, but would his lordship care for coffee, and snapped his fingers. Anna slid off the bed, disappeared and in an instant reappeared and floated up to Idi with a tray of thimbles full of hot, thick, sweet coffee, the fingers clicked again and Penny floated over to a bulkhead cupboard, pulled open a pair of doors and out folded a fully stocked bar complete with ice and crystal glasses. It was obvious that Idi had two vices, Scotch Whisky and girls. With half a bottle of Famous Grouse inside him and Anna and Penny draped outside him Idi was a pushover for the story that he was spun. Dusty explained that his miserable son of a camel engineer had allowed water into the fuel so his equally miserable Captain had the temerity to suggest that they sought sanctuary at the nearest moorings which as a place they had sighted on their way down to Dar-es-Salaam, which is where they were heading to effect repairs when Allah was gracious enough to allow his humble servant to be saved by such a brave and honourable personage. By the time Dusty had finished his exaltation so was the Famous Grouse. Idi, a little the worse for wear by this time, said he would tow them to the Naval

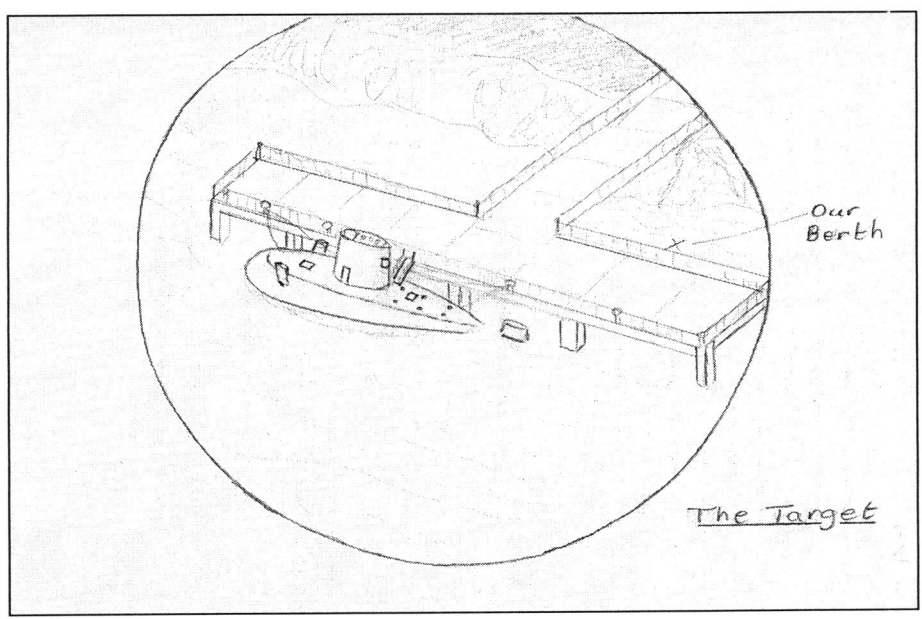

Base jetty to allow them to make good the defects but told him that leaving the vessel was forbidden, and that they must leave immediately the repairs were completed. Dusty laid it on with a trowel again, giving praise and thanks to Allah for being delivered by such a generous and magnificently masterful person as his Lordship, who with another bottle of Famous Grouse grasped firmly in his fist, shook off the females and staggered to the upper deck. He shouted and waved his arms at his men who disembarked helping Idi on his way. A tow line was passed and secured and off we went, kind permission of the opposition. We of the away team were let out much to our relief and everything was going better than expected. It was now a race against time to see if the towing speed of 4–5 knots would be sufficient to be able to beat the tide deadline. Huddled over the chart the two navigators came to the conclusion that the odds were not good. The snag was that if we didn't make it the whole exercise would be a huge failure and would have to be abandoned. At the speed of advance we were making it was estimated that we had 6 hours to prepare for whatever might be, and thinking positively, the diving sets, spare oxygen cylinders and associated tools, shot lines, explosive strings, and detonators were all checked over thoroughly and made ready to go. Our support teams in the Nimrod and *Hannibal* were informed in code by Curly of the situation. Good luck signals were returned, so now we were on our own.

As we eventually approached the Naval Base all eyes were straining to see what, if anything was alongside the jetty, because if nothing was there we'd have missed our chance and the operation would have to be abandoned. Stan had the best binoculars, and was concentrating on the horizon dead ahead, suddenly he readjusted the focus and locked onto a point just a couple of points to port and suddenly gave an explosive gasp.

'I don't believe it', and passed his binoculars to Sharky who, once he saw what Stan had seen looked as if he was going to do somersaults.

'What're you lot on about, anybody'd think you'd won the lottery or somat!' Nobby shouted angrily.

'Everybody, there's a boat alongside, not just any old boat, it's the 'V' boat, the bloody TARGET!' Stan shouted.

'It answers a lot of questions and makes our job that much easier and quicker.'

What Stan meant was that the target speed increase that wasn't understood at the time and caused so much confusion was now crystal clear, as Nuclear Propulsion is a lot faster than Diesel Electric, as the 'V' boat must have done a speed trial, or possibly was adjusting Base ETA. Another question that was answered was why the target had not gone up stream before the half hour high water window, the reason being that a 'V' boat is twice the diameter of a conventional boat and therefore a greater draught and consequently could only get upstream at near enough full flood tide. The big advantage though was the fact that we could do the job in one hit rather than having to hang about waiting for the main target to appear, which could have taken forever.

It was now for real, and everybody switched to automatic, another half hour and we would be alongside the jetty, and we four of the away team would be in the thick of it. We had changed out of our wet suits when the tow had got underway as they can become quite hot out of water especially at this latitude. So we now put them back on and rechecked our breathing sets yet again. Then as the patrol boat cast us off to allow us to drift into an inboard berth of the jetty and the heaving lines were thrown, Stan explained to us his intention to reconnoitre the best approach to the target as it was on an outboard berth further up the jetty.

The coffer dam was opened up, we donned our breathing sets and fins and slid over the rim into the water and the lid closed after us. Stan cleared his set and disappeared out of the shimmering glow of our oblong of light taking a lead line with him. He seemed to have been gone ages, and in the meantime the three of us, to conserve our breathing set, enriched it by bleeding storage cylinder oxygen into the void through a two stage reducer and silencer. When Stan eventually returned, he explained that the ebb tide was quite strong, and although the visibility was not too good and it did pose quite a problem regarding detection, as the water was quite shallow under the jetty, he had found a way through the support piles and had strung out the lead line as a guide, and proposed that we transported all the gear required to the outboard side of the jetty alongside the target with a view to transferring it across at dusk when we would be less vulnerable to detection. The intention was to split into two teams, Stan with H and Andy with me, and stash ourselves in each side of number 5 main ballast tanks. These tanks were the biggest with plenty of stiffening bulkheads with interconnecting free flood holes large enough for a body complete with breathing gear to pass through with ease. The idea behind splitting up was that if for any reason one team was detected or was unable to complete their task, the other team could at least inflict a damaging blow to delay, if not disable the dock for some time.

The plan was put into action straight away, nose clips on, breathing systems cleared and off we went, and as Stan had predicted it was difficult but the lead line was a great help, and when we arrived at the dump site you couldn't fail to be impressed by the sheer bulk that confronted you. We went back for the remainder of the gear, while Stan went to survey our final destination. It was just as well he did because that's when the plan started to go pear shaped. Stan was back in next to no time signalling for us to follow him, and headed off back to Baggy, and as we assembled in the Coffer Dam Stan immediately ripped off his mask and started making slow signals for help. While he was doing this he explained in a whisper that the free flood hole grills had been re-fitted barring the entrance to our hideout. Suddenly the signal light started flashing fast for danger. We found our later that the problem was that it coincided with some unwelcome visitors who came aboard Baggy and wanted to know the far end of a fart. Dusty and Ali managed to keep the nosy leader reasonably happy with their answers to his probing and then Dusty noticed the signal light flashing slow, so he enticed the uninvited guests to inspect the problem in the Engine Room. They were very impressed with Danny's happy state of chaos, with petrol and water swilling about all over the place and assorted pieces of pipe work strewn everywhere. The smell of petrol was overpowering and everybody was convinced by then that Baggy was genuinely badly disabled and wanted to get away from the smell, and more importantly the hazard, but while they were down there Sharky was able to give us the danger signal. Eventually after a few drinks and the gift of a bottle each the rubber-necking bums departed and the lads dashed down to see what we wanted, leaving Spike to keep an eye on things up top. We didn't get out but Stan called for Danny and while he was waiting explained to the crew the problem.

'When the first 'V' boat was commissioned, during silent running a strange low frequency humming noise was detected which, after a lot of tests and trials, was traced to the grills on the free flood apertures of the ballast tanks. So she was docked down and the grills removed, and no further problems of that nature were experienced, and in subsequent boats of that class the grills were omitted. So why the hell the opposition put them back is anybody's guess.'

With that Danny appeared and Stan grabbed me and we went into a huddle.

'Danny, we need socket spanners and tee bars, what size are the nuts Ted?'

'1 ½in AF (across the flats) we'll need two full sets and extensions for the tee bars, say 4 foot lengths of 1in bore Red Band steel pipe. If you haven't got 1 ½in AF sockets make one a 38 mm AF. If not, off set ring spanners of either size but cut the other end off so that the the extension piping can be used on the shafts.'

Danny shot off to see what he could rustle up, and I got hold of Stan and explained to him that once we had the grills off we had to go inside the ballast tanks and then put the grills BACK and disguise the fact that they'd been removed, 'cos the first thing you do once you've docked a boat down is to do a hull survey. I suggested that H and I should go and help Danny with his task and then get him to help us cobble something together to somehow disguise and then replace the grills from inside the tanks, as however we did it, it would have to be duplicated. It was agreed, so H and I climbed out, dried ourselves off and got to it. The first thing to do was to devise a method of getting the grills back into place once we were inside the tanks, and disguise the fact that they had been removed. Danny, being a good Tiff, had squirreled away more than a few 'come in handy' bits and pieces. Once we had removed the four securing nuts from the corners of the grill there was no way we could put them back so the omission would have to be disguised. Danny found a short length of 2 ½in x 2 ½in timber and cut eight 1in thick slices and drilled a 1in clear hole in the middle of each block and stained them black with ink from marker pens, but they would have to be shaped to fit. We decided it would be easier to remove the grills and transport them to Baggy where we would be able to work easier and be able to make a bit of noise without attracting attention. So we suited up again and got to it, we split up into our pairs and got stuck in. the one thing in our favour was the full moon which gave us a bit of visibility and the jetty lighting helped a bit. I took the socket spanner and tee bar, the handle of which was taped up to keep the noise down, and Andy carried the extension pipe and we attacked the port grill. The first problem we encountered, not unexpectedly, was getting the socket onto the paint encrusted nut. Normally it would have been given a good clouting with a hammer but this, for obvious reasons, was out of the question. What it needed was a rocking motion with lots of weight behind it which was impossible on your own in water, which is where Andy came in useful. He grabbed the grill with one hand and backed me up with the other. Eventually the paint gave way and we got the socket well on, and Andy slipped the extension pipe onto the tee bar handle then it was my turn to back him up as he put his back into it. The one thing you don't do when using a re-breathing set is start to pant as the soda lime cannot do its job properly, and I could feel Andy starting with the exertion, so I tapped him on the shoulder and signalled him to relax and take it easy for a bit. Then we attacked it again and Andy gave a huge lunge at it and it gave, after that we went round the other three and slacked them off easily by the same method, then it was just a case of spinning the nuts off with the tee bar. I then quietly scratched a mark in the middle of the front of the frame to be sure it went back the right way round.

Having stashed the nuts carefully for use later, we used the extension pipe as a crowbar and, end for end, prised the grill off the studs and with very little trouble it came away and dropped gently to the gravel sea bed. I passed Andy the spanner and pipe and signalled that I was going to see how the others were getting on, and told him to stay put and that I wouldn't be long. Ducking down and passing under to the stab'd side I caught Stan a bit on the hop, but he calmed down when he realized it was me. They'd only got two nuts slacked off so I showed them our method and the other two came loose no trouble, so I waited till they'd dropped their grill then signalled that I would meet them back at Baggy.

The next step was to hump the damned grill back to Baggy, the problem being not so much the weight as the size manoeuvring it through the jetty piles, but eventually we arrived back at the Coffer Dam, gave the signal and got instant response. Everybody lent a hand and the grills were dried off as much as possible and transported to the engine room, where Danny shaped the wooden blocks he had cut to fit the nut recesses, whilst I and H blacked out the bits that had been cut to fit, and then we glued them in place with Araldite, a two part epoxy adhesive. Time was of the essence as we didn't know exactly when the boat would start up river. In record time we had both grills doctored, and off we went again dragging them back to whence they came. While we'd been modding the grills Stan had solved the problem of securing the grills from the inside of the ballast tank. He remembered that when we had

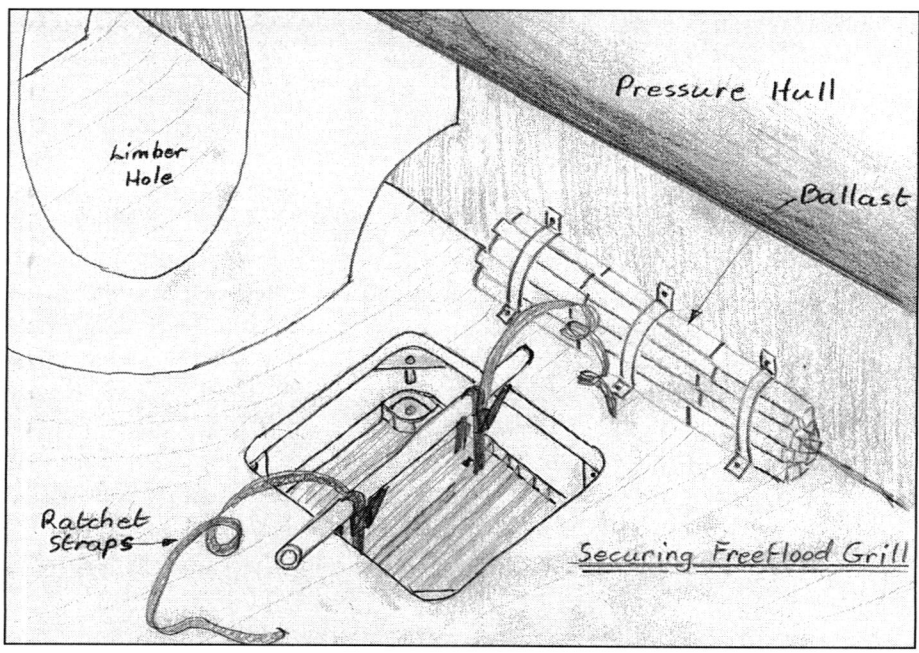

Securing Freeflood Grill

the problem in the Med. with bad weather, Baggy had to be strapped down more securely and some of the gear had to be secured with narrow ratchet straps. So he asked Danny what had happened to them and lo and behold he opened up a small stowage and out popped 1in wide ratchet straps, ideal when Danny had stained them black. I'd also had a word with Stan regarding communication between us in our respective tanks when we had boxed them up as, surrounded by steel, normal radio reception would be impossible. So Stan had a word with Sharky who had made up a direct cable connector to sling between the tanks.

Armed with a couple of ratchet straps per team we humped the grills back through the jetty piles and dropped them on the gravel bottom and got on with the job of loading all the gear into the tanks, before boxing up the grill with us inside it. Last job before boxing ourselves in was to connect up the radios, then we all climbed into our respective tanks and Andy and I stripped off our breathing gear and hauled up our grill on the tails of the straps which were loosely looped at either side of the grill. With the loops inside the tank the 4-foot extension bar was passed through the loops so that the grill was suspended just below the studs. The grill was then aligned as near as possible and then gently and as quietly as possible ratcheted up and, with a bit of juggling onto the studs and seated and then the excess webbing rolled up neatly and stowed safely, job completed. We transferred to the after bay through the lower limber hole, commissioned a light stick and in its eerie glow, sat back on the ballast and yarned in hushed tones.

We talked about all sorts of things, but one thing Andy said stood out in my mind as an example of the result of service life. It appears that he left the mob because his wife and child wanted to see more of him. His father-law got him the job at the builders, and it bored him to tears. Then his wife and child decided they were seeing too much of him. With us turning up and reminding him of earlier days in the mob, he'd decided that if he got through the current operation he'd sign back on again.

I in turn told him about the cushy job I'd had before Stan collared me and lumbered me with the present can of worms, and the fact that I had no idea what I was going to do when the shindig was over 'cos he'd burnt my bridges. We decided it was about time to test the radio link, which checked out fine, and they told us they were all set for the coming fray!

Chapter 10

In

The time was checked, and we calculated that we would have to be leaving within two hours if we were to make the next tide, so we settled ourselves back for a long boring wait.

Number 5 main ballast tank being aft of the fin had no free flood casing above it, so the after deck was the deckhead (ceiling) of the ballast tank so that any activity on the after deck could be distinctly heard.

Suddenly our long boring wait was rudely interrupted by lots of heavy footsteps thudding overhead signalling feverish crew activity. Then all at once there was such a cacophony of ear splitting sound and an oily mist enveloped us and frightened us both to death until I realized that the LP Blower had been started, and I was able to reassure Andy that things were OK. It was like a hot gale force wind and we had to hang on like grim death to the lighter gear. On reflection it was obvious that we were about to get underway as this was one of the preparatory routines to ensure maximum buoyancy. When the blower finally stopped and we'd calmed down it reminded me of the Shamals, the hot date-ripening winds coming off the deserts of the Persian Gulf.

We of the away team found out much later that as activity started on the boat, Idi had made a visit to Baggy and told Dusty to shift or be shifted, and he was backed up by an ugly bunch of well-armed thugs. Dusty thanked his Lordship for his generosity and indulgence and explained that at that very moment his miserable excuse for an engine minder was about to test the engines. With that there was a whirring sound and then suddenly an engine burbled into life, then a second one burst into life and a dirty scruffy, grinning Danny appeared at the engine room hatch to be berated in Arabic (which he didn't understand a word of) to get his miserable misbegotten filthy self back down where he belonged. Idi was given a couple of bottles of Famous Grouse, mooring lines were let go and Baggy was underway heading South. Sharky wanted to get well out of radar range before taking a sweeping swing out East and then back north so the ECM was re-hoisted and a strange radar contact was observed which appeared to be following them for quite some time, but then suddenly disappeared off the screen on a reciprocal course.

A signal was sent to Hoppy via the Nimrod informing him that the deployment of the away team was complete.

Meanwhile the activity above Andy and me, and of course Stan and H, was increasing to a frenzy, then the distinct judder of propeller movement and we were on our way, which according to our calculations was far too early. Again it was going to be sheer boredom, or so we thought, so again we sat on the ballast and chewed the fat. We had been underway for about twenty minutes which was far too long to be going upstream, and I was about to contact Stan on the radio to discuss the situation when our tranquillity was rudely shattered and all hell broke loose.

All at once there was a mechanical clatter, air pressure suddenly reduced, ear drums and sinus canals hurting like hell, and water absolutely erupted through the free flood hole grill like what can only be described as an upside-down waterfall. They'd pulled the plug and we were diving fast. I had a mad scramble to get to my breathing gear with no time to evacuate the system, just opened up the bottles, stuffed the mouthpiece in my gob and held my nose while I scrabbled to locate and fit my nose clip, then think about getting my harness on while being thrown head over heels in the manic flood. The one hope that raced through my mind, and the other three I'm sure, was that the boat wouldn't be taken too deep as the depth limit on pure oxygen was two atmospheres, or 33 feet, as below that depth there was a real fear of oxygen poisoning which causes debilitating symptoms and eventually death. The awful thing about this was that different people have variable thresholds to this problem.

I was being tossed about like a rag doll as the water boiled in, but managed to hang on to the rim of a limber hole until the turbulence had settled down a bit. It appeared that we were running at periscope depth as there was still some light coming through the free flood hole. My next problem was to locate Andy as he was nowhere to be seen and I was concerned for his welfare. I eventually found a couple of light sticks, broke and activated them and went looking for him and the radio in that order. I eventually located him near the top of the after bay where he'd been blown with the force of the inrushing water. He'd managed to grab his breathing set and use it but had damaged his right arm and hadn't been able to get into his harness, so I helped him with it and tucked his arm into the webbing to ease his discomfort. I then went hunting the radio so that I could check on the others when we surfaced.

But before I could do anything the unthinkable happened, we started to be taken deep. We came slowly to the realization as there was no perceptible bow down angle, just a slow dimming of the light coming from the free flood grill, and a slight increase in pressure on the eardrums.

Then we had to operate the bypass valve to bleed extra oxygen into the breathing system to compensate for the compression due to the increase in depth. That unfortunately was the last thing I remember because it appears we exceeded 100 foot depth and I succumbed to oxygen poisoning and passed out. Somehow Andy, with his one good hand, had managed to keep my mask on while I convulsed before lapsing into the oblivion of unconsciousness. It appears that we weren't too long at depth, which was just as well really because if Andy had succumbed to oxygen poisoning as well who knows what would have become of us. Anyway, the next thing I remember was Andy bent over and staring at me with a light stick jammed in his harness and slapping my face with his good hand to bring me round. It appears that we'd only been at depth for about 15 minutes and had then slowly regained periscope depth and then blown the ballast tanks and surfaces, which is where I came back into the land of the living, with a splitting headache and a horrible taste in my mouth. The first thing I needed to do was to contact Stan and H to see how they'd fared, so it was all hands to hunt the radio which was eventually located buried underneath the jumbled up mass of the rest of the gear. With fingers crossed, hoping that the watertight plug had held, I called up Stan, and after an interminable delay he answered stating that he and H were OK, he himself having suffered a damaged ankle. I explained that we were also still with it, but unfortunately Andy had suffered a damaged arm.

My next project when my head had cleared a bit more was to assess Andy's injury, so I commissioned another light stick and collared him and sat him down on the ballast and discovered, to our horror, that his arm was broken, both radius and ulna, the only saving grace being that it wasn't a compound fracture. So I broke up the lid of the light stick box to fashion splints and tore up a burlap sack, that had been used to transport some of the gear, to secure the splints, and immobilize his arm by lashing up a sling, then administered him pain killers. My next priority was to change the breathing set Soda Lime canisters as the contents of the existing units would exhaust prematurely because of our failure to evacuate the system in the rush. Our transport appeared to have increased speed and according to my calculation we were within half an hour of high water so it would appear that the race was on to make the narrows.

With our plan back on track it was time to sort the gear out from the jumbled mess that had been caused by the untimely dip that we had experienced. Once that was done Andy and I settled down to what we hoped would be an uneventful transit.

I had to think of some way to take Andy's mind off his injury, and mine off the problems that lay ahead because of it, so I decided to explain to him why I knew we were being rushed along. I knew because we were about to go 'on the step', which gives more speed on the surface with no increase in power consumption. I explained the reason that I knew it was going to happen was because the engine revolutions went up and a series of violent port and starb'd helm movements occurred. Normally to go on the step it only needed a slight swell, and maximum revs and fore planes to rise, but the Indian Ocean at this time was as flat as a pancake and therefore required heavy helm movement, which was discovered empirically. The whole idea being to create a bow wave configuration, which develops a large crest of water over the propeller, effectively putting the prop deeper and so reducing cavitation and therefore increasing efficiency. The reason it's called on the step is that as the prop digs in more efficiently and the speed increases the boat assumes a definite bow up angle as if it is on a step and the prop goes deeper and digs in even better.

I was getting a bit desperate as to what to talk about next when the revs dropped, and the boat dropped off the step, which hopefully was the prelude to negotiation of the narrows. Then slowly the light filtering through the free flood grill started to dim and as we peered down through it the gravel riverbed came up to meet us.

Then suddenly there was a cacophony of thrashing sounds and the riverbed turned to a jumbled muddy mass as tugs nudged us in the right direction through the worst part of the narrows. The reason for the assistance was the fact that, with a single screw, and at slow speed, this type of vessel was a pig to manoeuvre, and so for the rest of the trip up river and entry to the dock we were straddled and shepherded by these two vessels.

Entry into the dock took a couple of stabs, but eventually we were in and securely moored. The next stage was a bit dodgy for us, as divers would take to the water to check that as the dock was pumped out the boat settled on the keel blocks correctly. So I checked that the grill securing strap tails were stowed inboard, and that nothing was sculling about on the grill. Then I called Stan up on the radio to enquire how they were doing and remind him to check the same details which he confirmed had been done, and that things were not too bad with him, which to me didn't sound too good as he was the master of the understatement.

Chapter 11

Ungodly

Meanwhile, as we found out later, things weren't going too well for Baggy and her crew either. As may be recalled, the radar contact that was following and suddenly disappeared must have been us getting a ducking, and for Sharky and the boys and girls it was just a mystery and they went gaily on their way. They ran south until dawn and then swung east with a view to eventually looping back up north.

As night fell a radar contact appeared rapidly approaching on an intercept course from the south. On gaining a visual sighting at dawn it was shown on the radar to have slowed to just be gaining on Baggy. So Sharky called Dusty and Spike and explained developments to date, and what he thought the likely scenario would be.

'The area we're in is known hunting ground for pirates who are both efficient and barbaric, always disposing of all evidence and guaranteeing no survivors'.

'What makes you think they're pirates Sharky?' Dusty enquired.

'They appeared on our radar screen at dusk as we headed east, closing us at about 30 knots, but as soon as we became visual they've slowed right down but are still closing.'

'Well if you have serious doubts about the vessel's intentions I think we ought to formulate some contingency plans, don't you Dusty?' Spike enquired.

'What I've already done is had the radar secured and the scanner dismantled so that if they are the ungodly they hopefully won't be aware that we know of their fast approach and possible intentions.'

Dusty thought long and hard for quite a while and then agreed with them both that it would be prudent to prepare for the worst, and that even if it was a false alarm, it would be a good exercise to test the crews preparedness and training. So the crew were called together and Sharky addressed them.

'I won't beat about the bush, I hope I'm wrong but I believe we're being targeted by pirates.'

There was a quiet giggle from the girls who must have thought it quite romantic, which idea Sharky quickly dispelled.

'It's not funny, far from it. Modern pirates are completely ruthless and do not, I repeat do not take prisoners. I hope I'm wrong but Dusty and

I are taking no chances. So Spike will issue you with your arms and ammunition and allocate your station. We will carry on at this course and speed and wait and see what develops. Don't forget your training and Ali's signal of squatting on his haunches, elbows on knees hands together is preparatory, when hands go to outstretched it's execute, in more ways than one. Good luck to you all. Ladies can I have a quiet word with you.'

He took them below and explained to them in words of one syllable the dangers that could be in store, and the fact that they would be required to render first aid if required as they more certainly would have to do if his fears were realized. This made the girls realize the gravity of the possible situation and they went to work with a will collecting together all the medical equipment they could muster.

Meanwhile Spike was dishing out positions and arms, including grenades both fragmentary and stun, and gave specific target areas should the shit hit the fan. He then went to have a word with Sharky and Dusty suggesting that Sharky take the helm and not reduce speed no matter what and not allow the opposition to get within boarding distance. He then went to see Danny and suggested that he take the remote engine controls in the wheel house to give them the gun at the first sign of a manoeuvre of the baddies to get alongside and to take over from Sharky if required.

By now as the suspect vessel came within hailing distance everybody was nonchalantly in position with Ali ready to talk turkey and Spike stretched out with his back against the mainmast with his favourite weapon, an automatic with built in grenade launcher, concealed alongside him.

The vessel as it came closer was a very nice rather large motor cruiser with a very high flying bridge which gave a very good overview of Baggy's deck. A smartly dressed Arabic looking gent dressed in western clothes hailed Baggy from the bridge asking in Arabic if help could be given to a sick passenger. Ali quite surprisingly immediately assumed a squatting position but with hands together, which had everybody aware and alert.

'It is with great regret sir that my master has nobody onboard his humble vessel who has any medical expertise and therefore is not able to accede to your request.'

The visitor started to veer towards us so Sharky laid off a couple of points.

'But surely your master carries on his fine vessel first aid equipment and medication in case of emergencies.'

'Oh yes sir, my master's humble vessel does carry such equipment

"The Ungodly"

and medication as you so rightly point out but –'

The hands spread, palms up –. Then violence erupted with Spike's first grenade taking out the flying bridge with horrifyingly spectacular results. The bow of the intruder veered in towards the starb'd side, Danny realized what the intention was and slammed both engines full astern which made the enemy overshoot across Baggy's bow giving the rest of the crew a good broadside view target which they took full advantage of. Heads popped up all over the intruder and Dusty stationed in the bow gave the whole of the upper deck a good spraying of automatic fire as it slid past, having lobbed a grenade onto the bow with devastating results. Spike's next grenade exploded in the engine room setting it on fire. Meanwhile Ali in trying to take cover was shot in the shoulder, but managed to tumble down below to be administered to by the girls. Pancho, stationed to port, caught the arse end with a grenade and a burst of automatic fire as it overshot Baggy's bow. Sharky congratulated Danny on his quick thinking and got him to put the engines full ahead and swung Baggy to starb'd, away from the carnage when the wheelhouse suddenly exploded and Sharky took the full force of the missile which came through the port window, and slammed him into Danny who was left semi conscious and full of splinters. Curly, stationed to starb'd had lost sight of the enemy when he saw the wheelhouse disintegrate with Baggy going full chat ahead in a wide starb'd circle which he realized would quickly bring them back to the danger zone, so he shouted for Nobby to follow him and went into the mess that used to be the wheelhouse. Realizing that all the controls were shot to ribbons, he diverted to the emergency control position with Nobby. On the way he shouted for Penny to get to the wheelhouse to render whatever assistance she could. He realized that two things had to be done immediately, reverse the helm and control the engines. Having disengaged the remote linkage he used the emergency helm position to put port wheel on but the engines were a problem until suddenly a very bloody Danny appeared and took control of his engines, so Curly got Nobby to be his eyes and give him helm directions and Danny engine orders to keep Baggy out of trouble and away from the pirate vessel which was circling and burning furiously back aft.

Meanwhile Spike made his way back aft to assist in the wheelhouse only to find Penny kneeling alongside Sharky sobbing quietly. He did a quick pulse check to confirm that life was extinct and lifted Penny gently to her feet and shepherded her to the saloon and the comfort of Anna. He went back to the wheelhouse to tidy up and found Dusty doing just that. When they had accomplished what they could they started to make a survey of the rest of the injuries and damage, halfway through which there was a terrific bang which brought all those who could to the upper deck to see a pall of smoke where the oppositions vessel should have been. Dusty took charge and manoeuvred Baggy to the spot but found nothing but debris and a widening patch of oil.

Dusty and Spike carried on with the survey and the final result was: Sharky dead, Ali shot through the shoulder, no bones broken and a clean wound, Danny concussed, lots of splinter damage all over especially to the face, in need of extensive removal of foreign bodies and plenty of stitches.

Mechanical damage confined to the wheelhouse, which Danny was confident of being able to repair and re-commission helm and engine controls after the girls had rendered first aid.

Dusty called the rest of the crew together to explain the changed situation and future course of action.

'Ladies and gentlemen, I know you are all still in a state of shock, but we must for the sake of the away team and the exercise generally put the recent conflict behind us. I, as Deputy Leader, am taking over and I need everyone's help. I intend to signal Admiral Hopgood to advise him of the changed situation, and also advise us regarding Sharky. Meanwhile we continue on the planned track east and turn north at the appropriate time. Pancho, could you and Nobby give Danny a hand with the wheelhouse repairs. Curly, could you help me signal Hoppy please. Thank you all, carry on please.'

The signal sent read:

URGENT TOP SECRET F T A O ADMIRAL SIR A HOPGOOD

Ref Operation Docksunk

Have repelled attack by Pirates, no survivors.

Suffered one fatality, REA3 H. Ward please advise.

Curly encoded and sent it and then went to see if he could also help Danny. Meanwhile Dusty was surveying charts trying to get his head round the intricacies of navigation and calculated that it was time to alter course and head back up north. Shortly after which Curly received a reply to the signal which when decoded read:

DOCKSUNK SPECIAL FORCES

Ref Your Signal

Advise position @ 0400 tomorrow.

At that time heave to and hoist radar reflector.

It all seemed very strange and cryptic to Dusty but with Curly's help they managed to work out the position and encoded and transmitted the information as requested. After all the excitement and trauma Dusty decided to get his head down for a bit and left word that he was to be shaken at 0300.

Came the appointed time with Baggy hove to and the radar target hoisted, everybody was wide awake wondering what to expect as it wasn't quite dawn. Nobody saw it coming, this black mass just appeared alongside as if by magic. A voice called out to take a line and Baggy ended up secured alongside a conventional submarine, an O class Diesel Electric boat. A voice called out from the dark.

'Permission to come aboard.'

'Yes please' Dusty called back.

A lightweight brow was passed across and a tall slim gent in a duffel coat and battered off white hat appeared, got to Baggy's deck, turned smartly aft and chopped one off, a salute in true Naval tradition, turned back and, with an understanding smile, shook Dusty's hand and introduced himself as Lieutenant Commander Gale.

'And you must be Dusty, I'm Windy, permission to bring a couple of my lads aboard, let's go below and talk.' With that, without waiting for a reply he waved an arm and another three came down the brow, two

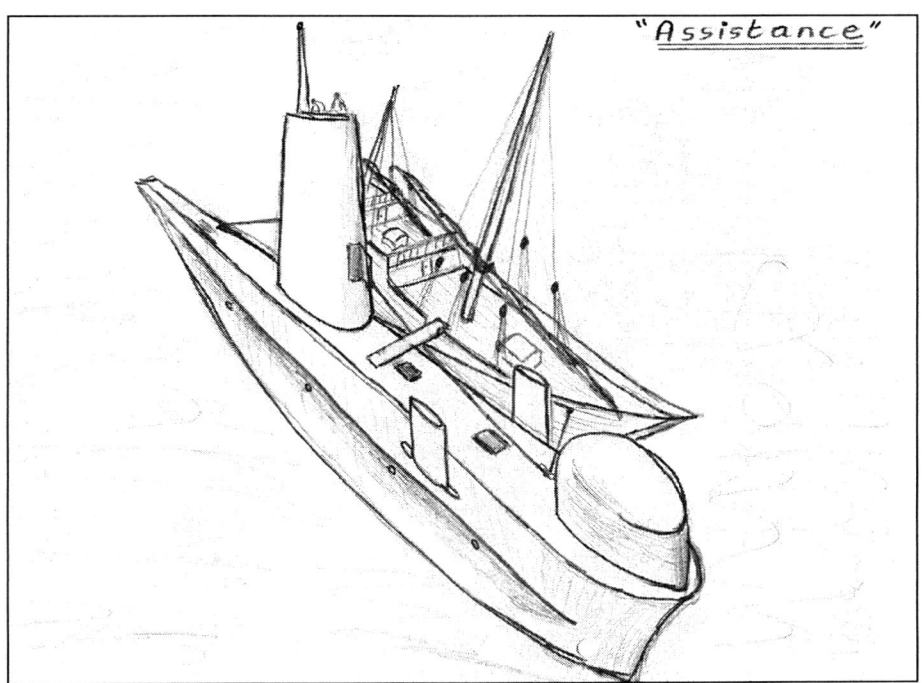

"Assistance"

of whom carried a Neil Robertson stretcher.

'Dusty could you arrange for someone to show these lads where you would like assistance?'

'Spike, do as Lieutenant Commander Gale requests please.'

The two then went below, but Dusty's head popped back up and called Curly to join them. All three sat round the saloon table to discuss the situation as they had lost a key member of the team. As Dusty pointed out, Ali Hassan could take over the position of Sailing Skipper and Curly could handle the electrical maintenance, but navigation was a bit of a black art to the rest of them.

Danny popped down the ladder, still looking the worse for wear, and asked if it would be possible to borrow a Tiff from the boat to help him square the damage up a bit.

'I think I can help you out on both counts,' Windy Gale volunteered. 'Is your Short Wave Radio still working?'

'I don't know Sir but I'll check' and Curly shot topside and confirmed that it was, at the same time the third hand from the 'O' boat asked him to inform his Skipper that his party was ready to disembark. He went below and passed on the information and Windy took the RT extension mike and called up his boat and spoke to his duty RO.

'This is the Captain, ask the First Lieutenant to open the Torpedo

Loading Hatch to allow the stretcher party back aboard, ask ERA Brown to assist in repairs to the vessel alongside, and instruct Sub Lieutenant Betts to join us below.'

While they were waiting Windy explained that the Subby who was to join them was the spare hand, and was the most awkward and clumsy lad he'd ever come across in his life, his only saving grace being that he was a wiz at navigation as it was his hobby, as was sailing, and had done some Americas Cup racing as a grinder and navigator.

Very shortly after, a fresh faced Subby appeared at the access hatch. Windy waved him down and this absolutely enormous youngster descended and tried unsuccessfully to uncoil himself and failed miserably, and was told brusquely to sit down. With his build he was a most unlikely candidate for boats service, as the only way he would be able to straighten out would be to stand with his head up inside the access to the conning tower, or horizontally. No wonder he was ungainly in such a confined environment.

'Betts, I want you to volunteer to help out Captain Miller and his crew OK?'

'YES Sir –eh –eh – what will my duties be exactly Sir?' he enquired rather pensively.

'Main duty will be Navigation and secondly sailing duties.' At which Sub Lieutenant Betts face split into a broad grin and looked all enthusiastic, spring to his feet with delight, cracked his skull with bone crunching ferocity and sat down again with a foolish grin on his face.

Windy shrugged his shoulders and gave a wry grin, then stood up and asked Dusty if he could be of any further use. Dusty thanked him for all his help and asked if he could retain Danny's assistant for a little while longer, which was agreed, so they shook hands, saluted each other and Windy took his leave.

Danny and ERA 'Buster' Brown, who was the 'O' boats wrecker worked long and hard, and eventually got the bridge mechanics in full working order again with a few jury rigs, and so Buster took his leave and the black beast cast off and disappeared into the darkness as silently and eerily as it had arrived. Danny went down below to see the girls to get the rest of his splinters removed and sticking plaster applied, and came away looking like a patchwork quilt.

Chapter 12

Docked

Meanwhile, back at the sharp end, things were getting a bit tense as the dock was being pumped out and divers were in the water as predicted to check that the boat settled correctly on the keel blocks. Then, once settled, the shores were floated out, positioned and, as the water receded the wedges were hammered into place to secure them and the boat and the rest of the water was pumped out. Then as the dock deck broke surface a load of rubbernecks started wandering around and poking at things so we kept our fingers crossed and, after what appeared to be an age dusk fell and they all decided to wait till midnight and then get together to discuss our changed situation. Stan decided that he and H would join Andy and me as Stan reckoned he was in better shape than Andy. Come the appointed hour we dropped the grills gently and quietly. I helped H replace their grill with the original nuts having discarded the wooden blanks after transferring all the gear over to the one side while Stan hobbled over to the other side, but had to wait for us to give him a bunk up into the tank. 'H' and I followed and replaced that grill and then got us all back aft to the rearmost bay, and broke a couple of light sticks, and I inspected Stan's ankle, which was a mess. There was no other way to describe it, you could feel bone crunching as it was manipulated and Stan was obviously in agony, so, disregarding his protests I administered morphine and told him bluntly that he was no use to the operation. Also, although Andy wasn't in so much pain, as his arm was now stabilized he was no good to us either so it was down to 'H' and I. After a lot of protests and opposition the other two agreed to revise and amend the plan of action.

What was also worrying me was our departure from the area which was up river and across the swamp to rendezvous with Baggy in the lee of Accar Island. I expressed my concern to Stan who promised he would give the problem his full attention so H and I got on with assembling the gear ready for the main part of the operation, the deployment of the explosive strings which was exactly what we did, but it didn't take us all that long and the same problem kept nagging at the back of my mind, so I broached the subject with Stan again. He confessed that he'd chewed it over long and hard but hadn't been able to come up with a feasible solution, but I suspected that the pain of his injury, combined with the effects of the morphine, were affecting him.

'Well,' I piped up, 'two things are for sure, we have to come up with a plan very soon, and our main problem is going to be our evacuation after the charges are laid, speed being essential and we sure as hell aren't going to manage that on our own. I therefore propose that we get in touch with Dusty and get him to organize a shore party to come out and meet us and assist us in our evacuation.'

'That's all very well Ted but how are you going to get in touch with Baggy? It's doubtful if the radio will have sufficient range from in here, and even if we tried the opposition's surveillance systems would more than likely pick up the transmission and put them on their toes and start them looking for us.'

'Yes I'm aware of that, which is why H or I have to go upstream with the radio and GPS and contact Baggy from a suitable spot to meet up in the swamp area, explain our problem give them the position and establish the mutual timing.'

Stan started to protest, but as I explained I couldn't think of any option other than to abandon the whole operation and struggle out on our own, and unless anybody could come up with a realistic alternative it was the only way. Stan reluctantly agreed and as Andy pointed out the thought of abandoning things at this stage was out of the question.

So H and I tossed for it and H won the doubtful privilege of going up stream and decided on just taking a snorkel rather than full diving gear, and assembled the radio, GPS and a side arm in a rucksack. By now it was coming up to 2a.m. which meant that he only had 4 hours of darkness to accomplish the mission, so off he shot with all our good wishes.

While the grill was down I decided that I could at least deploy the explosive strings and attach the magnets. Obviously I couldn't manage to connect them in the middle, that would be a two-handed job, but at least I could lay them on the river bed ready to rig when H returned. It proved easier said than done, each string weighed what seemed like a ton. Stan and Andy gave me a hand to lower them to the deck quietly, but then I was on my own. Dragging that dead-weight across the deck took forever with the added worry of keeping a lookout for native insomniacs. Eventually I arrived at the dock end, found the cleat end of the string and gently lowered it over the edge at the centreline and finally came to fix the magnet, which is where I came unstuck because butterfingers me dropped the bloody thing and down it sank. Because of this I decided on a different plan for number two, and having dragged it to the other end of the dock, I dangled the magnet end over the edge, dropped into the water myself, removed the keep and went to attach it. It took charge and frightened me to death, because it was that powerful it slammed into the tank side and made a noise like a hammer blow, which reverberated for what seemed like an age. I held my breath, I don't know why, it wouldn't have done any good, absolutely nothing happened so I climbed out eventually and slowly fed the string over the side and dropped the end over the side and scooted back to the safety of the ballast tank.

Stan greeted me by asking if I'd heard the loud bang, and was gobsmacked when I explained that it was me that had caused it. I also explained that I'd made a bog of the first one and would have to go back to rectify my mistake. Having taken a bit of a rest, I donned my breathing gear and trotted off to recover the magnet from the first string, but I armed myself with a bit of timber from the light stick box to try and prevent a repetition of the 'clanger' I dropped on the other one.

I'd have to get a wriggle on as dawn was fast approaching. I now appreciated my training in Rosyth Tug Basin with its Zero Viz. Over the side I went and quickly located the pile of the explosive string, and so the magnet, but I couldn't lift it to the surface. I jettisoned my back pack envelope of 4oz lead balls, which helped, but it still wasn't enough so I had to start cutting off the ballast weights from the string in sequence, and the more I cut off the higher up I managed to get, until finally I reached the surface with the damned thing. Having removed the keep from the magnet, (well away from the hull) I put the bit of timber on the face and offered it up to the tank side very gingerly and it gave a satisfying clunk. I then had to use my knife to prise one side of the magnet off to remove the board, then eased the knife back and wangled it from side to side to extricate it. By the time I'd finished pratting about there was a slight lightening in the eastern sky so I climbed out and scuttled back to the relative safety of the ballast tank fairly well exhausted. I'd hoped to find H back when I returned but no such luck, and we were all more than a little concerned for his safety and also for our own future.

Having got rid of my breathing gear I helped re-secure the grill, and after that I felt thoroughly knackered and Stan suggested that I got my head down. He tried to cheer Andy and me up by suggesting that he must have been delayed and caught out by dawn, and would have holed up to wait for the cover of darkness to return. We all agreed, but privately I wasn't too sure, and by the look on Andy's face, he wasn't either but there was nothing we could do about it so I curled up in a corner and died.

I was told later that I'd slept through a particularly hairy situation. It appears that a painting party had applied a coat of anti-fouling paint to the lower hull. They didn't do any cleaning, scraping or chipping to remove weed or animal growths, they just slapped it on willy nilly, but in so doing came perilously close to giving Stan and Andy heart failure. They both reckoned that the only thing that saved them from discovery was the fact that they were nattering that much between themselves they wouldn't have taken any notice even if they had been spotted.

When I did finally return to the land of the living it was mid afternoon and I was as stiff as a board with leg cramps and it took me ages to come round. Andy reckoned his arm was comfortable and not giving him too much trouble, but Stan looked dreadful and was obviously suffering, so I talked him into a low dose of morphine to take the edge off his pain. Then all three of us pigged out on water and chocolate, and sat around nattering, trying not to think of what might have happened to H. To pass the time we tried to lift our spirits by narrating some of our exploits to each other. Stan kicked off by telling us of the time he was torpedo officer on a 'P' boat doing a COQC (Commanding Officer's Qualifying Course).

'Prospective boat Skippers having done all the theory in the classroom and to practice in the Attack teachers, have then to go aboard a boat in a group and take turns at executing a for real attack, the only thing missing being live torpedoes. The bloke in charge of the course was a very senior ex boats Skipper, and a right bastard to the students. The crew on a COQC boat hate it because everybody's at attack stations all day for days on end, and everybody gets very on edge, especially the planesmen and helmsman who are moved about like a fiddler's elbow. At the end of the course the students are told there and then whether they've passed or failed and, depending on the results, everybody goes ashore in Rothsay to either celebrate or drown their sorrows, and I was invited to join in along with a couple of others out of the wardroom. We all got well smashed but some rotten sod had taken a large box of dhoby dust with them and stuck it all in the local fountain. You've never seen so many suds flowing down the main drag and the local constabulary were less than amused and the culprit didn't own up so we all got a right bollocking, but it was very spectacular just the same.'

Andy told us about his stint on HMS *Reclaim* the old RN Diving vessel before he went clearance diving. Him serving on *Reclaim* was a bit of a coincidence because in the dim distant past H and I had served on *Reclaim* for the duration of one exercise with the minesweepers we helped to repair while we were at *Lochinvar*. Anyway it appears that the divers' mess was as chaotic when Andy was aboard as it was when we were aboard. They had canteen messing, which meant that the mess caterer was allowed cash equal to the amount spent per person on normal central catering to be used however he wished. Andrew 'Legs' Diamond the Chief Diver was the Mess Caterer and you could get tea, coffee, milk and sugar any time of the day or night, as much as you wanted, but you couldn't get solid food for love nor money which is why they called it canteen messing 'cos you fed out of the NAAFI.

'We were in Chatty Chats doing a quick refit and all the routine tests had to be done and Dockyard Mateys were swarming all over the place. This particular day Legs went down to the diving flat to do a mandatory pressure test on the main re-compression pot. So he had a quick shufti in to check it was clear then slammed the access hatch, went over to the control panel and wanged on the requisite test pressure and sloped off to have sippers from his bottle and another coffee. Unbeknown to him a Dockyard Matey had found a nice comfy bunk in the inner chamber and had got his head down. He was on his second mug of coffee when a very worried looking Dockyard Gobby explained that one of his mates was looking very agitated in a vessel on the diving flat. Legs shot down the flat and peered through the viewing port and saw this bloke with a little trickle of blood running from one ear, doing a wall of death in the inner chamber (the one he hadn't checked). The poor sod had tried unsuccessfully to contact someone on the internal telephone to no avail and had ripped it off the bulkhead and it was reckoned that if he'd been left in a bit longer he'd have chipped ALL the paint off the inside of the pot with the handset. Thinking quickly Legs decided that if he let the pressure off slowly, on opening the hatch the occupant would very likely attack him, so he decided to drop it all at once, and wanged the exhaust valve wide open, unclipped and swung the hatch in, dragged the poor unfortunate out by the scruff of his neck and told him he was trespassing and to f ... off or he would be in serious trouble. The poor bloke was so dazed he staggered off semi comatose never to be seen on board again. I wonder why.'

My contribution was the saga of two good mates on a 'V' boat who shall remain nameless. The Engine room Tiff had been off sick and had just returned back aboard. His mate the Radio Electrical Tiff, was replacing a defective heating element in the Snort head valve. This valve on the top of the induction mast allowed air to be drawn into the boat while submerged at periscope depth. The heating elements were necessary to prevent the valve freezing up in sub zero conditions. On this type of boat the snort head valve was streamlined with the fin top when lowered. Therefore to be able to gain access to this valve's internals it had to be raised, but not too much, just sufficient, a couple of foot, but it meant that to do the job and be comfortable he had to sit on the top of the fin with his legs dangling in the hole left by the top of the valve. His BIG mistake was not putting a 'Do Not Operate' label on the control valve of the snort induction mast. The ERA swanning back from sick passed the panel and saw that the snort mast was not down according to the indicator and so decided to lower it. A loud shriek came down the conning tower hatches and he let go of the lever and dashed up the tower and saw his mate jammed in by the snort mast streamlining cover by his legs. He shot back down to the Control Room and belled the base Ambulance Service and explained that he had broken his best mate's legs and was utterly distraught. He took charge of the ambulance crew, much to their annoyance, untrapped his mate and saw him loaded into a Neil Robertson stretcher complaining all the time that he was OK and was told by his mate to shut up and let the medics do their stuff, lashed in the stretcher to get him lowered down the conning tower hatches. This type of stretcher was purpose built for just this type of evolution, the only exposed bits being the feet and hands. As he was being lowered through the first hatch he started to complain bitterly about pain and was told by his mate to stop moaning and not to be a wimp and started stomping on his shoulders to get him through the hatch. Eventually he ended up in hospital, his injuries, slightly bruised thighs and two broken wrists that had jammed on the hatch coaming.

Stan came back with one of my less happy incidents, which occurred on *Osprey* when he was Jimmy and I was Wrecking.

'We were at Harbour Stations about to take a load of visitors on a PR trip. It was just a day trip, so one watch was left inboard so that lots of visitors could be taken (boats only carried bare minimum escape equipment). Any time you take visitors they always congregate in the control room which is the last place you want them when you're closed up ready for leaving harbour, but all the usual checks had to be carried out regardless. One important job was for the Wrecker to check the correct operation of all the masts. The only exposed masts were the periscopes, for obvious reasons, and they were extremely complex. When lowered the very long ten inch diameter tube is housed in a well and when raised the ocular box (the bit at the bottom of the tube) can be adjusted for height by the Tiff on the panel, but for maintenance purposes can be locked in the raised position by inserting pins through hooked brackets on the crosshead of the ocular box and fixed eyelets in the deckhead. I heard the hydraulic hiss of masts being checked, and then I heard Ted's voice shout above the hubbub 'stand clear of the forrard periscope' and then the hydraulic hiss again, then suddenly a strangled scream. Looking in its direction I saw this civilian head and shoulders above the rest leaning forward with his head and shoulders jammed up against the deckhead. What had happened was that he had been standing too close with his back to the mast and as the crosshead came clear of the well the pin hook slid up inside the back of his jacket and hoisted him to that posture. Ted being only too well aware of what had happened decided to lower the poor unfortunate but in so doing, as he was very much leaning forward, proceeded to stuff him down the mast well, so another strangled scream emanated from the poor sod prompting Ted to stop so that the victim could be unhooked.'

A load of other subjects were discussed, but our prime concern was H's safety. We talked till the late hours but eventually I had to admit that the prospect of him returning was becoming more and more remote and told Stan and Andy that I had decided that shortly before midnight I intended to get rigged in breathing gear and attempt to deploy the strings by myself. The only concern I had, apart from H's fate, was wondering if I could manage the deployment on my own, but I was determined to give it a bash seeing as how we'd got this far.

Chapter 13

Fix

Come the appointed time and I started to get my gear together when suddenly we all froze as we heard a quiet tapping. We covered the activated light sticks and I crept through the limber holes and peered cautiously through the grill to see H peering up at me. I whispered to him to hang on a minute and called back to tell them the good news, and asked Andy to come forrard to give me a hand to lower the grill. We soon had an exhausted H inboard and the grill back in place. We fed him water and chocolate, and he came round a bit, and he gave us a synopsis of his day's escapade.

'My first mistake was that I picked the wrong time to set off because what we hadn't realized was the strength of the tide. The current was against me and I ended up walking the bank most of the way. The terrain is terrible and the first couple of miles is bristling with armed guards. After that stretch there's a bloody great razor-wire fence and I wished I'd had my breathing gear with me 'cos having surveyed it the only way I could see a way through was to take to the deep water with the flow against me and get under the soddin' thing, and damned near drowned in the attempt and had to hole up for some time to recover from the effort. By the time I'd come round sufficiently to carry on it was slack water, and I could have kicked myself because if I'd waited I could have saved myself all that effort. So I carried on with progress being a lot easier and the further up stream I got, as the tide turned, the easier it got. I eventually arrived at the swamp area just before dawn absolutely nif-naffed and decided to head into the swamp a bit before attempting to contact Baggy. It was lucky that I did, because I discovered that not only was it swamp, but there are areas of quicksand which is where I nearly came unstuck, as I blundered into one of them, but managed somehow to struggle and drag myself back out and skirted northerly, which, for the distance I travelled, seemed much safer hazard wise (as the Yanks would say).

The easiest bit was getting hold of Baggy on the blower. As soon as I made the callsign Curly came straight back at me. I explained our changed situation and the fact that we would need evacuation assistance. Curly acknowledged the request and replied that he would consult Dusty and get back to me asap. True to his word, within no more than ten minutes he called me back confirming that an away party would be available to set off within a couple of hours. I did a quick calculation and decided that the tide would be right to vacate the dock in the early hours of what was, at the time, tomorrow. The only problem I had was the rendezvous point, so I signed off explaining that I would advise within the hour, and set off back to the river. My thinking was that Stan would be better moving in water rather than over ground and so decided that the pick up point would be better at the water's edge. I travelled back due West knowing that I would hit the river eventually, hopefully just below the rapids.

Eventually having reached the river just before the lower end of the rapids I moved South and found the ideal spot, a slight curve in the river where it eddied and was an area of relatively calm water. I called Curly back and gave him the GPS co-ordinates and warned him to skirt to the northern extremity of the swamp to avoid quicksand areas, and having calculated the tides, timed the link up at 0600 which would be early dawn, a bit hairy, but couldn't be avoided as it was going to be a hell of a rush back at the dock. Dusty came on and acknowledged the details, promised us their help, and wished us good luck.

By the time I'd got that lot over with the tide had turned and it was easy peasy getting back to the fence, which is where I holed up till dark to avoid the guards. The snag has been that while waiting for the sun to go down the tide eased off ebbing and the last leg became an increasing struggle, and so here I am. How are you lazy lot getting on?'

'You cheeky sod,' I rejoined, 'I've half done your job for you here. Seriously though, are you up to finishing rigging the strings?'

'Yeah, let's give it a go, the sooner we get it rigged the sooner we're away from here. There's only one snag though Stan, what method do we use to detonate the things?'

'You'll have to remove the hydrostatic switches and discard them on the bottom and we'll have to rely on the Microwave jobs OK?'

So we got to it, rigged our breathing gear and then fixed ourselves a buddy line, exited the tank and helped Stan and Andy re-secure the grill, moved to the forrard end of the dock and slid gently into the water. H stayed forrard and I went aft and had to flange around a bit to find my pile of the string and eventually located it. It was a struggle to find the free end because this was the first one I deployed and the end was at the bottom of the pile. Eventually I found it and gave the buddy line a couple of tugs and got a couple in reply, so headed off in the direction of the line. It was still a shock when we bumped into each other but we joined up the Ingelfield clips and started to draw the ends through the self clenching cleats. It was surprising how heavy the strings were with the ballast weights still attached so it was out knives and as we drew away from each other pulling on the ends, we cut the weights off in sequence and as the string started to ascend we were able to draw the lines tighter. I got to the far end of my half of the string, removed the hydrostatic detonator and dumped it and pulled myself back to the middle on the line that I'd pulled through, and again met H in the centre. We gave the lines a final haul to ensure the explosives were snug against the bottom of the dock hull, tapped each other on the shoulder to say OK and went forrard climbed out and legged it back to the safety of the ballast tank. We'd both noticed that the tide had turned and it was time we departed.

When we got inboard Stan called us together and explained that he and Andy had also been a bit busy too.

'Andy came up with the idea and I don't know how he got up there with one arm, but he's set a charge on the Main Vent and another down here on the Emergency Diesel Generator cooling water line, which if my 'V' boat part three bilge diving serves me correctly is the inlet, and he assures me that the way he's rigged it, it will rupture the line inside the pressure hull blowing off the hull valve. He's also fitted them both with the same microwave detonators that are fitted to the main charges.

H and I both agreed that it was a great scam, and would certainly ensure massive internal flooding when the dock went up, but told them both in no uncertain terms it was time to piss off fast.

Chapter 14

Out

The grill was dropped, we helped Stan and Andy to rig their breathing sets, and checked that we hadn't left any identifiable gear, and gave Stan a shot of morphine to help ease his pain on the trip. We then got the invalids down onto the deck of the dock and replaced the grill with the original nuts and discarded the banks again. Andy made his way forrard whilst H and I virtually carried Stan to the edge. We connected ourselves up to a buddy line with H leading, as he knew the way, then Andy then me and dragging up the rear Stan as I was going to have to tow him. And so in we got and off we set. Only H knew where we were going as he kept taking a sight, the rest of us just stayed submerged and followed the river bed playing follow my leader. Eventually as we approached what I assumed was the perimeter fence it appeared to get lighter, and the closer we got the lighter it got until it seemed like broad daylight rather than the dead of night. H led us back the way we had come and found a secluded eddy pool away from the glare. He got us all surfaced and we conducted a council of war as it were.

'We can't go through the gap with it lit up like Blackpool because we have to break surface to get through it, and the opposition are all over the place, running round like headless chickens, and looking very trigger happy. Something's happened to stir them up. The only thing I can think of doing is to somehow disable the lighting.'

'How the hell are you going to do that with all this lot going on?' demanded Andy.

'How the f – do I know, all I know is that we have to try something, and if anybody's got a better idea let's hear it. The one thing in our favour is the fact that, knowing the local natives' mentality, and their technical ability especially with wiggely amps,* Ted and I are going to go looking for a weak spot and do a bit of sabotage, and if and when the lights go out you and Stan must somehow make it through the gap and we'll see you on the other side OK?'

Stan agreed, as he so rightly pointed out, there seemed to be no alternative, so it appeared that I was volunteered. So H explained in detail to Stan and Andy exactly how to locate the gap and negotiate it, and promised that he and I would do our very best, if successful, to meet them at the gap and help them through the obstacle and get them to deep water and then, hopefully on to team up with our very own heavy mob.

Stan and Andy wished us good luck and off we went, stowed our diving gear as near to the perimeter fence and river as we dare go when suddenly there was a sudden crescendo of beetle crushers, and we hit the deck. I swear to God a combat boot came down with great force no more than half an inch away from the top of my scull. We hugged Mother Earth with the grip of sheer desperation until the panic died down and the crunch of boots receded and finally ceased.

H started to tentatively get up but I dragged him back down, put a finger to my ear and put my head back down and could more feel rather than hear a mechanical rumble. H also confirmed that he'd detected it too. With a bit of flanging about we headed off surreptitiously in the noise's general direction and eventually came across a dimly lit building which must have been at least half a mile away from all the who-ha. We skegged about a bit and discovered that nobody was in attendance. The door was padlocked and the noise was coming from inside so we had somehow to get ourselves in. We had our side arms with us so stupid me stuck my pistol barrel in the hasp of the lock and twisted. It took a hell of an effort but eventually the lock gave way and so did my pistol barrel which would have shot round corners, or blown my hand off, and was absolutely useless, but at least we were in.

The noise was an irrigation or water supply pump of some description electrically driven, the noise being generated by a knackered pedestal bearing with the shaft gland peeing out, but on looking round the really good news was that the main purpose of the building was an electrical sub-station with an emergency generating set wired up to start up and switch on line automatically on a mains supply failure. Fool proof, you might say, not so for a couple of Tiffs. The distribution breakers, and the mains isolation breaker were sequential units with the old fashioned type coded key arrangement. The system was such that on making up the distribution board the main breaker was made up first by inserting the appropriate coded key and turning it to allow the breaker handle to be operated to make the breaker up, then the rest of the distribution breakers are made up in sequence in the same way using differently coded keys.

I went straight to the emergency genny, took off the air intake filter cover and stuffed a large wad of cotton waste down the intake and put the lid back on (shades of the shallow water diving course). Meanwhile H was busy weighing up the sequence of the breakers so that we could break them all in the right order, remove and nick the damn keys. The final breaker to operate was the incoming which when broken and the key removed, and also nicked, initiated the start sequence for the emergency genny, which hopefully would suck in the cotton waste and bring it to a grinding halt, fingers crossed. H explained the sequence to me and we did it together fast. We did the dastardly deed, kept the coded keys and legged it. We saw the lights in the sub-station dim and go out, then we heard the whirr of the engine starter motor, the overloaded sound of the diesel starting up, and then the satisfying sound of choking, then absolute silence, so off we shot hoping that we'd got the right joint because time was running out for the link up.

We retraced our steps as carefully and quickly as we could, and to our great delight, as we re-approached the barrier it was in complete darkness. We picked up our gear from its hiding place, donned it and entered the water, heaved the breaker coded keys into mid stream, and made our way to the barrier gap. We'd not been going long before we overtook Stan and Andy who were really struggling. Andy was about knackered and Stan was in great pain, so I gave him another shot of morphine. The snag was that although it eased his pain it made him much more lethargic and so, much more difficult to assist.

We linked up the buddy lines again and before we knew it we were at the pitch black barrier. H and Andy went through with a bit of difficulty because the tide had turned and the gap in the barrier was a man-made water race. I stayed behind and we manhandled Stan past this obstacle as gently as possible in the difficult conditions, and off we went again still thankfully in pitch blackness. Another problem manifested itself though because we had passed the high water mark and we were now in the main water flow from the rapids which was becoming stronger. It must have been raining further up stream. It was particularly strong at the narrower and shallower sections. It took H all his ingenuity to seek out the less turbulent and eddy areas, and in places we were literally dragging ourselves along the bottom with our bare hands on any rock or crevice we could grasp or jam a fist into. By now poor old Stan was about as handy as a one armed paper hanger as he had become almost a dead weight and we had to keep stopping in convenient eddy areas to make sure his face mask was still in place and that he was breathing after a fashion.

Eventually after what seemed like more than forever, we were told by H that we'd finally made the rendezvous point for which information we were extremely relived as we were all niff-naffed. We dragged Stan out of the water, but kept his re-breathing set on hoping that the oxygen might help him recover a bit. Then Andy and I flopped out while H attempted to contact Dusty to get the latest sit-rep.

Chapter 15

Cavalry

Curly was contacted by H and was told that they were at the rendezvous point and would lay up until help arrived as there was no way they could evacuate Stan on their own as he was in such a bad way and Andy had enough trouble struggling by himself.

'Roger H, standby.'

Curly immediately yelled for Dusty to the shack and then carried on with a three- way conference. Dusty assured H that they would get to them as soon as humanly possible but explained that realistically it was going to be some time because Baggy had just passed the village to the north of Accar Island. H reminded them to skirt to the northern limit of the swamp to avoid the quicksands. Then he asked for an ETA and was told that the best possible guesstimate was mid to late evening, and recommended that they hole up as best they could and switch on the UV beacon in the early evening, and then wished them the best of luck and signed off looking very grim.

Dusty then called all the crew together and quickly explained the desperate situation the away team was in.

Then gave out the orders, no more Mister nice guy. This was now the complete professional.

'Curly, full continuous radar watch, and stand by the radio, any contacts I want to know.'

'Sarnt Redwood, assemble sufficient arms and ammunition for a team of four, and take a few surprises.'

'Danny, get them engines of yours flat out, push them through the gate, or whatever you do, absolutely maximum speed is essential.'

'The recovery team will be :-
Me, leading
Sargeant Redwood 2IC
ERA Kaye
S/Lt Betts
In that order of command.'

Ali put his hand up.

'Yes Ali?'

'I want to come'

'Why?'

'I can be an interpreter and decoy if necessary so that you may be able to do your job better.'

'OK Ali, you're in, Sarnt Redwood, make that five. I've made out a revised Crew List to ensure individual duties are understood. Now let's all get to it. GO.' And they all shot off to their allotted duties.

Dusty then took the girls below, sat them down and explained that he wanted the very best backup and medical assistance for when they returned.

'It may not be necessary for all I know, but be prepared, like the boy sprouts say. Whatever happens I don't want any emotional outbursts. Instead I want Service professionalism, is that understood?' then left leaving them both gobsmacked, but with no illusions as to what he wanted and meant.

REVISED CREW LIST

Lt. Cdr. S. Westerman RN 'Stan'	Team Leader Indisposed. IC Away Team.
J. H. Smith ERA1 'H'	Away Team.
Me CERA 'Ted'	Away Team.
A. Bromfield PO Seaman. 'Andy'	Away Team. Semi Indisposed
Captain D. Miller RM 'Dusty'	IC Cavalry.
J. Redwood Sergeant RM 'Spike'	2IC Cavalry.
N. Kaye 'Danny'	ERA3 Cavalry.
D. Betts S/Lt. RN 'Betty'	Cavalry/Navigator.
A. Hassan Somali PO 'Ali'	Cavalry/Interpreter.

S. Powers Chief Diver. 'Pancho'	IC Caretaker Crew.
J. Clarke L/Seaman. 'Nobby'	2IC Caretaker Crew.
D. Hannam PO RO 'Curly'	Caretaker Crew. Radio/radar Operator.
P. Westerman 1st. Off. WRNS 'Penny'	Caretaker Crew. First Aid.
A. Kharche L/Writer WRNS 'Anna'	Caretaker Crew. First Aid.

Dusty then consulted Betty for an ETA of landfall which looked as if it was going to be within two hours calculated by the speed Danny had got his engines up to. This would mean daylight deployment and camouflage to suit.

He dug out Spike to appraise him of the fact, but had been beaten to it and was all organized. Another surprise he sprang on Dusty was a couple of new type rifles with grenade launcher attachments, quite a formidable weapon. Also the very latest laser sight automatic rifles, and night sight binoculars.

He took his leave having realized that he was in the way and wasting his time.

Dusty's next action was to go to the repaired bridge where Pancho was on the wheel, and Curly was glued to the radar screen with the RT close at hand. He called Curly and Nobby over to the wheel and explained to all three the fact that they were going to be in charge while the rest were on the mission and to keep the girls busy to stop them thinking the worst. The main task though was to have everything ready for a quick embarkation and departure.

'As fast as if you've got a rocket up your arse, understood?'

He turned to depart, then suddenly turned back on his heel.

'And Curly, for God sake keep a listening watch at all times even if you have to use the girls while you rest up, OK? and let Pancho and Nobby do the ship husbandry.'

He then went forrard and stood at the prow racking his brains to think of anything he had missed, forgotten or overlooked and also psyching himself up for the job ahead.

A shout from the wheelhouse brought him back to reality. It was Betty who, almost doubled up in the confines, informed him that it was less than half an hour to disembarkation.

'I've organized the kedge anchor to be deployed two hundred yards off shore because it'll be high tide when we arrive and the caretaker crew have been instructed to draw Baggy off the putty when we've gone. I'll disembark with the forrard anchor and find something that it can be secured to so that on our return all the caretakers have to do is haul it on the forrard anchor and ease off on the kedge and Baggy can be positioned correctly for our swift embarkation whatever the state of the tide, if that's in order Sir?'

'Perfectly in order Betty, in fact it's bloody marvellous, and the name's Dusty on this trip.'

'Right, my team to muster in the saloon to get rigged up for our little jaunt.'

And off they went below and came back a quarter of an hour later looking like a gang of Rambos, all armed to the teeth, with backpacks. Then it all happened, Betty let go the kedge and Baggy drove slowly for the steep beach with Pancho paying out the kedge line. Then Betty leapt forward and over the gunnel and stood on the rubbing strake, bent down and grabbed the shank of the anchor and then instructed Danny to unclench the anchor cable and he literally hauled the anchor cable onto his shoulder, then, sighting the bottom called for the engines to be cut and Baggy drifted in and gently nudged the putty. Betty then to everyone's absolute amazement just jumped in, complete with anchor and chain, and disappeared. The next thing to see was him stomping up the beach with more chain dragging along behind him. While the rest of the team were getting into the water, Danny did a Betty and leapt in and grabbed the anchor cable and assisted in its deployment. Having enough chain paid out, Betty took the anchor round the bole of a stout looking tree and clenched it on itself and signalled the caretakers to take in the slack on both anchors. Then the whole shore gang disappeared behind the tree line and it was time for the caretakers to secure Baggy in a more favourable position. So Pancho took Anna back aft to help with the kedge rope multiplier winch, and Nobby had Penny to help him on the anchor chain winch. After a few hiccups Baggy was positioned to everyone's satisfaction, midway between the anchors, the girls went below, made a brew and distributed it, and then they all went about their allotted duties.

Meanwhile, ashore, the gang had assembled and then set off, Dusty at point, Spike drag, as the Yanks say, and off they went. It wasn't long before Dusty had a prickly feeling at the back of his neck and called Spike to join him, who confirmed that they were not alone. Betty was called up and given Spike's pack and most of his gear and off they set again, but shortly after Spike was no more until Dusty came across him further along the trail, but he was not alone. A skinny, scantily clad native was in a stranglehold, not able to move or make a noise. Arms were cocked and the unfortunate was surrounded by the lads, with them looking outwards.

Ali was called up and tried a few dialects with Spike easing off the pressure slightly to try for a reaction and eventually hit on one that could be understood by both parties. Ali told the captive that he would not be harmed, but he would have to behave if he was to be released, to which he nodded as vigorously as he was able. Spike eased his grip quite tentatively, but the poor man, shaking like a leaf, said and did nothing apart from look absolutely petrified.

Ali asked him where he was from and eventually got from him that he lived in the village to the north. Asked why he was down here he explained that he was looking for food as his family and the rest of his villagers were starving. Asked why, he explained that the Devils from the Naval Base and around the Kanaga River had slaughtered all the wildlife for sport because for some reason they wanted the village emptied, but as he explained, they had nowhere to go.

Ali dived in his backpack and took out a bar of chocolate and tried to give it to the native, but he recoiled from it, so Ali had to eat a bit of it before his newfound friend was convinced and tried and liked chocolate.

From then on it got better and better, and Dusty knew that if he played it right he had a new and very useful ally, so got Ali to explain as simply as possible that they were here to rid them of their enemies and rescue some of their friends, and if he and some of his best village friends wanted to help they would be welcomed and fed. As Ali started to relay the message to the man, whose name was unpronounceable and, because of his strange dialect which included hollow clucking noises, was christened 'Click'. Anyway as the message started to get through a smile started to appear on his face and the further the message got across the wider the grin. By the time Ali had finished the man was beside himself, and went into a diatribe until Ali stopped him. As he explained to Dusty the man was so incensed by the treatment of his people that not only would he be willing to help in any way possible, but all the villagers would too.

Dusty asked Ali to tell him they wanted ten good men as soon as possible and to go with him and take some 'K' rations to distribute in the village.

Further instructions were cut short by the RT, Curly had an urgent message for 'Cavalry Leader' and sounded calm but concerned. Dusty grabbed the set and acknowledged Curly's call.

'Sea born Bogeys approaching slowly from the South. At present rate of progress ETA will be two, repeat TWO hours, please advise.'

'Standby Baggy', and Dusty, thinking fast, got Ali to ask Click how deep and wide their village stream was. The surprising answer came back that it was big enough to hide their dhow, so he'd obviously seen our performance at the landing site.

'Ali belay my last, Danny, go back to Baggy with Ali and Click, shove off and drive as hard as you can to the village stream. Unstep the masts on the way and get the villagers to help camouflage her as best you can. Distribute as many 'K' rations as possible. Get Ali and Click to choose ten or so of the fittest natives and take a GPS unit and RT and contact us when you're on your way and I'll give you our position for joining back up, go for it fast.'

'Cavalry Leader – Baggy.'

'Baggy.'

'Stand by to cast off immediately after embarking Danny who has instructions, plus two, understood?'

'Understood, standing by.'

Danny and Ali had dumped their back packs, having just kept their arms and took off, dragging Click with them. Ali attempted while they were on their way to explain to Click what was happening and what was wanted. Click suddenly found renewed energy and took the lead at a trot and took a different route and got them back to the beach in record time.

The caretaker crew had done an heroic job and had Baggy almost back up to the beach by the time an exhausted Danny and his team arrived. So they unclenched the anchor from round the tree and dragged it back to the waterline. Click disappeared which worried Danny more than a bit, but he soon reappeared with a large leafy branch and proceeded to eradicate all traces of human presence. Nobby and Penny started winching in the anchor cable while Danny, Ali and click climbed aboard.

Danny immediately went below and cracked up his engines and when they'd warmed up sufficiently, transferred control to the wheelhouse then went up there himself and explained the plan of action to Curly and told him to take the wheel and engine controls. Pancho and Anna started winching in on the kedge line. Danny went forrard and spelled Nobby on the anchor winch. When the anchor was clear of the bottom he went back aft to assist Pancho, and when he reckoned Baggy was far out enough to manoeuvre, took the emergency axe from its stowage and just chopped the kedge line and told Curly to head north, flat out.

Then Pancho took over the helm and Curly went back to his radar and radio. Ali took Click round everybody and introduced him and got the girls to break out some 'K' rations for him which he devoured ravenously in no particular order, but couldn't seem to get his head round the bog-wipe having tried to eat it at first, and no amount of explaining western customs by Ali would convince him of its intended purpose.

Ali was then collared by Danny and got him to explain to Click what was required of him when they arrived at the village as he had to reassure the natives that we were friendly. So Ali said he would take Click up to the bow at the appropriate time and feed him the words and get him to spread the good words about enemies, friends and food.

Danny's next problem was the masts, how to unstep them, last time they'd been stepped RFA *Hannibal's* crane was used. Having thought on a bit he decided that as the yards were already down and stowed it just left the masts themselves, so it was shit or bust time and started on the mizzen with his faithful emergency axe. Having rigged guide lines to the mast head, the idea was to not leave any traces of their existence floating around. So all hands, other than Pancho and Curly, manned the lines well forrard of the spar's trajectory. Danny then cut the forrard shrouds and slightly slacked off the after ones, then everyone keeping well clear, Danny made a good imitation of a Monty Python Lumberjack and in no time at all the mizzen started making splintering noises and lean further forrard so he cut the after shrouds and the mast sank slowly to the deck, in a reasonably controlled fashion, and it was secured.

Flushed with success, he adopted roughly the same method for the big bugger. Unfortunately his calculations showed that the mast was taller than its distance from the bow, so, thinking fast, decided to chop it off at the knees rather than the ankles, so to speak, and so rigged himself a platform to chop it off six foot high up. This meant that the teams holding the guidelines would have to be aft of the fall direction and so less controllable, especially with the added weight.

Anyway everything was rigged, the guideline teams were well back aft, the forrard shrouds were cut. As an added precaution Danny had rigged a rolling hitch in stout rope to the mast just above where he was going to chop, and although the hitch was self clenching he drove some large nails in just above the knot to be doubly sure it wouldn't slip. The ends of the rope were secured to forrard cleats at either side because, when cut through the mast was liable to shoot aft. Braces were added to the belt, safety pin and string, in that he had Pancho heave too, just in case it fell over the side, which would be disastrous if still under way.

'One final warning, I noticed that some on the guide lines last time had taken turns round their hands, please do not do this because if the mast suddenly goes you will not easily be able to let go and this one is a lot heavier. If in doubt tail end charley can take a turn round a convenient stanchion, OK?' And then he went to work with a will making an initial notch at the forrard face of the spar. He then attacked with the main cut using the full length of the axe handle to keep as far away from the danger area as possible. After a sustained attack of about a quarter of an hour an ominous creaking and splintering emanated from the area of Danny's attack, so he dashed and cut the rear shrouds having got the guide rope teams to take the strain. Another creak then suddenly an almighty crack and the whole damned thing lurched forrard, the guide-lines were let go and the severed end shot aft to be restrained by the braces after travelling about two foot. The mast head ended up hanging over the starb'd side, but the port guide rope crew dashed forrard and secured their line to a port cleat and then the rest of the gang were able to warp it inboard and secure it. So off they went again, arse down and away flat out for the village steam.

As promised Ali took Click up to the bow on the approach to the village shore. A few natives looked up from the beach and were about to disappear with fear but Click shouted assurances to them, prompted by Ali and a few more natives came down and gathered on the beach. Then, at the mouth of the stream Pancho hove to and through Ali, Click explained that the people with him were friends who had food for them and would help them get rid of their enemies, but what they wanted right away was help to tow their vessel up stream to hide it. By this time all the residents were out and listening, men, women and children. Bow lines were passed to port and starb'd and with assistance from Danny's engines just ticking over Baggy was guided up steam by the willing natives who all looked extremely malnourished.

Meanwhile Penny and Anna busied themselves digging out box after box of 'K' rations and Baggy was secured well up stream, and under instruction from Pancho and Nobby via Ali and Click, the natives cut local vegetation and she was well camouflaged.

The girls distributed the 'K' rations to the helpers and Click had them howling with laughter, obviously about the bog wipe.

Danny then went with Ali and Click back into the village to recruit ten or so volunteers, but what they found was that everyone wanted to help, so they had to be ruthless and picked twelve of the fittest looking men.

They were told to quickly get something down their necks, arm themselves as best they could and get back to the vessel as soon as possible.

Then Danny and Ali legged it back to Baggy to collect their arms, ammunition and rations, and started off back to meet up with Dusty and

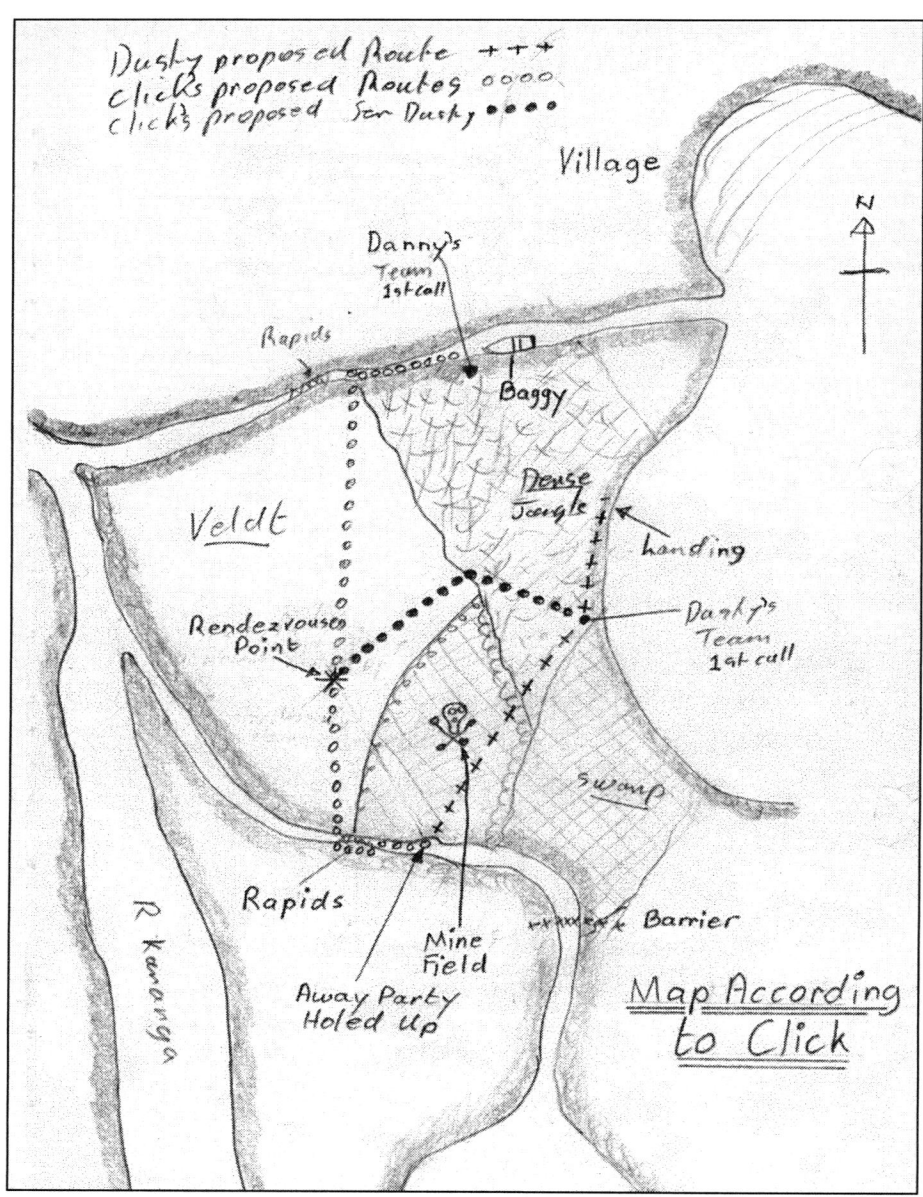

his mob, having told Click to collect his gang together and catch them up as soon as possible. The daft thing was that as they were about to set off Click's gang were waiting for them, armed to the teeth with spears and machetes. Danny picked up the GPS and RT and they all shot off at a steady trot. Danny called Dusty up on the blower giving his position, and vice-versa and he marked both positions on his map. He then asked

Dusty for a rendezvous position, which he then also marked on his map. Click started to take an interest in the map and enquired through Ali if he could have a look and asked where they were eventually heading, which Danny showed him on the map. Then he asked what route each party intended taking, which he was also shown. With that he went completely ape shit. Ali calmed him down and asked him what was wrong and all Click could do was throw his hands in the air shouting boom boom. Danny spread the map out and grabbed Click and got Ali to get him to draw in with pencil anything he wanted to. He drew a line from Dusty's position to the away team's hole up position and did his arms in the air and boom bit again.

'Ask him if it's bombs or mines or something else.'

Click demonstrated by treading very carefully and then doing the arms and boom bit again.

'Bloody hell, it's a minefield. Ask him how big an area it covers.' Click drew a line from halfway down the forest edge in an arc turning due south to join the river above the rapids West of where the away team were waiting.

'Ask him how he would get us to the away team safely and get them out again.'

Click drew a line west along the village stream to just before the rapids and just clear of the forest and then directly south to meet the lower stream just above the rapids, across the stream and east to clear the rapids, recross the stream and join the away team. He then explained via Ali that to evacuate, the route was simply reversed.

Danny then immediately belled Dusty to explain the latest development and discuss future planning.

'Danny – Cavalry'

'Cavalry.'

'Your chart is incorrect, do not, repeat do not head further south, you are standing into danger. Head two nine zero degrees true to forest edge,' and gave a coded GPS position.

'Then head two three zero degrees true to proposed rendezvous position,' and gave another coded GPS position.

'Will explain fully later, will also inform away team of problems.'

'Roger that Danny, Cavalry leader out.'

Danny then got Ali to tell Click that he was to lead the team and to take his proposed route to the away team. Click's chest swelled with pride, he grinned happily, then clicked and clacked out orders to his lads who miraculously produced dug out canoes. They all embarked and the natives paddled with a will, towing two spare canoes. In almost no time at all the canoe convoy were at the rapids where Danny took the opportunity to talk to H.

'Danny – Away Team.'

'Away Team.'

'Cavalry is on its way but delayed. You must not, repeat not go ashore on the north bank, will explain fully later.'

'Stand by Cavalry.'

H looked at me and we both wondered what the hell was going on as we were already ashore at the water's edge.

'I was going to walk back to the swamp area to dump the breathing gear in the quicksand, what do you think?'

I suggested that he got back on the blower and explain to Danny our present situation and future intentions and ask for advice as we know nowt of what's going on.

'Danny – Away Team.'

'Danny.'

'We are ashore on the north bank but not far inland. Had intended going overland to dispose of excess baggage in swamp, please advise.'

'Do not, repeat do not go further inland, stay where you are. If you have to dump gash, travel by water or on the south bank to the swamp area before crossing to the north bank.'

'Roger that Danny, hurry up, see you soon, out.'

Chapter 16

R&R

'Well, if the Cavalry are going to be delayed we'd better make ourselves as comfy as we can without moving about too much.' So spoke H, who invited me to help him modify a re-breathing set as an oxygen mask for Stan. So H and I turned to and rigged his demand valve to a free standing oxygen cylinder with the reducing valve attached. The demand valve discharge hose was cut away from the soda lime canister and the harness, and a non return valve was lashed up out of two pieces of mask rubber and stuck onto the cut end of the demand valve. We saved a couple of extra oxygen cylinders and let Stan have a bash at the jury rig which seemed to ease his discomfort, but all three of us were worried about his condition, which had developed into something more than a broken leg. We were all of the opinion that he had a respiratory problem of some sort so I gave him a small shot of morphine and he fell into a light sleep. The only snag was that our jury rig demand valve arrangement sounded like the quiet cries of a ruptured duck.

H called me to one side and told me he was going to take and dump the diving sets and the remains of Stan's plus fins and other assorted rubbish to the swamp and dump it all in the quicksand. I chowed at him and told him I was going with him, because Andy was still in relatively good shape and could take care of Stan well enough until we returned.

Regardless of H's protest I had a word with Andy who assured us that it would be OK and to sod off and do the job properly. So we dumped the lead ballast balls in the deepest bit of the stream, left the chocolate and water with Andy and set off down stream. It was really easy as the flow was with us and we just kept close into the northern bank. It started to rain very heavily but it didn't worry us much as it was warm rain, but it was later to almost prove our undoing.

H eventually signalled for us to enter the swamp, so we crawled into it dragging the gear behind us just in case anybody was on the prowl even though it was peeing down, then H pointed ahead at a particularly nasty looking bubbly area and whispered that it was the quicksands. When I said why are you whispering, he just shrugged his shoulders, grinned and started heaving the gear in so I helped him and we watched it being slowly devoured leaving no trace whatsoever.

So off we went retracing our steps and back into the water, but the stream had been transformed into a raging torrent with debris and rocks being washed down against us. We'd checked with Danny that the South bank was safe to go ashore on and we'd intended to do that on the return leg, but it was far too dangerous to cross over the cascade, so we had to struggle up the north bank as best we could, trying to pull ourselves through the water by the bank vegetation, which was not easy until suddenly H who was in the lead gave a strangled yell as he flung his arms in the air and leapt back into the main stream. I just managed to grab his collar and a substantial tree root and pivoted him back to the bank.

'What the hell was that all about?'

'I know why we're not to go ashore on this bank.'

'Why for God sake?'

'It's a bloody minefield, I've just grabbed one that had been eroded from the bank by this torrent. I missed blowing myself up by thous, and the dam thing just dislodged and shot past me into the main stream.'

To reinforce what he'd just said a huge explosion rent the stillness and a huge column of water shot into the air downstream of us as the mine hit, or was hit on the detonator as it must have tumbled through the water.

'Well that'll have got the opposition on their toes. We'd better get back as quick as possible and warn the cavalry to be more vigilant, and to make sure Stan and Andy are still safe and well hidden.'

Getting back to the lads was a nightmare and at times it was one forward and two back. Apart from the possibility of getting yourself dislodged by the force of water, there was the likelihood of being hit by assorted rubbish eroded and dislodged from upstream. The only relief we had was that every now and again we came across an eddy where the bank had washed away, usually on a bend, in a deep scour where the water swirled round but was relatively calm. In these areas we were able to take a breather and rest up a bit, but we daren't stay too long as the water force was getting stronger by the minute.

Eventually we both arrived back absolutely knackered to join Stan and Andy who were in a very precarious position, in fear of being washed away, as the quiet pool we'd left them alongside was now eroding the very bank they were parked on.

Once we'd got our breath back the first thing H did was to contact the Cavalry to tell them of the mine incident, and warn them that the opposition would be on the alert, and to be even more vigilant.

The next thing was for us to make our own position less precarious, and H and I decided that the only way we could go was inland which meant that we had to be sure the area we shifted to was mine free. So we took Andy to one side and explained that we were in a minefield and we wanted him to show us no-no's how to go about mine clearance. He though we were crackers but couldn't come up with an alternative, so he decided to co-operate. He explained that we would have to use our diver's knives as probes instead of the thin purpose-made proper jobs, and as he explained, the only saving grace was that our knives were non magnetic. First he asked H how big in diameter the mine that he saw was. H's reply was initially unprintable but, as Andy pointed out it was crucial to know so that probe spacing could be calculated so as not to miss a possible hazard.

The idea is to push the probe into the ground at an angle of between ten and fifteen degrees to the horizontal, the plan being to touch the side of the mine instead of the detonator on the top. When a possible device is encountered the ground is excavated in front of the unit and gently and carefully the spoil removed so that the device can be identified and the correct removal method adopted.

From H's description Andy decided we probed every six inches, so off we went, Andy insisting that if we thought we'd found something to give him a yell, figuratively speaking of course. Who had to be first to find something, yes, H, who called Andy over to show him how to clear away and eventually discovered a rock, as the ground was sandy with varying sizes of stones in it. We started to make good progress and Andy made a good job of marking out in pebbles the area we'd checked. After a few more false alarms we became quite blasé about the whole thing and I'd found another rock or so I thought, so I scratted away but suddenly saw a glint of metal and froze. Eventually I managed to squawk at Andy who came across and casually confirmed my find. While I tried to calm down, Andy asked H to retire to a safe distance and look after Stan and be sure he was safe, which really filled me with confidence, and then he came back to my side and proceeded to instruct me in the gentle art of mine disposal.

I had to clear away the earth round it without undermining it, if you'll pardon the pun, until it was clear all round. Andy identified it as a Mark 7 Anti Tank device of a very old design but very powerful and still very effective, which cheered me up not a lot.

Having cleared the sides I had then to clear the top that had these funny spiky things on top, which I wasn't supposed to touch, for obvious reasons. This done I then had to lift it out of its hole and put it somewhere safe and firm because Andy wanted me to defuse it. I did enquire as to why we couldn't just leave it somewhere safe, or just heave it into the stream, but Andy unfortunately and quite rightly pointed out that unless it was made safe it would be a hazard, and if we heaved it in the stream it might go off there and then and injure some or all of us, or go downstream some distance before it went up and further alert the foe, so he convinced me.

He showed me two slots in a ring in the centre if the thing which he said was the locking ring for the detonator, which he said was normally engaged with a pin spanner to unscrew it. All we had as tools were diving knives, so Andy said he was going to stand on the damned thing to keep it stable and he wanted me to use the pointed end of a diving knife in the slot on one side of the locking ring and bray the knife handle end with a rock. I thought he'd flipped his lid but he was deadly serious, and steadying himself on me put both feet on it either side of those spikes and told me to give it a bash, which I plucked up courage to do eventually, but Andy wasn't impressed and told me not to tickle it and to give it a good bash, so shit or bust I gave it a hefty clout which blunted the knife but I thought it gave a bit, so I told him I was going to go round and do the same on the other slot. I got set, took a deep breath and clouted it again and it definitely moved. I came back to the first side and as I put the knife blunt end into the slot again it just moved round. Andy stepped gingerly off and gave a huge sigh of relief and shook my hand and said he didn't think it would work. Then he pulled me back down to earth saying that I now had to unscrew the bloody thing and remove it. Just put your fingers flat in on the ring and it'll spin off quite easily, and it's captive so when it's unscrewed completely you can lift the whole detonator out by the ring. So, after more deep breathing exercises, I laid back down to have a go, and as Andy pointed out, as he went to a safe area, if anything went wrong I wouldn't feel a thing. So I called him a smart arsed git as he departed with a wry grin. True to his word though the ring spun off no problem and all I had to do was keep well away from the spiky bits and lifted it gently out of its hole by the lock ring and bingo, held it by its body and called Andy back.

'Right, all you have to do now is keep hold of it as you are doing, carry it to the water's edge and without catching any of the triggers, heave it into the Oggin.'

'Will it make a big bang then?'

'No, it's very low power, but there's enough explosive in it to blow your hand off.'

'Oh cheers,' I said, and gave it the float test. Nothing happened for a little while, then as we were turning away a little crump and a few bubbles and Andy said that was it.

'What do we do with the main body?' I asked naively.

'You can play football with it for all I care, it's as safe as houses.'

We realized that we had enough room to be able to settle down with relative comfort, as it had stopped raining, so we huddled together round a relocated Stan, who was awake and saying that he was feeling better, but we didn't believe him and he still sounded like a ruptured duck with his breathing rig, so we just chatted among ourselves.

We were supposed to be on R and R waiting for the Cavalry, so H decided to celebrate by lashing us up to the last of the chocolate, and the talk inevitably turned to food, and of course drink.

I kicked off with a run ashore I'd had in Gibraltar.

We'd been day running out of Gib in *Vectra* which meant that one watch per day could have a full day inboard and a good run ashore.

The snag was that me and a couple of others of the wrecking gang had to stay full time because the outside hydraulic system had been contaminated with sea water via a periscope ram leak. A Centrifuge had been shipped out to us from UK and we had to rig it in the AMS* and distilled water wash the hydraulic oil and centrifuge the emulsion to remove the water and salt to prevent corrosion of the hydraulic system internals. After a fortnight of this we managed to crack it and the Engineer Officer swung us a whole week's leave.

We found a small hotel just off Main Street, cheap and clean, and near to our favourite boozer cum eatery 'La Campana', the Bell, just off Main Street up Engineers Lane. We knew it as Eddie's Bar, and we could be found each morning sitting on his doorstep waiting for him to open up. When he did, his first move was to put a bottle of Bacardi and a few Cokes on the bar as freebees, after that we paid. Up a couple of steps to the rear of the joint you could get a good meal. Eddie was real good to us, he even made us special ice cubes that would fit down the neck of an ordinary thermos flask which we then topped up with Bacardi and Coke and a few twists of lemon. We'd have a few more bevies then wander down to the beach, buying a load of fresh fruit on the way, do a bit of sunbathing, eye up the talent and get pleasantly pissed.

This particular day though it was one of the lad's birthdays and we went a bit OTT, culminating in the birthday boy suffering a dislocated shoulder. He'd accidentally fallen between two parked cars and was laid on his back between them singing quietly to himself. His oppo* went back to assist and grabbed both wrists to pull him up. The snag was that the cars were parked fairly close together side by side, and his oppo's shoulders were wider than the gap with the inevitable result, but he didn't find out until the next morning, he was that handcarted. We all went back to Eddie's Bar to get big eats, and had a lovely seafood salad. The birthday boy managing to eat with one hand, complained that the battered onion rings were rubbery. His oppo called him a stupid b – – – .

'They aint onion rings them's octopus testicles.' He was famed for his Malapropisms.

'I remember him,' Stan piped up, and we all looked round rather surprised.

'Yes, I remember overhearing him telling one of his mates how clever his family doctor was. By, he said, he's a real clever fella e's got all these diplamats' angin' on is wall, an 'es got all this new tubeless furniture in is waitin room, an he keeps a couple of bloody big laburnam dogs int back yard, 'e's real clever, 'es even sown a new lawn an' its cumin' on a treat 'cos 'es used bird propellant on it.' Then he went back to sounding like a ruptured duck.

Andy then chipped in with his Singapore runs ashore.

'We'd just finished clearing the Suez and all of us clearance divers and back ups were knackered, some were even basket cases. So Their Lordships in their wisdom decided we were due R and R so they let us bum a lift on a destroyer to Singapore and were billeted in HMS *Terror*, The Butlins of the Far East.

We were green as grass and some of the barrack stanchions took us under their wing and showed us the ropes.

The weather was hot but very humid, so we couldn't get our heads round the fact that all the wardrobes had illuminated light bulbs in the bases day and night. One of the old lags showed us a suit that had been in an unilluminated wardrobe and it was green were food had been spilt. In the humidity mould grows at an alarming rate overnight. Drinking in the mess could be a nightmare if you weren't careful because you were always thirsty with the heat, so you went down the bar and got a beer, Tiger beer, bottles of it, and sank the first in one go and suddenly you had excruciating stomach cramp, because the beer was out of the fridge and damn near frozen. You learnt after the first time to take it slowly to start with.

Eating out was another experience not to be missed. One of the streets was all just shops and cafés. On the pavement outside was the Chef and his kitchen with his wok and charcoal brazier with all his making round him. You go into the shop and upstairs to the café area and we always used to go to the front so that you could look out, because there was no glass in the windows. You were brought a large pot of green tea and cups at no charge and asked if you wished to eat. If yes the menu was brought, you made your selection and ordered and then you watched out of the window as the chef prepared your meal. His equipment consisted of a razor sharp cleaver and a soup ladle with which he performed miracles and the food was superb.

My favourite dish was Stir Fry Steamroller Duck. The duck was called that by 'Jack'. It was preserved duck in the shape of a duck, complete with skin but with no bones in it, and had been preserved with the long neck formed into a hook shape by being pressed between two flat boards and when the process was completed it came out the shape of a duck, but only half an inch thick, which is why Jack called it Steamroller Duck, for obvious reasons, and these were hung up on a rail by their necks, hence the shaping.

If you wanted to eat in the evening a good and very interesting place to go was Bougiss Street. During the day it was a normal thoroughfare but in the evening the tables and chairs came out on it from the cafes and restaurants. My favourite dish there was king prawns. Half a dozen filled a big plate on their own and was a full meal with nothing else.

The place was a hotbed of theft, corruption and prostitution, three year old little girls would play you at noughts and crosses for money, you could draw if you were very lucky, but you never won.

Then there were the Ky-Tyes, Lady Boys, we'd been warned, but some hadn't. These creatures dressed in the very latest revealing fashion dresses, and acted and looked far better than the local girls. You could see the young Merchant Seamen making a play for them, and were they going to get a surprise, like a handful of nuts and bolts.'

H, to my dismay, told the story of yours truly and Chalky White and our run in with a certain Chief REM.

'This bloke, pointing at me, and his Second Dicky Chalky White were Wreckers on *Vectra* which was alongside *Adamant* where I was working in the periscope shop at the time of the incident. The Chief Radio Electrical Mechanition in question sported a full set in the style of King Harken of Norway, a blond pointed beard and matching waxed moustache, which were his pride and joy. Normally when inboard he used to twirl his tash with soap which when dried was well pointed and quite impressive, but on runs ashore he waxed it into long rigid spikes. He'd been ashore and had a good bevy and had settled into an armchair in the chief's mess and fallen asleep. The terrible duo also arrived back aboard after a good run ashore and espied said CREM decided to have him on a bit. Ted's hair was the same shade of blonde as the targets so he got a bit of his forelock and twisted it with pussers hard (soap) then snipped it off. For all the world it looked like one side of the victim's tash. Chalky then did the dastardly deed, but at this juncture I must point out that the said victim was known by all and sundry except our Dastardly Double Act to be AC–DC, especially when in drink. Chalky, naively, with the whole of the mess members now watching him with great interest, crept up behind the mark holding the dummy tash in his right hand also grabbed and tugged the real one to wake him up and then loudly snipped the scissors in his ear and let go the real one whilst displaying the fake. The bloke leapt to his feet saw the dummy tash and scissors in Chalky's hands and suffered instant humour failure, in fact he went absolutely ballistic and chased poor old Chalky all over the place, threatening to do very naughty and rude things to him. Eventually Chalky found a hiding place in the Wardroom Pantry 'cos the steward owed him a favour. The next day however, at tot time the CREM realized it was just a scam and saw the funny side of it and had a good laugh with Chalky. The long term effect though, was much different in that whenever Chiefy came off shore bevvied up and he knew that Chalky's boat was alongside the hunt was on, threatening to inflict dire and dastardly acts on him, and Chalky, when he heard on the bush telegraph that he was being hunted, used to go to extraordinary lengths to hide as best he could, whilst Jack-me -Tickler-Pump here, pointing at me, got away with it all scot-free.'

Stan had fallen into a shallow sleep, the rest of us had run out of stories, and it was getting dark, so H took the radio and recognition torch and told Andy and me that he would take the first watch and for us to get our heads down.

    Andy took no rocking and was zizzing within minutes, but sleep eluded me so I went to keep H company and have a quiet chat about the events of the last few days. During the conversation I mentioned that when we did the unplanned dive when the injuries occurred that it frightened the life out of me, and took me ages to calm down and get warm again. H said he was the same and that us two were lucky to escape injury, but that he'd found a quite warm pipe to sit on that heated him up really quickly after he'd helped Stan as best he could. With that I decided to try and get a few zeds myself, but something was nagging at the back of my mind, I couldn't put my finger on it but I knew deep down it was important, and went into a fitful sleep.

Chapter 17

Cavalry 2

When Danny and Ali dumped their back packs and legged it, Betty without being asked or told just picked them up and slung them over a shoulder and plodded on. Dusty thought to himself that the lad may be awkward in a boat but out here doing this he was ideal, and a real work horse. So now they were down to three and on they plodded South, keeping as far as possible to the water's edge as the jungle was very dense.

Dusty explained to the lads that the plan was to head this way until they encountered the swamp and then just skirt the edge of it till they hit the southern stream and then head West to the holing up point, and then get the lads out of their predicament. Which all sounded very noble and well meaning until the blower went and threw a spanner in the works, about 1 ½in Whitworth.

Dusty called the other two back to him.

'I've just had a baffling call from Danny saying that there's problems and danger ahead if we carry on in our present direction. He's told us to head west nor' west ish, which means we have to hack our way through the bloody jungle. I've no idea what's up but he was adamant about it, so I'm going to take his word for the fact that there's a problem. He's actually given us a couple of course changes for a rendezvous point, so we're gong to head 290 degrees true till we break out of the jungle. So machetes at the ready, let's go.'

The further they moved inland the more dense the jungle became so they adopted a spell system, in that they took it in turns to lead and cut a path. Each spell lasted about half an hour by which time the poor sod was about knackered, and well due a breather. The only saving grace being that all three were superbly fit and could hack it (pun intended). Their progress though was painfully slow and was further hampered by the wildlife, from large creepy crawlies through various sizes of reptiles to carnivores. Unexpected allies in the form of primates that put up such a racket on their approach, the gang were convinced that their cacophony scared a lot of potential danger away.

Meanwhile Danny's mob were making good progress having dragged the canoes ashore and stashed them and set off south at a good pace in the tall grass, with Click's lads as outriders. En-route Danny got talking to Click via Ali and among other things asked him how bad the jungle was. The reply convinced Danny that Dusty and the lads could do with help, as Click had pointed out that unless you knew jungle craft well it would be difficult. So Danny asked if Click and a couple of his lads went ahead could they help to get them out of the jungle quicker? The answer was a definite affirmative, so Danny asked Click to appoint a deputy, pick a team and go and help Danny as best they could. More clucks and clacks and then he and a couple of others just disappeared.

Danny then got on the blower.

'Danny – Cavalry.'

'Cavalry.'

'Click and party are on their way to assist you in passage to course change. Keep ear open for join up possibly Sta'bd side over.'

'Roger that Danny, out.'

Danny informed his team of the latest development, so they all tried to be extra vigilant but it was a bit difficult as they hacked their way on. The jungle was becoming more and more dense and consequently the speed of advance reduced until a halt was unanimously called, for a bit of a breather.

All three slumped down and started to relax, maybe a bit too much, because there was a bit of a rustling in the canopy, which they all assumed was some innocuous creepy-crawly or reptile. Then a bit more slightly louder rustling, then a loud snarl and down leapt a panther, straight for Spike, who went for his pistol but wasn't quick enough and it landed right on top of him, and as he said,

'I shit myself and saw my messy end in sight, but the bloody thing didn't move, it had knocked all the wind out of me and I couldn't breath because it was just a dead weight on top of me. I couldn't understand why it didn't move until the lads rolled it off me and I saw a large assegai sticking out of the side of its chest. Then out of the jungle came a grinning native followed by Click and one other, the team Danny had sent. Was I thankful, and what crap timing though, they could have made it a bit earlier.'

A long time later I introduced Spike to, I forget who, as the only bloke I've ever known to have been nearly squashed to death by a panther.

By way of explanation, panthers are black leopards. The usual spotted variety live in the bush and light undergrowth where their colouring is good camouflage. The black ones having adapted their colouring to the dense dark jungle.

Spike, when he'd got his breath back, shook the spear marksman by the hand as a thank you gesture, as if he hadn't been extremely accurate the lucky bootneck would most certainly have been a gonner.

When everybody had calmed down and sorted themselves out, and the marksman had taken his trophy from the carcass, Click signalled them to follow him and the three natives headed off, machetes flashing and slashing in a northerly direction. Dusty felt like pointing out that it was the wrong direction to be heading but decide to give it a little longer before saying anything. Quite suddenly though, a faint track was found, which the natives followed, although it wandered about a bit according to Dusty's compass but it generally headed in the right direction and was a hell of a lot easier and faster in the long run, and it didn't involve any hacking. What path clearing that was required, was done by Click's mates. They also warned everyone of possible wildlife hazards to avoid, which was a great help as the lads could relax more.

It was found out later that the track they were following was a migration route of a troop of chimpanzees, and Click and his gang knew all the tracks and trails in this jungle, as let's face facts it was their larder 'til the interlopers started to try and get rid of them by starving them out. Also asked later why they didn't do more fishing, Click had explained that the reason that Baggy had to be moved was that the vessel approaching was using hand grenades to kill the fish and scare them away, and did the run regularly every day. The reason they were in the area and saw them was the fact that they were waiting for the enemy to pass because sometimes some stunned fish washed up on that particular bit of beach because of a quirk of the tide.

Progress was still being made, and eventually the jungle gradually started to thin out and then the migration track veered off in completely the wrong direction and it was back to hacking their own trail, but it was a lot easier than earlier, and they all took turns. Finally the jungle thinned to stunted brush and then into a broad expanse of veldt with just tall grass to contend with.

Click then consulted with Dusty by sign language pointing to the compass and extending his arm in the general direction of the course recommended by Danny. So off they set on that course, and Dusty, while on the move in the relative open with easy travelling progress, checked with Danny for an updated rendezvous time and position.

'Cavalry – Danny.'

'Danny.'

'Have changed course and am at position – (and gave coded point). Advise updated rendezvous point and time.'

'Rendezvous will be (and gave coded fix and time), take care, out.'

All these codes had been worked out at the planning stage and were deemed necessary in case the opposition had facilities to scan radio transmission frequencies. Also, if they had up to date direction finding equipment positions may be able to be triangulated, but if the transmissions were kept short, that and the codes would at the very least slow them down a bit.

So Dusty knew his own position and he knew the rendezvous position and so could calculate the required course which involved a slight track adjustment, and the rate of advance required to make the target. So off they marched with the natives acting as sort of outriders just in case the opposition were about, the only encounter they did have though was with a small herd of elephants. Click and his lads closed in and signalled Dusty's team to crouch down and stay still. The noise of heavy footsteps and trumpeting got louder and louder, then above the tall grass appeared the head and shoulders of a large female elephant, obviously the matriarch of the group, in a very aggressive pose warning all and sundry to stay away. Then with a shake of its massive head, trunk curled aloft and a loud bellow spun round and lumbered off satisfied, they hoped, that there was no immediate threat to her charges.

Dusty ordered a short rest period to have a swig of water and a K ration snack, partly to calm everybody down, but also for sustenance to keep them up to the effort, Click and his lads richly deserving the food for their efforts. Then it was off again, keeping up a good pace, Dusty calculating that they were still maintaining the required rate of advance to meet up as planned.

Danny's lot, meanwhile, were making good progress and he also calculated from the last communication with Dusty that join up plans were realistic and on target. That was until Click's deputy spoke urgently to Ali who relayed to Danny that a group of the opposition had been spotted on patrol to the east of their position and were reported to be heading south, which would put them on a possible collision course with Dusty's group. One added negative factor was that it was now early dusk and visibility was becoming increasingly difficult, so Danny got back on the blower to warn Dusty of the possible hazard heading towards them from the north. Dusty acknowledged the warning and sent Click and his lads out scouting to find the threat and try to keep track of it. The natives once again proved their worth by both teams working together and reporting back to their respective Team Leaders and recommending slight course changes, so the threat was avoided, but as Click explained to Dusty later, that random patrols such as the one that had been avoided were not an unusual occurrence.

After that close encounter and slight readjustment of direction the two groups finally joined forces with lots of back slapping and quiet celebration. After a short rest break, the visibility was now poor, with a very hazy moon so Dusty asked Click to deploy his lads as outriders again with Click staying with the main group for liaison purposes, and off they set again. Dusty then got Betty to calculate an ETA with the away team. The bottom line came back that at the present rate of advance, two hours would see them at the target point which Dusty passed on to H, who acknowledged the good news, but reported that Stan's condition was further deteriorating. Ali, keeping Click up to speed with developments, mentioned that one of the group was in poor health and would require assistance with evacuation. Click immediately called in a couple of his team, gave them some instructions and off they trotted.

Chapter 18

Rendezvous

H passed on the good news that the Cavalry were only two hours away, and that there would be food and water in abundance very soon, which cheered us all up, including Stan who had woken from a fitful sleep. So, thinking about food, and to pass the time I told the gang about Shitty Vest West the senior Chef on *Vectra*.

'You remember Shitty Vest West don't you Stan?'

'Yes, he was the one who was good with pre-mix bread wasn't he?'

'That's him, he was as queer as a nine bob note, but he was harmless and didn't push his luck in that respect. How he ever got into the mob in the first place was a complete mystery as he was semiliterate, but surprisingly was also quite an artist and would write out the menu on a blackboard in beautiful copperplate print, but in Naval slang. For instance:

Breakfast
'Train Smash (Bacon and Arrigones (Tomatoes)) 'Shit on a Raft' (Saute Kidneys on Fried Bread). 'Cackle Berries' (Boiled eggs). 'Elephants Footprints' (Spam Fritters). 'Arrigones on a Shingle' (Tomatoes on toast).

Dinner
'Babies Heads' (Steak and Kidney Pudding). 'Tiddy Oggy' (Cornish Pasty). 'Pot Mess' (Stew). 'Figgy or Plum Duff' (Suet Pudding). 'Duff and Thickers' (Pudding and Condensed Milk).'

'Why call Steak and Kidney Pud "Babies Heads"?' enquired Andy.

'Steak and Kidney Pudding comes in tins as "Submarine Comforts"* and to get it out of the tin both ends of it are opened and the contents slide out as the Clacker* is water paste. The resultant lump is then delicately cut in half and both halves placed in a baking tray, contents side down. This procedure is repeated till the tray is loosely filled, to leave room for expansion. The tray is then placed in a preheated oven to bake the clacker and heat the contents of said clacker. When baking is complete the tray is removed from the oven, the clacker has expanded and the corners rounded and for all the world it looks like a tray full of babies heads. And very tasty too, served with Smash and two tinned veg and RBG, * Heaven.'

'But I digress, the real reason for this diatribe is to extol the prowess of Shitty Vest West's Bread. All RN Vessels carry in the deep freeze premix bread, which is all ready to bake apart from defrosting and adding yeast. This to be used when stocks of fresh bread ran out or went mouldy. Most times you must all agree premix bread was pretty dire and fit only for use in fishing, not as bait but as sinkers, and even Shitehawkes* turn their beaks up at it, but Shitty's bread was divine. He could make Cottage Loaves, Breakfast Buns, Plaits, Farmhouse Loaves, Bloomers, Tea Cakes, Hot Cross Buns, Fruit Loaf, you name it, he could and did do it. We even bartered his bread for dodgy films with the Aussies. The secret of his success we all concluded was the fact that when he left the final mixture to prove, he stripped off and covered it with his Shitty Vest.'

'That's how he did it is it?' Stan queried, then fell back into a light sleep.

'Don't talk to me about chefs,' from H, 'all they've done for me is give me grief. The final ignominy being the bunging up of the Pig's (Officer's) Head when I got conned into training as wrecker on the 'P' boat just before getting the periscope job. P and O boats Heads are luxury compared to the older A, T and S classes, in that instead of having to blow your own residues directly to sea, and running the risk of getting your own back if you got the method wrong, all such arisings are collected in an internal tank and discharged in bulk, when full and/or convenient, by blowing out using compressed air. The four heads were arranged in line just aft of the diving panel, three basic traps for the troops and sheer luxury for the Officers with not just a bog but a wash hand basin as well. Entrance to said Head was via bat wing doors situated opposite the galley and just forrard of the engine room bulkhead.

The problem was and always will be that it's too easy and convenient for the Chef to empty his slop* bucket down the nearest bog, and that one of course was the Officers' Head. The second problem was that the Chef very often left either a cleaning cloth or eating irons or both in the bottom of the bucket and pulled the flush handle before he realized what had gone down the hole. The third problem was the fact that the foreign objects never got to the tank and caused a blockage in the pipework, which caused a backup of subsequently discharged material from all the traps as it was a common line with the Officers' trap the last to join it, and therefore the one to concentrate on for clearance purposes.

'The clearance procedure, I was told, was tried and tested and worked well. The idea was to turn off the flush water, which ran when the pan flap valve was operated to discharge the arisings. The flap handle was then jammed down so that the pan was then open to the tank with the blockage between the two. The next stage was to cover the top of the pan with a gash bag and then put the lid down on it to secure it, then a slight pressure was applied to the sewage tank from the blow station situated by the engine room bulkhead door. Usually this is sufficient to cause a slight eruption under the gash bag and the foreign object can be removed from the bowl and the culprit confronted with it. Unfortunately for me this didn't happen, so I gave it another little burst of air and still nothing, so I went to ask the Wrecker what to do next, and all he said was to give it an extra burst, so I went back and gave it another burst, the over pressure relief valve started to feather and still nothing. That's when I made my big mistake. I peered through the gap in the bat wing doors to find that nothing was happening, so I poked my head through them to find if I could hear anything, then with no warning the damn thing just erupted. Like a fool I just tried to pull my head back but the doors were spring loaded and they jammed behind my ears. I got a six inch wide stripe of shit all the way down me and two lovely black eyes, which everybody took the piss out of me about. Talk about getting your own back, I got everybody else's as well.'

Time was marching on so H decided it was time to show the ultraviolet signal torch. Andy volunteered to do the biz with it because he said he felt like a spare one at a wedding and needed to feel a little bit useful, H said OK and to point it in the general direction of West as the cavalry would be coming down river.

The cavalry meantime had got to the river, the flow rate of which had abated somewhat but was still quite fast flowing. Spike took out a rope from his back pack and was about to try fording it when Betty volunteered to do it instead, which reminded him of the old adage, never look a gift horse in the mouth, or was it mug. Anyway, Betty tied a bowline round his waist and off he plodded as if he was taking an afternoon stroll and eventually signalled down the rope that his end was secured. So one at a time they crossed over with Spike bringing up the rear having made sure the rope was well secured at the start end. Then they all set off east leaving the rapids to their left, making good progress whilst keeping a weather eye open for the Baddies. Having cleared the rapids Spike donned the UV viewing goggles which would pick up the Away Teams homing signal. Dusty got on the blower to inform H that they were past the rapids via the west bank and in striking distance of them and to activate the signal lamp which H confirmed had already been done. Within minutes of the conversation Spike confirmed that he had a visual on the away teams signal which quickened their pace until the two groups were opposite each other across the still quite angry stream. Dusty weighed up the situation and decided on a plan of action.

'I'm going to cross first, then Spike and Danny to assist in evacuation. Betty, you stay here with Ali and the lads to co-ordinate reassembly on this side and defend the position if required. I'm going to go upstream to secure my rope so that I have a chance to get across before I get to the lads. If I miss I'll allow myself to be swept back to this side so that I can then try again. If and when I get across I'll signal you to follow by just going hand over hand on the rope and allow the water flow to help.'

So off he trotted with Spike in attendance and found a fairly substantial but stunted tree about fifty yards upstream and the rope secured, Dusty secured himself to the other end with a bowline and started wading in. It soon became too deep and fast flowing and he lost his footing and so started doing a typical Water Polo Crawl, like a horizontal windmill with lots of splashing, but making good progress, reaching the far bank and getting washed downstream to be grabbed by H and me and pulled up onto the bank. We had a quick hand shaking and back slapping sesh and then got down to the plan of action. It was obvious that the rope couldn't be secured at our side so us three able bodied ones had to hang onto the line like grim death. Dusty got Andy to give the signal to start the transfer and before we knew it Spike was with us shortly after which Danny joined us too.

Chapter 19

Evacuate

Now help had arrived and the gear was in place so it was time to evacuate. Danny then laid out his plan of action.

'Our prime concerns are Stan and Andy, and the trip across is going to be a bit rough, so I suggest that you, H or Ted cross first and check things out before we commit the wounded to the trip.'

So H and I tossed for it and I won.

'When you get over there Ted get on the blower to let me know how it was and any suggestions you may have to make it easier. I suggest that we give Stan and Andy a shot of morphine to ease the discomfort. Spike, you take Stan with you, Danny you take Andy then it'll be H, then I'll drag up the rear. There's enough rope to be able to tail you out and recover it once each trip is complete. Any comments? NO, then let's get to it.'

Dusty then went over to the injured and explained the plan of action. Stan was well out of it and didn't mind the idea of another jab, but Andy protested that he would be OK but was eventually persuaded that it would be less stressful if he also accepted a quick shot.

So I got ready and shackled myself to the end of the rope with a bowline, made sure the tailing line was attached, and launched myself into the Oggin. The first problem I had was to keep my head pointing upstream, which I achieved by holding the rope above my head. The next problem was trying to keep my head above water as its force kept rolling me over, but my main problem was when I came close to the far bank. I say close because the current kept buffeting me away from the bank and the lads ashore couldn't quite grab me until finally Betty produced his rope and threw me a length of it, which I managed to grab after a few tries and got hauled in feeling a bit like a drowned rat.

I gave Dusty a bell as promised and explained that we were going to attach another line to the main rope to assist the current in dragging the passengers across and landing them safely. I also explained that I wanted to inspect and check the security of the main anchorage as I thought it might have given a bit, and would let him know when to proceed. Betty volunteered to check it out and took one of the native lads with him, who came back alone shortly afterwards and gave a thumbs up signal, so I let Dusty know that it was OK to launch again.

Meanwhile, on the other bank a harness had been fashioned out of spare rope to strap Stan to Spike and Spike to the main rope, having taken onboard my comments about stability. He then lifted Stan as gently as possible and walked to the water's edge, took the strain on the main rope and slid as gently as possible into the stream, turned on his back, gave a signal on the haul rope and quickly disappeared in the maelstrom.

I got the signal on the haul-in line and the lads pulled with a will and in a matter of seconds Stan and Spike had been landed safely hardly any the worse for wear. Stan was then made as comfortable as possible. Danny managed to get Andy across with no problems, and then H and finally Dusty in quick succession. A quick congratulatory back slapping ensued, and then we wrapped everything up and set off back towards the rapids, coiling in the main rope as we went with Danny carrying Stan. We very quickly came upon the stunted anchor tree, which had been uprooted with Betty in the hole where the trees roots had been, dug in and lashed up like the anchor man in a tug-o-war team. Asked what had happened, he explained that when he got to the place to inspect the rope anchorage, the tree was just about uprooted.

'So, as there were no other substantial enough trees around I decided, so as not to delay the proceedings, to be the anchor myself, so I sent the native back to signal that everything was OK and just dug in and hung on. I'm glad to see everybody's together again.'

Dusty expressed his grateful thanks to Betty but went away shaking his head in disbelief at the man's incredible strength and extreme modesty. He then had the temerity to relieve Danny of the transport of Stan.

So on we all trekked and soon passed the rapids and on to the crossing point line, and started the transfer immediately, with Betty lugging Stan across with Danny in attendance as guide and backup. Dusty went next with Andy in tow, then Click and his lads with H and I following on after them along with Ali. Spike had been instructed by Dusty to unshackle the far end of the rope and we would haul him across on his signal.

But suddenly all hell broke loose with incoming automatic fire from the far bank, Dusty was about to recross to assist his sergeant when, in the next instant we heard about half a dozen stun grenades going off in quick succession, obviously launched by Spike, then a frantic signalling on the crossing line, so we hauled like mad and Spike came barrelling across as if his arse was on fire. He quickly explained to Dusty that he estimated that about ten of the opposition had surprised him but had given them a bit of a headache for a while and suggested that we made tracks while he conducted a rearguard action. Dusty asked for volunteers to assist Spike so H and I decided to help out, at which point he explained that the idea was to stop the baddies or at least slow them down, but try not to kill them if at all possible so as not to alienate us more than necessary in our efforts to thwart their operation.

Dusty then got Ali to arrange for Click to deploy a couple of his lads on the flanks to warn of any possible pincer movement. So off the main bunch went to be met soon after by the couple of natives Click had sent off on an errand before the first water crossing. They brought with them two long poles and some shorter ones, which they must have dashed to the forest to collect, which was some feat in the time that it took. They lashed them all together with some borrowed rope to form a litter with shoulder loops at each end. Some of the tall grass was cut and laid on the litter to form a mattress and Stan then transferred to it with the two natives insisting by sign language and through Ali that they wanted to take the first spell. They then gently lifted the loaded litter by the shoulder loops and broke into a steady and smooth trot, so giving Stan a more comfortable ride than with Betty.

Meanwhile H and I were taking instruction from Spike who positioned us nearly at the water's edge, prone in the tall grass, watching for any activity on the far bank. He explained that if needed, he wanted us to fire high in short bursts at any movement we detected, and he would back it up by launching stun grenades in the same direction to keep the opposition at bay.

It all got a bit boring, which reminded me of watch keeping. As I explained to Spike, in a situation like we were in, from sheer boredom to feverish activity could happen at any moment. In conventional boats a similar situation occurs when snorting, which is when the boat is at periscope depth and the main diesel engines are run drawing combustion air into the boat via an induction (snort) mast and exhausted through individual group exhaust valves. Emergency shutdown from snorting is critical as everything happens at once. One of the most critical actions of this evolution is to shut the group exhaust valves to prevent water flooding back into the engines. To this end, at snorting stations, two junior engine room personnel are stationed opposite each of the group exhaust valves that are fitted with large chrome plated hand wheels. When the stop snorting alarm goes off these two individuals have to leap across the gangway and spin the hand wheel to shut the valve. I had the misfortune to serve as an engine room watch keeper with a stoker who was a towny and whose snorting watch keeping station was the starb'd group exhaust valve. He had one unfortunate habit, in that he constantly picked his nose, and could produce some fearsome grollies. He also had a malevolent streak and got bored very easily, so to relieve his boredom and amuse himself at the same time he used to park his grollies on his oppo's hand wheel in the hope that the stop snorting order would come through when the hand wheel was fully loaded.

Our boredom ended when the native covering the left flank came back and by sign language conveyed to Spike that something untoward was happening downstream, so he left us to it and went to find out what was going on. He found that a small group of baddies were halfway across the rocks of the rapids, suddenly their support team on the far bank spotted Spike and loosed off some rather erratic automatic fire, to which he responded by firing stun grenades at both groups. The ones on the rocks dropped as if poleaxed and fell off and were washed down stream, the bank group dropped into the undergrowth and were seen to retreat quite some time later looking a bit the worse for wear.

Spike then returned to our position and explained that he reckoned the whole of the opposition group had been seen off at the rapids area and decided to follow the main group as a rearguard force, so he sent the native who had raised the alarm to round up his colleagues from the other flank. Once regrouped he spread us out in line abreast and off we trotted in a general northerly direction, keeping a weather eye open, especially to the rear.

Our progress was good and in no time at all we had caught up with the main group. To celebrate the event Dusty called a short R and R break where the last of the water and K rations were consumed. Dusty and Spike went into a short huddle and then explained to us all the latest plan of action.

'We know from what Spike and his lot have experienced recently that the enemy are aware of our presence and must know that we are up to no good as far as they are concerned. So they will be keen to capture as many of us as possible to find out what we're up to. Therefore Spike and his gang are going to continue in their rearguard mode as a buffer and early warning group for the main force. As we approach the northern stream where the canoes are stashed I'll call the rearguard in and we'll then all evacuate via the stream to Baggy, any questions?'

'Yes, Dusty,' Andy piped up. 'Now we're relying on manual detonation instead of the automatic hydrostatic jobs, when are we going to let her rip, because we surely want to be certain of maximum effect with both targets together, and we don't know how long the docking has been planned for, and the two may part at any moment.'

'I understand your concern Andy, but I want us all to be safe and clear of the area before I give the OK because I don't want anyone else hurt if it's at all possible. Anything else?'

'How much of a head start shall we give you?' Spike enquired.

'Oh, give us about half an hour Spike. Any more? No? OK then let's get to it then.' And off they trotted again.

So Spike, H, I and the two lads sat around twiddling our thumbs until Spike broke the silence by talking about patience and being patient.

'A good mate of mine was a patient fella. He's a Chef and at the time he was in barracks waiting for a seagoing draft and was pissed off at being detailed to do duties in the galley. Worst of all he was detailed off to do the early shift for breakfast and hated it. He had to turn to at 0400 to get things ready for reveille having, apart from everything else, to boil at least twenty dozen eggs.

What used to really piss him off was this one young lad who was always first and used to run down to the servery before the reveille bugle had finished, having not washed or shaved. So my mate used to wind him up a bit by blowing an egg and putting it in the tray with the boiled ones, and as the mark dashed towards the serving hatch, he picked up the blown one and threw it at his head, and of course the mark ducked in panic and the empty shell hit the deck and bounced down the gangway. This routine was repeated a few times and eventually the mark got used to it and started to head the blown egg each morning and got quite class at it.

My mate eventually got his Draft Chit, so on his last morning as duty Chef, instead of a blown egg he threw a full raw one with spectacularly messy results with the comment, "it serves you right you scruffy, scabby, gullible bastard".'

After a good laugh at the yarn we lapsed into uneasy boredom again until it was time to carry out our mission, so we deployed as before, spreading out as far as possible whilst keeping in touch with each other. Everything went well for quite some time until H having fallen behind a bit thought he heard voices to the rear, so he hung back a bit further until he spotted a couple of heavily armed, military looking natives following their tracks and talking to others he could not see. So quickly and quietly he sneaked away and caught up with Spike and told him we were being followed.

Spike then called the rest of us in and we legged it to put some distance between us and our followers, and Spike was at the same time racking his brains thinking of ways we could stop them or at least slow them down. Then one of the natives came up to Spike and pointed to his backpack, so he took it off and the lad opened it up and took out the K ration waterproof packet of matches. We all looked a bit confused, so he pointed to the sky, puffed his cheeks out and blew, then mimed striking a match.

Suddenly we all twigged that he was suggesting giving the antagonists a quick roasting, which seemed to be our best option because, as Spike pointed out, we didn't know how many there were or how spread out they were, and the grass was nice and tall and dry, and the wind was in a nice gentle NNE direction. So we legged it north as fast as we could for a while to put some distance between us and the foe, and then headed up wind gathering bundles of grass on the way, to twist and plait into torches the way the natives showed us. Then we spread out, lit our torches and set light to the undergrowth and grass. The result was spectacular as the whole front suddenly burst into flames with very little smoke and advanced slowly and steadily downwind towards our trackers. We, for our part regrouped and Spike decided that we should join the main force early to rush them along and get the hell out of it as soon as possible, so we again legged it as fast as we could. Spike got on the blower en route and appraised Dusty of the deteriorating situation.

Chapter 20

Meanwhile

When Danny, Ali, Click and his lads finally left, Pancho gathered his caretaker crew together and asked Penny to go with Curly to get a run through of the radio and radar installations so that she could spell him when necessary. He then asked Nobby to assist him in putting the finishing touches to the camouflage and generally check Baggy's overall condition, and asked Anna if she would go ashore and try conversing with the natives as she was the linguist of the crew.

'If you want me to do that I'm going to need some help and moral support, because I'm going to have to use a bit of bribery,' Anna explained.

'OK then, I'll look after Baggy, Nobby you assist Anna to try and communicate with the villagers, OK everybody?'

So off they went about their various duties. Anna got Nobby to put some chocolate and K rations in a backpack and off they went ashore and into the centre of the village where they attracted quite a crowd. They were both struck by the generally poor physical condition of the vast majority of the villagers, who after their initial hesitation were keen to accept the handouts, not for themselves but for their children and the less well, and they both concluded that these were kind and gentle people.

Anna started trying to converse rather than use sign language and went through her whole repertoire without any success until one in the group of ladies holding a small child came forward and took hold of Anna's hand and persuaded her to follow with Nobby dragging up the rear.

They were led to a small hut on the outskirts of the village where the native lady called gently through the open doorway. Eventually a shy looking girl appeared who looked more Asian than African. Anna tried speaking Urdu with no effect and so tried Hindi with instant success. After a fairly lengthy conversation, Anna discovered that this girl had been sold into slavery to an Arab dealer some nine months earlier and was being transported to Africa. She had thrown herself overboard rather than submit to the slaver's demands, so he had abandoned her and left her to drown, but by a strange twist of fate she had been washed ashore barely alive and was looked after and nursed back to health by the lady who had introduced them. In the nine months that followed she had managed to pick up most of the strange native language and when asked was only too willing to act as interpreter.

She said her name was Raisa Partak and was originally from just outside Nagpur a very poor area in Central India, which is why she had been sold, as girls are considered an encumbrance. She introduced the lady, who had got them together, as the head Wife of the Chief of the village who was also the one who was leading the native group who were helping the other foreigners.

Anna asked Raisa to accompany her and to bring the Head Lady to meet the rest of her colleagues, so off they went followed by a crowd of happy but rather emaciated youngsters who thought that Nobby was the bees knees because he kept dishing out chocolate. The whole group clewed up at Baggy where the introductions had barely been completed when suddenly a series of explosions reverberated from the direction of the open sea and shattered the calm and sent all the birds into the air. Poncho started to organize defensive action but was stopped by Anna, who had been advised by Raisa that this was a regular daily occurrence, and that it was the foe killing all the fish in the area in an attempt to starve the villagers out of the area, and explained that when the patrol boat responsible for the explosions had cleared the area, some of the fitter villagers would launch canoes and search the area for stunned and dead fish for food, but the pickings were getting less and less as time went on. This being partly due to the fish staying away, but partly because they weren't as quick as the local sharks that had sussed out the situation.

After the initial who-ha when things had calmed down, Penny took a shine to the Head Lady's baby and vice-versa, so she held out her arms hands outspread and the child readily transferred her affections. She noticed that the very bonny baby was quite thin with a rather distended tummy, so through Anna she asked Raisa the general state of health of the rest of the babies. She was told that most babies were undernourished and that the child mortality rate was high because mothers' milk quickly dried up because of malnutrition, and that at the moment diarrhoea was rife in the baby population, with some fatalities already.

Penny immediately sprang to life, handed the baby back to her mother, and got Anna to tell the head lady that they had the cure to diarrhoea and to ask her if they had access to good fresh water and salt.

'Yes, the village well has very good clean clear water, and salt was plentiful as it is used as currency,' came back the answer via Raisa.

'Good, Pancho get all the sugar you can muster from the K rations and the tea boat, we're going to perform miracles. Anna, collect as many spoons and beakers as you can together. Nobby please go below and get one of our full plastic five gallon containers of water, oh and Pancho, bring along some water purification tablets.'

With that they all trooped back to the centre of the village and Penny set up shop getting Anna to get Raisa organizing the gathering of all the village ladies with babies suffering from diarrhoeal disease to bring them for treatment. The first lady that came was a little apprehensive but was reassured when she saw that the treatment only involved the feeding of her baby with no more than a drink of a solution of sugar and salt in the right proportions. Word quickly spread and before very long a queue had formed and a production line had been set up and in no time all the babies had been treated and the mothers had gone away with a beaker full of medicine and a spoon to administer it with, and already the babies were starting to get better. Penny asked Nobby to refill the water container from the well and put a couple of Pancho's purification tablets in it and give the rest to Raisa with instructions on how to use them along with the rest of the sugar and salt. With that all hell broke loose as Curly legged it over to tell them that he'd just received a message from Dusty to say that they were on their way and to prepare Baggy for a swift departure. Pancho acting on Curly's information asked Anna to get Raisa to spread the word that assistance was required to turn Baggy round and get her as far up stream as possible to make the Cavalry's journey as short as possible, and therefore the getaway time earlier.

By the time the caretaker team had got back aboard the villagers had started assembling and in no time flat almost the whole of the village had turned out, including sons and daughters, mothers and babies. Pancho's first job was to allow Baggy to drift back downstream to a point where it was wide enough to swing her round using the water flow to assist. The native men were good seamen and realized immediately what was required and were of great help, and the evolution was carried out with no problem. The hard bit was to go upstream against the water flow, so Pancho chanced his arm and started the engines as Danny had shown him. He left them to warm up for a while then transferred control to the bridge then went up top and put the astern clutches in. In the meantime Nobby had deployed the stern lines one to each bank ready to do the towing and guiding job. Pancho got Anna to station herself at the stern to keep an eye on the water depth to warn him if it got too shallow, he then gave the signal to the bank teams and gave the engines a few revs and off they went up stream slowly and steadily. The natives were very good and kept Baggy in the dead centre of the stream and were making good progress until eventually Anna signalled that the water was getting a bit shallow. Pancho was about to shut the engines down and secure Baggy to the Southern bank when a commotion on the northern bank caught his attention and distracted him, and before he realized what had happened both engines had stopped themselves. At the same time Baggy suddenly lurched to the southern bank and back downstream until she bumped the bank and stopped. On investigation it was found that both props had been badly fouled by the northern bank tow line which had parted. Very fortunately the team on the south bank realized what had happened and had quickly secured their tow line, otherwise Baggy would have drifted downstream out of control with possibly disastrous results. Pancho quickly realized what had happened and got another line onto the South bank to be sure Baggy was well secured.

He then got down to the tricky job of assessing the extent of the problem with the fouled props, hoping against hope that no permanent damage had been caused, which would be a disaster. He quickly dressed in a spare wet suit, rigged himself out with a re-breathing set and safety line and instructed Nobby to take the line ashore and go upstream, take a turn round a tree and control his position against the current, and be sure he wasn't washed downstream.

Armed with a good sharp diver's knife he went over the side to tackle the problem. Fortunately being a very good and experienced diver who had done this type of job lots of times before. He surfaced after about twenty minutes for a bit of a breather as it was very tiring fighting against the water flow whilst sawing away at the bar taut fouling rope. After a ten minute break he went over the side again, and after another half hour came back inboard thoroughly exhausted but happy that he had successfully cleared the props and couldn't detect any permanent damage, which he was very relieved about. To be absolutely certain that no damage had been caused he got Nobby to help him double up the mooring lines and then flashed up the engines and rotated the props one at a time, both ahead and astern with no excessive vibration which was further good news, and even greater good news for Pancho.

In the meantime Penny and Anna had been collecting together all the powdered milk they could find and tins of Thickers (condensed and evaporated milk) and passed the lot over to Mrs Click Senior to distribute among the mothers with small babies, having shown her how to use the K ration tin openers and beer can spanners.

And then it was just a case of hanging about waiting for the cavalry to appear, so the caretaker gang just sat around drinking black, unsweetened tea and coffee, yarning. Pancho kicked off by telling about a Killick diver who served under him on *Reclaim*.

'He was a bit of a ladies' man and they used to hang around him like flies round a lump of you know what, the type that always pulled when you went ashore which left everybody else feeling very inadequate, and hating him for it, mainly because we didn't understand what he had that we didn't.

'His party trick was to hang upside-down from a hammock bar, or similar structure, by his toes. His one proviso for performing this feat of athleticism was that whoever he showed off to had to help him down afterwards. He'd left *Reclaim* for barracks waiting for a seagoing draft, and the next time I saw him was when I was invited by an old mate of mine to the Chief's mess in barracks while *Reclaim* was in the dockyard for a short refit, and who do you think I bumped into. You've guessed it, the said Killick with both arms in plaster, and like a fool I asked him what had happened to him, and was of course told that he'd done his party trick, but the rotten bastards who had encouraged him to show them his trick had pissed off and left him dangling with the inevitable result. But as he explained it had its compensations, because when he was first treated he was in BMH* for a while with all the nice female nurses to help him with his ablutions and bodily functions. Typical Jack, always remembering the good bits.'

A general discussion ensued about why each other joined the mob in the first place, the most fascinating reason coming from Curly who said he had to join up.

'What do you mean you had to?' asked Anna.

'I had a choice, either join the Armed Forces or go to jail, as easy as that.'

'Why, for God sake?'

'Well if you must know it was because of the first job I got at this builder's yard on the outskirts of Pompey. Me dad got me the job 'cos a mate of his knew the foreman at the yard. All I did all day was sweep up and generally prat about, until one day one of the gaffers dashed into the yard when I was the only one around. He grabbed me and asked if I could drive, I said yes, so he told me to take a diesel driven road roller to a building site down by the dockyard asap. I forgot to tell him that I was only fifteen years old and didn't have a driving licence. For those who don't know, a diesel roller doesn't have any brakes and has just a forward and reverse crash gearbox. I managed to start it OK, selected the forward gear and got it out onto the road. As I said, the yard was on the outskirts of Pompey at the top of Portsdown Hill, which is not too steep but very long, and I had to go down it, and it was really slow going. That's when I made my big mistake, I took the damn thing out of gear and it picked up speed, so I tried and failed to put it back into gear, because it was a crash gearbox, not syncromesh like a car. As I overtook this car the driver of which looked more than a bit surprised, to say the least, and I eventually came to rest a the bottom of the hill, with the police following carefully behind. I was charged with dangerous driving, and speeding in a road roller whilst under age and not insured. The beak gave me the choice of going to jail or joining the forces, so I signed on.'

After that scintillating yarn everybody fell into a quiet stupor as if waiting for something to happen, then after a few minutes, all of a sudden Stan leapt to his hind legs and shouted,

'What the hell are we doing here, we should be rustling up some more canoes and native help and go upstream to help the away team back downstream, they must be exhausted, especially having to manage the injured.'

'Bloody good idea,' Pancho exclaimed, leaping to his feet, 'let's get going and get this show on the road.'

'Stan', Penny piped up, 'I think it might be a good idea if Anna and I stayed behind and got things ready to help the wounded.'

'Yes please Penny, I'm sorry I just wasn't thinking, now the rest of you, as Pancho said, let's get going and get this show on the road.'

Everybody leapt to it with a will, pleased to be doing something useful instead of sitting around chewing the fat.

Chapter 21

Kidnapped

Shortly after we had set off back to join the main force again, having checked that the fire was burning brightly, Spike called H and me over and explained to us that he had had an idea and was going to take a detour for a bit, and asked us to carry on in the same direction, and that he wouldn't be long and would rejoin us later. No amount of questioning would draw him, and he disappeared into the undergrowth so there was nothing for it but for us to bash on. So we called the native lads in and trekked on in a northerly direction to catch up with the main party.

As we went on our way I started thinking about what was niggling at the back of my mind about H. it was something to do with what he had said when we were holed up waiting for the cavalry after we'd got rid of the mine and had nattered about a few things and I'd mentioned how long it had taken me to get warmed up after our disastrous unscheduled drive. H had said that he didn't take too long to warm up because he'd found a nice warm pipe to sit on and it helped a lot – that was it.

'H, you know when you said that after our unplanned dip you found a warm pipe to help revive you, was it a four inch line just inside the second bay running from the pressure hull to outboard?'

'Yes, why?'

'No wonder it was warm, I've just realized what's been nagging in the back of my mind, it was warm because of radiation, you were sat on the Reactor primary loop over pressure safety relief valve pipeline.'

'It may have been the radiation keeping it warm but surely the pipe would be sufficient shielding?'

'For Alpha and Beta radiation yes, but not Gamma, so depending on the type of contamination in the line depends on the magnitude of the radiation dose you've received. Promise me that when we get back to the UK you'll go straight to BMH* and get a thorough check up.'

'OK if you say so, just stop nattering, you're sounding like the trouble and strife, let's get on.'

So we cracked on and eventually had the main party in view when suddenly out of the undergrowth appeared two very black individuals to which we were alerted by the native lads. H and I dropped prone with weapons cocked ready to take them out when the taller of the two waved and shouted,

'It's me, Spike, ya pillocks, don't shoot.'

It sounded like Spike but it certainly didn't look like him. H shouted for them to come ahead, but we kept our guard up until we were certain it really was Spike looking very sooty and singed with very little hair and eyebrows left.

'What the hell have you been doing with yourself and who the hell's that you've got with you?' I enquired.

'You've never met but this is the pillock who caused us a lot of aggravation and consumed a lot of our good whisky because he was in charge of security at the Naval Base. We christened him Idi because he looks and acted like the despotic Dictator Idi Amin. He doesn't look much like him now though does he?'

That was definitely an understatement, to start with, apart from his natural colour he was definitely 'sooty'. His smart uniform was in charred tatters and he was barefoot, his boots having been too badly burnt. His hair was also badly singed and his eyebrows non existent. But to put the top hat on it Spike had him trussed up very well with his hands crossed and tied behind his back and angled upwards so that his wrists were just below his shoulder blades. A line was attached to the binding of his wrists and a round turn taken of his neck and back to the wrist binding, which under normal circumstances was not too uncomfortable, but if he struggled he tended to choke himself. To complete the picture, him being very overweight, and being scared shitless, he resembled a singed wobbling jelly, if that's not a contradiction in terms.

'What the hell have you dragged him along for?' H enquired. 'He'll be a bit of a lumber won't he?'

'I think not, look what I've got,' and he produced a radio telephone. 'He's the gaffer in charge of our pursuers. With this gadget we can get him to call off his dogs, and a few other things come to mind, but I'll save those for Stan and Dusty to decide on.'

'Did you go out with the intention of getting him?' I enquired.

'No I just wanted a hostage to bargain with, finding him was a real bonus, and we now have real bargaining power.'

'How did you find him?'

'Oh, I just skirted round to the east, ran hard and caught up with the fire front, skirted along its active perimeter and came upon this wreck. He's that fat that he obviously couldn't outrun the advancing fire and was overtaken by it. He'd fallen into a hollow and must have been overcome by smoke and the fire passed over him, singeing him more than a bit in the process. I though he was dead to start with but as luck would have it he was still with us, so I made him secure before I revived him and invited him to accompany me back to meet everybody, some for the second time. So let's get on and catch up with the others and show them the news and get a decision on what to do with him.'

Off we trotted and after a while Spike, to break the monotony, waxed a bit philosophical and banged on a bit about World Power and keeping a balance to stop the Idi's of the world getting too big for their boots.

'I know of a certain RN Officer who shall remain nameless who had a sharp lesson in balancing power and people,' broke in H.

'He joined the 'P' boat I was wrecking on as Jimmy and immediately got everybody's back up. Officers aren't meant to be liked, but in boats a certain tolerance and benevolence is expected. Our new Jimmy though, started by cracking eggs with a big stick, nothing suited and he did a lot of nit picking, which pissed everybody off.

'His one Achilles Heel was that he was absolutely hopeless at catching a trim and keeping it.'

Catching a trim means getting the overall weight of the boat right so that when dives it is not only neutrally buoyant but also that it is balanced fore and aft, and it is the job of the First Lieutenant to catch the initial trim on the first dive.

'He wouldn't take advice from anyone regarding trimming and at times it was all hell and no notion, with the ballast pump operator in the engine room leaping about like a lunatic, cursing all the time with the intercom running red hot, and the planesmen sweating cobs trying to maintain depth. The boat all the time porpoising and assuming odd fore and aft angles.

'His comeuppance came in the shape of a circus seesawing performance in the guise of a tightrope act with a cyclist on it. Some wag just before said Jimmy was due on his dived watch as OOW, had rigged piano wire tightly between the two periscope masts and put a little balanced bicycle with grooved wheels on it, with a rider whose feet were attached to the pedals, and articulated legs.

'Immediately after being handed over the watch, without noticing the little bike, he started re-trimming with the inevitable results of lost trim, and the cyclist started pedalling backwards and forwards between the two masts.

The buzz went round like wildfire and quite a crowd started gathering quietly in the control room, the stokers from back aft and the dabtoes from forrard all watching this little fella zooming backwards and forwards ever more urgently until his little legs were going like pistons accelerating to a blur in mid traverse. Some of the lads couldn't contain themselves any longer and started with a little giggle that very quickly ended up in roars of uncontrollable laughter which alerted Jimmy to the situation at the same time as the Skipper came out of his cabin to see what all the commotion was about.

'Number One was never the same again and was replaced shortly after this incident, but I understand that he stayed in boats, having calmed down and eventually made a very good Skipper.'

By the time H had finished his yarn we had caught up with the main force because they were being slowed down by the injured members, so an R and R was called to give everybody a spell and Spike could discuss possible uses of his captive with Dusty as Stan was out of it.

Chapter 22

Evacuate 2

On meeting up again, there was a lot of back slapping, hand shaking and general joviality after which we enquired into the state of the wounded. Andy was uncomfortable but OK generally, but Stan's health was giving great cause for concern as he was becoming increasingly delirious.

Spike went into a huddle with Dusty about the use and fate of Idi and came up with a plan to send the opposition on a wild goose chase. It went like this, Dusty and Spike wrote out a script for Idi to broadcast to his gang on his own radio telephone, instructing his gang to quickly head east in a broad sweep to catch up with and capture the fleeing (phantom) intruders and to stay in touch and report back progress and any results. This script was then translated by Ali into Idi's dialect. Idi was then taken to one side by Spike and 'persuaded' to co-operate and also volunteer the name of his 2IC and the call sign of the day. Then the charade was played out with Ali listening in to ensure that the script was strictly adhered to with Spike hovering intimidatingly over the proceedings ready to pounce should Ali signal any deviation from the script. After a quick rehearsal the plan was executed without a hitch, with Idi's 2IC accepting his instructions without hesitation or reservation, which just showed how powerful and autocratic the fat swinish bully was.

This accomplished Dusty rallied the whole team for one more effort to get to the river and the stashed canoes and hence back to Baggy and the village. So off we all trotted, with Spike, H and I again as the rearguard. With everybody again on the move Dusty called up Curly to give him the latest Sit Rep and ETA of approximately two hours which Curly acknowledged and passed on to the rest of his gang.

The whole group made real good progress because of the increasingly good terrain, and also the added incentive that we were on the last lap. When we of the rearguard arrived at the river bank there was lots of exhilaration and congratulations as the base team had come upstream to greet us and assist in the evacuation downstream to Baggy.

Without further ado and with lots of native help the wounded were quickly and very gently loaded. They then took great delight in inviting, none too gently, the ample bulk of Idi to load up, and we all set off apace and in no time at all we were boarding Baggy.

Penny was devastated and visibly distressed when she first saw the state of Stan, but soon resumed her composure and became very professional, got a couple of natives to gently get him below and started administering to his immediate needs. Meanwhile Anna was attempting to help Andy who was not at all used to the fuss, but was told in no uncertain terms to shut up and behave.

Once the injured members had been organized Dusty called the rest of us round to give a Sit Rep and explain the future plan of action.

'The situation thus far is good, we have achieved our objectives in all respects so far. We have overcome some severe difficulties, have lost nobody, on either side to the best of my knowledge, and have left no trace of our identity. This success in no small measure to our native friends.'

Ali translated this to Click who passed it on to his Tribesmen who became all shy and pleasantly embarrassed through a round of our applause. Ali listened to a short remark that Click whispered in his ear which translated as 'We helped each other' which drew another round of applause causing more embarrassment.

'We really need, in a rush, to get out to sea to be evacuated by the RN so I'm straight after this natter going to jack it up. Also I'll be trying to jack up for some of us to become airborne to do and witness the detonation before the damned target is re-floated and slips, so time is of the essence, any questions?'

'Yes Dusty,' from Spike. 'What are we going to do with our fat friend Idi?'

'He'll be going with us to undergo a bit of good old-fashioned debriefing to see if we can find out any more about the perpetrators behind this scam.'

'Can we give Baggy to the villagers when we get picked up?' asked Anna.

'I don't see any reason why not Anna, but I'll seek advice OK?'

'Is there any more we can do to help the locals, it seems such a shame if we have to just abandon them to their miserable existence after all they've done to help us?' So spoke up Ali to nods and murmurs of agreement.

'I have every intention of doing so Ali, but thank you and all of you for reinforcing my resolve in this matter. Now is there anything else quickly as we must crack on, no? OK, all hands to rig Baggy for sea, leave the camouflage on but take her as close to open water as you dare. Betty, Ted and Curly come with me to the radio shack. We'll get in contact with Admiral Hopgood and formulate our future plans.'

It took very little time at all to prepare Baggy for sea and warp her nearer to open water. Stan had been made comfortable, his wound properly treated and dressed, drugs administered along with lots of TLC, and was sleeping peacefully. Andy, meantime, had been dealt with in no uncertain terms, so all that could be done was to brew up and chew the fat.

'This is all a bit tame and boring after the past excitement ain't it?' piped up Danny.

'It's strange and sometimes bizarre when you can get up to when you're bored.' H conceded.

'When I was serving on my first 'P' boat as Wrecker, I used to get constant earache from the engineer about the leaking Torpedo Loading Hatch. I'd tried everything to cure it and it was always OK at periscope depth, but below that the deeper we went the worse it got. It never really got that bad, it was just a nuisance.

'The basic problem was that the loading hatch was set at an angle to the pressure hull axis to enable Fish to be shipped in one long piece. Unfortunately this means that although the hatch is round the hole in the pressure hull is elliptical which is a weakness. To combat this, when the hatch is battened down, Strongbacks (large tight fitting bars) are slotted into crutches across the aperture to prevent hull distortion due to pressure at depth.

'It was a nuisance because as you went through the fore ends access hatch to go forrard up the centres, you always got a neck full. One Skipper's rounds, the Captain got the dreaded neck full and rounded on the Killick fore end man to "do something about it" so he did. On a long boring 3 month Fishplay exercise said Killick started by diverting the steady trickle to one side using a suspended piece of lagging sheathing (half a 2 inch diameter tube of thin aluminium). From then on, every time the skipper did his rounds another bit had been added with considerable ingenuity, and it ended up like a Heath Robinson sculpture with water wheels, tipping scales, little animated animals and roundabouts, seesaws and assorted other gizmos, until finally disappearing into the bilge to be returned from whence it came, to the ogwash. The Skipper couldn't in all fairness complain because his last order was being obeyed.'

'I wasn't so much bored, more frustrated at the inactivity,' Nobby volunteered.

'I'd been stuck in Pompey Barracks for what seemed like forever, working down the Dockyard on my latest Draft for a trip to the Far East. The refit was running behind schedule and all leave was cancelled, not that I as a no badge F-all could do anything about it.

'The snag was that my best mate and Towny's leave wasn't cancelled and on that last weekend leave came back bragging as usual but in the conversation it slipped out that he'd seen my long term girlfriend with some smoothy or other, and I ended up in DQs*'

'What do you mean you ended up in DQs, why?' Pancho queried.

'I took an unofficial trip up homers and duffed up the opposition.'

'You mean you went AWOL* and administered GBH?'

'Yes but it worked.'

'What do you mean it worked?'

'I got out of the Far East draft and I married her and we're very happy.'

'Come on Pancho, what's your boring claim to fame?' Ali queried.

'Oh there's only one I can think of but it wasn't me who was bored, it was the rest of my idle crew. I was at the time Chief Diver of HMS *Reclaim*, the official RN Diving Vessel. We were at anchor, I forget where, but it was somewhere nice and warm. We were supposed to be doing routine maintenance checks on all the diving gear. But the lads were bored and lounging about waiting for stand easy. At the time the main diving bell was deployed over the side and I was in it checking the equipment. The bell has hatches top and bottom and can either be used as an enclosed vessel or open at the bottom to allow exit and entry at depth. The top hatch is for crew entry which is a little difficult as the umbilical and a triple chain set are strung over it. At this particular time, unusually, both hatches were open when some clown accidentally (I hoped) slipped the chain safety clip with the crane fall drum in free run.

'The chamber dropped like a stone, the oggin spouted in at a rate of knots, faster than up the outside because of the differential diameters. The column of water shot me straight out of the top hatch, missing the triple chain, I don't know how, and I managed to grab the coaming of the side entry to the diving flat, where the watertight door had been left open. I dragged myself into the diving flat, soaking wet and bloody furious, and hot footed it to the upper deck to find the whole of the diving crew fully awake and leaning over the rail, caps in hand shaking their heads until I bellowed at them and called them naughty names. It's the closest call I've had for a while I can tell you.'

Chapter 23

Exit

Dusty took Betty, Curly and me into the Radio Shack to knuckle under and formulate a plan of action to extricate ourselves from our present position. The first thing we agreed was to acquaint Hoppy (Admiral Hopgood) with our present position and status – it read:

    FTAO Admiral Hopgood   Ref DOCKSUNK

1) Target primed with Ultra Sonics
2) Attack team evacuated, no fatalities
3) Two (2) casualties, one walking, one stretcher
   Urgent medical assistance required
4) One hostage for interrogation
5) Request one Visitor
6) Can Baggy be donated to Villagers
7) Advise detonation method and possibility of observers
8) Ready for immediate evacuation – Advise
9) Advise rendezvous position

Curly encrypted and transmitted the signal, and Hoppy and his team must have worked double time because suddenly the teleprinter was clattering out a nonsense of letter groups which Curly knuckled under to decipher. It read:

    To Docksunk 2IC   From Hopgood

1)&2) Well done
3) Medical assist avail immediate on evacuation
4) Good
5) Yes
6) Negative, must be completely destroyed in deep water

7) Detonation from air – Observers welcome

  8) Advise opposition activity in immediate area

  9) Evacuate in own time heading N/E – advise when clear of danger area

We looked at each other for a while because some of the answers we didn't expect, but Dusty stood up and suggested that we get on with it.

'Betty, you plot a course out of here and mark a possible RV* point. Curly you keep a listening watch and I'll send somebody up shortly to relieve you while Ted and I get some answers together.'

'Well I've got to agree with 6), we can't afford to leave even the slightest bit of evidence related or linking us to this exercise, but I reckon we could squeeze somebody to lash them up to some sort of help or assistance.' I offered.

'Yes, I suppose you're right, but Anna's going to be not well pleased, but nevertheless more importantly when do we bite the bullet and go?'

'We know the land forces are no immediate threat, but we don't know about the seaborne mining gang, they usually come round just a couple of hours before dusk, but they're a bit inconsistent.'

Dusty fell silent for a while, chewing things over, then piped up.

'If we go now we should be a couple of hours ahead of the mining party and there's nothing else to stop us is there?'

'No, let's do it, by the way what was 5) about?'

'Oh I thought of asking Click if he wanted to come with us to watch the fun.'

'Good idea, you'd better check with Betty to see how far he's got, I'll go and pass on the good and bad news OK?'

Dusty nodded in agreement so I went down to the saloon where everybody had congregated to see how Stan was getting on.

'Listen up people please, I've got some good news and some bad news. The bad news is that we have to dispose of Baggy completely.'

Anna looked stunned, so I carried on quickly before she had a chance to have a go at me.

'But the good news is that we think we may be able to offer other better aid and assistance to the villagers. It has been decided that we slip as soon as possible to avoid the mining vessel because if we wait we won't be able to go till after they've left and it'll be dusk, also the sooner the better for Stan. There is still a possibility of an encounter with the opposition because they are unpredictable, so all weapons to be checked and fully loaded.

Penny, the other very good news is that full medical assistance will be available as soon as we are met. This brought the witness of a smile to her rather strained expression, and a quiet ripple of applause from the rest.

'Oh, one other thing, Ali will you find Click for me so that I can have a word with him. Right, let's get to it, Danny how's your engines, OK I hope?'

Danny nodded and went to his engine room, everybody else dispersed to organize their own things. Eventually Ali turned up with Click in tow looking all worried.

'Ali tell him it's nothing bad.'

The clicking went on a bit and a smile returned to Click's face.

'Now ask him if he would like to come with us to witness the destruction of the cause of his people's problems. Tell him we'll bring him back afterwards.'

As the translated conversation progressed Click's face changed to amazement, then credulity and then sheer joy which gave me the answer without a word being spoken.

Dusty and Betty emerged from the Radio Shack with the estimated time and position of a possible pick up point dependant on our time of departure. So nothing more could be done on that score. But Dusty expressed concern about leaving traces of our presence in the village, and I suddenly thought about all the 'K' ration packaging. The solution though was far simpler than I had expected. Dusty called Click in and asked him through Ali if he would get his tribe's people to scour the whole area to collect anything connected with us, including the bog wipe, which he organized with surprising speed and efficiency. The arisings, which were surprisingly large, were loaded aboard in weighted sacks ready for committing to the deep six* (given the float test*).

Dusty then called a meeting on the upper deck and asked us all if we were ready for the off, to which everybody agreed.

'Right then, there's a remote chance that we may encounter the opposition so anyone on deck must be dressed as before in native attire with arms. Lookouts on deck at all times. We will be keeping a continuous radar watch to give us as much prior warning of an intruder as possible. The rules of engagement are the same as for the run in, OK? As we slip we will be contacting Admiral Hopgood to inform him of the time and he should come back with a rendezvous position and time. Any questions? No, well let's get to it, cast off, Danny flash them engines up, Curly send the time signal, Betty when clear of the channel steer 045, as they say in 'Rawhide' Git em up, Move em out, Yah.'

And off we set with the whole of the village turned out to cheer and dance and wave, especially for Click who was loving every minute of it.

Guess who?

Main Armament Ahmilla Patrol

Idi had been locked in the peak stowage locker, safe out of harm's way. We had hardly any food left as we had given most of it away, but we had tea (no sugar) so Anna made a brew, which was very welcome. We weren't too worried about the food situation because we would soon be picked up, all being well.

Course was set, good speed was being maintained, Danny's engine sounded as sweet as a nut, the weather was glorious, and everything was going according to plan. The weather was that good that everybody ended up on the upper deck to take advantage of it.

I ended up chewing the fat with Ali talking about our experiences of the 'Ahmilla Patrol.' A pathetic attempt by the RN to police the Persian Gulf and general area. It appears that we, on our respective vessels, relieved each other. He told me about the time of the first Iran-Iraq conflict where UK Nationals employed by the Oil Industry were at risk in the Basra area and his vessel was sent to the mouth of the Shat-el-Arab on immediate notice for steam ready to dash up river to carry out an evacuation if required.

'The worst thing was that it was the time of the Shamals, the date-ripening winds coming off the desert, the hottest part of the year. The Deck Apes sat around in the shade fishing, dozing and generally lazing around, while the boiler and engine room gangs were on full watch keeping routine, with pressure up on both boilers and engines turned over every ten minutes, all sweating their little socks off. It caused more than a bit of animosity and a few near punch ups. It was that hot down the machinery spaces that two stokers had eventually to be evacuated, suffering from acute heat exhaustion, the rest of us just kept drinking gallons and eating loads of salt tablets.'

I told him about the time we were anchored off Bahrain, as in those days there was no deep water harbour, the run ashore was dismal with nothing to do and nowhere to go, so most stayed aboard consuming loads of liquid and chucking the empties over the side. These bottles and cans were of some value to the impoverished local community, and pearl divers used to come out in dugouts and small dhows to dive for them around the anchorage using a very ingenious method. A pole was rigged over the side projecting about a couple of feet. A large rock was attached to a length of rope. From the crew of two the elected diver jumps over the side and his mate hands him the rock and the rope is looped over the pole, the diver grasping the bight of the rope and stands on the rock. When ready the diver takes a deep breath, lets go of the bight and allows the rock to carry him to the sea bed, where he steps off and swims around gathering anything of value before he has to surface for air. In the meantime his oppo had hauled up the rock ready for the next dip.

One amusing incident concerning these activities involved our own vessels qualified Shallow Water Diver. Every RN Vessel has at least one qualified diver for obvious security reasons, and they have to keep qualified by doing regular training exercises. Out in the Persian Gulf the water is very often blood heat but it is recommended that a suit be worn to protect the wearer from jelly fish and other stinging creatures. One particularly painful animal looks very much like pulled out orange knitting which tends to drape over the body and stings everywhere it touches.

Anyway this particular time the diver got dressed in a dry suit and re-breathing gear, told his oppos to keep an eye on a couple diving off the Stbd side, and went in over the Port side. He dropped to the bottom and hugging it approached the pearl diver from the rear and tapped him gently on the shoulder. Relating the incident later, our diver said his target's head swung round, caught sight of this big black thing, his eyes nearly popped out like a cartoon character and shot to the surface as if jet propelled. According to rubberneckers on the quarterdeck, the guy shot straight out of the oggin into the boat as if he was on fire and paddled like hell for the shore.'

Our relaxed humorous conversation was rudely interrupted by Curly shouting for Dusty to get to the radar shack.

'We have a radar contact approaching bearing 180.'

'Secure the radar set, action stations everybody, Ali the same signal applies. Ted, you and H don't know the routine we've perfected, and there's no time to explain. Keep your heads down and when the shit hits do your best.'

So H and I armed ourselves, made ourselves as inconspicuous as possible and waited for the inevitable to unfold.

The contact turned out to be, as predicted, the mining vessel, with very bad timing, and it was obvious that it had spotted us and was bearing down fast on us.

Dusty decided on us acting the lame duck because, as he explained later, the opposition had to be stopped, as to try and outrun them would be long and protracted and would lead to all sorts of complications with regard to the rendezvous being delayed. So the scene was set for yet another confrontation with possible nasty complications, Spike and Dusty went into a huddle to discuss tactics, then Dusty hurriedly called a full emergency meeting.

'Pay attention, time is short, we can't afford to hang about for all sorts of good reasons, not the least of which is Stan's condition. The approaching vessel is large enough to carry adequate life saving equipment on board so we are going to sink it under them and let them take to the life rafts or whatever to maintain our policy of preventing loss of life. If they use small arms from the rafts we respond vigorously.'

'How do we sink the damned thing?' Piped up Danny.

'We issue all six grenade launchers we have and aim for the water line on Spike's order to fire, Spike explain.'

'Dusty, myself, H, Ted, Nobby and Pancho will have the launchers, aim for the waterline particularly back aft where the engine room and fuel are if possible. You have 303 facilities on the launchers in case we take incoming fire. Wait for my signal as the launchers have limited range.'

'Thanks Spike, Ali make sure you keep Click safe. Curly you take the wheel and engine controls and try to manoeuvre in such a way as to expose their beam to us, and when the action starts try and round their stern. Penny keep a listening watch on the radio and let me know if anything important comes in. Betty we haven't any native clobber to fit you so just stay out of sight because you'll stick out like a sore thumb. Any questions, no, OK then let's get to it.'

Slowly and inextricably the inevitable unfolded before us and the fear and adrenaline started to come to the fore. Dusty told Ali to stall them as long as possible and tell them we had steering problems or some such bull dung.

Spike then gave the six launcher owners a quick briefing on their operation and the stage was set with everybody apparently loafing about on deck.

A loud hailer rent the apparent calm of the day. Ali stood up slowly and cupped his hands to his ears faking deafness, which drew the opposition a bit further in. Again the loud hailer blasted the air telling us to heave too, to which Ali replied in a different dialect with a typical eastern shake of the head, which put them into a state of confusion and closer still. They tried another dialect to which Ali just shrugged which caused even more confusion and consternation and a huddle on the foredeck, which dragged the deck gunner away from his charge and into the discussion. Then they all leant on the handrail calling in all sorts of different dialects for Ali to respond to, and drew them ever closer.

Spike was keeping a careful eye on things and suddenly in a low voice called

'Stand by.'

A few more yards and Curly put a couple of points of starb'd wheel on to ease us even closer. A few more yards and,

'NOW'

And all hell broke loose. Curly slammed the engines full astern and wheel hard over to close the range and get them to expose their beam. Explosions rent the waterline, the deck gunner went to go back to his charge but was dissuaded by a burst of 303 from Dusty. Danny was chuffed to get a grenade hit on a fuel tank, which set the stern on fire. The whole vessel started to list into the damage and the fire started to migrate forrard which caused panic to set in. Another grenade from Spike demolished the wheel house as Curly put the engines ahead and veered away from a potential explosion, and the disorganized crew decided to abandon ship which, with the general panic was accomplished by a minor miracle. It appears that there were only minor injuries and no fatalities, which was the whole object of the exercise. The wreaked vessel slid slowly underwater leaving a scattering of debris and an ever widening oil slick.

The only mistake that was made in this part of the fracas was the supervision of Idi, who had somehow managed to get free just before the fun started. What happened next is a little unclear, but it appears that as the shooting started he had jumped over the side away from the action and started to swim round and head towards his colleagues. We were all too busy to notice his disappearance until after the cease-fire. The alarm was raised by Anna who informed Dusty, but by that time we saw some thrashing in the water, then we saw the unfortunate Idi who had also seen the menace. Unfortunately, by this time he was midway between havens and hadn't a cat in hell's chance of reaching either. The sharks had initially been attracted to the area as a direct result of the mining operation providing easy pickings of dead and stunned fish. Unfortunately Idi was now easy food as his hideous screams indicated, and eventually attracted three or four more sharks to the grisly feast, much to our dismay and horror, and his colleagues' fright and fear for their own safety.

After a short while to weigh up the situation, Dusty got us to cautiously approach the rafts keeping them under constant armed surveillance, but they were in a deep state of shock and not going to cause any trouble. We lashed them up to first aid equipment after checking that none of them had any arms or ammunition and left them to their fate with the natives in the village.

For our part, after our adrenaline rush and all the excitement and mayhem, we set course N/E once again for a rendezvous point, which was still to be determined, so Dusty called Curly and Betty to the radio shack to acquaint Admiral Hopgood of the present situation, so a signal was drafted which read:

FTAO Admiral Hopgood   Ref DOCKSUNK

1) Negative Opposition this Area

2) Will be clear of area in 3 hours

3) Position @ that time – (position given)

4) Please advise

Curly encrypted and transmitted it and again in no time at all the teleprinter was away again. Curly deciphered it and it read:

To DOCKSUNK 2. IC					From Hopgood

1) 	Set Demolition charges
2) 	Deploy radar Reflector
3) 	Heave to when @ predicted position and stand by.

Chapter 24

Lift

With Betty's help we arrived at our RV position and hove to as instructed. The radar reflector was hoisted on a jury* rigged mast, and Dusty and Spike disappeared below to lay demolition charges to Andy's instructions. The problem with it, as Andy explained was that a wooden vessel is very difficult to sink, and the only way to destroy any evidence is to completely disintegrate it, which requires massive amounts of explosives which we didn't have. His solution was to rig all the small arms ammunition, hand grenades and launcher grenades along with containers of fuel and the remains of the plastic explosive primed and scattered throughout the hull, so that the combination of explosions and resultant fires would destroy all evidence of Baggy's existence.

Stan was brought to the upper deck and an awning rigged to shade him. He didn't look too bad but was as high as a kite on drugs. The oggin was like a mill pond, not even a slight swell or a ripple, to coin a phrase, like glass. Evening was fast approaching and the air cooling down to a comfortable degree. The rest of us just loafed about drinking black unsweetened tea, kind permission of Anna, but we were beginning to hate the taste.

We were all getting bored with waiting and getting frustrated at the delay, which reminded me of an incident that occurred on my first 'O' boat, so I thought I'd tell the tale to break the boredom a bit:

'In conventional boats the scarcest commodity is fresh water as the storage tanks are of very limited capacity and the electric distillation units are about as handy as a chocolate fire guard, and most of what's available is used by the chef. It's a well known fact in boats circles that the ones with the cleanest jobs washed the most. I was Panel* watch keeper at the time and this poncy Ping Bosun* was stomping up and down the after passage with his little towel round his neck and his soap bag in his sticky little fist, past me and kept looking down into the troops' bathroom (two wash hand basins) and chuntering to himself. Eventually he got on my nerves so much that I stopped him and asked him why he was wearing a groove in the decking and what the chuff was up. He pointed down the ladder to the bathroom entrance and said,

"He's been down there about half an hour, and if he doesn't shift soon I'm going to go down and shift him.'

'I looked down and all I could see was this large lump of pink flesh in the entrance to the bathroom but nothing else, then I got called away to do a panel operation. After another ten minutes Ping gave a snort of rage and shot down the ladder to sort things out, then suddenly there were roars of laughter coming from below. It appears that the Coxswain* had decided to treat the lads as it was his birthday and so had taken this monster turkey out of the deep freeze and had put it in the wash hand basin to thaw out.

'The outcome was that we all enjoyed our turkey dinner.'

This story prompted H to tell the one about the magic torch.

'I was on my first 'P' boat and was wreaking at the time and the story involved Snorting. For the uninitiated snorting is the process of running the main Diesel Engines while submerged by drawing combustion air down a mast called the snort induction. The reason for doing this is to enable the battery capacity to be conserved or even charged up whilst avoiding radar detection.

'This particular time we were running deep and the Skipper ordered the OOW to initiate snorting. So the Jimmy who was OOW picked up the rubber covered microphone from its stowage between the two planesmen and ordered over the Tannoy.

"Stand by to Snort, go to black lighting."

'Black Lighting was in fact pin points of red light used to acclimatize the Control room crew to the darkness up top. The rest of the boat staying with normal lighting. Jimmy then told the planesmen to come slowly to periscope depth and on the way up had Asdics do an all round sweep to check the area clear. On gaining periscope depth the Skipper had an all round look with the search scope to further check the area was clear to continue with the snort exercise. At this time it was the change of watch and the new Subby* took over from the Jimmy.

'The normal position for the microphone was laid across the stowage for convenience sake, but just before black lighting Jimmy had been looking for a small suspected water leak behind the main panel and used a waterproof rubber torch to look for it, but the batteries failed, so at black lighting he put the microphone in its stowage and the duff torch on top with the intention of changing batteries as soon as convenient.

'The radar mast was raised and the screen checked clear so the Skipper told the Subby to start snorting, so Subby picked up what he thought was the microphone to transmit all the complex instructions required to perform this evolution, but was in fact the duff torch which I spotted. So I grabbed the Chef and explained the situation and he set up a command chain to the Donk Shop Horse and Ballast Pump* Operator so that all instructions supposedly over the Tannoy were transmitted verbally and all responses to the orders came back to the control room via the tannoy as normal. On securing from Snorting all orders were again transmitted verbally. Eventually the Skipper ordered the Subby to go deep and revert to white lighting.

'The lights came on, the Subby went to put the microphone back in its stowage and realized it was a torch. Looking absolutely horrified, he had a quick all round sweep to see if anyone else had noticed. When he thought nobody had, as everybody involved in the scam had melted away he surreptitiously replaced the torch on top of the storage and carried on as if nothing unusual had happened and to this day I'm sure he's still confused.'

We were still waiting for something to happen, so Ali and I got nattering some more and it appears he was out the Persian Gulf the same time-ish that I was. The reason we realized this was that he happened to mention the incident involving the collision of two tankers in the Indian Ocean and I said *Ferdinand Gilabert* and *Melika,* and we were both amazed because he said yes that was them. We both agreed that it was almost beyond belief that in that day and age with all the technology and all that oggin in the Indian Ocean and in broad daylight, that two huge vessels could collide. The *Melika* had a hole in her side that you could park four double decker buses alongside each other. She'd caught fire back aft so the crew had abandoned her and left her steaming into the distance. The only reason she stopped was that the oil fired boiler ran out of fuel. *Ferdinand Gilabert*'s bow had been completely stove in and only the deck was still intact, but flapping badly in the swell.

I got a double wammy from the incident because I, as a junior Tiff, was detailed off to accompany a senior Tiff to repair the fire damaged fridge gear on the *Melika* so that it could be re-stored because the crew wouldn't return aboard until it had been done. The job was a pain in the arse because apart from having to climb aboard up a never ending rope ladder, the fridge pipe work was lagged with cork and we both ended up as black as the hobs of hell, good stuff burnt cork, ask Al Jolson. Then once that was done we were ordered to tow *Ferdinand Gilabert* to Karachi. Because of the damaged bow we had to tow her stern first to prevent excess pressure on the exposed bulkhead. The whole crew turned to to hump anchor cable back aft, two links per man, to weigh down the tow line. The snag was that the rudder was jammed hard over to starb'd, she kept veering over to our port to an alarming angle before shooting back on track and then doing it all over again. To try to keep on track and combat this effect we had to run the port engine at maximum revs and starb'd just ticking over. Then I got the second wammy because they wanted me to be part of the boarding party to try and centre the rudder. We'd been joined by a couple of destroyers and a carrier and they were going to shift us by helicopter and land us on the floppy foredeck. The helicopter winched our gear and tools aboard and then plans were changed and we all lost our gear. Another set of lads were landed on and eventually centred the rudder, but found that the fresh water was contaminated so they broke into the bonded store and quenched their thirst on wine. It appears that by the time we reached Karachi they were all rat arsed. When we eventually got to Karachi the Port Authority refused us entry because our charge was leaking fuel slightly, so our Skipper informed them that after a very difficult towing operation, if they didn't accept the vessel he'd put a 4in brick in it and sink the damned thing in the harbour entrance shallows, so the Authorities allowed us to leave it with them.

The good bit that came out of it was that I got £35 as a 4th class Tiff which was a lot of money for those days. I'm led to believe that the salvage money for this occurrence is still the highest paid to the RN and was in the multi-millions, and as a bonus we were all presented with tankards for donating blood to treat the injured.

It was early evening by this time and everybody was a bit fed up hanging about waiting expectantly when Ali, who had very acute hearing, looked skyward to the north east and held up a hand for silence. From the far distance a very quiet thrashing sound emanated, becoming slowly louder then the flashing lights were sighted and then into view came a whole flock of helicopters. We recognized the pair of big Sikorsky Sea Kings first, then a couple of fully armed Huey Cobra Gun Ships as escort which made us all wonder what the Yanks were doing in this neck of the woods. We also all thought we would have to be winched off into the Sea Kings which wouldn't help Stan's condition much, but one came very close to us, close enough for us to feel the down wash and proceeded to deploy flotation aids and landed on the oggin.

A large RIB* was launched from it and a crew member piloted it across to us. Stan and Andy went first with Betty, who gently manhandled Stan with Penny in attendance. They were loaded aboard the Sea King and the RIB came back for the rest of us, needless to say that Click was at his wits' end and Ali was hard pushed to reassure him that everything was all right and normal. As we boarded the chopper a broadly grinning Flight Lieutenant Bob Khan greeted us all, but Anna in a more friendly way. H, ever the John Blunt, enquired,

'What the hell are you doing hanging around here, up to no good I suppose?'

'I've come to see how Anna is.'

'How did you get here then?'

'Ah, that's classified, you'll have to wait and see,' he said with a glint in his eye and a grin and a wink.

Dusty, as gaffer, was lashed up to headphones and microphone and plugged into the intercom system and spoke to the Captain. The Sea King's engines wound up, a slight, urgent type vibration started and we slowly unglued from the sea surface in a flurry of fine spray, did a wide sweep round and took up station about two hundred yards to the north of Baggy. Dusty produced the detonator remote unit and handed it to Andy who with great reverence pressed the tit and we all watched as Baggy disappeared in a cloud of black and orange. We all felt the pressure wave and slight after shock before the eruption subsided and revealed just a widening area of little bits and pieces that were Baggy, our home for the last few days, and we all felt a great sense of loss.

Then with a wide sweep round we headed off into the semi-dusk flanked by the other Sea King and the two gun ships which gave us all a very secure feeling.

After what didn't seem very long we looked out on the incredible sight of a huge American Nuclear Powered Super Carrier, and in no time at all we had landed on and it was even bigger than we thought possible. The reception party treated us like royalty in typical American fashion. Stan and Andy, with Penny still in attendance, were whisked away to the sick bay and we were ushered into a beautifully furnished conference room, and in our scruffy state, felt a bit out of place.

A door opened at the far end of the compartment and in strode none other than Admiral Hopgood, grinning like a Cheshire cat, followed by his Flags* and a few others including Bob Khan. Hoppy came round and shook everybody by the hand and delivered a few words.

'Well done everybody, a magnificent effort under very difficult conditions, the finale will be played out shortly. We have surveillance over the target and everything is well in hand and you have sufficient time for a wash and brush up and a nice meal. I'm sure you will all agree with me that our American friends have pulled out all the stops to co-operate and assist us in our endeavours to combat terrorism, for which the UK Government is extremely grateful, and I'm sure you will be looked after very well indeed. Now I would like to introduce you all to our host Admiral Alwyn L. Shults, Officer commanding the American Eastern Fleet.'

With that a rather dapper chap in full Admiral's uniform and lots of Fruit Salad* stepped forward and was very short and sweet.

'I will not take up much of your time. Welcome, very well done, I aim to make sure you finish the job you started. Anything you want is yours, please take full advantage of our hospitality, thank you again.' And we all gave him a round of applause.

He was true to his word, all we had to do was ask and we got it, and we were all unanimous in asking for a cup of tea with milk and sugar, and it was nectar. While we were supping it H found out that Bob on his return to Cyprus found out that a volunteer was required to fly escort to a Transport Command Aircraft carrying some bigwig into the Indian Ocean. He put two and two together, made a few discreet enquiries, and went for it for now obvious reasons.

Next on the agenda was a wash and brush up in the palatial bathrooms, where we luxuriated far too long. Then we were lashed up* to the very finest American lagging*, and then on to the scran*. I've never seen so much good food in all my life, the quality superb, the quantity enormous, suffice to say we overindulged ourselves. You can imagine how overwhelmed Click was, and Ali was having a bit of a problem too.

H and I decided to visit Stan and Andy, so our guide took us to the Sick Bay, which was more like a full blown hospital. We found Penny and Andy waiting in a rest room for Stan to come out of the operating theatre, where they were assured that a top Orthopaedic Surgeon was sorting him out. Andy confirmed that he had been sorted out and his arm was in plaster and was told by the Doctor that it was A-OK and that there would be no complications, which was good news.

To take Penny's mind off the present I related the trip we did in my 'O' boat to Norfolk Virginia.

'We started out from Gare Loch to surface transit across the Pond*. But as soon as we stuck our nose out after Ireland we hit roughers* and I grabbed my bucket to contain my mal-de-mare. Problems arose almost immediately because we were the first boat to be fitted with a fibreglass casing* and it had started to break up. We kept going with the OOW keeping a careful eye on the damages progress. It became critical when the after-escape buoy aerial deployed and started transmitting our Subsunk distress call. The skipper was informed and went up top to look for himself, having told the radio shack to transmit a cancellation of the distress signal and then ordered a couple of Dabtoes* to get rigged in safety gear and harnesses and go and sort the thing out. We then hove too and as the lads got onto the casing and clipped on the whole of the restraining covers flew off and the buoy popped out and over the side still transmitting. It was eventually recovered and silenced, but the casing problem persisted so the Skipper, to limit the damage, ordered a surface snort transit. This involved the induction mast raised for Engine Combustion air but with the conning tower hatch left open and normal

Roughers on the 'Pond'

watch keepers on the fin with the boat trimmed down to cut through the waves rather than ride them. It helped reduce the casing damage but the poor sods on the fin kept taking green ones and the control room didn't fare much better as columns of oggin kept shooting down into it, the poor sod on the helm taking the worst of the soaking.

'Eventually the weather abated and the extend of the damaged casing was assessed and a signal sent to Their Lordships requesting replacement sections which were waiting for us when we eventually arrived. We fitted it all with help from some of our Buddy boat crew in sweltering weather. The American Buddy boat system was great and I hope it still exists because it made visitors to the States feel very welcome. The idea was that your boat was moored alongside a USN boat and their crew looked after yours, and they did it very well too, pandering to your every whim, and quite often taking you up homers*. They also organized group activities like barbecues and baseball matches. All in all we had a wonderful time after a lousy start.'

A short while after that little story Stan was booled out followed by his surgeon who took Penny to one side and explained what was wrong and what had been done to put it right. She came over afterwards and gave us the gist of the discussion. The surgeon said that the first aid that had been administered had been most effective, for which all three of us were very thankful and relieved. The infection was under control and the prognosis was good. So we left Stan, who was still anaesthetized, to come round with Penny by his side, and rejoined the main party who were real pleased to hear the good news and also pleased to see Andy looking fit and well, apart from the pot.

We were then invited to take a Cook's tour of the carrier, which was incredible because of the facilities that were available. The crew wanted for nothing, they worked very hard it's true, but off watch the amenities were second to none. Every conceivable recreational facility was available, and the PX put our equivalent NAAFI to shame, it was like an up market superstore, in fact the whole vessel was run like a small town.

We had been fed and watered and cleaned up and clothed and now we were allocated billets and invited to get our heads down, having been assured that the final act would be played out in the morning.

I for one slept like a log, I hadn't realized how weary I had become and I think everybody else in the party felt the same.

Chapter 25

Shufti*

So come the morrow we were all raring to go after a superb breakfast with a choice of absolutely anything you fancied. A lot of the crew I noticed had a huge steak with eggs on top.

I slid off and visited the sick bay to find Penny and Stan having a good natter. Stan looked an awful lot better than the last time I'd seen him, and told me he was feeling great, but couldn't remember much about the immediate past. Penny looked extremely weary but absolutely over the moon at Stan's improved condition and told me that the surgeon had said that given plenty of time and lots of TLC he would be as good as new. So I left them to it and went back to give the rest of the gang the good news, which put everybody in a good humour.

We were then invited to join Admirals Shultz and Hopgood on the Island Bridge where we watched the activities of the flight deck crew who were highly efficient. The takeoffs were fascinating and highly organized, but the landings were something else, they came in at incredible speed and unless waved off, just cut the throttles and dropped like a stone in what seemed to us to be a controlled crash, and came to a shuddering halt with the arrester wire as if a brick wall had been hit, and I take my hat off to the Jockeys. But for me the greatest spectacle of all was when the aircraft about to land had made a bad approach and was waved off and the pilot gave it full throttle to go round again. The noise, even inside the double glazed bridge, was horrendous, you didn't so much hear the noise as feel it, as the very air rattled and shook, you have to experience it to really understand what I mean.

During the course of our rubbernecking Flags brought Penny up to join us and got a little round of applause as she greeted everybody and explained that Stan was an awful lot better and had ordered her to join us. Flags then moved over to Hoppy and quietly passed on some information. Shortly after which Hoppy called for our attention.

'Ladies and Gentlemen, it's a real pleasure to welcome Penny back with us, especially with the good news about Captain Westerman's much improved health.' A round of applause followed the news of Stan's promotion.

'Now if you cast your gaze forrard you may soon spot your transport which is winging its way to us at this very moment.'

We all turned our gaze up front and strained to see what he was talking about, and then in the distance we saw a dot trailing a faint smoke haze which grew bigger and bigger and eventually developed into a rather large Transport Aircraft. By the time it did a flypast for a landing approach it looked almost too large to fit on the flight deck, but it came on in anyway and made a perfect touchdown. With our bird's eye view of it we realized it was an AWACS* Aircraft. You know the sort, a large aeroplane with what looks like a big umbrella on top of it. We were informed that its official designation was a 'Northrop Grumman E–2C Hawkeye' equipped with two Allinson T56-A–427 Turboprop Engines which were fitted with reversible pitch constant speed propellers. No sooner had it touched down than it was descended on by all the servicing and refuelling crews. It was explained that a quick turn round was essential to ensure continuity of surveillance.

We were all then led away to be rigged up in flying gear, which Click found most uncomfortable because he was used to running about semi-naked, but Ali managed to persuade him that it was necessary. When we were ready and the AWACS had been prepared we all trooped across the flight deck led by Hoppy and entered the strange world of surveillance. The whole of the inside of the aircraft was lined with electronic instruments, an incredible sight. We were allocated seats with head restraints facing forrard and secured tightly with full harnesses. The Captain came across the intercom telling us to stand by for take off, the engines wound up to screaming pitch and the whole airframe trembled, then suddenly the steam catapult* was actuated and it was as if you had been hit in the back with a sledge hammer, then as soon as it started things calmed down and we were airborne and gaining height rapidly.

The Captain came back aft and introduced himself and informed us that we were approaching operating altitude and that we would be over the operating area in twenty minutes and that we could now unbuckle and stretch our legs and ask questions if we wished. So we ended up with another Cook's Tour, this time round the inside of a flying eye in the sky, the umbrella being the high resolution radar, but to me the more important gadget was the downward looking camera the image of which was displayed on a large screen which would be handy at the appropriate time.

I showed Dusty and Spike the camera system and they agreed with me that it would be handy to witness the results of our handiwork. Then we got nattering and Spike got me going by asking me what year I was out the Persian Gulf.

'I finished my apprenticeship '57-'58 – why?'

'A mate of mine was out there about that time and he reckoned he and some crazy sailor built a canoe out of an old packing crate.'

'That crazy sailor was me, and you're talking about Jumper Collins.'

'Bloody hell you're right, it's a small world ain't it, did you really build a canoe?'

'Yes, it's all a bit bizarre really, we were anchored off Bahrein and as I've already said it was a rubbish run ashore in those days, but there was a canteen just off the jetty. This particular evening our Chief Stoker went ashore and got absolutely rat arsed and on his way back aboard through the yard saw a self contained air condition unit, and being a big lad he thought, in his confused state, that the Captain might like it for his day cabin. So he hoisted it onto his shoulder and carried on to the end of the jetty for the last Liberty boat* which was waiting for him. He peered down, saw the boat, shouted Below* and dropped it aboard from a great height. The reason that it was from a great height was the fact that the tide had gone out and the AC unit hit the prop shaft at a rate of knots and bent it like a banana. Another sea boat had to be sent to tow the damaged Liberty boat back together with the Chief Stoker. Chiefy was on Captain's Report for being adrift and damaging Pussers* property. What didn't help his cause very much was meeting the Captain first thing the next morning when the Skipper was having his morning constitutional and saying to him in a jovial fashion,

'Good morning Sir, you look about as bad as I feel.' Which went down like a lead fart, and for which he was suitably punished, but we all had a good laugh about it in the end.

'The sequel to the incident was that a new prop shaft had to be requisitioned and was eventually shipped out to us, and caught up with us when we were tied up alongside the jetty in Kuwait.

'I was the Tiff who was detailed off to fit the new shaft, and possession being nine tenths of the law, I commandeered the packing crate it came in. I took it apart very carefully because, although it was only softwood, it was good quality and reasonably knot free, and just the right length for a two man canoe. I conned a Bootneck* (Jumper Collins) into helping me, but I think he was keener than me. We borrowed a rip saw off the Chippy* and laboriously and sweatily cut the planks into strips to make stringers, and bummed marine ply offcuts from the Chippy for formers (frames) and canvas and paint of the Buffer* for skinning and waterproofing, and we proceeded to build a canoe.

'Most of the crew thought we were crackers, some took the urine, and some were amused and kept asking what we were going to call it. Being thoroughly teed off with the stupid question, in desperation one day when the same question was asked Jumper, without thinking called it Fred.'

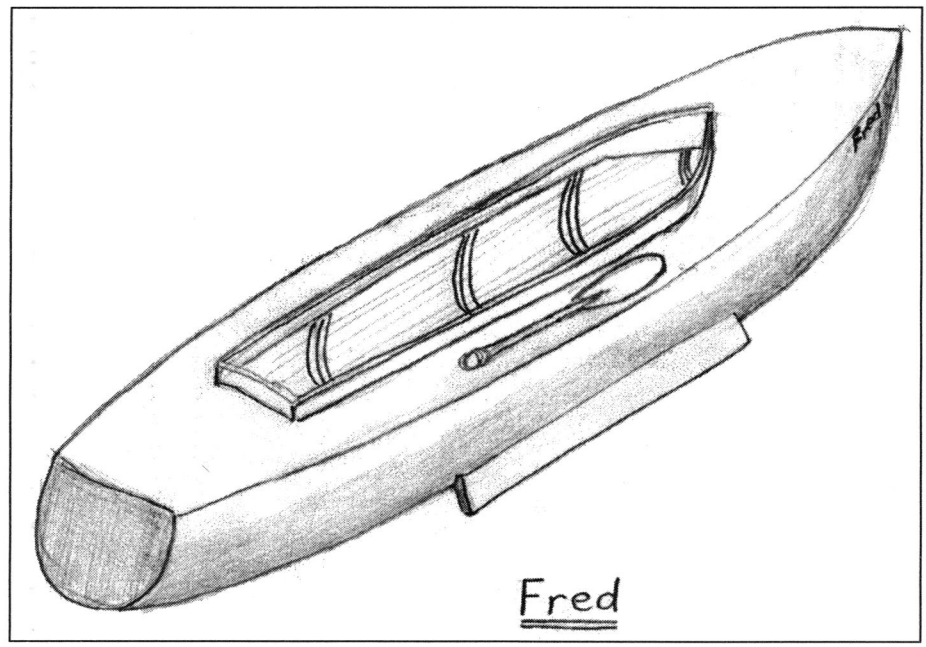

'Fred,' Dusty almost shouted, 'and we thought he was making it up and spinning us a line!'

'Yup, Fred it was, and from then on the name stuck and rubber neckers would regularly come by to see how Fred was coming along.

'We eventually gave it a good coat of paint and Jumper did a fair job of painting Fred Flintstone on the bow, a couple of paddles were fashioned and Fred was finished and it looked good even though I say it myself, and Jumper and I had some real good fun in it. But initially we had a bit of a stability problem in that it tended to capsize. After a bit of thinking and consultation with the Chippy we attached a couple of bilge keels and the problem was solved.

'We showed how good it was by going on longer and longer voyages, with permission of course, and on one occasion ended up on some rich people's private beach, but instead of being booted off we were invited to join the party they were having and were fascinated to learn about our home-made vessel. We eventually left having eaten our fill and a little the worse for wear booze wise, but managed somehow to paddle our way back with no mishaps.

'Interest increased amongst the crew and we eventually started to lend it out and it became a very popular recreational activity. Unfortunately on one occasion one of the pair that borrowed it this particular time was very fair skinned and very susceptible to sunburn, and having suffered badly in the past, always covered up well. Unfortunately this particular time he wore one of the, then new, nylon shirts which, unbeknown to him offered next to no protection. The pair had a good canoeing trip and on returning and restowing Fred, went below for a shower and the poor unfortunate on removing his shirt also removed most of the skin from his back which had stuck to it. He ended up in great pain and on a fizzer* for negligence.

The only real snag with Fred was that it weighed a ton mainly because of the heavy duty canvas used and the large quantity of paint we had to use to make it watertight. We were ordered to stow it on the boat deck which was quite high up. It was not too bad for launching but to haul it back up afterwards was more than hard work and a pain in the bum. I can't remember exactly what happened to it but I think we donated it to some children from Bahrein.'

My thoughts were interrupted by the Skipper of the Hawkeye who announced on the intercom that we were about to climb into some high cloud so as to approach the target area undetected.

This information reminded H of an exercise he was on in his 'P' boat involving the American Atlantic Fleet with all their up to the minute Vessels and equipment.

'We were operating off the north West coast of Ireland, and our job was to avoid the destroyer screen and attack the aircraft carrier that they were protecting. Easier said than done because apart from the destroyers having modern Sonar, the carrier's armament included helicopters equipped with 'Dunking' Sonar. The idea of Dunking Sonar was that the helicopters were directed to possible contact areas by the destroyers and having arrived come to the hover and winch down a Sonar sensor and dunk it in the oggin where a specialist crew member checks for contacts and directs destroyers on depth charge runs accordingly. The helicopters also adopted team tactics to check larger area.

'What our Skipper did to outwit the opposition was worked out the mean course of the Flotilla as it was zig zagging and circled round in front of its track. When we had achieved this he ordered Silent Routine and all machinery was stopped, carpets laid on steel decks, fluorescent lights switched off (they buzz) and all crew off watch turned in. The only thing left running was the hover pump, a small silent pump adding or discharging ballast water to maintain neutral buoyancy and depth.

'Our passive hydrophones were used to track the fleet's progress and eventually detected that the Van* had passed over us and we had avoided detection. The Skipper allowed a short while to elapse and then ordered slow ahead, periscope depth, and we crept slowly up heading for the carrier.

'Let's Twist Again'

'I was Wrecking at the time and had just desiccated* the Attack Periscope and our REM*. Bogey Knight who was a photography nut had recently serviced the periscope camera which was lucky for us both because the Captain ordered the camera to be loaded with film and attached to the Attack periscope.

'After what seemed like an age and a few quick shufties and all round sweeps through the attack scope the Skipper informed the crew over the intercom that the Capital Ship (carrier) was about to run over us. He then ordered one hundred foot depth, and before long we heard faint prop noises from the Target. We went back to Silent Routine and the Gaffer called Scratcher* to the Control Room and gave him specific instructions. We found out afterwards that as a music buff Scratch was ordered to rig his record player up close to the Underwater Telephone* and sort out the record of Bill Haley and the Comets. Then at the precise time that the carrier was overhead the Skipper ordered the Underwater Telephone switched on and turned up to full volume and 'Let's Twist Again' shattered the depths. It was switched off after the first two lines and we went back to Silent Routine and the Sonar Shack reported that all the escorts had turned in towards the carrier.

'The object of the exercise was for the destroyers to try and locate us and if successful to drop hand grenades on us and when we considered we were hit we were to discharge a smoke candle, but nothing came anywhere near close to warrant a candle although they must have wasted hundreds of grenades. So after a while the Gaffer took us up slowly and silently to Periscope depth, had a quick all round sweep with the attack Scope and then proceeded to take photographs and used the whole roll of film up.

'We then went deep and the camera was given to the REA with instructions to process the film and print anything that looked interesting. What Bogey did was truly magnificent, the whole roll of film was printed and some more interesting shots he enlarged. I managed to thieve a couple of small prints but most of them were a lot better quality.

'There were lots of shots of the carrier, lots more of the escort destroyers, but the best ones were of the helicopters. In some of the shots you could see that the Pilot was Joe Bloggs as his head was hanging out of the cockpit and you could see the 'Electric String' dangling down with a Dunking Sonar on the end of it.

'After any Naval exercise there is always what is called a washup* where all participating Skippers and their entourage gather with charts, tracks and logs etc., to analyse the outcome of the exercise. The Senior Officer, in this case the American Admiral of the carrier, is always the Chairman in charge of the washup. After lengthy discussions and pourings over all the evidence presented, the Admiral concluded that the Americans had won and that 'there were no British submarines in my carrier's area.' Whereupon our Skipper reportedly opened his briefcase, dug out a large handful of very large photographs and flung them towards the Admiral who, on inspecting them, went a funny shade of puce, looked as if he was about to explode, and stormed out of the room with all his hangers on scurrying along behind him. We all reckoned that Joe Bloggs was in for more than a bit of an upping, and the Skipper of Destroyer 824 and the Jockey of Helicopter number 59 we reckoned were not going to get away scot free.'

Shortly after the telling of the tale the Aircraft Captain came over the intercom to inform us that we were about to over fly the specified area.

Chapter 26

Boom

With the announcement from the Hawkeye Skipper, the atmosphere was becoming more and more charged with expectation. We all converged on the large screen as we came below the thin high clouds. Click suddenly started jumping up and down as he recognized the approaches to his village and Accra Island. Then we passed over the Naval Base when suddenly one of the operators reported an incoming missile of unknown type. The aircraft immediately took violent evasive action banking hard to port, throwing us into a big heap, whilst a crew member discharged decoy flares, which thankfully worked, but the ensuing blast was a bit too close for comfort and gave the Hawkeye a bit of a shake-up and got everybody's adrenaline flowing well. The skipper, having successfully evaded this particular attack, decided to clear the area and regain higher safer altitude.

This reminded me of a story one of our Stokers on *Vectra* told us about when he was serving on his first 'P' boat. This particular incident happened when this boat was doing discharge trials in Loch Long on the West coast of Scotland. Discharge trials were exercised to test the efficiency of the Fore Ends crew and equipment firing and reloading torpedoes.

Loch Long as its name implies is long and straight, ideal for launching torpedoes which are fitted with blowing heads instead of explosives so that they surface when they run out of fuel and are recovered by civilian MFV's seconded to the RN.

Anyway it appears that halfway through the trials the hydraulic reload system became unserviceable and the old fashioned block and tackle method had to be resorted to, so off watch Stokers were 'volunteered' to make up the numbers, including our green storyteller. Being new to the job he was tail end charley on the haul line so he was nearest to the short ladder leading to the Watertight Bulkhead Door.

Things were going quite well although, understandably, a little slower than normal so orders were given to speed things up. Unfortunately on the very next reload the Fish stuck halfway up the spout, so an extra effort was called for and the gang gave an extra special 2 – 6 heave and the Fish slid forward at a rate of knots, overshot the top stop (which was supposed to lock it in position) and hit the outer door with a loud clang, springing it off its watertight seat momentarily. The result was the sound of rushing water and a gout of oggin shot from round the Fish.

The next thing our Stoker knew was that he was laying face down at the bottom of the ladder with the bulkhead door being slammed shut and clipped with pain and footprints in the middle of his back. Being green our poor unfortunate didn't realize the implications of the overshoot, but the old hands knew the possible scenario and took immediate evacuation action and, because he wasn't fast enough, used him as a stepping stone.

The moral of the story is, know when and how to take evasive action.

The AWACS regained the higher altitude light cloud and came in for another pass with the whole of the crew on full alert ready for further possible aggressive action. We all crowded round the screen again and as we passed over the target area again we vaguely saw the ex-AFD through the cloud. The skipper came on the intercom again and explained that the target area had been filmed and we would swing round and make just one more pass and advised us to initiate the detonation as he was not prepared to take another run over the area for safety reasons.

Dusty then produced the detonator and handed it to Admiral Hopgood and invited him to do the honours which he accepted, he said, on behalf of Commander Westerman as this was the culmination of his meticulous and so far successful planning.

As we re-approached the area the thin cloud broke, Hoppy pressed the tit and we all stared at the screen willing it to show us a spectacular eruption, but all we saw was a slight disturbance around the dock, and then the cloud closed back in on us again, and another incoming missile was reported with decoy flares and evasive manoeuvres and us in a big heap ensuing again, but this time there was more warning, and the missile was detonated well away from us.

The flight back was very subdued and not at all what we had anticipated, but Hoppy tried to cheer us up by saying that the films would be processed and analysed and he was sure that the more detailed inspection of the results would reveal a positive outcome, but it didn't do much to raise our hopes, and I quite frankly was not at all convinced.

In my already depressed state, one experience I didn't enjoy on the return to the carrier was the landing, which quite honestly frightened me to death. The unfortunate thing was that H and I were invited to the flight deck to sit in dicky seats and strapped in to experience the landing. I think H's reaction was worse than mine by the look and pallor of him.

Have you ever been in a Hi-Rider or Man Lift, gone up high and looked down at the bit that is supporting you and thought how unsafe and small it looks? Landing on that carrier, it looks ten times smaller. The aircraft was lined up on the postage stamp and we came in high and fast, then the gear came down at the same time as full flaps were applied and it felt like we'd hit a brick wall. Then the postage stamp came up to meet us and we hit the deck with spine shattering force, and I wondered how the landing gear had not collapsed, then the props screamed in full reverse pitch and we snagged an arrester wire and the whole airframe shook and tried to throw us forward out of our seats. Then everything went still and we were manoeuvred to the servicing area. I had to admit to the Skipper that I'd near shit myself.

'Oh' he said, 'that was a real good one, you ought to try some of the not so good ones, like in the dark when it's pissing down in a gale force wind and heavy seas, and you think you've missed the Fercristsake Wire*.

I shook his hand and told him in no uncertain terms that it wasn't anything personal, but flying with him again would be one too many.

The Hawkeye had a change of crew, was refuelled and departed for surveillance patrol again. H and I made a quick visit to sick bay to see how Stan was getting on and found him in good form considering his ordeal, and we had a good natter with him until Penny turned up, so we made our excuses and left them to it. We were fed and watered and then addressed by Admiral Alwyn L. Shults who hoped we had enjoyed our stay and also hoped that our mission had been successful and wished us bon voyage and told us that our transport was now ready and waiting on the flight deck. He shook Hoppy's hand and passed over a briefcase containing all the film taken by the Hawkeye. Hoppy thanked the Admiral on our behalf for all his hospitality and excellent assistance, and then we all trooped up and out onto the flight deck to board a long range Northrop Grumman E-2B which took us all to Cyprus. We then transferred to an RAF Transport Command Aircraft which Bob Khan on Hoppy's orders had arranged and would be Co-Piloting to Glasgow International Airport with us.

En-route to Glasgow we kept passing over water which reminded me of my experience of conducting discharge trials in Loch Long in the 'O' boat I served in, not because of the trials themselves but the perks, because the MFV Crew were full time fishermen and part time RN employees and after a stint of torpedo recovery always came alongside with a box full of assorted seafood in exchange for a bottle of whisky from the Wardroom*. That being so the Wardroom Steward always had the pick of the box and the remainder was donated to us plebs, but we of the lower deck had a secret weapon up our sleeve on the form of Killick* Stoker Frederick 'Soapy' Watson who in earlier life had been a very good fishmonger, who took what the steward considered to be rubbish and knocked up some incredible meals for us in collaboration with Shitty Vest West, such as Bouillabaisse, Kalamari, Pizza Di Mare and Paella.

One of the funniest stories about discharge trials I've heard though was the one about the Mk21 that suffered a malfunctioned gyro, the bit that controls direction. Loch Long is not only long it is also beautiful, which is why whisky magnates and the like build mansions with billiard table smooth lawns on its banks. The Mk21 is driven at high speed by an internal combustion engine fuelled by shale oil and compressed air with contra-rotating props. This particular wayward Tin Fish* decided to head for this particularly nice lawn which came right down to the water's edge and proceeded to plough its way towards the big house, coming to rest within feet of the conservatory.

The really embarrassing bit was that Jolly Jack had to take a gang and a Wagon round to the Big House and knock on the front door and say 'Please may we have our torpedo back.'

It's rumoured that the Admiralty had to pay out thousands of pounds in compensation and insurance claims, and the lawn was never quite the same again.

We landed at Glasgow International at night and were met by a fleet of Fast Blacks* and a Blood Wagon* for Stan, all with Bootneck guards, and whisked away back to Faslane and escorted to the conference room where we were given a reminder of the Official Secrets Act and the need to keep the reason for our little trip to ourselves by Hoppy, who also advised us to get a good night's sleep because we were all required to attend a washup* in the morning.

The snag was that we had all slept well on the flights back, and, as it was not yet closing time, most of us reassembled in the NAAFI Canteen for a night-cap with the exception of Stan and Penny, now in sick bay, Bob and Anna who we reckoned were now an item, and Ali who had taken Click in hand and shared his double cabin with him, but Click preferred the deck to the bed. The rest of us just chilled out without a mention of the past few days, and after a few wets went our separate ways to reassemble bright eyed and bushy tailed in the morning.

Chapter 27

Washup 1

I don't know about the others, but I didn't sleep at all well because every time I dozed off I suffered this recurring nightmare of the detonation where nothing much happened and woke in a cold sweat. This made me think that the previous chapter should have been entitled Pop not Boom. Anyway, the Washup was convened as planned, the only absentee unfortunately being Stan, but who was represented by Penny, who reported that he was going from strength to strength, and was upset and annoyed at not being able to attend.

Admiral Sir Arthur 'Hoppy' Hopgood chaired the meeting, and having interviewed all the participants individually, which is where I got a lot of my information from about the activities of the other parties, ran the films taken by the Hawkeye and invited comments.

Most of the observations were quite negative but Andy tried to be positive.

'Sir, I don't know if you remember, but when we were doing our training at rigging the explosive string on the pontoon ...'

'Yes I remember, it was a complete success as I recall, was it not?'

'Yes Sir it was, but if you remember the actual detonation was at night and warnings went out to all the security services about possible loud controlled explosions, but when it happened the result was very unspectacular. In fact, we all assumed it had failed so we abandoned the exercise as a bad job and went back the next morning and discovered that it had been a complete success.'

'Yes I remember,' retorted Hoppy, sounding a little miffed, 'what's your point?'

'You don't have to have lots of snot and shit flying all over the place to produce results with explosives and there's no reason to suppose that this isn't the case here.'

'I still would have expected a bit more of a show though, wouldn't you?' Dusty chipped in.

Danny stood up and addressed Hoppy.

'Sir, didn't we get some still shots of before and after that we can compare?'

'Yes and I've had them blown up as well, here we are, pass them round.'

We all got copies and, using magnifying glasses we peered at the before and after shots till we were blue in the face, but nothing conclusive came of it, and it made me even more annoyed and depressed and I needed to do something positive to clear up the doubt one way and another.

'Well, I think it's a bit of a bastard that we've all gone to all this trouble to clear up without a positive result, it's really pissing me off,' burst out H as he tried to take a lump out of the table with his fist.

'It's no good taking it out on the table, what we need is constructive suggestions not destructive gestures,' threw in Curly.

'What the F in H are you bleating about?' H came back.

'Order, order,' Hoppy broke in, 'this is getting us nowhere, I can understand everyone's frustration as I have the same feeling, but has anybody got any questions or answers?'

'I've got a question Sir,' as Ali stood up, 'what's going to happen to Click, he really needs to be getting back to his people, he's getting more than a little homesick.'

'Ah, yes Ali, we'll have to be thinking seriously about his future.' But everyone could see that the Admiral was losing it as his eyes glazed over and his face started to blank out.

'I have the solution to all our problems.'

All eyes turned on me and Hoppy's face came back to life and he gestured for me to continue, so I thought here goes, shit or bust.

'We all want to know how successful the operation was, me more than most. So I propose that one or two of us escort Click back home and supply his people with the sea transport that Penny had promised them.'

'But that isn't going to solve much is it?' enquired Spike.

'Well what we could do, as we'd be out there anyway, would be to have a little shufti round about to see what's what.'

Hoppy looked a bit confused to start with, but it suddenly dawned on him what I was trying to achieve.

'All right then Ted, let's adjourn and reconvene in the morning and see if you can come up with a plan of action that will solve our problems OK?'

'Yes Sir.'

'Any other business then?'

'Yes Sir,' and we all turned to see a very nervous Betty on his hind legs.

'Yes, Sub Lieutenant."

'Would it be possible for me to transfer to the Royal Marines Sir please?'

With that we all burst out laughing, not because of anything other than sheer joy at knowing that at last Betty had found his proper role in life, and the laughter turned to a round of applause.

Dusty and Spike heartily approved the request and Hoppy promised to arrange it.

So finally we all dispersed feeling a little happier than earlier and I buttonholed Dusty and suggested that we went to consult with Stan, if he was up to it, to help formulate an action plan that was already germinating in my head.

When I explained to Stan what we wanted to talk to him about he was very enthusiastic and cursed the fact that he wouldn't be able to come with us. So I started to give them my thoughts on the return trip.

'My idea is for a small force to initially get Click back to his village and use it as our HQ as we'll be able to glean some intelligence from the natives. That means that we need Ali as interpreter, and as it's mainly a land based operation, you Dusty to lead the operation and have Spike as your 2IC.' Stan and Dusty both nodded approval.

'And H and I come along for the ride as it'll be a seaborne invasion.' Again nods of approval, so I decided to go the whole hog.

'We need fast transport and I do mean FAST and I know of just the job, it's getting hold of the thing that's going to be the problem.'

'What do you want and what's the problem?' Stan enquired.

'Well what I want is a 'Bold' Vessel, and the problem is they were experimental and are about to be decommissioned and scrapped.'

'What's so good about this type then?' asked Dusty.

'I can answer that,' Stan piped up, 'they're experimental gas turbine driven vessels and the fastest thing on the water bar none, and I reckon that if we jiggle up Hoppy he'll be able to swing it for us, so let's just assume it's fixed and carry on with the scenario.'

'OK then H and I either have to do a quick conversion to Brave Class vessels or drag along one of their ex-skippers. I suggest taking a couple of Pussers Whalers with a full complement of oars and canvas for the villagers, and a big deck cargo of fuel for increased range. What do you all think?'

There was a pregnant pause for quite a long time, and then they all, all at once, heartily approved and promised to back the plan.

Again I didn't sleep too well, again trying to think of things that could go wrong knowing full well that it was a total unknown. So came the dawn and we reconvened as planned. Just before Hoppy brought the meeting to order the door burst open and the heavily plastered and bandaged leg appeared, followed closely by a wheelchair-bound Stan, the motive force being Penny, to be greeted by a joyful round of applause.

Hoppy eventually regained control and invited me to kick off, but Stan requested permission to open the discussion.

'I was involved yesterday in a discussion with Ted and Dusty, and Ted gave us the bones of a great plan of action which Dusty and I heartily endorse and recommend.' So I got on my hind legs and ran through the outline of the plan, but purposely not going into detail of the mode of transport.

Ali explained to Click what was going on and looked over the moon at the prospect of going home. Spike was chuffed, H told me he was going to get me at playtime, and all the others were disappointed, but at the same time pleased that something positive was being done to get answers.

The meeting was adjourned with Hoppy again reminding everybody of the Official Secrets Act and then everybody wished us good luck, but unbeknown to them the tricky bit was still to come, talking Hoppy into arm twisting for the Bold vessel. So we requested a meeting with the big man and were invited into his stateroom with his personal steward hovering about.

'So what do you want now?' Not being one to mince words. So I jumped in with both feet.

'We would like you to intervene in the scrapping of 'Bold Pathfinder', an experimental Gas Turbine Driven Torpedo boat and use it as transport to get us out to the area with a couple of Whalers for the natives, but above all we want either an experienced Bold type Skipper or H and I to have a quick familiarization course on the type.'

'Is that all?' he said sarcastically, 'you'll have to leave it with me and I'll get back to you as soon as possible.'

That night I didn't sleep too well again but only because I dreamt of an incident that happened on the 'O' boat again. These boats were, as I've mentioned before, were Diesel Electric which meant that there were no shaft clutches and all manoeuvring was done by Greenies* in the motor control room, but all Officers and Senior rates had to qualify on the motor control panel as a precaution in case of emergency. Telegraph orders were transmitted to the control panel for propeller movements. As a precaution a large red warning light was fitted to make the operator aware if they ran the motors in the wrong direction. The Big Red Light had a label above it which read, unsurprisingly, WRONG DIRECTION, but some Greenie wag had in a quiet bored moment removed the red lenses and made little card cut outs and placed them behind the lenses and replaced them. Unfortunately, some say, the next crew member to re-qualify was the Captain and, guess what, he selected the wrong direction, and the big red light lit and told the Skipper that he had selected the wrong direction with a very very naughty word of female anatomy and he was not amused, in fact he was very dischuffed and had an almost permanent humour failure.

Came the dawn and Hoppy's runner had Dusty and I hot footing it round to the conference room again. Shortly after we arrived the big man swept in and immediately launched into the results of his efforts the previous evening.

'Your Bold vessel is at this moment on its way up here on a Queen Mary* from Pompey, that's the good news. The bad news is that you're on your own going back out there in it, but I have managed to recruit one of the civilian development engineers of the old class who is coming up with the vessel to show you the ropes. The rest is up to you.'

'H and I can cope with the mechanics of the vessel if as you say we have an expert to run us through the intricacies, but what about the seamanship side of things?'

'What about Betty?' Dusty popped in.

'Good thinking. So when is it going to arrive?' I enquired of Hoppy.

'It set off last night under police escort with two driving crews, so it should arrive about tot time, therefore I suggest you get your act together and let me know when you're likely to be ready to depart and I'll arrange transport for you.' And out he swept.

So off we trotted. I went to grab H to somehow rustle up a couple of Pussers Whalers complete with spars, rigging and sails. Dusty went to dig out Betty to 'volunteer' him for Skipper and Navigator on the operation, and then root out Spike to get him to organize stores, arms and ammunition.

A little bit of history now to explain some of the background to the gas turbine in the RN. These engines were already very successful in the aviation world, so the bold project was initiated to evaluate the use of them for sea borne use. The advantages being high power-to-weight ratio, good fuel economy and relatively safe, easily handled fuel readily available worldwide compared to the old furnace fuel oil used for steam driven vessels. FFO had to be preheated to be able to transport, transfer and burn it to produce steam a lot less efficiently than gas oil.

Now all modern RN vessels are gas turbine driven which is why the Royal Yacht was not used as a Hospital Ship in the Falklands crisis as it used FFO and would have had to have its own tanker for refuelling.

On a purely personal note I cannot understand why their Lordships and the Government did not have RY *Britannia* converted to Gas Turbine Propulsion, rather than have her end up as a pathetic tourist attraction, because she was a wonderful, beautiful vessel and did much for the Monarchy, PR, and sheer spectacle.

I joined HMS *Killisport*, which was undergoing a refit in Pompey Dockyard, straight from training, and walking from barracks to her drydock I passed *Britannia* in her drydock looking absolutely fabulous, gleaming like a jewel and exuding class.

Back to the plot though, I went back to Hoppy to acquire another chitty giving the bearer authority to requisition stores and equipment. Armed with one of these Spike went to the Royal Marines Base Stores, buttonholed the QM and raided his arms store and came away with a veritable arsenal.

H, ever the quick flip to the front, went to the top in the form of the CO of the Royal Naval College Dartmouth, rang him and explained that he had the authority of Admiral Hopgood, and could he please requisition two good condition Whalers complete with spars, sails, rigging and oars, as he knew that Dartmouth Cadets did extensive sail training.

After some initial reluctance, and being sent an official signal from Hoppy's office, the requested items were assembled, loaded on wagons and dispatched in record time.

Tot time came and went and we all assembled in the NAAFI Canteen Bar, including Betty who, on being asked to volunteer for the mission, was beside himself with excitement. Dusty had just got the round in when one of the security guards approached him and told him that a Sam Hall was at the Main Gate Security Shack asking for him, so having just got the round in he detailed Spike to go off and find out what was what and get rid if possible. Arriving at the main gate, more than a little pissed off at having been dragged away from his beer he enquired where this Sam Hall was, and was ushered into the interview room, where he was confronted by a very beautiful and very angry female.

'I'm awfully sorry, I'm looking for some one called Sam Hall.'

'I'm Samantha Hall,' she exploded, 'and I'm not at all happy about being locked up in here.'

'My apologies Mrs Hall, but this establishment has extremely tight security, I am Sergeant Redwood, how may I help?'

'It's Miss, Doctor Hall and I've been told that I have to report to Captain Miller.'

'May I enquire what reason you have to report to Captain Miller?'

'I am a Development Engineer on Gas Turbines with Metro Vickers,' and handed Spike her business card.

'Oh, I'm really pleased to meet you and so will Captain Miller, please come with me and all will be made clear in no time at all.'

The first thing we knew of all this was when Spike appeared at the canteen entrance and ushered this dolly bird in. They came over and Spike introduced her to Dusty who introduced all the rest of us. With a drink in her hand she started to relax a little, so Dusty explained that we were about to be delivered of a Bold vessel for a special operation and had requested some expert advice on the engines fitted in it.

'Well this could be your lucky day,' Sam said, 'because I was one of the Project Engineers developing the Gatric engine, the type fitted to the Bold class.'

So Spike explained that H and I were the engineering types who would have to look after them. He then contacted Penny who came to the canteen, was introduced to Sam and ushered her away to sort out accommodation, then Dusty turned all gooey, much to the amusement of the rest of us, and his embarrassment.

All that was needed now was the Queen Mary and Pathfinder to appear, and shortly after Penny and Sam departed we were informed that it had appeared at the main gate so H and I accompanied by Dusty went to sign it in and direct it to the slipway for unloading.

So all was set for another foray into the unknown, which was rather a tenuous link to H's shipmates run ashore which could also be described as a slide, rather than a foray, into the unknown. H's boat had come alongside the Faslane Base after a three month Fishplay Exercise in the Gulf Stream area and all were raring for a good run ashore and piss up.

The base at this time was very basic, with HMS *Maidstone* alongside the jetty and boats alongside her with an LCT alongside forrard of her used as an auxiliary store. The rest of the base was a compound surrounded by a chain link fence, the Guard House being part of the topworks of an old Merchantman, begged from the breakers yard just North of the base.

A sizeable section of the crew went ashore en-mass led by the legendary Yorky Crossman, the boat's Chief Tiff, whose passion was horseracing, and whose intercom reports were always in racing terms. For instance, during routine servicing the OOW might enquire how the main engine repairs were progressing, the answer would be something like, 'Port's evy goin 'n Starbd's a non runner.' Anyway back to the plot, off they trooped to the lads' canteen whose manageress was Miss Crystal, but more of her later. All in Yorky's gang got well ratted and at closing time meandered their way slowly back to the Guard Room to pick up their Station Cards when Scratcher happened to see one of the lad's Pay Book on the desk, and in his pissed state, demanded it as he was the deputy Coxswain and he would deal with it. But the RPO* in charge of the watch disagreed and an ugly argument ensued. The RPO's written report reads:

Petty Officer Second Coxswain S. Wright O/N. P/8865372 was finally Restrained by L/Patrolman Small sitting on his head, whilst CERA Crossman attempted to bribe RPO P. Hall with '400 fags, 50 cigars, and As much rum as he could drink.' Whilst all the time L. Seaman H. Tull Climbed to the top of the fence shouting down 'leave him alone you Three Badge* F – all shiny arm Bastard' and many other profanities.

The outcome of it all was that they all got various terms of stoppage of leave and other privileges, but as the boat was away in a couple of days it didn't matter much. We all had a good laugh over the incident as there was no love lost between boats Crews and the Regulating Branch and Crushers* in general.

While we were directing the Queen Mary to the slipway Dusty cornered me.

'Ted, we've done all this, but one thing's bugging me, I didn't realize how big this vessel was going to be, how are we going to get the thing to the Indian Ocean?'

'We steam it down there through the Med and Suez!'

'How do we get through the canal without arousing suspicion?'

'You'll have to do the organizational details and paperwork through Hoppy, but my plan would be to go as a civvy vessel on a jolly and we disguise the 'Pathfinder' as such.'

'How do we do that?'

'Easy, we repaint her, modify the funnels to be able to dismantle them, alter the trellis mast and run on the auxiliary diesels through the canal, and once clear re-rig the funnels and away we go and bunker up from an RFA once clear of Aden.'

Dusty wandered away with a puzzled look on his face, deep in thought. Eventually he came back to me and said,

'I'd better go and make an appointment to see the Admiral then and do a bit of arm twisting and get some documentation to support our guise and get some help to do the mods you want!' and away he trotted, still looking confused.

We finally got the trailer positioned to our liking and so decided to adjourn to the canteen to celebrate our progress to date with a nightcap before the canteen shut.

'That reminds me of the time I got lumbered with a shore patrol duty,' piped up H.

'It was when I was spare crew waiting for Porpoise to come in. It wasn't too bad really, apart from the final duty, which was to close the troops canteen, which had to be dead on time because the canteen manageress,

Miss Crystal, was a stickler for punctuality. She was a rather large lady who didn't take prisoners.

'As ill luck would have it a couple of boats had that same day come alongside after a long and arduous patrol. So me and a couple of sailors were going to have our work cut out to maintain order and close on time.

'Five minutes before closing I took my patrol into the lion's den so to speak, to be greeted by a raucous cheer. I automatically checked the clock above the bar, whose glass was missing, and noticed to my horror that it was ten minutes slow! So when the cheering had subsided I shouted that the clock was wrong, grabbed a chair, stood on it and advanced the clock to the right time to the accompaniment of loud boos. As I stepped down and turned to face the onslaught the boos turned to cheers as some wag had, quick as a flash, jumped up and put the thing back to ten minutes slow again.

'All I could do was smile and took my patrol into the back private area to confront Miss Crystal and explain that the canteen would have to close ten minutes late. She was not well pleased, in fact she complained bitterly and told me she was going to report me. I said that it was her prerogative and that I would take full responsibility. In due course the canteen closed late with very little trouble, and I was reported and severely reprimanded.

'The sequel to the story is that a similar situation occurred to some other poor sod but Miss Crystal insisted on closing dead on time and the place was wrecked and then burnt to the ground, so she was out of a job and the troops had no canteen.

Sods Law Eh!'

Chapter 28

Preparatory 2

The arrival of the Queen Mary heralded the beginning of the end of the whole operation. When Bold Pathfinder was uncovered our hopes took a dive, the pathetic sight that confronted us was of scruffy weed and barnacle encrusted hull, and paint peeling top works. The only good thing in its favour was that the main armament of four torpedo tubes had been removed, which would make the stowage of the deck cargo of extra fuel and two Whalers a lot easier. I suggested to Dusty that we leave it in its cradle on the low loader while we got it ready to go into the water, which was agreed much to the consternation of the tractor driver, but a quick flash of Hoppy's Chitty convinced him and he departed bobtailed.

One good thing that came from Pathfinder's condition was that the rest of the original gang rallied round and volunteered to assist in the restoration work. One other plus was the fact that she had been mothballed, which involved chemically inerting the interior and then sealing it off below decks. So all hands turned to removing hull fouling and upper deck cocooning and ventilating the interior.

After overnight ventilation, tests confirmed that the atmosphere was safe so we went below to have a look round and were surprised and delighted at its really good condition, apart from the musty smell. Sam took H and me down to the engine room and explained what was what and also what preservation measures had to be reversed, such as all inhibiting fluids to be exchanged for recommended lubricants and coolants, as Sam pointed out, especially the high ratio gearboxes which were the critical items in the propulsion system.

In a surprisingly short space of time the old tub was looking a lot more shipshape. Even the Whalers turned up, so H disappeared for a while to check the general condition of them and that the associated equipment was complete which it was, in fact most of the gear was brand new and Dartmouth had certainly done us proud.

Sam took H and I into the classroom and gave us a crash course in Gas Turbine design and the Gatric in particular which was very interesting and informative. The next step was to get the vessel in the water, wind the engines up and give the whole rig a run up the Loch to see what bugs there were, and sort them out as quickly as possible. So the big crane was manoeuvred alongside the trailer the slings rigged and P5720 Bold Pathfinder was put back into her element, the tripod mast was re-stepped and we all had to admit she did look the business. Danny had been commissioned to arrange the manufacture of the auxiliary fuel tanks and a fuel bowser had been arranged from Glasgow International Airport and duly arrived and bunkered Pathfinder up, the remainder of the tankers load discharged to a holding tank to await Danny's auxiliary units.

Now it was time to light the blue touch paper as it were, I for my part was shit scared, I don't know how H felt, but Sam seemed absolutely nonplussed and exuded complete confidence. Both engines were fired up and Sam showed us the relevant critical temperatures and pressures that required to be constantly monitored. Dusty, Spike and Betty joined us aboard, we cast off, the clutches were engaged, a bit of ahead pitch was applied and we slowly left the wall. With Betty at the helm, he suggested that we headed for Garelochhead so that we could have a good run south before Rhu narrows, so Dusty as Skipper approved, and off we went. H and I took a quick shufti round the engine room where everything was as Sam predicted with the Gatrics running as smooth as silk, so we went topside to admire the view. As the prop pitch was increased slightly and speed picked up, the only effect on the engines was a slight increase in noise level. A sweeping turn at Garelochhead and with the pointed end facing south the pitch controls were eased to maximum, the engines started to growl and the speed picked up and suddenly we were flying, it was incredible. At the washup it was estimated that our speed was well in excess of 40 knots.

Mind you, talking of incredible exhilarating speed, when I was helping Danny race his Manx Norton, after a major overhaul we used to test it on a local disused airfield. On one such occasion Danny, who was usually very protective of the Manx, suddenly suggested that I had a ride on it, to which I reluctantly agreed. My instruction was to wait until the rev counter got to 4000 RPM when it would go onto the mega (tuned exhaust) then I could let her rip! I got sat astride the thing and he shoved me off, the engine spluttered into life slowly accelerating and sounding like a bag of hammers with the rev counter slowly rising. Eventually nearing the supposed magic number I had become quite blasé, and then it happened, it got to 4000 and the bloody thing took off and nearly shot out from under me. Only by hanging onto the handlebar was I able to stay on, but in so doing had opened the throttle fully and couldn't shut it down until I'd pulled myself back into the saddle. I'd gone at God knows what speed, over revved the engine, incurred Danny's wrath, and damn near shit myself, all in the matter of a few seconds. That was the last time I ever straddled anything other than a pushbike.

Returning to the jetty, there were congratulations all round, then Sam took H and me below to show us how to shut the turbines down properly to prevent heat distortion. On reappearing on the upper deck Dusty was waiting for me.

'I've had a word with Hoppy and he wants to see us both right away.'

So off we trotted to be grilled by the big man himself. His ADC met us and ushered us in having warned us that he was in a filthy mood.

'What's all this nonsense about conversions and modifications, and whose bright idea is it to sail the damn thing down there?'

'Mine I'm afraid Sir,' I piped up.

'Well you'd better have a good explanation.'

'Yes Sir, the Brave boat's displacement is nearly 200 tons and there is no way we can transport that sort of weight other than by its own volition. If we do this it had to be via the Suez Canal because (A) we can't risk such a small vessel going round the Cape and (B) we wouldn't be able to carry enough fuel. Therefore to prevent the Arab Mafia in Port Said putting two and two together and getting five we will have to go as civvies with a civvy boat which will require slight modification as a vessel with large twin abeam funnels, a tripod mast and painted battleship grey, flying the White Ensign might be a bit of a give-away.'

'All right Chief, there's no need to be sarcastic, you've made your point, I'll arrange the paperwork and fuelling requirements. You have my permission to carry out any mods that you deem essential but hurry up, time is of the essence.'

So we scuttled out of his office as fast as our legs could shift us. Dusty gave an explosive exhale.

'I thought you'd really blown it that time Ted.'

'So did I, but it's no good beating about the bush at this stage of the game, we've got to cut the crap, and as Hoppy said get on with it 'cos time's awasting.'

So with the Admiral's words ringing in his ears Dusty called a meeting of all the old gang and asked for volunteers to help convert and tart up Pathfinder. Everybody wanted to help, even the girls, including Sam, so they were put to work below to make it more like a civvy motor cruiser. Danny was still hard at work organizing the auxiliary fuel tanks. H took on the funnel mod's, Betty took on the tripod mast alterations, so I took on the stowage of the Whalers and their camouflage. The rest of the gang, including Click, turned to with a will to paint the ship. The colour scheme chosen was White topworks, Royal Blue boot topping and Powder Blue hull.

Everybody was cracking on well with their allotted tasks except for

'Q' Ship The Conversion

me. I was seriously stuck, so I decided to have a word with Stan to see if he could come up with any ideas.

Stan listened to my bleatings for a bit, mulled it all over for a bit and then:

'What you need is a quick conversion job similar to what we did with Baggy, but on the upper deck instead of down below.'

'I don't get you Stan, what on earth can be done to hide funnels, fuel tanks and whalers?'

'You're not thinking big enough Ted, what's wanted is some topworks built to hide what you don't want to be seen. Remember the 'Q' ships in the Second World War. Close in the bridge with plenty of toughened glass and top it with a nice solid civvy style raked mast with a civvy style radar scanner.'

He then proceeded to sketch his thoughts, the main idea being to build false topworks behind the bridge. A sliding section to cover the Turbine air intakes and exhausts and hide the dismantled funnels and auxiliary fuel tanks, and two hinged panels aft to cover the whalers and associated spars and rigging, and two extra fuel tanks. To complete the illusion he suggested false access doors aft and lots of portholes either side.

'I tell you what' he said 'you get the senior Chippy* to come and see me and I'll see his DO* to smooth the way for the conversion OK?'

True to his word, all of a sudden what appeared to be the whole of the Shipwright Department descended on Pathfinder, and in conjunction with Danny, H and Betty, stripped the upper deck of all extraneous bits and pieces and proceeded to make Stan's sketches a reality.

Danny explained to the Chippies the need for civvy finished, which meant lots of shiny bits and bull dung to make it look good, and in no time the job was done and she looked a picture. Suggestions were put forward for a name for the 'new' vessel, but Stan came up with the perfect solution, a combination of Baggy and Gas turbine, hence *'Gasbag'* which all and sundry wholeheartedly approved. So *Gasbag* was officially registered in Goole, a sleepy hollow on the South Bank of the River Humber, well away from the RN and any other Armed Forces.

Unbeknown to us Stan had been busy on our behalf and again called Dusty and I to a meeting with Hoppy again.

'Gentlemen, I have arranged with Admiral Hopgood's permission for you and your vessel to hitch a ride as far as just out of sight of Port Said.'

Dusty and I in unison enquired how and what with?

'HMS *Fearless* is due to exercise with NATO in the Mediterranean and is shortly to depart Guz*. You will steam full belt south on main Gas Turbines to rendezvous with her west of the Isles of Scilly where she will take you aboard, for you to be transported to nearer your area of operation.'

'What the hell is *Fearless*?' Dusty enquired.

'She is an Amphibious Transport Dock (LPD) built to transport assault craft and troops to areas of conflict. So remove digits and get down there as *Fearless* won't wait for ever. It'll also be a good shakedown trip to sort out any bugs there may be with *'Gasbag.' Fearless* will do a Show the Flag* in Malta before dumping you south of Cyprus OK, so off you trot, chop chop!!

Ah, 'Malta', that name conjured up memories of early days on HMS *Killisport* en-route to the Persian Gulf. Our entrance to Grand Harbour, which I'd heard and read so much about, was awesome. A large proportion of the Mediterranean fleet were assembled in the heady days before Dom Mintoff. The Dyso's* milling about running errands and transporting Jack ashore. Then up the very shaky Barraca Lift to Valetta.

I was greener than grass, and my Mess Mates took charge and showed me what it was all about. I'd heard all about 'Straight Street' and didn't believe most of what was said until I was taken down the 'Gut' and was overwhelmed by all the offers from the resident 'Ladies'.

Four other things made a lasting impression on me, the dust and stone buildings, old ladies in black widows' weeds begging on the streets, very old cars still going strong with not a trace of metal moths*, and last and most vivid suffering belly ache and the trots with 'Malta Dog'.

We both went back to the jetty and explained the situation to everybody, and efforts were re-doubled and *Gasbag* was ready to slip in less than 24 hours.

So Dusty called all hands to a meeting in the canteen, bought everybody a drink and called for order.

'To start with I want to thank everybody for your unstinting efforts. Now comes the difficult bit, I have chosen the crew to man this operation, the object of which is to assess the measure of success of operation Dock Sunk and also return Click and offer what assistance we can to him and his people. I'm sorry for those not chosen, but the crew will consist of:

Myself	OIC
Betty	Skipper and Navigator
Spike	2IC and Armaments
H	Engineering Watchkeeping
Ted	Engineering Watchkeeping
Ali	Deck Hand and Interpreter
Click	Passenger

'We have to make a fast transit on main turbines so I am requesting Samantha to accompany us to our RV point as insurance against engine problems en-route, that is if she is willing?' A big grin and emphatic nodding from Sam.

'We will be slipping at first light tomorrow and we all need our beauty sleep, so thank you all again for your help and good night.'

As Dusty turned away a spontaneous round of applause erupted from the rest of the gang, which was very touching.

Came the dawn, having not had a very good night, I gave H a shake, we picked up our gear, which included our diving sets and associated charging gear, just in case, went down to the jetty, put our gear aboard and went down below and did engine checks on both the Turbines and the auxiliary Diesels. That completed we went up to the Bridge where the rest of the crew were now assembled. Dusty nodded to Betty, who in turn asked H and me to start main engines. So off we trotted below with Sam supervising, and both Turbines were flashed up and settled down with no trouble at all. Once we were happy that everything was as should be, engine control was transferred to the bridge and after a final check round, all three of us returned to the Bridge. To our surprise quite a crowd of the old gang and a few others had assembled to wave us off.

Betty, now full of confidence, ordered mooring lines to be singled up, then cast off fore and aft, let go the forrard spring, clutches in, minimum ahead pitch and the bow swung out slightly then the stern spring was let go and we were slowly away from the jetty to a loud cheer from Stan and the rest of the lads and lasses. And so we were off again on a new chapter in this long running saga, pitch was increased and we picked up speed to about fifteen knots, which was maintained through the Rhu narrows and into the Clyde past Inverkip, and then Betty opened her up and we creamed away at 40 knots with the oggin as flat as a mill pond.

Chapter 29

Passage 2

We creamed our way South making terrific time, but as we approached Little Cumbrae the wind started to pick up and the oggin started to get a bit choppy, so Betty asked Ali to contact Inverkip Marina for an up to date local weather forecast. The answer was not good news, with a wind and rain front tracking east which we would meet if we took the Irish Sea route, so Betty planned to make the track decision as we reached Plada. The weather was definitely going down hill just south of Plada and speed had to be reduced because of the choppy conditions, so the decision was made to head WSW to pass south of Sanda Island and the Mull of Kintyre. As we did so it appeared that we had passed through the front as the wind and rain abated slightly. Betty then made the decision to head for the Atlantic as the Irish Sea could be treacherous in the predicted conditions. So we cut across the top of Ireland and then left hand down and head due south in a long low Atlantic swell which although uncomfortable *Gasbag* was able to increase speed to near maximum. The main engines performed faultlessly and in no time at all, it seemed, we were approaching the rendezvous position. In fact, the transit was quite uneventful really, the only incident that was of any interest to relieve the boredom was the interaction between Sam and Dusty. Dusty, well known for his shyness and difficulty communicating with girls, was obviously attracted to Samantha, who didn't seem to mind his clumsy stilted approach and by the time we reached our RV position there was a definite mutual attraction.

The only bloke I ever came across who was even more inept than Dusty at attracting the opposite sex was POME (Stoker PO) Robert 'Shiner' Wright, who at Tot Time* in the Spare Crew Mess of *Adamant* finally admitted his shortcomings and related the ultimate in humiliation.

Poor old Shiner wasn't a bad looking lad, a bit of a loner, good at his job and always a neat and natty never gaudy dresser who was always on the lookout for, and very unlucky with, female company. His boat *Seraph* one of the last of the little 'S' boats, had just returned to Faslane after a long and arduous exercise in the north Sea. He took ages tarting himself up for a run ashore in Helensburgh, and after a quick snifter of his bottled neaters*, (strictly illegal), sallied forth. He clewed up the only customer in the bar of a very exclusive Hotel trying to drown his poor progress sorrows. Then a very attractive lady swept in and parked herself at the other end of the bar, ordered and started to sip a drink, then looked round to survey her surroundings and smiled sweetly at Shiner, whose heart rate and expectation soared. He smiled back and started planning his next move, possibly offer her a drink, or wander across nonchalantly and introduce himself. Not being able to make up his mind, she ordered another drink and gave him another smile which he responded to with fervour, and he was about to make his move. But suddenly she picked up her drink and elegantly strolled towards him and parked herself on the bar stool next to him. His heart was pounding so much it felt as if it was going to crush the fags in his inside breast pocket. She turned to him, smiled sweetly again, and said in a lovely low sultry voice.

'Hello, are you in submarines?'

Quick as a flash, not believing his great good fortune he replied.

'Yes, I am, how did you guess?'

'Oh, it was no guess, my husband is the First Lieutenant on *Oracle*, I could smell you!!!'

Fearless was waiting for us at the specified position and was already flooded down ready to accept *Gasbag*. The turbines were shut down and we manoeuvred into the dock area on auxiliary diesels, and no sooner had we secured than this deceptively large vessel was under way and we were heading south again.

We were all invited to the bridge and introduced to Captain Cunningham, who welcomed us, and hoped our stay with his vessel would not be too arduous, for which Dusty thanked him. The captain then arranged for his Jimmy* to show us to our mess and then give us a Cook's tour of the vessel which was a most unusual and versatile design. The weather was superb and we all spent a lot of time on the upper deck. The food was good and plentiful and our accommodation was excellent, what more could we want.

The Bay of Biscay behaved itself and was transited with no trouble thankfully, and before we knew it we were passing the Pillars of Hercules leaving Gibraltar to port and on into the Mediterranean. The weather remained fine and we were making good time, the only hiccup was when Dusty was instructed over the tannoy to report to the Captain's cabin.

On his return to the mess he called us all together to explain the outcome of the meeting.

'Captain Cunningham informed me that he had received a signal from

Their Lordships ordering *Fearless* to remain at Malta to host a meeting of environmentalists which will last a week, which means that we will be very badly delayed. Has anybody got any comments to make at this stage?'

'Yes' H piped up, 'why the hell don't we bunker up fully at Malta, and as long as the weather holds, make our own way to Suez because we'll be faster than *Fearless* anyway?'

So I added my ten pen'orth by agreeing with H.

Betty also agreed and said he would enjoy the navigational challenge.

'I'm glad you all agree to H's suggestion because I was going to suggest just that if no one else had.'

So Spike went back to the Captain and informed him of the revised plan of action and requested a fuel fill up, he also requested that *Gasbag* be disembarked out of range of Malta and prying eyes. The Captain agreed but went one step further explaining that his arrival in Grand Harbour was timed for 0800 the following morning and as they were ahead of schedule, so instead of slowing down he would overshoot by an hour and let us loose east of Malta at 0700 to help us on our way.

So Dusty came back and explained the latest plan and suggested that we got a good night's sleep so that we could be up bright eyed and bushy tailed ready for departure.

'Oh and by the way,' Dusty added, 'I've asked Samantha to accompany us as an extra Engineer and she has agreed if that's alright with you all?' which caused the rest of us to give a cheer, and brought a gentle smile to both their faces, say no more, nod nod, wink wink.

'Has anybody got anything else to talk about?'

'I've got a question,' piped up Spike. 'How the hell are we going to fool the Gypoes into letting us through the Canal and what about all the bum boats that are going to pester us, and the lighting parties that will raid us?'

'Good question.' Dusty looked a bit crestfallen. 'I'm working on it.'

'Exactly how far have you got then?'

'Not very far I'm afraid.'

So I thought I'd put my two pennyworth in.

'I've thought of a plan to keep the robbers and nosy Parkers at bay. We fly the Quarantine Flag, have someone dress up as a Doctor and have Sam dressed as a Nurse. A signal is sent to the Canal Company HQ shortly before our ETA that we have a suspected case of 'whatever' and have to get the patient to Aden to consult his personal physician and arrange very urgent treatment.'

'It all sounds good to me,' Dusty said looking quite relieved and puzzled at the same time, 'but what's the patient going to be suffering from and how do we get the dressing up gear?'

'You'll just have to chat up *Fearless*'s senior quack who I understand is a Surgeon Commander. You should be able to flannel your way round him. Ask him what contagious disease is feared by the Egyptians, and also bum some quack's lagging quoting Admiral Hopgood and showing him the Chitty*, that should do the trick.' So we all left him to it, and wishing him the best of luck.

Before we turned in H and I went and arranged the bunkering and also bummed a few jerry cans of fuel as extra reserves from the Chief Tiff IC* Dock Area. We also did the routine engine checks in preparation for the morrow.

After another restless night I went below to the dock early as I couldn't sleep, and just re-checked all the levels on both the Turbines and the Diesels, but I wasn't alone for long as the rest of the crew started to turn up, so we just sat around in the wheelhouse nattering till Dusty and Sam appeared with lots of hospital garb. Then the tannoy blasted out our instruction to cast off and slip so H and I wound up the turbines and Betty manoeuvred *Gasbag* out of the Dock stern first, and when well clear, went ahead and turned East. As we started to increase speed we received a cryptic signal, 'Good Luck – Good Hunting.'

Dusty replied 'Thank You' and away we went slowly increasing speed to near maximum, which put a great bone in *Gasbag*'s teeth. The weather as predicted was ideal and again the transit was completed uneventfully, apart from the rehearsal of the Doctor Nurse Patient routine, which at the time was quite amusing, but the serious part was to convince the canal people and so enable us to pass through into the Indian Ocean.

On the subject of faking it, the previous example reminded me of an escapade on *Vectra*. Their Lordships decided that the crews dental health was suffering because of the prolonged periods at sea and so decided to lash us up to a dentist to augment the Medical and Health Physics Department.

Therefore on our next call at Faslane a very young Sub Lieutenant joined us together with a whole host of tools and equipment. Knocker and I as Outside Wreckers were detailed off to rig his gear and install him in the Health Physics Lab. This involved the securing of a rather large dentist's chair with power and plumbing, and more interestingly a state of the art Air Turbine Drill which as its name implies required clean compressed air and a cooling water supply.

The Air Turbine was a wonderful gadget, which made tooth drilling much less uncomfortable and painful. The only snag was that it had three minor drawbacks. To start with it made a really high pitched whine, secondly it produced an acrid smell of burning plastic, and finally the water to cool the cutter and the tooth had to be sucked away with a vacuum pipe which was hooked into the side of the patient's mouth.

Sub Lieutenant Andrew 'Andy' Smart was not only good at his job, he was also a good run ashore with the lads, which tended to be frowned on by the Wardroom, but Andy didn't give a toss as he was only on a short service Commission.

Eventually the crew's teeth were considered to be 100% and Andy was to be drafted elsewhere, so a few of us Senior Rates took him on a final run ashore, got him well smashed, smuggled him back aboard and down to the Health Physics Lab, and to his surprise strapped him in his own chair.

Knocker and I, having installed all his gear, also knew how it worked and how to use it. Poor sucker Andy thought it was all quite amusing until we prised his mouth open and kept it wide open with an expandable clamp, then he started to change colour a bit. Knocker got one of his tooth band clamps, the sort used to contain filling amalgam material until it sets, but this time, unbeknown to the victim, we used it to clamp a piece of perspex, which we'd prepared earlier, to one of his incisors, then I got to work with the Air Turbine. At this time the victim's colour vanished and his complexion resembled alabaster. I started grinding away at the perspex which was in close contact with his tooth, which made it appear that his tushy peg was being whittled away. He was now acting like a sweaty chameleon as his colour had changed to a pale shade of yellow. I redoubled my efforts on the perspex causing the burning smell to become very pungent and steam wafted past his now saucer wide eyes with an accompanying change of colour to puce. We finally called a halt and unshacked the perspex and took the jaw clamp out, but by this time he'd had a complete humour failure, but the look of relief on his face was a picture. He did eventually forgive us, but at the time he admitted that he had been scared shitless, and was stone cold sober.

The rehearsal started with Dusty showing us the bag of goodies he had managed to bum from *Fearless*. He was going to have to be the Doctor as he was the only one who could speak Arabic, with Ali as reserve interpreter. So he had a nice crisp white coat with matching stethoscope. For Nurse Sam he had acquired a rather fetching white trouser suit with nurse's white cardboard titfer and matching white slippers. He also produced some face masks to complete the picture. For the patient, Spike, he had borrowed rouge and a water mist spray to give the flushed sweaty look and as a finishing touch, blankets to half bury him.

'While I was filching this lot I suddenly thought about how to show that we were carriers of a highly contagious complaint, the inboard quack had suggested smallpox, as the natives dread even the mention of the name and he suggested that I contact the Communications Branch to find out about how to signal the fact. The OIC Communications got the Chief Bunting Tosser* to help. The outcome is that we signal the Port Authorities of our contagious passenger once we've entered the holding dock and not before, so that we are hemmed in and trapped by vessels entering after us and therefore the only way out being through the Canal. At the same time as we send the signal we hoist "Quebec Quebec"!'

'What the hell are you talking about?' we more or less all asked in unison.

'I thought that might wake you all up and get you going,' and produced two oblong yellow flags.

'These flags are 'Q' or Quebec in the phonetic alphabet and two are hoisted six foot apart to indicate to other vessels and authorities that we are in quarantine. So you Tiffs are going to have to rig an extra length of mast to use when we hoist the signal. You're also going to have to rig two lights for night time, red above white six foot apart, that should keep the buggers worried and at bay.'

H and I being squirrels at heart had 'borrowed' a few offcuts of the Chippy's nice teak deck planking so we split one down, fixed a pulley at the top, slotted some cordage through it and spliced it into a continuous loop and screwed it to the existing raked mast. The two flags were bent* on at the required interval and were ready to be hoisted in a hurry. We also rustled up a spare port navigation lamp and a spare bow lamp and wired them at the appropriate distance apart to a wandering lead able to be bent onto the flag halyard if and when required.

We now just had to wait for Betty to tell us when we were near enough to launch into our now well rehearsed plan, all quite boring really.

Talking about boring reminded me of the last Fishplay exercise I was on with Oberon, which involved swanning about the Gulf Stream for three months sweating cobs where everybody, including the Skipper, wore rag sack specials. You dived into the ready use rag sack and dug out the largest piece of cloth you could find and used it as a sarong, nothing else, just a lump of rag wrapped round your waist, nice and cool for the nether regions!

Anyway, to ease the boredom, one of the for end men decided to produce a newspaper. He used large sheets of chart correction paper and hand printed all the items and even drew photographs to go with some of the items. One of the items I remember was 'Uncle Clancy's Kiddies Corner' (Clancy McGrail was the Coxswain) with a junior crossword, games and cartoons.

The general gist was spreading buzzes and extracting the urine from all and sundry, all very cleverly done, they must have taken hours to compile let alone think up.

One section I recall vividly in one edition was 'Letters To The Editor' one letter I recall in particular was:

To The Captain
HMS/M Oberon.
From The Headmistress
Evesham College for Young Ladies.

Dear Sir,

Thank you ever so much for showing our Senior Girls round your Converted Sewer Pipe. Please may we have them back now?

Yours hopefully,

I believe the Skipper actually collected them up and saved them as souvenirs of a very happy commission.

Just before we arrived off Port Said a rehearsal was held of the forthcoming performance, the sick bed was installed in what used to be the original Skipper's day cabin, the problem being that *Gasbag* was mostly all engines with very little room left for crew accommodation. The full dress rehearsal went very well and to us looked very convincing, so hopefully it would fool the Canal Staff, and we were about to find out, as Betty ordered the Turbines shut down and cooled down and propulsion transferred to the diesels. When all was cooled down H and I unrigged and stowed the funnels, slid the cover over them and slotted the blanks into the air intakes and in no time at all we were entering the assembly area with a large menacing Tanker coming up astern of us. We were soon well hemmed in so Betty suggested that Dusty contacted the Port Authorities and appraise them of our supposed suspected case of smallpox onboard, at which the bloke at the other end of the radio telephone sounded as if he was having a seizure. With that Betty ordered Q Q to be hoisted as the bum boats were about to descend on us. To counter the imminent invasion Sam and Betty appeared on the upper deck in all the gear complete with face masks, waved their arms and shouted 'smallpox!' with remarkable results. They all suddenly disappeared from around us as if by magic. The next thing was a Gypo in a peaked hat shouting something unintelligible at us through a loud hailer that was suffering from a bad case of feedback, who was joined by a few more individuals who started jumping up and down on the jetty. Finally the radio telephone came alive again and Dusty managed to explain that the patient had to be delivered ASAP to his personal physician in Aden as he was suspected of contracting smallpox but it could be something worse! The guy with the bullhorn was still at it so Betty put the diesels slow ahead and pointed *Gasbag* towards him. With that he started to wave us away but as Sam and Betty offered to talk to him as we got nearer he jacked it in and legged it.

The RT came to life again and we were instructed to follow a decrepit old Tramp Steamer at an increased distance, and nothing came close to us, not even the huge tanker behind us. We didn't even get inundated by lighting crews, and were instructed to show navigation lights at all times.

There were lots of binoculars trained on us and our nice yellow flags and white clad doctor and nurse who appeared on the upper deck at regular intervals, just to keep the pot boiling so to speak. Spike was very dischuffed because he hadn't been able to display his acting ability, but Dusty jokingly told him not to be such a prima donna and think himself lucky that we'd got away with it so far, and to keep his fingers crossed for the future, and added that he would have overacted anyway.

So eventually the Convoy got underway and it was just a case of follow my leader, all very boring really, passing the time, occasionally doing the doctor nurse parade, nattering, supping tea and eating nutritious but dull K rations. Which reminded me of *Oberon*'s overflowing freezer.

One trip involved us in an exercise in mid Atlantic to be a very boring target for a multi-national NATO Surface Fleet. Eventually arriving at the allotted area the exercise started and, most unusually, we were immediately detected as signalled by a hand grenade. Starting another run we were again almost immediately detected, which was a bit more than coincidence and suspicions were roused. Surfacing to do a fast transit to the new start position the OOW called the Captain to the bridge and pointed out an oil slick in our wake, so the skipper ordered a 360 degree loop round and as we regained our original course the smell of diesel fuel was overpowering.

That's when I was called to the bridge as I was the Wrecker and I was joined by the chief Tiff to try and establish where the leak was coming from. The only answer I could come up with was the cooling water discharge from the Refrigeration Units which controlled the temperatures of the Air Conditioning, Fridge and Deep Freeze. The Chief couldn't be sure so we had to consult the drawing which confirmed my diagnosis that the discharge line ran through an external (to the pressure hull) fuel tank. To ensure that this really was the case the Chief and I suggested that as the sea surface was calm the boat be stopped to see where the fuel rose from. The Skipper agreed and called down all stop and as we lost way and came to a stop sure enough a lot of fuel globules welled up from the location we had predicted and quickly spread into a large area slick. No wonder we were being sussed out so fast, all they had to do was follow the oil slick, cheating gits! The skipper sent signals off reporting our condition and we were recalled to Faslane and good old AFD 58 to effect repairs.

So we headed for home and the Skipper got Jimmy* to check with Scratch* the paperwork regarding the contents of the Fridge and Deep Freeze, the reason being that the Cox'n (grocer) was on compassionate leave. In the meantime the Chief Tiff got the Donk Shop Horse* to draw fuel only from the defective tank to try to limit the losses and pollution. According to Clancy's books there wasn't much grub in either the Fridge or Freezer, so with the Chef in tow Jimmy went to see what could be consumed before we got to Faslane, as the things would have to be de-stored. The Fridge yielded just a bit more than was listed, but as they opened the Deep Freeze it all fell out at them. It was ram jam full of meat of all descriptions, unbelievable!

Needless to say that on the way back all there was to eat was meat. If chicken was on the menu, that's what you got, a chicken, nothing else, just a whole chicken on its own. Breakfast was bacon, sausage, kidney, steak and chops, lamb and pork. By the time we arrived in Gareloch the whole crew was sick of the sight of meat, but it avoided questions being asked inboard, although Clancy got a mild bollocking for not keeping true records. We all agreed though that he was a good grocer who fed us a lot better than most other boats.

Eventually the Convoy emerged into the Red Sea where all vessels set course and speed independently again. Betty took us to the west of the main shipping routes and in no time at all we were on our own and we were able to re-rig the funnels, wind up the Turbines and get under way on a fast transit, keeping a keen Radar watch to maintain plenty of distance between us and the rest of the Convoy and any other stray vessels.

Chapter 30

Re-visit

Approaching the narrows by Aden we throttled back as we were in radar range of shore and didn't want to attract unwanted attention, but as soon as we were in the Indian Ocean proper it was arse down and away again.

Now was the time that Dusty called us all together to discuss tactics for the coming few days.

'I'm going to outline the plan as I see it,' he started, 'if anybody has any suggestions, comments or criticisms please save them to the end.'

'On arrival in the area we must hope for the best but expect and be prepared for the very worst, therefore we will approach the village under cover of darkness. A fully armed recce group will enter the village whilst the rest of us will retire with *Gasbag* to the lee of Accar Island.'

'The shore party will be Spike IC, Click, Ali and one other volunteer, and will row the dinghy to the village, hide it upstream, infiltrate the village and, without causing any undue disturbance establish the state of play regarding opposition activity. The contents of that sit-rep will dictate our future actions! Any comments?'

H and I both at the same time volunteered for the shore party so we drew straws and I won. There were no other takers and no other comments, so we all bashed on with our own preparations. Spike delved into his armoury and issued the shore party with a great array of weaponry and camouflage gear and then proceeded to drill the whole crew in all sorts of wicked ways, including Samantha who appeared to quite enjoy the experience. Although it was pointed out that Dusty was also in the group.

After Spike's spell of tuition it was just a matter of patience waiting for the time and miles to pass before action was required.

Patience was what was needed when we took *Oberon* to Manchester. Yes Manchester, up the Ship Canal which caused quite a stir with the populace along its length observing this big sinister black beast silently sliding past. Unfortunately it was mid summer with glorious sunshine and nil rainfall for some considerable time which accounted for no change in the canal contents. As we made our way up the black liquid and broke the surface the smell of hydrogen sulphide was appalling. We had just completed a lengthy exercise in tropical waters and the hull was badly fouled with weed and barnacles, but halfway to Manchester in the

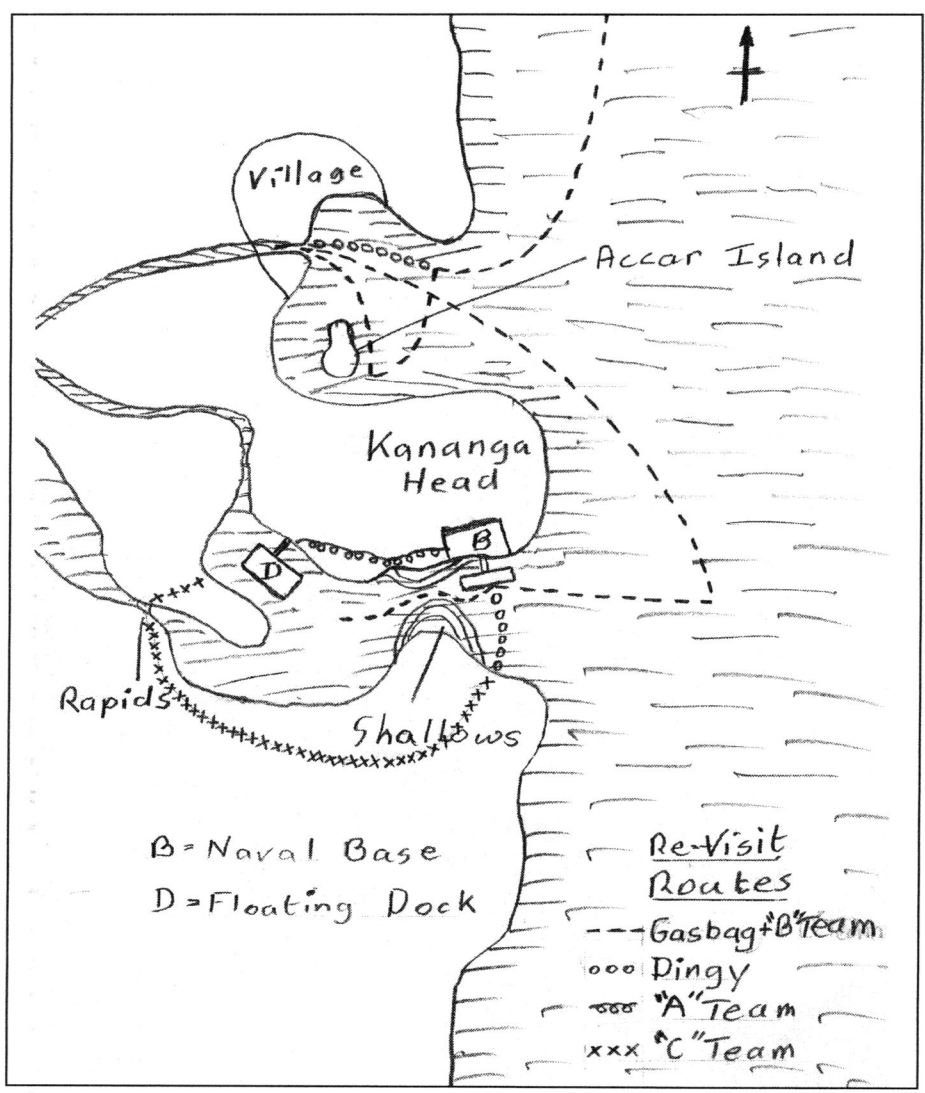

acidic canal left our bottom bare metal, even the anti fouling paint had been stripped off.

Having arrived at the docks and tied up, a tremendous crowd had assembled waiting to come aboard and have a look round, and were upset to find that visiting wasn't till the next day, as we all had to make everything clean and shiny with all personal gear stowed away. Then the next day all but a skeleton crew had to be sent ashore as there was only one passageway, so only guides were allowed to stay aboard.

It appears that record for the largest number of visitors through a conventional boat was well and truly broken on this show the flag trip. Quite a few stories of large people getting stuck in hatches were prevalent, and lots of complaints about the smell and the clutter of pipe and valves, but the general consensus was that it was an informative and good day out.

The downside was that accommodation for the lads and senior rates should have been arranged ashore, but due to an administrative error (cock up) had been overlooked. Senior Rates arranged B&B or similar, but Jack ended up spending the early nights getting well pissed and then getting their heads down upstairs at the back of all night buses, but the bus crews didn't seem to mind too much. In those circumstances the lads had to have lots of patience and a sense of humour, and most of us were glad when we made our farewells and got back to sea and normal.

Eventually after pushing the Gatrics hard we arrived at a position where we switched to auxiliary diesels and slowly and quietly closed in to shore as near as Dusty dare get to the village river mouth. At 0300 the inflatable dinghy was launched by the light of a very thin new moon and our team, loaded down with arms and ammunition, embarked and nearly swamped the poor little thing, but eventually we settled down, 'trimmed the dish' and started paddling quietly and purposefully towards the shore. Click was beside himself with excitement in anticipation of being reunited with his family and subjects and had to be subdued from time to time by Ali to prevent him capsizing us. After what seemed to be an age of strenuous padding we eventually entered the river mouth, secreted the dinghy in the undergrowth a couple of hundred yards upstream. Click then led us through the village to his family abode where he was restrained while Spike entered to check the interior out. There was a muffled shriek and then after a couple of minutes he re-emerged and beckoned us all inside where, by the dim glow of the fire embers Click was reunited with his wife and family, a very moving scene!

By now dawn was breaking, so Spike got Ali to get Click to interrogate his family as to the whereabouts and strength of the opposition. The answer was not at all good, as it appeared that raiding parties kept harassing the village perimeter and the grenading of the bay had resumed with renewed vigour. Spike insisted that Ali ask again with exactly the same answer. It appeared that things had got worse instead of better after our original operation.

The village came to life as dawn broke and as our presence was discovered we were mobbed, and I noticed Raisa Partak the young Indian girl in the crowd. I pointed her out to Ali, we drew her to one side and

Ali asked her about the situation and she confirmed what we had already been told.

So Spike got on the blower and informed the *Gasbag* mob the bad news and informed Dusty that it was all clear to steam to the village and up river, but with extreme caution and they arrived to be greeted by a silent crowd of semi-starving villagers, who helped to camouflage *Gasbag*.

The rest of the crew just couldn't disguise their dismay at seeing the abject misery that pervaded the whole village. Dusty managed eventually to bring us all back to reality by explaining that the object of the exercise was to ascertain the present situation and the conditions of the foreign installations and the navel facilities on the Kananga River, but ordered that all our rations be unloaded and distributed to the natives, then called us all together.

'We're here to do a job and that is to suss out the effects of the last occasion we were here. Because conflict has resumed in this area means it could be worse elsewhere. I propose that we have a meal here and now and then embark a few of the fittest native men and steam round there and find out what has, and maybe still is going on, extreme caution being the order of the day.'

So within the hour we re-boarded *Gasbag*, took aboard a dozen native volunteers including Click, cast off and Betty headed us S. S. E. on main engines and took us out and past the mouth of the Kananga so that we could observe the Naval Base from a distance. No movement was seen, so Dusty ordered us to arm ourselves and instructed Betty to approach the jetty slowly while we kept it and the base under close observation.

Eventually we clewed up alongside the jetty and secured, with still no sign of life, so Dusty ordered two search parties to go ashore. We split up, Dusty leading one group and Spike the other, dividing the native force between them, leaving Betty and Sam with engines ticking over and loop moorings ready for a quick departure if required. So fully armed we cautiously negotiated the jetty roadway and split up to search the base and joined up at the rear having encountered no one but agreed that the joint had been vacated in a hurry as there was lots of personal gear left sculling about.

Returning back aboard *Gasbag*, Dusty convened another meeting to discuss tactics for the next bit we had to inspect.

'Let's face it,' Dusty addressed the assembled mob, 'this is the bit we really came to eyeball, to determine what damage, if any, had been inflicted after the last foray and whether the terrorists' plans had been thwarted or are still ongoing. I believe that this is crunch time and if there are any opposition members left they will be upstream.'

'Can I make a suggestion?' Betty blurted out, which caught Dusty on the hop and surprised the rest of us as well as he was usually very reserved.

'Yes Betty what is it?'

'I'd like to propose that we do a three pronged recce, two groups, one on either bank and *Gasbag* in the stream up the middle. You lot split into two groups with half a dozen natives each as scouts. The south bank group to go ashore by dinghy and gain the high ground on the headland and, when we're all set and in touch by radio, advance slowly as one unit, with me and *Gasbag* along with Sam, Click and Ali.'

Dusty looking slightly amused, started clapping which was infectious and we all joined in with a little round of applause, which caused Betty to colour up and look rather embarrassed.

'Very good young Betty, I couldn't have thought of better myself.' Dusty admitted, slapping him vigorously on the back, 'one small alteration if I may though. H you stay aboard *Gasbag* as the fighting unit and Ali will take your place ashore if that's OK?' and there were nods of approval.

'RT communications to be kept to a minimum, Spike you're 'A' team, Betty you're 'B' team, and I'm 'C' team, the opposition is 'X' OK – so you heard the man, let's do it!'

So we split up, Dusty and I with half the natives, and Spike with Ali and the other half, and fully armed we all went to it with a will. Dusty and I took the dinghy, the natives preferred to swim, not that they could have all got in the inflatable anyway, and we landed on the south bank, checked with the other teams by radio, then off we trotted.

Our group had a long trek to get above the Kananga River rapids in order to cross over to the north bank of the Isthmus. So we were the critical group and would therefore be responsible for launching the operation with the other two groups once we were in position on the high ground overlooking the Dock area itself.

The terrain was relatively easy and we made good progress, keeping away from the coast in the tall undergrowth to be sure that we were hidden from prying eyes until we were hidden from view by the Isthmus.

We eventually gained cover with the promentary so we headed nearer the water where the going was even easier, and in no time at all we were at the rapids which had all but dried up, so we were able to cross with relative ease. Dusty suggested that we carried on up north until we could observe the dock without ourselves running the risk of being detected by the opposition.

'Then we can call up the other teams and as they advance we can observe their progress and warn them of any developments or possible danger and conflict, as we'll have a panoramic view of the proceedings, what d'ya think?'

'It's OK by me and sound a good plan.' I agreed.

So off we trotted with the native lads scouting in front and the sides, up a fairly gentle rise until we reached the highest point and, using sparse undergrowth and vegetation as cover beheld a most depressing sight and our hearts sank. The dock, the damned thing we'd come to see in bits and a mess looked perfectly OK, a bit rust stained, but looking at it side on, the only bit we could see, appeared absolutely normal and upright.

As I pointed out to Dusty, the only thing that was different was that the cranes were missing, but as I explained they could have been dismantled for repair and maintenance.

'Ah well, we'd better get this show on the road,' and called up the other two and told them the bad news.

'Advance with extreme caution and we'll keep a weather eye open and warn you of any activity hostile or otherwise. Stay alert and good luck!'

'Stay Alert', that phrase reminded me of an incident in Poole Harbour, and while we were waiting for the rest of our mob to come into view I related to Dusty the action of a guy who was less than alert at the time.

Torpedoes are launched using a slug of compressed air in conventional boats, (water ram on Nuclears) and to prevent detection the firing air is returned inboard as the fish leaves the tube through the AIV (automatic inboard vent). It's all quite complicated and accuracy of set-up is critical, as most of the gear involved is totally or partially immersed in salt water, so whilst in harbour the systems are tested with 'Air Shots'.

Air shots, instead of firing a torpedo, shoot out just a tube full of water, which has the same effect with the system. The one thing the TG* must do is to check that the tube he is about to test is empty! To this end the tube rear door has a label holder to display the contents but the rear door should still be opened to confirm the label is correct just in case.

The poor unfortunate who was about to perform such an air shot must have had a heavy night or something, and only firing on three cylinders. No label was in the holder of the tube he was about to cycle so he just assumed that it was empty.

The boat was about to depart for sunnier climes and had just completed taking stores aboard for the duration, but the TG had other things on his mind and flooded the tube, opened the bow cap, pushed the button and let her rip, and everything worked perfectly. So he couldn't understand why the Cox'n barrelled down the forends and started giving him an ear bashing and reading his horoscope.

'What the hell's up?' the poor unfortunate pleaded.

'Come with me.' And literally frog-marched him to the casing where the rest of the crew were assembled.

'LOOK' and spread his arms wide.

All you could see was eggs, no oggin just eggs.

'You have just discharged the whole of the next trip's egg supply into Poole Harbour, I don't think you're going to be very popular apart from with the Shitehawks.'

By way of explanation, eggs keep for quite a while if stored in a cool place. They are also very popular with the lads who call them Cackle Berries. They are also very bulky to store which is why, with the Wardroom's permission, the Cox'n ordered the Chef to load the said tube with the eggs making sure that the boxes were tied together so that they could be retrieved when required. Ten boxes X two compartments / box X seven trays / compartment X eighty-one eggs tray / 11,340 eggs which float in salt water. What a picture and what a mess!

Suddenly we were brought back to reality by the RT yammering away before any group had come into view. It was Spike on the north bank.

'A to C have located X's water transport moored up, please advise.'

'C to A immobilize item only, do not destroy.'

'How?'

'Wait. C to B, how close are you to A?'

'In sight.'

'H advise Team A.'

So Betty manoeuvred *Gasbag* close into the north bank to within hailing distance, and conversation ensued between H and Spike culminating in H stripping off and swimming over to the enemy vessel to be hauled out by Ali and the lads. He immediately went to the engine compartment, located the fuel solenoid valves and cut the electrical supply wire in an obscure place.

'There y'ar, that'll do it.'

'How does that work then?' enquired Spike.

'When you turn the start key the first step puts power through the wire I've cut, to the solenoid valve and opens it against a spring allowing fuel to get to the engine, the next step of the key engages the starter motor which turns the engine and starts it. When you turn the key back power is cut off to the valve, the spring takes over and shuts it and cuts off fuel to the engine and hey presto, it stops. It'll take somebody a long time to suss out that I've cut the wire and where. But to rectify will only take a couple of seconds if you know where it's cut, you just have to bare both ends and twist them together, OK!'

'Anyway I'd better get back, see y'a.' And with a wave he dived in and swam back to *Gasbag* and was hauled out by Betty who looked rather relieved to see him back again, and got on the blower to inform Dusty that the job was done, and that the advance was resuming.

Having listened to all the comings and goings over the ether reminded me of an incident regarding disabling a vessel.

The Admiralty issue 'Notices to Shipping' signals, some of which regard prohibited areas where submarine exercises are to be held and when. Such a notice was issued for a specified area off Portland Bill. The area was regularly used for boats discharge trials, as was in this case.

Discharge trials involve testing Torpedoes and Tubes and Crew in firing them as in chapter 27. The boat in question was the purpose built target boat Otter, which was armoured to be able to withstand practice torpedo hits, and was skippered by a very forceful and ambitious individual. All was set with the recovery vessel at the end of the range. The boat closed up and dived to periscope depth ready for the first run when the OOW on the search scope spotted a small vessel halfway down the centre of the range.

In fact the vessel in question was a small MFV skippered by an elderly local and crewed by his younger relations, none of whom had read or were informed of the said Notice to Shipping.

The boat's skipper was informed of the intruder, and got the Sparks to instruct the recovery vessel to approach the offender, and get him to shift out of the way. This was duly done and the recovery vessel resumed its position, but the offender stayed where he was, in the way!

In exasperation the boat's Skipper decided to tell the old fool himself, and ordered the Wrecker to blow main ballast and stopped blowing with minimal positive buoyancy, opened up the conning tower hatches, climbed to the bridge and ordered course and high speed on motors to close the MFV and, using a loud hailer came close alongside and read the riot act to the offender and told him to sod off in no uncertain terms.

That done the Skipper ordered hard a Starb'd group up, dive-dive-dive, gave the klaxon tit a good couple of bursts, dropped down the hole and shut the lid. Then ordered periscope depth and course back to the start line, where having turned down range and seeing nothing assumed that the old duffer had cleared off, carried on with the trials.

Unbeknown to him, as he had turned and dived the boat, its arse had broken surface because of the vicious manoeuvre and the port aft hydroplane guard had stuffed a great gash in the side of the MFV at water level and was sinking fast. The skipper transmitted a May Day and the crew inflated and launched the emergency dinghy.

Having dived, the boat's Skipper was unaware of the drama he had created, but the RAF Search and Rescue Station at Portland Bill had picked up the May Day and had dispatched their rescue launch to the scene.

The MFV Skipper seeing the RAF Launch let go a signal rocket which went the wrong way and sank his dinghy from under them. Nevertheless all of them were eventually rescued.

Their Lordships were not at all well pleased when the local rag the next day ran the story with the headlines

'LOCAL HERO SUNK BY RN RESCUED BY RAF'

And the boat's Skipper was suitably dealt with.

Chapter 31

Attack

While all this was going on I was keeping binoculars focused on the Dock below, when suddenly a couple of bodies appeared on the upper decks of both sides and started shouting and gesticulating at each other. They were then joined by others on each side and a full scale slanging match appeared to ensue. I got Dusty's attention and between us we observed at least sixteen bodies in all. They eventually dispersed and disappeared back down below, and Dusty advised the other two groups of the situation and instructed them to halt their advance, hold position, and await instructions. He and I then had a short discussion on the state of play, which led to him informing the others of his plan of action.

'C to A and B.' And both groups responded.

'We have assessed minimum one six Xs and believe that some or all will pass east to A's position to acquire disabled unit at or before dusk. A to detain, interrogate and advise C of result. B to retreat from view of A's position and await instruction which may be to assist A.'

The plan was for us of C team to wait till dusk or dark to board the dock, but if any of the gang decided to go back to their base they would want to use the now disabled launch, and Spike's team would be able to ambush them and possibly find out the score regarding personnel numbers, future plans and general dock and boat conditions.

It was now just a matter of waiting and watching, which Dusty and I took in turns as it was very tiring and any lapse of concentration could result in something important being missed, which could have serious consequences.

While I was waiting my turn of I-spy it reminded me that it was just such a lack of concentration that could have cost a few lives, if not the loss of an entire boat.

When a boat comes in from an extended patrol there are usually plenty of defects and it was usual to send down assistance from inboard (Depot Ship) to assist, and for all fitting work Spare Crew personnel are used as they are qualified boats Tiffs.

One particular individual, who shall remain nameless, obviously had something other than work on his mind. The job he was given was to replace a slightly leaking hydraulic actuator seal on number seven Diving Main Vent, the single one right back aft. The routine in any job on Main Vents is to ensure that the boat's safety is paramount and that the vent is fully shut, cottered and locked before commencing the job. The cotter is inserted to ensure the vent is mechanically locked shut and with it fitted not even the hydraulics can open it. Next the hydraulic supply and return of the items has to be isolated and any residual pressure locked in vented off, which as will be remembered from science class at school is easy, because liquids are incompressible, so one little drop released and the pressures all gone. The Fitter decided that as the seal was leaking he didn't deem it necessary to do this, as he assumed that it had already depressurized. If he had followed procedure with this type of repair, none of the following would have happened.

The one major thing that our fitter failed to do was to vent off the air side of the Air Loaded Accumulator. These units are fitted to any hydraulically operated unit that maintains hull integrity and are fitted so that they cannot be isolated from that unit. It is fitted to ensure that in the unlikely event of a loss of hydraulic pressure the Air Loaded Accumulator will take over and ensure the item it is connected to stays in its appropriate position. In the case of a main vent this means shut, as it has, as its name implies, air pressure on top of a quantity of oil. The correct procedure at this stage would have been to drain the air from the Air Loaded Accumulator which unfortunately was omitted.

To progress the repair the fitter had to undo an hydraulic union, which on this boat was sealed with polymer 'O' rings. If the main 'O' ring starts to leak a small hole in the union nut starts to weep and indicates that it has to be repaired at the next available opportunity. Our Tiff gaily started to undo the union nut, but 'O' seals are notorious in that they give way suddenly when it is undone with pressure behind it. The pressure by the way is 4,000 psi (four thousand pounds to every square inch) which is the equivalent of 20 large men all standing on an area the size of a fifty pence piece.

As was inevitable the 'O' seal eventually gave way and the hydraulic oil shot out of the tell tale in a vaporized stream. It could have hit the bulkhead and made a mess, it could have hit the Tiff and given him an embolism with possible fatal consequences, but sod's law dictated that it went straight into the centre of a switched on electric fire and immediately burst into a roaring inferno, which was fortunately extinguished in record time by others, but causing extensive damage. The perpetrator after a full enquiry was returned to General Service.

Back to watching and waiting and I was back with the binoculars in the late afternoon, when a couple of blokes appeared on the far deck, walked to the east end and disappeared. I informed Dusty and we waited for a while but they didn't reappear, and we deduced that they may be departing, so Dusty got on the blower to Spike.

'C to A.'

'C'

'Movement of two times X, suggest you scout west to investigate.

'Will do.'

No more movement was seen from our vantage point, but just under an hour later Spike reported back.

'Have been forward with one native and witnessed approximately ten times Xs ashore and heading for tethered craft. We are now preparing welcoming committee.'

H told me later what had gone on. It appears that Spike and his scout legged it back to where the launch was moored and he and H had loaded their grenade launcher automatics with stun granades and got the natives to conceal themselves in the sparse bush. Spike then by sign language explained to them to wait for his signal. Eventually a rag tag bunch were heard arguing vehemently well before they came into view. When at last they hove into sight, the last thing on their minds was the idea of being attacked. Spike waited till most of them were aboard their vessel and then he and H lobbed stun grenades in among them and then covered them with the automatics while Click's men went at them with a will, and had them trussed up before they had time to recover their senses.

H and Spike then realized that they had no way of communicating with their captives, so Spike called Dusty up and explained the situation, who came back with the solution. *Gasbag* was ordered to go alongside the enemy vessel when it was dusk and embark the captives and captors and retreat to its original safe hiding place for interrogations, question and answer sessions with the aid of Ali.

This seemed to Spike and H to be an excellent solution, but just to get the captives in the right frame of mind whilst waiting for the light to fade, Spike decided to perform what might be described as a war dance with the aid of a pair of deadly looking knives, back and forth along the line of the poor unfortunates who seemed to take it all very much to heart by the look of their terrified expressions. Even some of our natives also looked a bit worried at times.

Dusty instructed Betty regarding the transfer of the captives along with Spike and H at dusk, and *Gasbag* duly arrived slowly and silently on auxiliary diesels. The transfer was completed and Betty took them back to his start point, then the serious stuff began.

The International Court of Human Rights may not have approved but considering what these animals had inflicted on a whole community over a prolonged period, some might consider Spike's methods relatively mild. Nevertheless, his method of divide and conquer did bear fruit, and once he realized that the majority of the interviewees, pain threshold was very low, even the threat of violence on most brought forth abject pleadings for mercy, and having chosen the weakest and most voluble of these he started a systematic question and answer programme with surprisingly frank results. He quickly came to the conclusion that for the majority their heart really wasn't in the job.

The results of the 'interviews' was that there were another five personnel left onboard the dock as night-watchmen on the boat. The gang we had in custody were just caretakers trying to clear up the mess that had been caused by the first attack. They were waiting for a relief team to supposedly mend the damage, but the general consensus was that it was all beyond repair as the dock was virtually in two halves. It appears that the explosion caused the docksides to fall inwards which dislodged the cranes, and as it settled on the bottom, the two sides straightened up again to appear intact.

As regards the boat, none of the captives had been allowed anywhere near it. When asked about armaments i. e. torpedoes, none of them knew anything of that side of things, the only positive thing that came out of this line of questioning was that there was some sort of high security underground storage area back at the base.

Information was more forthcoming about the remaining five individuals who they seemed to think were submariners and a very different kettle of fish. It seems that they kept themselves to themselves and didn't mix, but were also waiting for an extra gang to join them to assist in whatever they were up to, but they didn't know what. All they did know was that some damage had been inflicted on the boat and some compartments had been flooded. What did come to light was that the remaining gang were living in the north wall of the dock, which would help in their apprehension.

All this information was transmitted to Dusty and me who, after a short conflab decided that the Gang on the dock must be rounded up as soon as possible, as suspicion would very likely already have been roused by the stun grenade noise. So Betty was ordered to return Spike and H to where they were picked up, and also disembark Ali and Click, embark all but one of the natives to act as guards over the captives and Betty then to take *Gasbag* back to the village and dump them, to be left to the 'tender care' of the residents and get back to his original position ready to take part in the assault on the dock and its residents as soon as possible, if not sooner.

Betty put the gas turbines to good use once out of earshot of the dock and having dumped the captives with the villagers, was back in record time and raring to get stuck in. So in no time at all everybody was back in their original positions and ready to go.

Dusty then got on the blower again to instruct all parties on the attack details.

'On the Go order 'C' team to make their way up the north bank towards the dock. 'B' to steam up river to keep pace with 'C' and give them covering fire if required. We of 'A' team will meet 'C' team at the access area to the dock north wall. Stand by for instruction to execute.'

'I hate to ask,' I interrupted, 'but how the hell do we get to the dock?'

'We swim, come on,' and we legged it down the far side of the headland.

Arriving at the water's edge, Dusty got on the blower again and gave the order to execute and received acknowledgement from both groups, and we took to the oggin at a point to the west of the dock to ensure that the river flow would drift us down onto it. Eventually we rounded the far corner of the dock and immediately sighted 'C' team, and also saw that access to the dock wall was by a brow to a pontoon and then a vertical steel ladder. Dusty signalled Spike to follow him up the ladder, and the rest of us to follow quietly, and off they shot vertically.

I was next, followed by Ali and then the natives, and as I reached the upper deck I heard a stun grenade go off, then shortly after another, and then some small arms fire, and as we all crowded round the access hatch the head and shoulders of a dazed stranger appeared. The next thing, quick as a flash, as I remember was that Click's lads pounced on him, dragged him out onto the deck and had him trussed like a chicken before he realized what was happening.

Spike's head popped up a moment or two later, grinning like a Cheshire cat, and called for some assistance, so Ali, I and a couple of natives obliged and followed him two decks down and into a filthy looking mess compartment with the rest of the opposition liked up against the far bulkhead with Dusty covering them. The natives set to work with a will and had all five of them trussed in a trice with hands together behind the back and a loop round the neck, which meant that if they struggled too much they tended to choke. Dusty ordered them to be taken to the upper deck and called *Gasbag* in alongside the pontoon to transfer the prisoners and called for H to join him and me, and bring a radiation detector and torches to enable us to take a shufti aboard the boat.

While we were waiting for all this to happen, Spike gave us a run down on what occurred.

'Dusty was like a ferret down a rabbit hole and it took me all my time to keep up. We could hear a heated conversation coming from down below us and we just followed the noise. He had a stun grenade at the ready with the pin pulled as we approached the compartment where all the noise was coming from. I got a stun grenade at the ready too as we paused outside the slightly open door to peer in. Then he slipped his grenade in through the door and slammed it shut. The detonation for us was bad enough, so you can imagine what it was like for the poor sods inside. Dusty then opened the door, saw some movement so invited me to lob my grenade in and slammed the door shut again, which seemed to bulge outwards with the detonation. We re-entered the mess to find, through the murk, five bodies in various states of concussion. At about the same time, out of the corner of my eye, I caught sight of a body dashing past the open doorway (which was the sixth), so I sent him on his way with a short burst of small arms fire in the hope that it would warn your gang of the escapee, which in fact you sorted no trouble. We had our captives facing the bulkhead, arms up leaning outwards, legs spread Yankee style when you joined us.

'Spike,' Dusty yelled, 'Do your knife juggling act on the prisoners for a bit and see what you can find out. I'm going with H and Ted aboard the boat 'cos they know what they're looking at and I want to have a shufti for the torpedoes, and see what damage there is generally to the hull and fittings.'

There was a brow* down onto the boat's slightly listing casing and the torpedo loading hatch was open, so we dropped down into the fore ends*, had a good look round and found no fish, either in the stowage spaces or up the spout (in the tubes), and there was no radiation detected in the compartment.

We worked our way back aft to the control room which didn't seem to be in too bad a condition, so we carefully opened the air lock to the tunnel, the heavily shielded access across the reactor compartment to get back aft, and checked for radiation which was well within limits, so we went through into the Auxiliary Machinery Space which was a shambles with all the reactor control electronics and main electrical distribution gear badly fire damaged. The compartment had also suffered severe flood damage which was very likely the results of Andy's handiwork from the previous attack.

Further back aft the engine room seemed pretty intact but that could easily be 'rectified.' So we retraced our steps and boarded *Gasbag* and Dusty ordered our evacuation back to the village, where en route he convened a meeting to discuss our next move.

Chapter 32

Search

The meeting opened with Spike giving us a rundown on what he had managed to squeeze out of our reluctant guest, explaining that having obtained information about a supposed secret underground storage facility at the Naval Base from the first group of prisoners, and also knowing that some other experts were about to join the project, he had an edge on the latest captives and under interrogation using this information weeded out the weakest one, the one who had tried to leg it, and when 'interviewed' again on his own was persuaded to show us what he knew as long as the rest of his gang didn't get to know, but admitted that he hadn't a clue when the new team would be arriving.

'That's good,' Dusty broke in, 'we can organize a search party to locate the storage and investigate its contents and then if necessary seek guidance on disposal.

The other problem we have is the condition of the boat, which according to H and Ted is not too badly damaged apart from the Auxiliary Machinery Space. They advise me that they have a plan so please explain to us what you propose.'

'Ted and I have decided that large lumps will have to be disabled as the AMS* electrical gear is relatively small items which can relatively easily be repaired or replaced. Therefore the large lumps we should damage would be the turbo-generator rotors and gear boxes and the main engine turbine rotors and their reduction gear box. These large lumps could only be replaced by large engineering groups in the UK and would obviously not be made available, so consequently re-commissioning the boat would not be a viable project.

We are sure that Dusty and Spike will be able to assist us to lay the explosives in the appropriate positions for maximum effect.'

'Thanks H, we'd be happy to oblige, has anybody got any questions? Yes Sam?'

'What do we do if we find Nuclear devices?'

'We will signal Admiral Hopgood, and he will seek professional advice, as he is surrounded by experts on all sorts of subjects OK Anything else?'

Nothing else was forthcoming so we carried on steaming full tilt for the village.

On arrival the prisoners were unloaded and handed over, the same as the first bunch, to the tender mercies of the villagers. They weren't treated cruelly but firmly and worked hard under very strict supervision.

As there would be no more grenade attacks on the sea life Click was presented with the Whalers and all the gear and rigging that went with them. Click and his fishermen were over the moon and H and I helped them launch them both and showed them how they were rigged, as we had as apprentices done a lot of whaler sailing and racing under canvas and pulling. The lads were quick learners and were away in mid bay fishing in no time at all.

We for our part had a brew up and a bite to eat and while we were at it H reminded me of our time as apprentices and some of the tricks we got up to.

Our first taste of workshop life, at the tender age of fifteen, was wood butchering (shipwrighting). One of the tricks to wind one of the lads up was to distract him at stand easy (tea break) so that he left his full pint enamel mug on the wooden bench. Once he was out of sight the co-conspirators decanted his name marked mug into another one, drove a 4in nail through the bottom of it into the bench and refilled it with his tea. The result was usually quite spectacular, and would almost result in a dislocated finger. The other bad move was to nail some poor unfortunate's hat to the bench if he was so lax as to leave it unattended.

Both unfortunate recipients would also be in the rattle* for misappropriation on Naval property and also have to pay for replacements.

Dusty decided that the priority was for us to locate the underground storage facility if it existed and then, if located, search the area for nuclear arms and if any were found to signal Nore Command and seek advice on safe dismantling and disposal. Then while waiting for a reply proceed to the boat and do the demolition bit.

The snag was that we would have to move fast and keep a weather eye open as we knew that enemy reinforcements were due to arrive at any time. So *Gasbag* was steamed full tilt back where we came from with our Grass in tow and landed at the Naval Base jetty and went about finding the buried treasure, leaving Betty and Sam as *Gasbag*'s minders while keeping a radio listening watch.

The Grass led us to the rear of what looked very like the Admin. Block to what appeared to be DQ cells complete with barred gates. With no keys the only option was to blow the lock. So Spike got to work with a little blob of plastic explosive and a time delay detonator, retired us to a safe distance and boom. When the dust settled we piled in, looked round and found a couple of wooden doors in the rear, which gave way to

Dusty's boot. The second one revealed an overhead lifting rail and on closer inspection a pair of large trapdoors in the deck.

It took two of us to lift each one open to reveal some concrete steps leading down into blackness. Good old Ali found a light switch and a huge underground workshop and storage area was illuminated, and there in their glory were a dozen torpedoes.

On closer inspection the propulsion units were old type Mk21s driven by compression ignition (diesel) engines fuelled by shale oil and compressed air. But the warheads which were not connected to the drive units were a different kettle of fish, with Arabic and Cyrillic markings and the well known nuclear signs.

Bingo, we'd hit pay dirt, but Click had disappeared, then suddenly we heard him calling from some distance away. Following the voice we came across a tunnel with narrow gauge railway lines let into the deck with Click at the end of the line struggling to open what looked like a very heavy steel door. We all lent a hand and after a struggle swung it wide to reveal the oggin and the underside of the jetty and *Gasbag* alongside at the end of it, so that's how they got the fish in. We closed the steel door and retraced our steps taking careful note of the hieroglyphics plastered all over the warheads on our way out, and legged it back to *Gasbag*.

Dusty immediately coded a signal regarding our findings and the markings on them, and requested urgent instructions as to disposal of same, and transmitted it to Hoppy.

Acknowledgement was received almost immediately with instruction to standby and wait.

So Dusty decided that we ought to do the demolition job on the boat before any reinforcements arrived.

By now it was becoming dusk so everybody re-boarded *Gasbag*, cast off and headed up river back to the Dock where Dusty, Spike, H and I transferred to it loaded down with plastic explosive, detonators, cortex, tools and torches. Re-boarding the boat we travelled back aft into the engine room. H and I removed lagging and inspection panels for Dusty and Spike to lay the charges and detonators in the best places and link them together. We decided to include the TG* Governor Valves and the Main Engine ahead and astern throttles as well as the Generators, Rotors and Gearboxes.

The last finishing touches were being applied when the blower exploded into life with a desperate Betty screaming that they could hear a helicopter approaching. Spike told him to calm down and asked him if he could tell which direction it was coming from, at the same time as H and I packed up while Spike finished fixing the electronic master detonator, while Betty told Spike he thought it was coming from the east. Then we all legged it back the way we came, and shot up the ladders to the open hatch of the dockside deck. Spike peered out into the now moon-less night and saw the navigation lights of the distant helicopter heading for the main base jetty. Dusty got on the blower to Betty and told him to bring *Gasbag* round the dock under the south side to the upstream end on the auxiliary diesels slowly without navigation lights and black lighting* on the Bridge.

We four then shinned down the dockside onto the access brow and waited for *Gasbag* to creep round the corner while we kept a careful eye on the Paraffin Budgie* and saw it land on the jetty and identified it as a twin rotor Boeing Chinook, and witnessed a number of bodies disembarking. We counted at least ten personnel but were not too sure of the final count.

Then we saw *Gasbag* coming round the corner of the dock and approaching us slowly and silently and we embarked.

'Has Nore Command come back to us with any answers yet Betty?'

'No Dusty not a peep as yet,' Betty replied.

'OK then, we've got to see if we can find out what's happening back at the base with the opposition. H, can you and Ted suit up and take a dip and pop round the dock corner and see what you can see?' Dusty queried.

'I don't see why not, we'll use wet suits and the re-breathing gear just in case we have to hide or retreat, OK?'

So he and I got rigged up and dropped into the oggin with our sets sealed and ready for use if required. We made our way round the northwest corner of the dock, under the brow to the Eastern end but the river bank obscured our view of the jetty, so we headed into midstream on a southeast course and eventually got a good view of proceedings.

All we could see was the now shutdown Chinook, and lights on in the base, and nothing else, which H reported back to Dusty.

'We'll stay in mid-stream and head nearer to the jetty to get a better view to see if we spot what's happening.'

'OK but don't take any unnecessary risks.'

So we hung about in the tepid water which felt quite pleasant really, a far cry from Rosyth Tug Basin or Caledonia's Swimming Bath which was usually a bit chilly. We had a bit of a laugh about it as we'd been used to it both in qualifying as Shallow Water Divers, and before that as apprentices when swimming was compulsory.

We had a bit of a laugh about our apprentice days, and in the course of conversation H reminded me of the time we helped out a fellow apprentice who was a Kiwi and a real good hand.

He was over six foot tall, and built like a brick toilet, a good boxer and an excellent rugby player, and an absolutely crap fitter, who had somehow managed to struggle and scrape his way to his passing out test job which he was making a right pig's ear of. The problem was that if he failed this particular test piece he would fail the whole Apprenticeship and would be returned to New Zealand in disgrace.

H was the good deep thinking one, I was the good fitter. I wasn't bragging, just stating a fact, so what H did was organize the rescue operation of the said Kiwi.

First of all H organized a few of us to 'borrow' files and tools from the workshop and store them in the communal hobbies room. The next problem he had was to purloin the said crap test job before it was ruined completely by our friend. I don't know how but manage it he did. The other great problem was that every piece of the test job had to have an identifying mark stamped on it with a sharp blow with a hammer on a hardened steel type stamp, which left a symbol on it specifically issued for that job.

If you were going to start work on the face with the mark on it you had to approach the Instructor to have another face stamped before you removed the original mark. If the Instructor couldn't find the previous mark before he remarked it (you had removed it by mistake), you either failed there and then or were given a new blank piece of material and had to start it again, which consequently earned you time penalties.

To this day I don't know how, but suddenly, just before the weekend break the relevant steel stamp with the correct mark appeared in the hobbies room, so I spent that night and the weekend grafting to try and resurrect the mess our buddy had made. I was even brought food and drinks to the hobbies room while a guard was stationed out side the door to keep nosy parkers with prying eyes away.

Somehow, at the end of the weekend I'd done my best to rectify the damage, and come Monday morning back at the workshop H had managed to arrange the Test Jobs reappearance.

The outcome was that our Kiwi friend passed his Block Strap Gib and Cotter Test Job with a reasonable margin. He was so gobsmacked, pleased and happy that he grabbed me, slung me on his shoulders and ran from dorm to dorm screaming that he'd passed, to loud applause, the only snag being that him being over six foot tall had me almost getting brained every time we went through a doorway. I only avoided severe injury by laying back horizontally each time.

Just before I got banged up I was told by I forget who, that our Kiwi friend had eventually risen to the dizzy height of Engineering Lieutenant Commander.

''Ello 'ello, look out, they're on the move.'

H brought me back to the present and reality, and pointed out a few flashing torches milling about on the jetty by the chopper, and then in line astern they headed back off the jetty and set off along the river bank in the direction of the dock.

'Dusty, movement at our end, they're on the way over to the dock on foot by the look of them.'

'Got that, can you try and get a head count?'

'OK stand by.'

We both tried counting bodies, but all we could guarantee was the number of torches and agreed that we could only be positive about the minimum number. After about ten minutes we decided on seven, which was less than the original estimate.

'We can only count seven Dusty, but all we can count are the torches they're using, so seven is minimum.'

'OK come back to *Gasbag* as quick as you can, but try and keep me posted on their progress if you can. I've decided that we'll detonate the boat when they go aboard it and then try and trap them in the dock using the same routine as the last time.'

Fortunately the tide had turned and was now in our favour and we made good time to the dock just ahead of the opposition, so we decided to go back the way we came, up the north side of the dock, and clear our sets and submerge under the brow and wait for the shore party to cross, so that we could possibly get an accurate head count. We informed Dusty of our intentions of which he approved with the proviso that we got back to *Gasbag* safely ASAP.

Just in time we parked ourselves, dived at the dock end of the brow with an occasional sly shufti to check the shore party's progress. In no time at all they were on the brow, so, hugging the dock hull either side of the brow we peered up leaving as little as possible visible.

When all movement had ceased we dived and made our way back East and surfaced at the corner of the dock and both agreed that the accurate count was definitely seven which meant that if Dusty's number was correct there were three bodies left at the base.

We informed Dusty of the count and the fact that they were aboard the dock and that we were heading back to join them and to expect us very shortly. Then we dived again, to be sure we wouldn't be spotted, and made our way round the dock corner and eventually came upon *Gasbag* and were helped aboard, and it was such a relief to be able to get rid of the breathing gear and the suit, as we'd been in it for quite some time. Dusty congratulated us for our efforts.

'Thanks Dusty, but where's Spike?'

'He's at the corner of the dock keeping an eye on the boat's brow so that we can blow the thing when they are aboard.'

'Any news from Hoppy?'

'Yes it came through while you were keeping an eye on the chopper. The warheads are the real thing all right. The snag is he wants us to try and recover them. How the hell we're going to do it is another matter. The other thing that's worrying me is that our head count doesn't tally. I reckon there are two or three bodies still at the base and they could possibly be the crew of the chopper. By the by, did you happen to notice if any of the team you counted were carrying arms?'

''Fraid not, we had enough trouble counting the bodies, let alone see what they were carrying. By the way, I hate to say this but I reckon that we might be in for a long wait 'cos there's a big possibility that they'll spend the night in the dock and inspect the boats condition in the morning, as they'll want to do an external survey first. That's what I would do if it was me anyway.'

'I think you could be right, so you and H get your heads down for a bit and later on I'll relieve Spike.'

'Would anybody like a cuppa?' Sam shouted from somewhere in the bowels.

'What a good idea, I thought you'd never ask.' H shouted back, so we had a sup and a wedge, then I dozed on and off for a bit but couldn't sleep. But when I did doze my mind wandered to *Killisport* and hammocks.

I think we must have been one of the last vessels in the RN to still sling them. Slinging a hammock was a pain in the bum, but once rigged properly it could be quite comfortable, but fraught with disaster if not. Poor rigging can cause all sorts of problems and pitfalls, for instance if the nettles aren't tied to the eyelets correctly they slowly let go one at a time while you are crashed out. Eventually the last couple give way and down you go. Depending on which end gives way first depends which end hits the steel deck first. If it's the head end a severe headache is guaranteed. Another problem is if the head end nettles are left too long and/or the stretcher is too short. As the occupant tosses and turns eventually the stretcher lets go like an arrow from a bow and is lethal for the neighbours, and buries the contents as the sides close in, which makes it difficult to evacuate. Some who thought to make their lives easier by using slip knots to speed up the rigging and unrigging of their sleeping appliance often came unstuck by their own messmates who, coming aboard from a good run ashore, a little merry and playful, would ease the slip knots undone, place the loose ends in the slumbering occupants hands and then wake him up, and stand back to watch the poor unfortunate seesawing until his grip gave way with bone crushing results.

An alarming incident occurred on *Killisport* while in the Indian Ocean one early morning during reveille when one of our Celanese* chefs, for some unknown reason, went berserk with a very sharp carving knife in the Chief and PO's Mess. He ran amuck underneath the rows of hammocks slashing the bulging undersides crosswise, fortunately not drawing any blood, but it was quite a sight with so many arses poking through.

The worst bit really, for us non sailor types, was the five minutes seamanship last thing at night unlashing and rigging, and first thing in the morning lashing and stowing the dammed thing. You were supposed to have seven lashings round it to ensure a neat and tidy tube effect with all your bedding and cordage inside, and neatly stowed vertically in the hammock netting. Usually our mess's netting looked like a scran bag* full of sacks of spuds with bits hanging out.

I was rudely brought back to reality by Ali asking me to join Dusty on the bridge, so off I trotted and found the rest of the team all assembled.

'Thank you all for joining me, I know we're all really tired but I've had an idea and I've worked out a plan, but I want to float it past you to see what you think and see if you approve.'

'My preoccupation has been with Nore Command's request for us to recover the warhead, and it suddenly came to me that the perfect solution is parked on the end of the jetty.'

'What, you mean the furious palm tree*?' H enquired.

'Exactly, the problem is who's going to drive it? Well if my guess is correct the two or three bodies left at the base are the chopper crew. If they're not, we're in the crap and we'll have to think again, but I think it's worth the risk, and if I am right we either befriend them or force them to help us at gun point, what do we all think?'

Everybody agreed that it was worth a try, and as I pointed out there was nothing to lose, and if it came off a lot of problems would be solved.

'OK then we're all agreed that it's worth a go, but then a problem arises in that I don't want the gang on the dock to be made aware of our presence until as late as possible, therefore while the main party go and kidnap the Paraffin Budgie* and crew, somebody has got to stay behind to do the detonation bit when the party on the dock decide to inspect the boat.'

Quick as a flash Ali put himself forward.

'Click and I'll do that so that you lot can get on with the important stuff.'

'Are you sure Ali?'

'Absolutely, even I can press a button, the only hard bit is going to be staying awake and alert, so Click and I can spell each other.'

'OK then that's settled, the next thing is the actual attack on the Chinook and what to do when this lot here decide to board the boat. We're gong to have to take *Gasbag* so I propose that Click's lads split into two groups, half with us and half with Ali and Click. Ali and Click to relieve Spike and get him back here, the lads to go ashore and stay hidden until the boat inspection party realize all is not well and decide to return to the base, which will very likely be after Ali has pressed the tit and blown the engine room to bits. Don't forget Ali, do the deed when they are aboard, but before they get right back aft, OK? Once done get ashore and wait with your party for the inspection party to depart the dock and follow them without being detected and inform me by radio of the fact that they are heading in our direction.

We for our part will hopefully secure the chopper and the bodies left with it. Any questions? No, well let's get to it then and good luck.

Chapter 33

Takeover

Having recovered Spike and deployed Ali and his team, we set off in *Gasbag* back to the Base under cover of darkness as fast as possible on diesels. Dusty called us all together.

'I propose to do a pincer movement to capture the remaining bodies, H if you come with me, and Ted you go with Spike. H and I will land on the Jetty, you and Spike will go under the jetty and enter the underground storage area by the access door we found. We go in fully armed and assume that whoever we meet is hostile, but we don't want them killed because they may be useful to us, the natives will stay with Betty and Sam who will land us on the jetty, if the coast is clear, as quietly as possible and then lay off ready to re-berth as and when required. Any questions?'

'Yes' Sam chipped in, 'anybody want a drink?' which caused a little ripple of laughter, and we all had a brew.

Then on the subject of liquid refreshment H told us about his experience of the disappearing Ky. Ky was a ritual for the silent hour watches (middle and morning), the Pussers* version of cocoa or hot chocolate made by painstakingly finely flaking a large block of dark unsweetened chocolate into a large Fanny*, then large quantities of sugar and condensed milk are added and topped off to final quantity with water (not a lot) then the whole lot is boiled up by injecting live steam from a drain in the engine room which is kept especially clean for that purpose.

The drain used on Bigbury Bay according to H was the steam drain off the operating cylinder of the port vacuum pump.

Came the Middle Watch and Ky time the engine room watch had just finished theirs when a lot of manoeuvring orders started coming down and were all a bit preoccupied when a young sailor came down with the upper deck's Ky for boiling up. He asked H where the steam drain was and H pointed in the direction of the vacuum pump, not realizing that the sailor was new at the job. The next thing that happened was that the port salinity alarms went off indicating contaminated boiler feed water which was serious as the boilers could prime and cause real damage. Then it just so happened that the young sailor came back into the centres looking confused and tearful.

'What the hell's up with you?' H barked.

'Me Ky's disappeared!'

'Oh shit, dump the port vacuum pump discharge fast,' he barked, and the leading stoker of the watch leapt to open the drain valve.

'You stupid git, you used the wrong drain, you got the vacuum side, piss off out of my sight.'

'What do I do about the Ky?'

'Tell your watch Chief what happened and expect a good kickin,' and carried on trying to clear the salinity alarm which is set off by any contaminants.

Betty declutched the engines and allowed the tide, which had just turned, to take us gently and silently alongside the jetty. A quick all round sweep with the night glasses yielded nothing dodgy so Spike and I, now rigged in wet suits, went over the side with our arms over our heads and swam towards the underground storage door. Meanwhile Dusty and H made their way round the Chinook, taking a quick peer inside to ensure it was uninhabited, and as quickly and silently as possible legged it down the jetty.

Spike and I swam under the jetty and heard the slight noise of Dusty and H above us. We got to the steel door and with difficulty forced it open slightly and had a shufti inside and checked that it was all clear, so we swung it wide enough to pass through and closed it behind us. Using the torches on our weapons we made our way to the concrete steps and the trapdoors where we paused to listen for any activity the other side. Hearing nothing Spike put his back to the right hand door and eased it open enough for me to take a peek and, seeing the coast clear, we swung the door back, climbed out and eased it back down again. We got as far as the barred barrier and had just exited it when we heard what sounded like Dusty shouting something, quickly followed by the detonation of a stun grenade. Simultaneously the door to our area burst open and a heavily armed individual dashed through. I froze but Spike was with it, shouting for the individual to stop. Then, almost in slow motion, I saw the man start to raise his side arm towards us. Spike, who already had his weapon to his shoulder squeezed off a shot, and the target spun to his right and lost the grip on his firearm. With that Spike was across the gap towards the man, kicking his weapon away and dropping down to kneel on the middle of his back with the muzzle of his weapon at the back of his head. He called me over to check him for any other weapons and I found all sorts as he had been armed to the teeth. Dusty shot through the same door, saw us and broke into a wry grin.

'Everything OK?'

'Yea, put one in his shoulder. How are you doing?'

'Got two, unarmed though, I think this one was their minder, but we'll soon find out when they get their senses back.' With that Spike told me to take over the gun to the head bit while he ty-rapped his hands behind his back. Then we turned him over and got him to his feet to reveal a rather tall athletic Arabic type.

Spike then drew his fighting knife and went towards his victim who flinched backwards, but Spike grabbed him and told him to stand still, and proceeded to cut away the clothing from his injured shoulder to reveal a clean wound with the round passing straight through the fleshy part. So he cleaned it up and applied a field dressing to it and told him to stand in the corner facing the wall, and got me to stand guard over him. I was glad he was facing the wall because his almost handsome face was distorted by what looked like a permanent sneer, which really teed me off, making me feel as if I wanted to remove it.

We found out that Dusty and H's experience started when they made it to the main buildings front door, had a sneaky look in, and saw three individuals in heated conversation, so Dusty, having warned H of his intentions, burst in with his rifle at the ready and shouted for them to stand still. Two did, the other went for the back door so the stun grenade went in and Dusty exited the door and shut it, re-entering after the eruption to hear the small arms shot, with the remaining two decidedly disorientated and bewildered.

Having checked that things were all in hand with us, Dusty went back to his own captives and once they had recovered their senses started to interrogate them and discovered that they were indeed the Chinook's crew, in fact they owned it. They were in fact Zimbabweans, ex Air Force who had become very disillusioned with the regime and had gone private, having pinched the Chinook and a whole load of spares to go with it. They had gone into business for themselves and it appears that they had been quite successful up until this particular job which had gone from bad to worse, culminating in their present situation. They had been hired to transport a supposed repair team to an oil installation, and bring out the team that they were relieving, at least that's what they were told. They said that they had their doubts when the one who had been shot was left with them and the others, fully armed, went off in a westerly direction.

'How many bodies did you bring in with you all together, and where did you pick them up from?'

'We picked up eight including the one you have from Mogadishu in Somalia and stopped somewhere well south of that for a re-fuel, but I don't know where it was as it was out in the sticks.'

'OK then, so who are you both?'

'I'm Ex-Flight Lieutenant Dan Masters, and this is Ex-Flight Sergeant Tony Mays my Co-Pilot and Mechanic.'

'Well you don't really want to know who we are, but how would you like to be hired by the good guys for a change?' Dusty enquired.

'We'll do it for zilch if it gets us out of the mess we're in at the moment.'

'How are you off for fuel then?'

'We're carrying a load in drums, enough to top up to a full load.'

'Well go and do just that then and consider yourselves hired, OK?'

'Will do.' And away they trotted looking very relieved indeed. Dusty beckoned Spike over.

'Go with 'em and keep an eye on 'em, I don't fully trust them at this stage. If you can, grill them a bit and see if you can learn anything else about them. Oh and if either of them so much as tries to start the engines, shoot them, but only to injure them and don't damage the shithouse.' He grinned.

Dusty then called Betty up and explained that the base had been secured, and to bring *Gasbag* back alongside the jetty, and told him to ask Sam to put a brew on.

He then got on the blower to Ali to see if there was any action at his end, but the reply was negative. They all then assembled on the jetty and in no time at all *Gasbag* was back alongside and everybody piled aboard, including the prisoner who was released from his ty-rap, but instead handcuffed by the wrist of his good arm to a very solid part of *Gasbag*s plumbing.

A quick brew was consumed and nearly everybody tried to get a bit of shuteye as it had been a long day. That is apart from Dusty and Betty, who penned, encoded and transmitted a signal to Hoppy.

URGENT TOP SECRET F. T. A. O. ADMIRAL SIR A HOPGOOD
Ref. Operation Docksunk.
(A) HAVE LOCATED TWELVE (12) NUCLEAR WARHEADS
MINUS FIRING PISTOLS
(B) HAVE HIRED CHINOOK HELICOPTER TO TRANSPORT (A)
(C) ADVISE PLANS FOR DESTINATION OF (A)
(D) HAVE ONE (1) SLIGHTLY INJURED PRISONER
(E) SEVEN (7) OTHER OPPOSITION NOT YET DEALT WITH
BUT EXPECT CONFRONTATION SOON
(F) ADVISE DISPOSAL OF (D) AND (E)

Then it was their turn to try and get a few Zeds* as Sam had volunteered to man the radio in case of a reply from Hoppy.

H and I were in a huddle talking about old times. H related the problem they had on Bigbury Bay with the Air Conditioning. They were exercising in the Equator area of the Atlantic and it was as hot as hell. The vessel was equipped with lots of individual Air Conditioning Units. The snag was that the Bootnecks were always complaining that their unit wasn't working and their mess was as hot as hell. The real reason was that their mess was in the fore peak where the deckhead was fully exposed to the sun, you could fry an egg on the fore peak deck. In desperation the Chief Tiff told the Tiff in charge of the Refrigeration and Air Conditioning with H as his second dicky, to shift the expansion valve of their unit up into the mess so that they could watch the refrigerant expanding (which causes the cooling effect) through the sight glass of the valve, and also see the discharge pipe from it with a large lump of ice and frost on it. The refrigeration cooling effect was obviously no better and possibly slightly worse, but the Bootnecks swore blind that it was much improved and no more complaints were received.

I recounted the story of REA Bunny Warren, a very clever and competent Tiff who was top notch at his job. His main job was to look after the state of the art ASDIC Gear on *Vectra*, the workings of which I've already explained. One of his minor duties was to service and maintain the depth recorders of which there were a few. One of them was an upward pointing unit to record our actual depth and as a spin off the ice thickness when in those climes, so it was a very important unit.

During a deep transit this unit became US* and was reported to Bunny who came up to the control room to fix it. I was on watch at the Panel* and heard a lot of swearing and cursing coming from the other side of the compartment so, as it was quiet, I wandered across to see what all the commotion was about. There was Bunny trying to prise an electronic bottle about two inches in diameter out of the face of the unit. The end of it was flush with the face of the recorder and about six inches long. He'd been trying to prise it out with a pair of screwdrivers by digging holes in the sides of it and levering, but the thin aluminium casing just kept splitting through the front and he was getting desperate and very frustrated. I volunteered to get it out for him, he looked a bit unconvinced but agreed to let me have a go, so I called over the watch Stoker and asked him to go forrard and get me a couple of yards of cod line. Bunny asked me rather scornfully what I intended doing with a bit of string, and I told him to wait and see. The Stoker returned with the cod line and I formed a timber hitch by forming two loops and putting the second behind the first and slotted it over the butchered end of the bottle. I borrowed Bunny's screwdriver and pushed the loops about two inches down the tube, pulled both ends tight with a bit of jiggling, then took a firm hold of both ends and gave a hefty yank and out popped the whole thing. Bunny's expression was a mixture of disbelief, surprise and relief, he turned to me and said:

'Cor thanks Ted, that's great, but nobody likes a smart arse!!!'

What a put down eh?

With that we both settled down and dozed off for a well deserved ziz.

It was a couple of hours later, but seemed like five minutes that we were roused by Ali on the blower warning us that there were signs of activity on the dock, and Dusty got back to him.

'Hi Ali, what exactly is happening?'

'A couple have just appeared on the brow to the boat, had a good look round, I think maybe checking to see if it's daylight enough for inspection purposes, and disappeared back into the dock.'

'OK Ali, well done, stay alert and keep me posted.'

Then Sam came up with yet another brew and a wedge of Herrings In* which went down a treat.

While we were feeding our faces the Teleprinter started yammering with a reply from Hoppy which read:-

DOCKSUNK SPECIAL FORCES
Ref. Your Signal

(1)   DESTINATION OF (A) TO BE DETERMINED WHEN SOLUTION TO (E) COMPLETE

(2)   DISARM AND RELEASE (D) AND (E) RETAIN SENIOR OIC

So we were now reliant on Ali to finally be able to see the end of the operation, and by now it was almost full daylight and we all expected Ali to come on the blower at any minute but it was quite some time before he did eventually call.

'Hello Dusty,' the loud speaker bellowed, 'the whole gang are coming out onto the deck of the dock but their going to have to get a wriggle on 'cos the tide's turned and they're going to get their feet wet if they're not careful.'

'Ali, whatever you do don't get spotted and wait till they're just aboard the boat before you detonate OK?'

'Understood Dusty, they've disappeared into the dock again.'

There was then quite a long wait before Ali came back on the blower.

'They're out on the boat's brow now making their way along the Fore Casing and are now going down the torpedo loading hatch, I'll give the last one a couple of minutes before I press the tit.'

A pregnant pause and then,

'Here we go, three, two, one now – bloody hell that sounded good.'

Then the sound reached us, and he was indeed right, there was such a cracking, like a lot of shotguns going off almost together.

'I bet that gave them a bit of a headache,' another very long pause, and then,

'They're exiting the boat looking much the worst for wear and going back into the dock.'

'Ali I expect them to hotfoot it back to the Base, so let me know when they do, and then follow them but keep a good distance behind. I don't want you being detected as they're armed and you're not.'

'OK Dusty, will do, oh ho they're heading your way right now, going fast and looking angry.'

'We'll sign off now Ali, and prepare a welcoming committee.'

Then Dusty rapped out a stream of orders and we all went to it with a will. Spike and I took up position behind the front doors of the main building, while Dusty and H went outside the base perimeter and camouflaged themselves in the sparse bush in a position where they could keep the footpath under surveillance, our natives melted into the bush, and we all waited patiently. Betty and Sam laid off in *Gasbag*.

Again the intercom broke the silence with Ali telling us that the gang had stopped at their disabled boat and were attempting to start it, eventually giving up and carrying on back towards the base, so we knew that they weren't far away and the adrenaline started to flow quite freely.

Then suddenly Spike and I heard the sound of a turbine winding up, and we looked at each other and suddenly both realized that it was the Shithouse starting up.

'The bastards are trying to chicken out in the chopper!' Spike yelled to Dusty over the intercom.

'We're going to stop them, you'd better look after the others yourselves.'

With that he shouted at me to follow him, and before I knew what I was doing I was legging it along the jetty, but Spike was going like a greyhound, and arrived at the chopper miles in front of me, and in one enormous bound leapt onto the extended radome nose, shoved the muzzle of his automatic up against the windscreen aiming at Masters, and screamed at the top of his voice.

'Shut that engine down or I'll blow your F – -in' head off, NOW!'

That's when I arrived and saw the sheer terror in the man's eyes as he looked into Spike's anger-distorted face. The engine whine started to die and Spike in the same distorted voice screamed at me.

'Ted, get that other bastard out of there and face down on the deck and shove your rifle hard into the back of his neck.'

And before I knew it I'd gone in, grabbed Mays by his collar and dragged him out onto the deck and had my knee in the middle of his back with my gun muzzle making a big dent in his neck. I really surprised myself!

As soon as Spike saw I had things under control he beckoned Masters out of the chopper, and as he came out slowly looking slightly worried Spike jumped down from his perch and as Masters started to speak Spike smashed him full in the face with his rifle butt, so hard you could hear the crunch of bone. He dropped like a stone with a low moan and lay motionless completely out of it. He looked over at my captive and said simply:

'If you want the same just make one peep OK, now move over very slowly to your oppo here.' And then he handcuffed them together. Then in his normal voice got on the blower.

'All secure Dusty, how is it with you?'

'It's a mess, the gang scattered when they saw you two legging it, at least three are holed up in the main building, the rest are in the bush somewhere, if you two could get those three we'll get the rest.'

'Will do, Good Luck!'

'Come on then Ted, you did good back there but we've got more work to do.'

'I just did as you told me, I don't know how they feel but you frightened me to death, would you really have shot him?'

'You're damn right I would, you don't make empty threats in our game. Come on we've more work to do.'

He then called Betty up and instructed him to bring *Gasbag* alongside the jetty, and warned him to be cautious as the opposition was on the loose.

I was getting to be a little worried as to what we were going to have to do next, so I asked him.

'Hey Spike, how the hell are we going to get all the way down the jetty without getting shot at?'

'I'll show you.'

With that *Gasbag* came alongside and we jumped aboard, immediately Spike went below and reappeared a few moments later with the prisoner handcuffed behind his back again.

'You've heard of human shields, well this is ours,' and jumped back onto the jetty and dragged his captive with him and using the chopper as cover, shouted back to Betty.

'Don't go anywhere near these two, pointing to the helicopter crew, but if either of them so much as sneezes out of turn shoot the pair of them, that's an order!'

'Come on Ted, stay tight up behind me, keep your weapon ready and if you see any movement ahead shoot at it over my shoulder.' And off we marched in line astern along the jetty directly towards the main building with Spike forcing his captive forward in the van.

We were halfway to the building when there was a crack and a shot whistled past close to our left. With that our shield started yelling loudly at the building, another shot rang out and zoomed to our right, and with that the poor sod started screaming what sounded very much like profanities. By this time we were three quarters of the way there when a third shot rang out and the man slumped in Spike's arms, so he picked the limp body up and started running with him, with me trying to keep up. Then I suddenly saw movement at a window so I fired a long burst in the general direction without taking aim, but it had the desired effect and the movement and shots ceased.

'Ted, when I shout, you break left and go for the building and I'll go right, OK?'

We ran line astern for a few more yards and then,

'NOW', and the next thing I remember is breathing heavily with my back up against the building wall. Spike had dropped the body in the middle of the jetty and was doing the same as me at the other side of the building. Then I saw him load a stun grenade and there was the sound of breaking glass as he shoved his rifle through a window and then a tremendous reverberation as the grenade went off. In the wake of the explosion Spike dashed through the front door in a diving roll, so I followed him in, doing the same and rolling in the opposite direction.

We both saw two bodies, one just stunned, the other looking decidedly dead near the window that I'd shot at, but no sign of the third member of the party. Spike leapt at the stunned individual and quickly shackled him to a radiator and kicked his weapon out of his reach and beckoned me to follow him as we systematically searched the rooms for number three, but he was proving very elusive.

Eventually we clewed up at the doors to the underground storage area, and Spike beckoned to me and whispered.

'Go back outside onto the jetty and get in position to get a clear shot at the exit door and if it opens take a shot and don't worry if you miss 'cos he's bound to duck back in and I'll get him, OK?'

I nodded and retraced my steps to the jetty, but couldn't find a suitable spot to get a good line of sight on the door, so shit or bust, I jumped into the oggin and managed to keep my rifle dry. I sort of dog paddled over to a suitable support pile and cradled myself in a cross member and drew a bead on the door and just waited.

But I didn't have long to wait, the door suddenly started to open before I had time to take good aim, so I just gave a quick burst of fire in the general direction of the part open door which slammed shut in rather a hurry. A moment later the door started to open again and I was ready for it this time and was about to squeeze an accurate shot off when Spike yelled through the partially open door for me to relax as he had number three secured, and to get to the door and join him, so I dog paddled to the door and he dragged me in.

The first thing I saw, as I drip dried, was number three, who looked very much the worse for wear hanging by handcuffs looped round an overhead pipe.

Spike then got on the blower to Dusty.

'Dusty, we're all secure here, two fatalities, two captives, how are you doing?'

Not very good Spike, the baddies have scattered but Click and his lads have volunteered to round them up for us so we've left them to it, so I suggest that we regroup on the jetty and try and sort out the chopper crew problem.'

So it was that we all met up again by the Chinook where Mays and Masters were looking decidedly unhappy, especially Masters whose face was covered in partially dried blood. Dusty started talking to them to try and find out what had motivated them.

'I thought you were on our side, you threatened to jeopardize the whole of our operation instead of assisting it, so what have you got to say for yourselves?'

'He's broken my nose!' Masters blurted out in a very nasal voice, staring hard at Spike.

'I'll break your F – in' neck if you don't shut up bleating and answer the Officer's question, you chicken shit bastard.' And gave him a boot up his arse to reinforce the threat.

Mays indicated that he'd like to say something so Dusty invited him to speak.

'Masters talked me into going AWOL* with him as I was dischuffed with the Zimbabwean regime, and he promised me great rewards and all he's done is given me loads of graft and even more grief, and I'm sick to death of it and him.'

'So what happened to get you to try and clear off?'

'He just said that things were getting too heavy and I could either go with him or stay and get involved in a load of grief, so I stayed with him, more's the pity, and now I've got even more grief, and all I want is a quiet life.'

'Well at the moment you're in the wrong place for that. Spike, unshackle them and take them to the Base building, unshackle the other two prisoners and get the four of them to transport the two bodies to a cool place, then bring them back here and we'll interrogate the other two. Ted you go with him while we try and get hold of Ali to find out how he's doing.'

Masters started to complain that he was just not well enough to assist, to which Spike replied that if he didn't shift himself fast he'd make very sure that he wasn't fit to help, which got him moving rather quickly.

As we approached the building again, who should we see but Ali, Click, and Click's lads with three very bedraggled individuals, two of whom were carrying a home made stretcher with the fourth member of the team on it. We herded our two over and asked Ali how they were doing. He smiled and said it was easy as Click and the lads did all the work.

'Is he dead?' Spike enquired of the one on the stretcher.

'No, but he's been speared a bit because he tried to make a run for it. The snag is my intercom has packed in so Dusty doesn't know how we've done.'

'Don't worry, I'll let him know while you bash on and join him. We've got a little job to do and then we'll be with you.'

'What happened to him?' Ali asked, pointing to Masters' face.

'He was trying to be a naughty boy and hit his face on my rifle butt, see you in a bit.' Spike then got on the blower and told Dusty the good news about Ali and the other four escapees. We then herded our two to the body of the human shield and got them to transport him to inside the main building and down the concrete steps to the storage basement, which was relatively cool. We then took them back up to collect the body by the window and transport him to alongside his colleague. Spike then unshackled his captive from the overhead pipe work and re-cuffed his hands behind his back. We then retraced our steps to unshackle the other one from his radiator and again re-cuffed him. He saw Masters eyeing up the weapon that he'd kicked out of reach of the captive.

'Go on then chicken shit, go for it and I'll have great pleasure in topping you!'

'Then you'd have nobody to fly the Chinook,' he retorted in a sneering voice.

'I couldn't give a shit, I'd just enjoy blowing your stupid head off!' then gave him a hard jab in the guts with his rifle butt, which put him on his knees badly winded.

'Get on your hind legs or I'll give you some more and you might learn to keep your big trap shut in future, now move it.'

The other two captives watching all this realized that they weren't dealing with a pussy cat and without a word headed off in the direction of the jetty.

Eventually everybody assembled on the jetty by *Gasbag*, and Dusty drew Spike to one side.

'I think we ought to take these six down below, Sam can tend the injured man's wounds while we find out who's in charge, and any other intelligence we can glean. Ted, would you and H go and repair their motor launch and motor up to the dock and take a look at the results of our handiwork on the boat and see if we've done sufficient or if you require a replay? Then you can motor back and bring it alongside here please.'

So off we trotted and left them to it, and on the way we told each other of memorable runs ashore that we'd had.

H told me about the time he ended up in jail in Cape Town. It appears that a group of Chiefs and POs had gone on a run ashore together and had clewed up in a night club and H had pulled this lovely tall slim sunburnt lass and eventually he was invited up Homers. So off they went with H thinking his luck was definitely in, strolling along with their arms around each other. Then suddenly a police siren sounded and then a cop car screeched to a halt in front of them. Two Yarpy* Scuffers jumped out, grabbed him and bundled him into the car and shot off to the station and bunged him into a holding cell with a crowd of ne'er do wells. He was allowed a phone call so he called Bigbury Bay and got hold of his DO* who promised to try and sort something out. H said he hoped it wouldn't be long because he was banged up with some very unsavoury characters.

Eventually his DO turned up with somebody from the British Embassy who asked him what had happened so he told it as it was, and the guy went off to have a word with the fuzz and came back with the DO grinning like cheshire cats saying he was free to go. So what the hell was it all about he enquired. Well the Embassy wallah explained that he was in civvies so the police didn't know he was an English visitor in the RN and was not aware of the law. What law he enquired. The law regarding segregation and apartheid, you're not allowed to consort with coloureds. She wasn't coloured he protested, and it was explained to him that she was classed as a Cape Coloured, a half breed. And he was shopped by one of the bar staff in the night club where they had met.

'Well it's a stupid law 'cos she was gorgeous and I thought that she was just well sunburnt, what a bummer.' And I had to agree with him.

So for my part I related my run ashore in Basrah. As I've explained before *Killisport* was the Armilla patrol and it was at the time when Iran and Iraq were sabre rattling, which was well before the first real bust up and real war. We were anchored at the mouth of the Shatt al Arab at the north end of the Persian Gulf, which is the confluence of the Tigris and

Euphrates. Anyway it was as hot as hell and we were at half an hour's notice for steam so we had to keep the main engines turned over every ten minutes, which meant that the boiler room had to be manned as well, and the Dabtoes were sunning themselves and fishing on the upper deck, with us down below sweating our bits off. We were told it was necessary, as if the shit hit the fan we were to immediately steam up river and evacuate the British Nationals.

Anyway it all calmed down eventually and as a thank you for our vigilance we were invited to Basrah and me and a couple of mates got invited up homers to this beautiful villa which boasted a swimming pool and air conditioning, the works, heaven.

One of the snags was that the man of the house, a high up oil company executive, was away in the UK on business. The second snag was that the lady of the house, although clocking on a bit, was very frustrated and man daft if you get my drift. The third problem was that she was an avid fan of Tommy Steele and had all his records and was a founder member of his fan club. The fourth and main problem was that she thought I looked the spitting image of him and wouldn't leave me alone, especially in the swimming pool, and I had a terrible time fighting her off, much to the amusement of my so called Oppos, and I was greatly relieved to escape from the house. Her parting gesture was to invite me back, but on my own next time!!

By this time we'd arrived at the launch and H quickly reconnected the fuel solenoid valves, turned the key, and a satisfying burble resulted. So off we set to the dock and moored up at the brow and taking the key with us climbed the internals to the boats brow and went aboard.

The first thing we noticed as we entered the Torpedo Loading Hatch was the acrid smell of detonated explosives. The further back aft we went the stronger the whiff and when we got through the tunnel it was almost overpowering in the AMS and the engine room was almost impossible, but there was no doubt about the results of our handiwork, the place was a shambles. Everything we wanted damaged was absolutely wrecked and definitely beyond repair. Having assessed this we beat a hasty retreat before we choked, re-boarded the launch and enjoyed a nice fresh air cruise back down to the jetty and tied up alongside *Gasbag*.

Chapter 34

Exodus

H and I boarded *Gasbag*, and went below to find it all happening. Spike had done some interrogating, in his own inimitable fashion, and had found out that the guy I'd shot at from under the jetty was the leader of the technical group sent to assess the damage to the boat and recommend to his 'superiors' the feasibility of repair. The one with the hole in his shoulder who was shot by his team-mate was a management thug sent to keep the rest of them in line, so as far as they were concerned he was no great loss.

He had also interviewed Masters regarding his background, which was looking increasingly iffy, but mainly regarding the transport of the warheads and had determined that to transport them all and our own personnel would take at least two trips to a maximum range of 120 nautical miles. *

Meanwhile Dusty was in the process of compiling a signal to update Hoppy and also ask some pertinent questions which read:-

> URGENT TOP SECRET FTAO ADMIRAL SIR A HOPGOOD
> Ref. Operation Docksunk
>
> (1)   ITEM (D) DECEASED
>
> (2)   ITEM (E) SOLVED OIC RETAINED
>
> (3)   DESTINATION OF (A) REQUIRED MAX DISTANCE 120 NM*
>
> (4)   TWO R 2 TRIPS REQUIRED TO TRANSPORT TOTAL (A)
>
> (5)   FUEL CARGO 900 IG* REQUIRED TO COMPLETE RUN 2
>
> (6)   CHINOOK PILOT EX F/LT MASTERS DANIEL ZIMBABWEAN AIR FORCE. RUN FULL CHECK AND ADVISE.

And then it was just a case of waiting for a reply, so yet another brew was organized by Sam, and we had a good old natter about books this time. It came about because Dusty asked her how she had come to be involved in noisy smelly engines.

'My dad, god rest him was a Pilot in the RAF and had flown Spitfires in the latter part of the Second World War and enthused about them so I became really interested in their history and development and became a bit of an expert on them. I just happened to be browsing through some WW2 books in the library and took one out for my dad and he enjoyed it so much that I read it as well and it changed my life. It was called *Cry for a Merlin*, all about the design and development of the Rolls Royce Merlin engine which not only powered the Spit, but the Lancaster Bomber and others. In actual fact the first Merlin developed just 990 hp, but with urgent development during the war brought the Griffon 61 engine, the successor to the Merlin to develop 2035 hp. How's that for improvement! Anyway I got so interested in the Merlin and other engines that when I got an Engineering Degree, I got a job with Vickers and have been faffing about with noisy smelly engines ever since and thoroughly enjoyed it.' And then laughingly poked her tongue out at Dusty.

Dusty then put his two pennyworth in.

'The best book I've read in a long time has been *Jack Speak* by Surgeon Commander Rick Jolly with cartoons by Tugg of Navy News fame. It's a dictionary of RN and RM slang, historical language and out and out humour, some of it very near the bone if you get my drift. The good bit about it apart from the humour is the fact that a percentage of the sales go to RN charity.'

So I leapt in with my choice.

'The best and also the worst book it's been my privilege to read is *The Admiralty Regrets*. Which is the tragic and poignant account of the loss of HM S/M. *Thetis* in Liverpool Bay and the loss of those aboard her, and the fact that her stern was visible the whole time of the failed rescue attempt. She was subsequently salvaged and recommissioned and renamed *Thunderbolt* and after great success in the Mediterranean was lost to an Italian sloop in the waters west of Sicily. The reason for the initial loss was the flooding of the fore ends through a defective torpedo tube, which once the rear door was opened could not be closed against the water flow. What it doesn't tell you in the book is that subsequently a modification was designed and fitted to all rear doors to prevent a reccurrence of the tragedy, and was called the Safety Swing Bolt, but we all knew it as the Thetis Clip.'

Then the Teleprinter started yammering away, so Dusty and I scurried to the radio shack, and as expected, it was indeed a signal from Hoppy, which when decoded read:

TO DOCKSUNK SPECIAL FORCES
Ref. Your Signal

(A)   ITEM (1) UNFORTUNATE

(B)   VESSEL BEING DIVERTED, WILL BE WITHIN 100NM OF YOU IN 24 HRS. ADVISE DEPARTURE TIME AND HEAD DUE EAST: ITEM (5) FUEL CARGO WILL BE AVAILABLE PASSWORD GERONIMO

(C)   ITEM (6) KEEP UNDER SURVEILLANCE AT ALL R ALL TIMES

So there it was, we had 24 hours to organize the first of the two difficult trips with a dodgy Pilot, so Dusty took Spike to one side, showed him the signal and charged him with the responsibility of keeping a close eye on his 'friend' Danny boy.

H and I were charged with the task of devising a method of getting the warheads up onto the jetty and loading them onto the Chinook.

So we scouted round the various rooms and lobbies of the building and found rope and canvas and also discovered a stout wooden shed in the rear grounds, so we did a partial demolition job and borrowed a few of the planks and a few battens from inside. With this gear we decided on the reverse procedure of brewery dray men in that we planned to haul the warheads up planks laid over the concrete steps by means of ropes anchored to the access steel barrier and the bight looped round the warhead and back up the steps, with a turn round the same bars. Two men on each rope and one guiding the way up the planks. For getting them to the Chinook we cobbled together a sort of loose hammock with battens on either side and one crossways in the middle, so that six blokes could carry it, similar to the way they transport dolphins to and from aquariums.

Click's natives volunteered to give it a go up the steps and after an initial wobble and a lot of clicking and gabbling, where one side was going faster than the other, it went up a treat nice and slow and steady and relatively easily.

So while the lads were doing their thing, we decided to try the other rig for humping them along the jetty to the chopper. H and I led with Masters behind me still complaining bitterly, but with Spike behind him to stop him bitching and Masters mucker on the other side with Dusty behind him. Dusty in true Bootneck fashion gave our crisp clear orders.

'Stand by to lift, LIFT, by the right quick MARCH, L R L R L,' etceteras and it was a doddle, apart from Masters who was threatened by Spike that if he didn't start pulling his weight he'd get a bit more of the same treatment he'd already had a dose of. Dusty ordered a breather halfway down the jetty, then off we went again and at the end of it straight up the open Chinook ramp. By the time we got back to the base building the lads had another unit up top for us, and so on it went, like clockwork until we had six loaded aboard and the other six all ready and waiting above ground, just inside the main building.

Dusty decided that we'd done enough for the time being, so we repaired to *Gasbag* where he ran through the next stage of the action plan.

'The first group to go will be Spike, Ali, the prisoner and Sam,' and looking directly at Sam said,

'and no arguments!'

Then he drew Spike aside and explained that the prisoner was a pussy cat and that his main problem was Masters.

'Make sure he behaves himself even if you have to kill him and get Mays to take over OK? But before you leave us we're going to lay a few charges in the Base building so that when I depart I'm going to blow the whole facility to smithereens to prevent it being reused.'

'Well before you do, and while there's still time, do you mind if I take a bath in that lovely blueroom* H and Ted found while they were scouting round for shifting gear?'

'No, go on help yourself, and let me know when you're done and Sam and I'll give it a go, and don't look at me like that, I mean separately so that I can stand guard OK?'

Which is where we met him because H and I had got there first, and while he was waiting we told him about the Rosyth Dockyard communal ablution facilities. H explained that the heads* were the real old fashioned type, just a long row of traps, each with it's own top plank with the regulation sized oval aperture in it. The receptacle of the overhead action was a long deep trough with a large cistern at one end and downhill at the other a connection to the main sewer. The cistern was automatically filled and discharged to flush the trough at regular intervals.

When the facility was to be used it was advisable to use the upstream trap if at all possible, the reason being that there was always some rotten shit of a joker who, wanting to get his own back on an oppo, or enemy would get upstream of him when his need arose, make a paper boat, wait for the cistern to flush, light the boat and sail it down stream with scorching results.

But the bit that I liked was when you'd had a long hard dirty sweaty day, up to your eyeballs in oil and grease, there was nothing like a nice hot bath down the blue rooms. The bathroom was very long and fully tiled throughout with a lot of full length enamel baths in a row. The idea was to take a towel and a packet of Daz or Tide or whatever other you fancied into the bathroom having removed watch, shoes and pocket contents, fill the bath to the required temperature but leave the taps running, pour sufficient wash powder in to create a decent lather, then climb in and soak thoroughly.

Once fully soaked and comfortable start to disrobe in any order and crunch out each item and discard over the side. When fully stripped lay back and relax until the water overflows clear and clean and the skin is nice and wrinkled, turn off taps and bale out.

Then it was back to reality, a quick bite to eat then another briefing from Dusty.

'Betty, you take *Gasbag* and deliver H and Ted to the Motor Cruiser so that they can repair it, bring it back here and load up the remaining prisoners and deliver them to the village and the care of Click's subjects.

'You then re-secure *Gasbag* alongside here, and H and Ted return the Cruiser here after dumping the prisoners. Then you can get your heads down till departure number one time.'

And so it was, I don't know about the rest of the gang, but when H and I got back after our delivery we were absolutely cream crackered, and we took no rocking when we eventually got our heads down.

It seemed like only a couple of minutes' sleep before we were roused by Sam with a cuppa, to tell us that departure time number one was imminent, and Spike was already supervising Masters with his pre-flight checks, and then the increasing pitch whine as the engines were wound up and fired. Then the passengers were walked aboard by Mays with Sam looking very upset at being parted from Dusty, and Ali keeping a careful eye on the prisoner. Dusty then went aboard to instruct Spike to load a drum of diesel fuel for the launch and K rations for the prisoners to sustain them on their way back to wherever, he then gave Sam a quick hug and returned to the jetty. The rear door reared up and closed with a satisfying clunk, then the whine increased to a crescendo, the dust flew a bit, the suspension stretched and then the whole huge thing rose from the jetty, gave a little side shimmy, with violent downdraft and veered off in a banking turn and headed east.

The rest of us busied ourselves by getting the remaining warheads onto the jetty ready for the next trip. Then Dusty explained the rest of the plan he had in mind.

'I'll now wait here for the chopper to return so that me, the chopper crew and a couple of Click's lads will load the remaining half dozen warheads. You Betty with H will take *Gasbag* to the village, and you Ted will follow in the launch, and take the rest of the lads between you. When you arrive at the village get Click to organize his lads into clearing an area as near as possible to the village, large enough for the chopper to land. Betty, when we land in the clearing you will fuel up and store the launch with the gear we will bring with us. Ted and H, you will take Click and a couple of lads and tow one of the whalers with *Gasbag* and scuttle her somewhere where she cannot be recovered! Then we'll give the prisoners the choice of staying in the village or using the launch to make their way back to whence they came, but they are not to be released until a week after we've left.'

So we left Dusty to his own devices and steamed north in convoy, and arrived at the village where we were accorded a great celebration feast with lots of fish on the menu. After which we explained to Click, who now understood pidgin English and sign language, what was wanted, so he set his lads to work making the clearing, and then we launched a whaler, tied it astern of *Gasbag* and set course for Accar Island where H and I had decided earlier to secrete *Gasbag* rather than scuttle her, as she might come in handy in the future!! So with Click and his boys sworn to secrecy we camouflaged her well with tree branches and undergrowth and we knew that in days the jungle would envelope the whole thing, so we battened down as much as we could and then departed and enjoyed a leisurely sail back to the village, which brought back memories of our apprentice days.

We had a choice of outward bound activities at the week end, either camping or sailing. We always chose sailing a dinghy which only required a minimum of three crew and devised a strategy which best suited us. We recruited a rather slow junior apprentice as the third crew member, and instead of packing food and survival gear we took civvies, sailed directly south from Rosyth Dockyard across the Forth, moored in South Queensferry's little harbour, changed into civvies, told our crew member to keep his trap shut and look after things, thumbed a lift into Edinburgh and went on the raz where H was usually more successful than me.

Come the end of the weekend, it was back to the harbour using the thumb again, change back into sailing gear and sail back over to the dockyard and tell everybody that you'd had a great time roughing it.

Now back to reality, we arrived at the village again to find a good landing area already cleared for the chopper, so all we had to do was relax and wait for the return of Dusty and the second trip.

Chapter 35

Trip 1

The radio finally announced the imminent arrival of Dusty and the Chinook, so we repaired to the clearing, lit a coloured flare and soon heard the unmistakable thrashing sound and in she swept, reared back to a stop over the clearing and slowly descended and touched down arse first, then settled on all fours, so to speak. Then the engines shut down, the rotors gradually slowed and came to a standstill, the rear door hinged down and out strode Dusty accompanied by an unexpected but welcomed individual in the form of Bob Khan. Him of Harrier fame on the first mission.

'Hiya Bob how ya diddlin?' H exploded.

'What the hell are you doing here, and how's Anna?'

'It's a long story, Dusty'll tell you all about it over a cuppa.'

Then the rest of the village lads appeared from the bowels of the chopper and then Mays.

'Where's Masters?' I enquired.

'Oh, he's in DQ's* Dusty explained, 'it's an even longer story, let's go with Bob's suggestion, we'll have a brew and I'll tell you all I know.' And so that's how it was, but it was all a bit garbled because of all the interruptions with questions, so I'll edit it for simplicity's sake.

It appears that shortly after take off and out of sight of land, Spike became a little suspicious about the course Masters was steering so he checked with his own orienteering compass and discovered that they were way off course and gradually veering further to port. So he went up to the flight deck and peered over Master's shoulder at the Gyro repeater which indicated due east. He then calmly asked Mays to take over control for a while as he wanted a quiet word with Masters and led him down into the hold.

Once there he turned to face Masters, grabbed him by the throat with one hand and slammed him up against the bulkhead and just about lifted him off his feet. He drew his knife with the other hand and held the very sharp point half an inch away from his right eye and in a low growl said that if he didn't explain immediately how and why he'd managed to change course while still showing due east on the Gyro he would loose the sight of one eye, and if he still refused, the knife would carry on going into his brain which would give him great satisfaction.

The knife point started to advance and close the gap and Masters screamed OK and in a terrified voice explained that he'd slowly added small offsets on the Gyro repeater. The knife advanced still further until it was almost touching the eyeball, and Spike said that he was almost inclined to kill the chicken shit bastard anyway and be shut of him, but that instead told him in no uncertain terms that he wanted the course to be altered so as to get them back on the correct track. He then added that if he so much as blinked out of turn it would be the last thing he did, let go of his throat and dragged him back to the flight deck, sat him back in his seat and supervised his every move with the knife point pricking the back of his neck dead centre, ready to sever his spine with one thrust. Masters by this time was shaking rather badly and wasn't so much white as a sheet, more like almost transparent, but he started making the course alteration and readjusted the Gyro repeater.

Spike checked that he'd overcompensated to be able to come back to the original track and then come back to due east, and had checked it with his own compass and it seemed correct, so all he could do was stay on Masters' case and hope that the correct track had been re-acquired.

He was quite relieved and his fears were allayed when suddenly the radio burst into life with GERONIMO and two Sea King helicopters appeared either side of the Chinook, then the radio blurted out 'Follow Me' and off they went line astern.

In no time at all, on the horizon appeared a large vessel which turned out to be an aircraft carrier, the radio came alive again and gave landing instructions, and with the knife still in position, and before they knew it they were on the deck and surrounded by what looked like the whole of the Regulating Department crew, with a very large formidable looking Jaunty* in charge. Masters was immediately grabbed and led away, which was a great relief to Spike as it relieved him of the arduous duty, then the boffins came round and inspected the cargo and confirmed that they were in fact state of the art Nuclear Devices. They then relieved Ali of his prisoner, and he and the Boffins were escorted below by some of the Jaunty's gang, no doubt to be interrogated to see if any useful intelligence could be gleaned.

Then all the home team were led up to the Captain's flat where they were introduced to no other than Admiral Sir Arthur Hopgood who was full of questions, but took a real keen interest in Sam and really took her under his wing, I hasten to add in a most fatherly way. Spike ventured to express, for all of them, their surprise and delight at meeting him and then had the temerity to enquire how he'd got down to this neck of the woods so quickly. The reply came as a bit of a shock as he was introduced to his personal chauffeur who turned out to be no other than Bob

Kahn, who had been seconded to the Admiral's staff as he knew of the operation and had been personally involved in the first phase of the operation.

It appears that the Admiral had requested Bob and a lift out to the Indian Ocean and had been granted the use of both Bob and a very rare two seater Harrier demonstration aircraft. They had refuelled in mid Mediterranean and dropped in on *Invincible* which had been in transit to an exercise area off Karachi, which the Admiral had diverted to their present position.

Asked about Masters he explained that on investigation, Mister/Lieutenant Masters had been a very naughty boy as he had been selling military secrets to dodgy regimes and a lot of other iffy deals, and was near the top of MI6's most wanted list. His second dicky Mays was a very reluctant accomplice as he was being blackmailed by Masters on a totally false fabricated misdemeanour.

Then Sam, looking very worried, asked Hoppy how on earth the second trip was to be made as the pilot was now in custody. Hoppy called over Bob Khan and introduced him to Samantha and explained that he was to be the new pilot, as he was qualified on Harriers, Sea Kings and also Chinooks.

Then Bob asked if he could be excused as he wished to supervise the preparation of the Chinook for the next trip, and took Tony Mays with him, because as he explained he was the one who had maintained the chopper and would be the one who would know of any subtle defects. When they arrived at the hanger deck, the Chinook was well on in its service routine, under the careful charge of one of the chief AA's*, who had previously done a lot on Chinooks.

Chapter 36

Trip 2

The Chinook was not the smartest looking aircraft aboard, but mechanically with a few minor adjustments and work and Tony Mays information and help, was now in perfect working order.

It was then fully fuelled, the cargo bay was loaded with drums of fuel sufficient for the return journey and a 45 gallon drum of diesel fuel was loaded and secured in the cargo bay, along with enough K rations to feed a small army, because some kind person thought the Natives might like the excess, also Sam had suggested some basic medical supplies, after she had had a heart to heart with Raisa.

Then the lift warning bells rang and the lift slowly rose till it was flush with the flight deck, the rotor blades were swung into position and locked, and the Chinook Flight Crew were piped to Flying Stations and out trotted Bob and Tony, climbed aboard and started pre-flight checks. At the same time an RN Sea King took to the air as the safety aircraft.

Then Bob wound up the Chinook engines, requested and was granted permission to take off and in no time at all was in the air and curling round to head off due west, accompanied by the Sea King, which flew alongside for a few miles and then called them up on the radio, wished them good hunting and veered off to return to Mother.

The flight carried on remarkably uneventfully and eventually the unmistakable shoreline of Accar Island and the Kananga River appeared on the radar screen long range setting. Bob made a slight course adjustment and carried on in, and when on the radar high resolution range setting Tony was able to point out the jetty where Dusty would be waiting patiently with the remaining natives.

In no time at all the coast line came into view, and they were dead centre for the jetty and a waving group of blokes on it who quickly evacuated as the Chinook let down with a perfect landing, with Bob congratulating himself on having enjoyed a successful flight.

As the engines shut down and the rear ramp was lowered, the first aboard was Dusty who was extremely and pleasantly surprised to see Bob and enquired the reason, so Bob explained that Masters had been arrested not only because he had been a bad lad previously, but because it appeared he had given Spike some trouble on the first flight, which was the reason why he was the pilot. To which Dusty replied that he wasn't surprised as he considered that Masters was a scumbag and a liability. Then he organized the refuelling of the Chinook from the drums by semi-rotary pumps and the loading and securing of the remaining war heads, because as he explained, it would be better if they could be on their way back to the Carrier before dark, which Bob agreed with wholeheartedly.

With great effort, in next to no time all was in and secure and the chopper was in the air and heading for the clearing that Click's lads had organized, which is where we heard the sound of the chopper and were informed over the radio of the imminent arrival and when we lit the flare.

And that's how it went.

'Hiya Bob, how ya diddlin, what the hell are you doing here, and how's Anna?' and we all went and had a quick brew and a natter, which was rudely interrupted by one of Click's lads grabbing Dusty by the arm and dragging him in the general direction of the village centre, amid a volley of clicks and unintelligible utterances. So H and I went along, leaving Bob and Tony to guard the chopper, to see what all the fuss was about. He led us straight to the communal meeting hut where a crowd had gathered. As we approached, the crowd parted to reveal one of the prisoners being restrained by a couple of villagers with Click overseeing the proceedings. He looked very relieved on seeing us, and in fractured English and sign language explained that the individual in question had been seen skulking about near the helicopter as it landed in the clearing, and had shuftied the interior when we'd retired for a cuppa, and was then seen in the undergrowth talking into a box, which Click then produced.

The box turned out to be a small state of the art long- range two way radio, and the owner was one of the first group to be captured. Dusty enquired of Click if he knew if the bloke spoke English, the reply being a shrug of the shoulders, so Dusty in a loud voice said to me,

'I think I'll just kill the bastard,' and grabbed him roughly, and the guy's eyes nearly popped out of his head and he started protesting in pretty good English, which cleared up that question.

'I think I'll take him away anyway and do a Spike type interrogation,' said Dusty, and dragged him away into an empty hut.

A short while later they both reappeared, after some rather chilling sounds had emanated from within the building, with a grim faced Dusty and a terrified looking prisoner. He passed the wretch back over to his keepers and we followed him back to the chopper, where he gathered us round and explained that we were in a bit of trouble.

'The individual I've just interviewed has admitted that he's been in touch with his superiors, and it's obvious that he's eyeballed the warheads, so we can assume that they know what our cargo is. I am informed that Hoppy's aboard *Invincible*, so I intend to contact him so that he can organize some form of protection as the Chinook is unarmed and we only have small arms, which are next to useless against a determined air attack. Any questions?'

'Well OK then, H and Ted, you get the other prisoners and give them the option of staying here or returning to the base, and get those returning to shift the barrel of fuel and fill up the launch, and load sufficient K rations for their needs and distribute the rest and the medical supplies as you see fit. Bob and I are going back to the chopper and taking the spy with us, and we're going to draw up a plain language signal to transmit to Hoppy for him to arrange some form of protection, and we'll see you back at the chopper, and be as quick as you can.' And so it was, the prisoners being split, half staying, half leaving.

We decided that the best way with the surplus K rations and the medical gear was to give them to Click's missus and Raisa and let them do the distribution, as they knew of the most needy. We then legged it back to the chopper to find Dusty and Bob finishing off transmitting, in plain language, the bad news to Hoppy which read:

F. T. A. O. ADMIRAL HOPGOOD V. URGENT

HAVE DISCOVERED OPPOSITION AGENT C/W RADIO TRANSMITTER AND IS STRONG POSSIBILITY THAT HE HAS INFORMED HIS SPONSORS OF CARGO. WE EXPECT MILITARY REACTION AND NO SIGNIFICANT DEFENSIVE ARMAMENT. PLEASE ADVISE.

In next to no time the teleprinter was hammering away with the reply:

OPERATION DOCKSUNK

TAKE OFF ASAP HEADING EAST, BRING AGENT WITH YOU. ARMED ESCORT BEING SCRAMBLED NOW. GOOD LUCK.

So then it was a mad scramble to get everybody aboard, get the prisoner secured, get the tailgate up and light the blue touch paper on the engines all at the same time. With that all done, and with the engines now at full chat, Bob wanged full pitch on and the old crate lived up to its RM nickname and shot into the air like a rocket, then he pitched it forward and did a vicious banking left turn and we were heading East flat out at all of 161 Knots.

Everything was going well according to plan, or so we thought, when suddenly Tony Mays shouted at the top of his voice,

'BREAK LEFT', and by pure training reaction Bob threw the controls, and us in the arse end clewed up in a big heap with a couple of the warheads coming loose. They took a lot of resecuring by H and me, while Dusty went up forrard to see what was happening on the flight deck.

'What the hell was all that about?' Dusty exploded.

'Bandits gaining on us astern, Tony spotted them abeam of us and it was the only way we could turn, and now we're heading back west.'

'What are they then?'

'They look to me like a couple of Apache gun ships, but I can't be sure.'

'OK, lower the tailgate, we'll shackle ourselves in and have a shufti and use our small arms and try to dissuade them as much as we can.'

He came back aft and told us the 'good' news as the tailgate came down and we just had enough time to shackle ourselves onto safety lines, and Dusty confirmed that the opposition were in fact Apaches and coming into range fast!

'Use your small arms and the remaining grenades in the launchers to try and put them off. I've got an idea, so I'm going back up to the flight deck to see what I can sort out, but stand by for some heavy manoeuvres.' He told H and me and disappeared forrard again and left us to it. So all we could do was lay prone on the tailgate and take pot-shots as they approached even closer. One small crumb of comfort was that the Apache's side pods had no missiles loaded, otherwise we would all have been dead meat in no time at all, but we soon felt the hot wind and heard the zing of incoming munitions. We started firing back with next to no effect until H lobbed a grenade very high, and although it didn't hit, it exploded near enough to the foremost Apache for it to take extreme evasive action, which nearly ended in a near mid-air collision with his trailing oppo which caused them both to drop back out of range for a while.

Then suddenly Bob started taking a lot of evasive action, violently changing altitude and course, which put the opposition's aim off, but didn't help us either. Suddenly though there was a subtle change in the evasive action, as we started to gain altitude fast, then zoomed down in a great banking turn, and we could see the oggin coming up a bit too fast for my liking. Then we pulled out of the swoop and suddenly we were passing over the Base jetty and then perilously low over the main building.

The next thing I remember was one hell of an explosion and an enormous blast of hot air, which lifted our whole machine and tipped it forward. It took us a while to gather our wits about us, but as Bob regained an even keel, we looked back on a scene of utter devastation. The whole of the jetty and building complex had disappeared in a heap of smouldering rubble, with a downed Apache in the middle of it looking decidedly badly bent with, at this stage, no sign of its partner.

It suddenly dawned on us what had happened. Dusty had said that he was going to blow the base to smithereens, so had directed Bob low over the joint and had timed his detonation to perfection, and had taken out at least one of the baddies.

Bob then banked us round and headed us out to sea again, and then the most glorious sight met our gaze. It was what appeared to us to be a monster slowly descending in our wake in the form of a Harrier and the pilot, grinning like a Cheshire cat, chopped us off a very smart salute, cheeky git, which prompted H to give him a very rude hand gesture, then stabbing his index finger repeatedly at his watch. We think he got the message, 'cos he gave us another huge grin and then veered off and left us to carry on our merry way. Dusty came back aft with a very satisfied look on his face, got us to stand clear of the tailgate which then closed. He reckoned that the Harrier had gone hunting the other Apache, as it had to be downed to prevent its country of origin identifying the UK as their antagonists.

The rest of the flight was thankfully uneventful, as we'd had more than enough excitement for one day. Halfway to our destination the Harrier passed us and gave a wing waggle, and then it was our turn to land, with Bob making a perfect touchdown.

As the rotors slowed to a standstill, the ramp was let down and a reception committee led by Hoppy himself came out to meet us and, after the formal saluting our hands were shaken, and it was congratulations all round. Then the Crushers led our prisoner away for interrogation, and we were then led away for a wash and brush up, while the boffins inspected their latest cargo, and Sam attempted to suffocate Dusty to a round of applause and cheering from the rest of us, much to Dusty's embarrassment.

Just before we disappeared into the bowels we were reminded that a Washup* would be convened after a short rest, while our memories were still sharp. Then the monster we were aboard started to throb as her props dug in deep and fast to get us away from the area to prevent identification.

CHAPTER 37

Washup

Eventually, after a glorious wash and brush up and fresh lagging and short rest period, we were called to the Conference Compartment where we talked among ourselves. Eventually Admiral Sir Arthur Hopgood swept in followed closely by *Invincible*'s Skipper and Jimmy* plus a couple of Boffins and the regulation Regulating Department, if you'll pardon the pun, in the shape of the Jaunty and a couple of his crushers, with a couple more standing guard outside the compartment.

They all took their places at the conference table with a bit of shuffling about, and then Hoppy called the meeting to order.

'Gentlemen, this is a closed meeting and no official record will be made, and I hope I need not remind you that you are still party to the Official Secrets Act. We are here to assess the success or otherwise of Operation Docksunk. I now call on Captain Miller RM to give us his considered opinion on the final outcome of the operation. Miller.'

'Thank you Sir, may I first congratulate all the party on great teamwork and efficiency. In general, after initial doubts about the success of the first operation, this present follow up instalment, in my opinion has been a complete and utter success. For the opposition to re-group and re-organize a similar style operation would take years, if not decades, and the Intelligence Services are now well aware and informed of its type and origin.

'I would like to call on CERA Bass to explain the technical side of the operation.'

'Thank you Captain Miller. From a purely technical aspect, although the first phase should have been sufficient to render the vessel and its facility irreparable, the photographic evidence was inconclusive, which is why this particular phase was instigated.

'On first inspection the Dry Dock was a write-off, but other facilities could possibly have been used. The boat on the other hand, although badly damaged, could with some hard work, have been re-commisioned as what was damaged was relatively small easily replaced units.

'What was needed was great damage to large irreplaceable units. With Bootneck – sorry Sir – I mean Royal Marine expertise in explosives and our machinery knowledge, charges were laid in strategic poosition and the results were extremely satisfying and terminal.

The conclusion in ERA Smith's and my opinion is that both boat and docking facility are complete and utter write-offs. The bonus as far as we were concerned was our escape from a very difficult situation, with a brilliant plan by Captain Miller and well executed by Flight Lieutenant Khan. This resulted in the complete destruction of the backup facility, the downing of an attacking aircraft, and even more important, the saving of our skins.

'One of the bonuses as far as I and the team agree, on is the recovery of the warheads, which we believe will enable a lot of people to sleep easier in their beds. On a non-technical matter, I think we would all like to thank Sergeant Redwood for his diligence in watching our backs at all times, and who was instrumental in our coming out of it in one piece.'

'Thank you Chief, I heartily approve of your last comment,' Dusty agreed.

'May I now commend the rest of the team, Sub Lieutenant Betts for excellent navigation and enthusiasm, PO Hassan who did a lot more for us than interpreting, but also did a fine PR job, and co-ordinated all the great efforts of the villagers by direct communication with their Chief. Next there is Flight Lieutenant Khan who has stepped into the breech more than once at short notice, and through his skill and versatility has been invaluable. And then of course there are our 'Tiffs' Smith and Bass. These tradesmen have been the lynch pin of both exercises and through their ingenuity and daring have carried both exercises through. Also Doctor Hall who is, as a civilian, not in attendance, but who nevertheless did not confine her expertise to just the engines, but helped out in many other ways.' Which brought a little twitch to the corners of a few mouths, and a slight smile from Dusty.

'And penultimately the whole of the first operation team, ably planned and led by Commander Westerman, who unfortunately could not lead us on this operation, due to injuries sustained.

'And last but not least, I am sure both teams would like to thank the home team for their unstinting back up, and in particular you Sir Arthur, for giving us the confidence to know that you were always available and able to help us out in emergency.' With that he sat down to a ripple of approving applause.

Hoppy stood up, tapped the table gently for silence,

'Thank you Captain, now can we have a word from Professor Thorenson who is a senior official in charge of research at UKAEA, and who, by the way was a Development Engineer with the Submarine Prototype up at Dounreay near Thurso in the Highland region.'

'Thank you Sir Arthur, firstly I must congratulate the team for recovering these lethal warheads as they represent an awfully large and dirty destructive force, and in the wrong hands, which they obviously were, could have caused an awful lot of grief.

'I agree wholeheartedly with the Chief that lots of people will be able to sleep easier in their beds.

'I'm sure you will all be interested in the fate of these units. They will be transported in secure containers under armed guard to our facility at Sellafield in Cumbria, there they will be carefully dismantled and the fissile material, the explosive part, will be removed and the remains will be passed over to forensic experts. They should then be able, by inspecting the internals, to be able to establish a country of origin and appropriate actions and/or sanctions taken to curtail their activities. Thank you again gentlemen for your courage and tenacity.'

'Thank you Professor. Master at Arms will you now please ask our other guest to join us please?' and with alacrity the Jaunty leapt to the door, disappeared for a moment then reappeared with a rather grey looking gentleman who, without invitation went and stood alongside Hoppy and waited for the hubbub to die down, cleared his throat and simply said in a grey monotone voice to suite his grey complexion and his grey suit.

'Gentlemen I am with MI and I have been speaking with the chap you brought with you, and we have gained some very important and valuable information with his help. I thank you for your efforts, my organization thanks you and HM Government thanks you. I have also had a word with the gentleman who I understand was your original pilot. He has also been very helpful, and will also be in the future we think.' With that, he gave a little nod in Hoppy's direction and left the compartment escorted by the Joss Man.*

Sir Arthur cleared his throat and tapped the table again.

'Well gentlemen, I think that about wraps it up.'

'Sir, before we adjourn, may I ask a question of Professor Thorenson?' Dusty enquired.

'By all means, but I warn you he may not be at liberty to answer.'

'No, no Sir Arthur, please allow him to ask.'

'Well Sir, I and some others may be interested to know the final fate of the material you refer to as 'fissile'?'

'Oh yes Captain, that is easy, it will be reprocessed and refined and used as replacement fuel rods in either Nuclear Power Stations or Nuclear Submarine Reactors.'

'Thank you very much Sir.'

With that, everybody drifted away after Hoppy had departed with the other scrambled egg. H and I wandered down to the Chief's Mess where the members lashed us up to a couple of beers and a tot apiece, and that's the last we remember for about twenty four hours.

Chapter 38

Epilogue

Us Tiffs eventually surfaced from a sleep of the dead, and I told H he looked like shit. He replied that I didn't look too bonny either.

I ate a hearty breakfast, he said he wasn't hungry and had a cup of tea, and almost immediately spewed it up, so I asked him if he'd see a quack, as I'd asked him to do ages ago, and he told me, predictably, to piss off and mind my own business.

Desperate situations demand drastic measures I remember hearing somewhere, so while he was away having another big spit* I earholed the Chief Sick Bay Tiff* (CSBA) who promised to look into things for me, 'cos he could see that I was worried, and he could also see that H wasn't well. So on the strength of that promise I explained what I thought was the cause, which strengthened his resolve to sort him out.

To cut a long story short, he was eventually dragged kicking and screaming to the Sick Bay to consult the Surgeon Commander, threatening me with dire consequences and calling me a treacherous bastard (I really resented the traitor bit). He was diagnosed, as was predicted, with what we now know was the big 'C' and you know the eventual outcome.

HMS *Invincible* carried on her merry planned way after its interrupted trip, a little behind schedule, to the Seychelles for a Show the Flag and Jolly*, so a few more revs were put on and we arrived off Cascade on the Island of Mabe' spot on time.

This was very convenient because the Island has an airport close to Cascade and Hoppy had chartered a rather large civil aircraft to whisk him and us back to dear old Sweaty Sock Land, and after a short Sea boat trip and a ride in a couple of Fast Blacks we were on our way.

Having been pampered something rotten en-route, in what seemed like next to no time, we landed at Glasgow Airport just above Paisley, and were met by more Fast Blacks, the quick ride across the Erskine Bridge and back up to Faslane with the familiar and very welcome rain pissing down!

We were greeted by the whole of the original crew, even Anna was waiting for Bob with very predictable results, Stan was almost 100% under the gentle thumb of Penny, Andy had come up from Hull and admitted that his job wasn't that bad after all.

We all had a great reunion, and most had the little man with the hammer inside their heads the next morning, but we all agreed it was well worth it.

Then we all went our own ways and did our own thing. H of course had forgiven me and had resigned himself very reluctantly to treatment, which in the first instance seemed to be working, but as we know, the outcome was somewhat different, enough said.

This has been hard work, writing I mean, and getting stuck in has taken a lot of will power at times, but now you have it.

I'll be let out soon. I've kept in touch with Spike, who's pissed off as he's dischuffed with civvy street, and I've told him about *Gasbag*, and we've developed a few ideas!!

FIN